• VICTORY, VIRUS, VOTES •

· 1917 – 1920 ·

· VICTORY, VIRUS, VOTES ·
· 1917–1920 ·

ELLEN M. LEVY

Deborah and Miriam's Boston Marriage Series

Halo PUBLISHING INTERNATIONAL

Halo Publishing International
7550 W IH-10 #800, PMB 2069,
San Antonio, TX 78229

First Edition, October 2024
ISBN: 978-1-63765-587-0
Library of Congress Control Number: 2024905825

Halo Publishing International is a self-publishing company that publishes adult fiction and non-fiction, children's literature, self-help, spiritual, and faith-based books. We continually strive to help authors reach their publishing goals and provide many different services that help them do so. We do not publish books that are deemed to be politically, religiously, or socially disrespectful, or books that are sexually provocative, including erotica. Halo reserves the right to refuse publication of any manuscript if it is deemed not to be in line with our principles. Do you have a book idea you would like us to consider publishing? Please visit www.halopublishing.com for more information.

This book is dedicated to my close friend of fifty-seven years, Carolyn Heusemann, who has been a great support during my entire writing career, and to Phyliss Guiliano, who edited earlier books and added a story for the foreword of this book. Neither of them lived long enough to see this book in print. I am grateful for their encouragement and assistance; they enriched my books with their love.

Contents

Foreword

The years from 1917 to 1920 were significant ones in United States history; the Great War, the fight for women's suffrage, and the influenza of 1918 influenced everyone's lives. Deborah and Miriam's personal struggles added intensity to this period.

The United States entered the First World War in April 1917. American Expeditionary Forces arrived in Europe by transport ships beginning in June and served overseas until the Allied victory on November 11, 1918. Though this was a comparatively short period, there was not a family in the United States untouched by this war. Four million Americans served their country; over 100,000 lost their lives. Those at home struggled with not only the loss of loved ones, but also the disruption to every aspect of their lives. Women went to work, replacing those men shipped off to war. Some ran their family farms to avert a food shortage, some volunteered with the American Red Cross, and others knitted socks or rolled bandages for soldiers. The United States relied heavily on propaganda campaigns to persuade people to curb food consumption, so soldiers would have enough. Food played a critical role in the balance of power between the warring factions. War was on everyone's mind.

During this time, the struggle for women's suffrage was at its peak. The National American Woman Suffrage Association stirred women to fight for voting rights following their convention in 1904, at which they adopted the Declaration of Principles. By 1917, eight states had adopted women's suffrage, but even though President Wilson switched his position in favor of it in 1916, and the House of Representatives granted women the right to vote through passage of the Nineteenth Amendment in 1918, the US Senate continued to deny women suffrage.

Also of great significance throughout the world, during this time period, was the influenza of 1918. Spread by soldiers with the grippe, the deadly sickness reached almost every country. Initially dubbed "the Spanish flu," this pandemic caused more than twenty-one million deaths around the globe. Influenza struck down Americans in great numbers. Americans saw a great resurgence of the disease when the Great War ended, as Armistice Day celebrations fueled additional breakouts. The United States lost 675,000 people to the flu, more casualties than from World War I, World War II, the Korean War, and the Vietnam War combined. Comparatively, in the 2020s so far, there have been over six million COVID-19 hospitalizations in the United States and over a million deaths. Almost seven million people have died worldwide.

To highlight the impact of the influenza of 1918 on families, Phyllis Guiliano recalled her personal family saga:

> In the early 1900s, my Sicilian grandparents emigrated from a small mountain town near Palermo, Italy, to the Little Italy neighborhood of Newark, New Jersey. In 1918, my grandmother, having just given birth to her eighth child, easily succumbed to the rapidly spreading Spanish flu. Her death set in motion events that would affect my then eight-year-old father, the cohesiveness of his family, and of course his life as an adult and parent.
>
> My grandfather, a young immigrant widower, was left to care for eight young children while supporting the family. When he proved unable to manage this impossible task, the state shipped the children to various foster homes. Two years later, the oldest girl was deemed capable of assuming the role of mother, and the children were reunited. Two years of this difficult role was all the oldest girl could bear, so she escaped by getting married.
>
> My father went to work at fourteen and later joined the navy. His trade as a fur-garment dyer disappeared in the early 1950s, as did any meaningful work for the rest of his life. Raising his own family and experiencing satisfaction and joy was a deep struggle for my father, who had survived a motherless childhood and a lack of role models.
>
> The flu pandemic changed the trajectory of this big family. None of the children got an education, they struggled to stay close, and one brother spent time in prison. A colorful spot was the old family house, which had been broken into many apartments, with

outdoor privies, coal stoves, basement winemaking, and loving characters. It remained a gathering place for fabulous Sicilian feasts well into my childhood.

However, my father's pain and his early story were buried in silence, but plainly showed that the pandemic had lasting effects well beyond 1918.

This book follows Deborah, Miriam, and their extended family through three years of dramatic shifts in the world as they derive inspiration from the world around them. I conducted intensive research to give life to historical events they experienced. I read many books and articles and viewed endless movies and clips of the era, though much of the information was culled down to a couple of pages or even a short paragraph.

Not being a historian myself, I can't guarantee the accuracy of the facts and figures. I did not verify the information sourced online. In fact, I've encountered discrepancies between articles, leading me to occasionally rely on approximations or averages. My aim is to infuse historical data into my characters' experiences to bring history to life. I apologize for any inaccuracies that may arise as a result.

I learned the value of working with librarians who delved deep into historical questions with me. A local librarian found maps of Deborah and Miriam's neighborhood from the 1910s, which led to the story about the actual stables that existed a couple of blocks from their home. Another librarian, Julie Travers, helped me discover the Gloucester, Massachusetts, vacation camp for the Saturday Evening Girls and found the current owner of the property, Bob Wayne. He gave me a tour of the campgrounds and showed me Helen Storrow's original deed and blueprints of the original camp. He also introduced me to his eight-year-old granddaughter, Lia Wayne, who wrote the incredible poem I attributed to Deborah and Miriam's daughter Ida.

My writing was enhanced by visiting the places I describe. I drove by Mayor Curley's home, stopped at the original site of the Great Molasses Flood, walked through the neighborhood where Denison House stood, went inside United Limb and Brace Company of Boston (now known as United Prosthetics), and viewed the synagogue Deborah and Miriam attended. I asked several rabbis about the Jewish practices of Deborah, Miriam, and their families, to assure that my descriptions fit the time and culture of the early 1900s. Throughout the book are italicized Hebrew and Yiddish words. Definitions can be found in the glossary at the end of the book.

Enjoy your immersion into the years of 1917 to 1920. It is nice to have you along for my trip back into this explosive era and Deborah and Miriam's lives.

Preface

This book follows my beloved characters of Deborah, Miriam, and their imagined, extended family, through three years of dramatic shifts in the world. The Great War, the fight for women's suffrage, and the influenza of 1918, turbulent history of the years from 1917 to 1920 in the United States, affected everyone's lives. My fictional characters, Deborah and Miriam, are affected by actual history, interwoven with their personal struggles. Being a Jewish lesbian couple adds an intense, intimate glimpse into this period. My research intends to give life to actual historical events through their experiences. I verified the facts and figures as best as possible.

Four million Americans served their country, and more than 100,000 lost their lives after the United States entered the First World War in April 1917. Beginning in June 1917, American Expeditionary Forces arrived in Europe by transport ships. Americans stayed engaged overseas until the Allied victory on November 11, 1918. Though this was a comparatively short period, not one family in the United States was untouched by this war.

Those here at home grappled not only with the loss or absence of loved ones, but also with the disruption to every aspect of ordinary existence. Women went to work, replacing those men who were off at war. Some women volunteered with the American Red Cross, some worked in factories, some knitted socks, and some rolled bandages for soldiers. The United States relied heavily on propaganda campaigns to persuade people to curb their food consumption so that soldiers would have enough. Some women ran their family farms to avert a food shortage. Food played a critical role in the balance of power between the warring factions.

During this time, the fight for women's suffrage was at its peak. The National American Woman Suffrage Association stirred women to stand up for voting rights following their convention in 1904, at which they adopted the Declaration of Principles. By 1917, eight states had incorporated women's suffrage. Even though President Wilson switched his position and the House of Representatives granted women the right to vote by delivering the Nineteenth Amendment in 1918, the US Senate continued to deny women that right.

In addition to war, the influenza pandemic of 1918 devastated the world. Influenza struck down Americans in considerable numbers. The United States lost 675,000 people to this flu, which is more casualties than from World War I, World War II, the Korean War, and the Vietnam War combined. Soldiers spread the grippe, as it was called. The deadly sickness reached almost every country. Initially dubbed "the Spanish flu," this pandemic caused more than twenty-one million deaths around the globe. Americans saw another resurgence of the influenza when The Great War ended. Armistice Day celebrations fueled additional breakouts. (Comparatively, in the 2020s so far, over six million COVID-19 people have been hospitalized in the United States, with over a million deaths. Worldwide, almost seven million people have died of COVID-19.)

While writing, I learned the value of working with librarians, and I applaud them. After selecting a location for Deborah and Miriam's home, a local librarian found neighborhood maps from the 1910s. That in turn led to integrating the story about the actual animal stables that existed a couple of blocks from their "home." Another librarian helped me discover the Gloucester, Massachusetts vacation camp for the Saturday Evening Girls. She found the current owner of the property, who gave me a tour of the campgrounds; and he showed me Helen Storrow's original deed and blueprints of the original camp. He also introduced me to his eight-year-old granddaughter, Lia Wayne, who wrote the incredible poem that I attributed to Deborah and Miriam's daughter, Ida. I also viewed pieces of the magnificent Arts and Crafts style pottery created by the Saturday Evening Girls in the North End of Boston.

By visiting the places I describe in historical fiction, I put a foundation to my characters and story. I drove by Mayor Curley's home, and I stopped at the original site

of the Great Molasses Flood. I walked through the neighborhood where Denison House stood. I went inside United Limb and Brace Company of Boston (now known as United Prosthetics), and I viewed the original Mishkan Tefilla, the synagogue where I placed Deborah and Miriam for worship.

I also made many personal connections which enriched my work. Melissa Burrage, Ph.D in American Studies, shared her book, *The Karl Muck Scandal: Classical Music and Xenophobia in World War I America,* making my chapter about the colorful conductor of the Boston Symphony Orchestra one of my favorites. She also assisted me with a thorough edit of the history of the era. Caroline Timbie, the granddaughter of the true to life character of Grace Banker and overseer of the Banker Foundation, taught me of Grace's tastes and activities, information which enhanced the information I gathered from books and articles. My friend Phyllis Guiliano told me of about the dramatic effects of her grandmother's death in the Pandemic of 1918, causing her eight children to be sent into foster care. I asked several rabbis about the Jewish practices that my characters and their families would have had, to better match the time and culture of the early 1900s. Throughout the book are italicized Hebrew and Yiddish words; definitions can be found in the glossary at the end of the book.

Enjoy your immersion into the years of 1917 to 1920. It is nice to have you along for my trip back into this explosive era as we conjure the lives of Deborah, Miriam, and their friends and families.

Acknowledgments

My most significant appreciation goes to Fay Jacobs, my mentor and guide. Fay turned my words into readable prose as she guided me to tell my story succinctly and required me to learn the mechanics of writing. I'll always appreciate Fay's willingness to take a fledgling writer and turn her into an author. Thank you, Fay.

Also significant was Melissa Burrage. I had the pleasure of meeting Melissa at the Cape Cod Writers Center Conference, where I learned about her book, *The Karl Muck Scandal: Classical Music and Xenophobia in World War I America*. Melissa kindly edited this book from the perspective of a historian, adding much information regarding the issues of the era. I greatly value her insights.

I turned to many others to assist in the completion of this book. Great praise goes to the magnificent Sara Yager, a layout designer, cover designer, and photography editor rolled into one. She brings the book to life with her creative spirit and technological wizardry. Margaret Kelner provided my first copy edit, adding her remarkable skills to a very rough draft.

The Writers Circle at the Resort on Carefree Boulevard, led by Dana Finnegan for many years, encouraged me to become a better writer by insisting I make Deborah and Miriam's tale more accessible to those who could not read my mind. Recently, under the tutelage of the fine writers of this group and that of the accomplished writer Becky Bohan, who taught me about cliff-hangers, my career as a writer has grown.

I also wish to acknowledge many friends who've endured hours of dramatic readings in which I have read every word aloud. Hearing my writing helps me greatly with dialogue and with the flow of the story. My listeners have caught repetitive words, incorrect dates, poorly chosen phrases, and missing links in the storyline.

The first person to hear my ramblings was Jan Eichen, who listened to the entire manuscript when it was just disconnected stories I needed to form into a story. Each of the next trifecta of readers noticed different aspects of my book and directed me to think about my writing from various perspectives. The author, editor, and wise woman Jeanine, Dr. Jazz Normand, through the process of reworking one chapter at a time, has also become a beloved friend. Jeanine collaborated with me as if she were the author, intimately befriending my characters as if they were her own friends. Shelly added new perspectives, listening patiently as I reworked chapter after chapter. My good friend Marian Grace, who under the pen name of Cameron Grae authored an early lesbian mystery series, added great insights and noticed many details I'd overlooked.

Varied writers' groups and educational programs have enhanced my writing. I am grateful to the women from Lesbians Writeon, a Zoom group of talented writers who teach me by example. I've appreciated the opportunity to conduct presentations at the online *Lesbian Fiction Campfire*, expertly led by Elena Graf, and at the internationally acclaimed lesbian writers' conference, Readout. Rainbow Lifelong Learning Institute gave me the opportunity to teach a course, Discrimination in Post-Victorian Boston, based on my extensive research. From each of these venues, I learned as much as I taught.

Carolyn Timbie and the Grace Banker Family Foundation offered me a great deal of insight into the life of Carolyn's grandmother, Grace Banker, who led the US Army Signal Corps's switchboard operators, the Hello Girls, in France during the Great War. I also want to thank my friend Judy Young, who, along with her partner, Meg Chalmers, wrote the book *The Saturday Evening Girls: Paul Revere Pottery,* stirring my interest about this wonderful Bostonian story. This Progressive Era library club in the North End of Boston became well known for their Arts and Crafts pottery. It was exciting when Judy showed me from her collection some actual pottery created by these talented artisans.

Also related to the Saturday Evening Girls was the property in Gloucester, Massachusetts; Helen Storrow purchased it to build a summer camp for the Saturday Evening Girls. Bob Wayne, the current owner of the land and an avid historian about Helen Storrow's purchase of the property, showed me around, noting where each building had been.

Finally, I'm grateful to my friend Phyllis Giuliano, who told me of the dramatic impact the influenza of 1918 had on her family.

I would be remiss if I missed an opportunity to thank my dedicated readers who have joined me on Deborah and Miriam's journey. Their tale continues…

Family Tree

(Ages as of January 1917)

Levines—Manhattan; Great Barrington, Massachusetts

Mr. Levine
(46)

Mrs. Levine
(44)

Deborah
(24)
(born late August 1892)

Milton
(20)

Anna
(17)

Sylvia (4)
Deborah and Miriam's child
(born April 16, 1912)

Ida
(1)
Deborah and Miriam's child
(born April 18, 1916)

Family Tree

(Ages as of January 1917)

Bubbie
(*died August 16, 1914*)

Mr. Cohen ————— Mrs. Cohen
(*died July 22, 1913*)   (*died July 27, 1914*)

William
(32)
(*Ruth's husband*)

Hannah
(27)

Sylvia (4)
Deborah and Miriam's child
(*born April 16, 1912*)

Ida
(1)
Deborah and Miriam's child
(born April 18, 1916)

Sarah (2)
Hannah and William's child
(*born June 3, 1914*)

Family Tree

(Ages as of January 1917)

GOLDS—MANHATTAN; GREAT BARRINGTON, MASSACHUSETTS

Ruth
(24)

Michael
(25)
(*Ruth's husband*)

Family Tree

(Ages as of January 1917)

BERKOWITZES—MANHATTAN; LENOX, MASSACHUSETTS

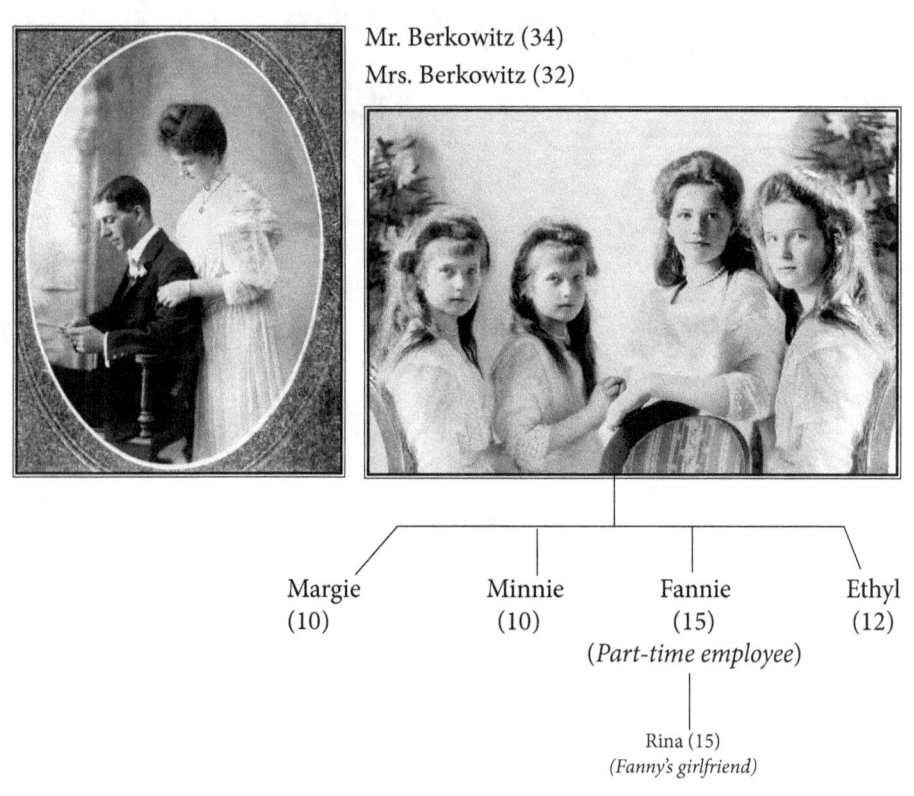

Mr. Berkowitz (34)
Mrs. Berkowitz (32)

Margie	Minnie	Fannie	Ethyl
(10)	(10)	(15)	(12)

(Part-time employee)

Rina (15)
(Fanny's girlfriend)

Friends

(Ages in December 1914)

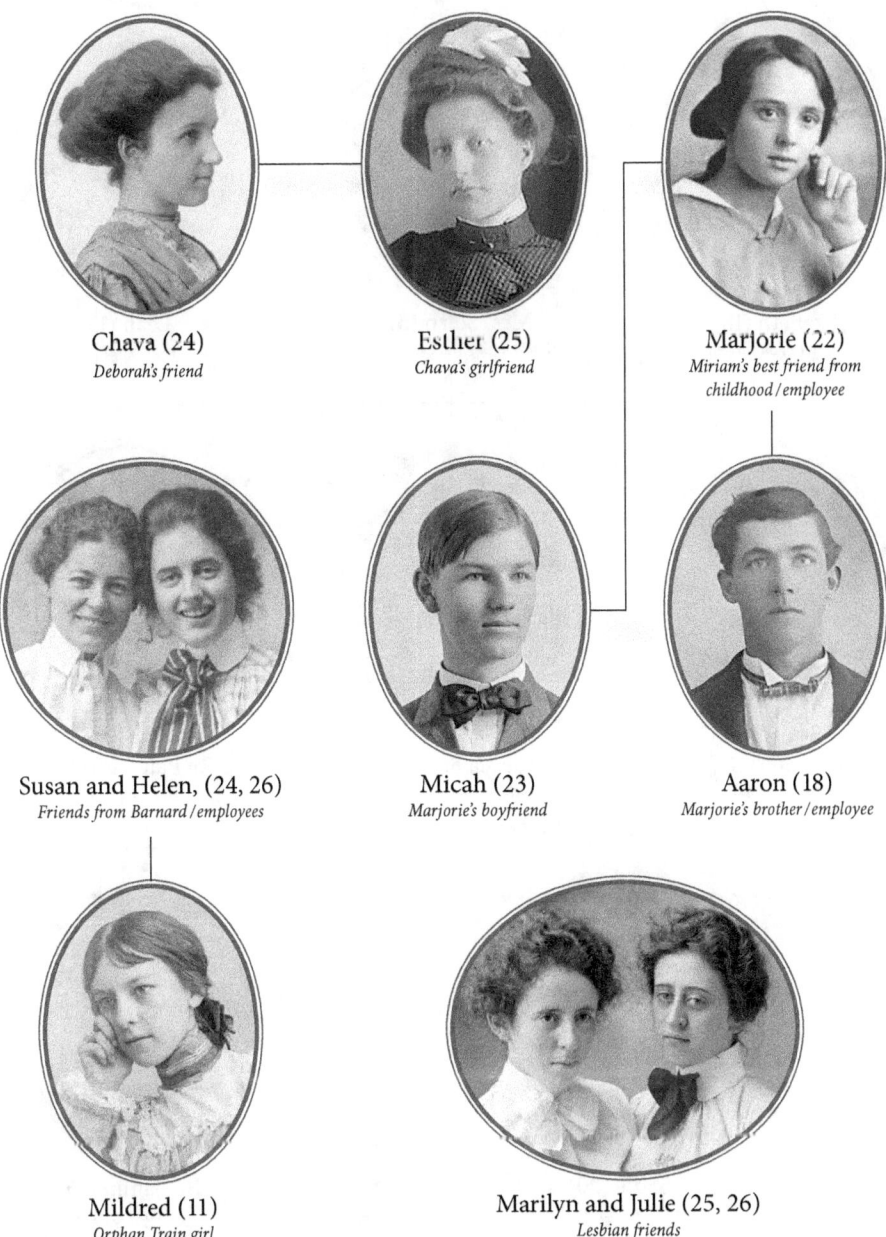

Chava (24)
Deborah's friend

Esther (25)
Chava's girlfriend

Marjorie (22)
Miriam's best friend from childhood / employee

Susan and Helen, (24, 26)
Friends from Barnard / employees

Micah (23)
Marjorie's boyfriend

Aaron (18)
Marjorie's brother / employee

Mildred (11)
Orphan Train girl

Marilyn and Julie (25, 26)
Lesbian friends

For Deborah and Miriam, securing a family is paramount. Following the loss of their beloved Bubbie and Miriam's mother, they pull their friends into a tighter circle. These courageous friends become part of their new and unorthodox family.

Other Characters
(Ages in December 1914)

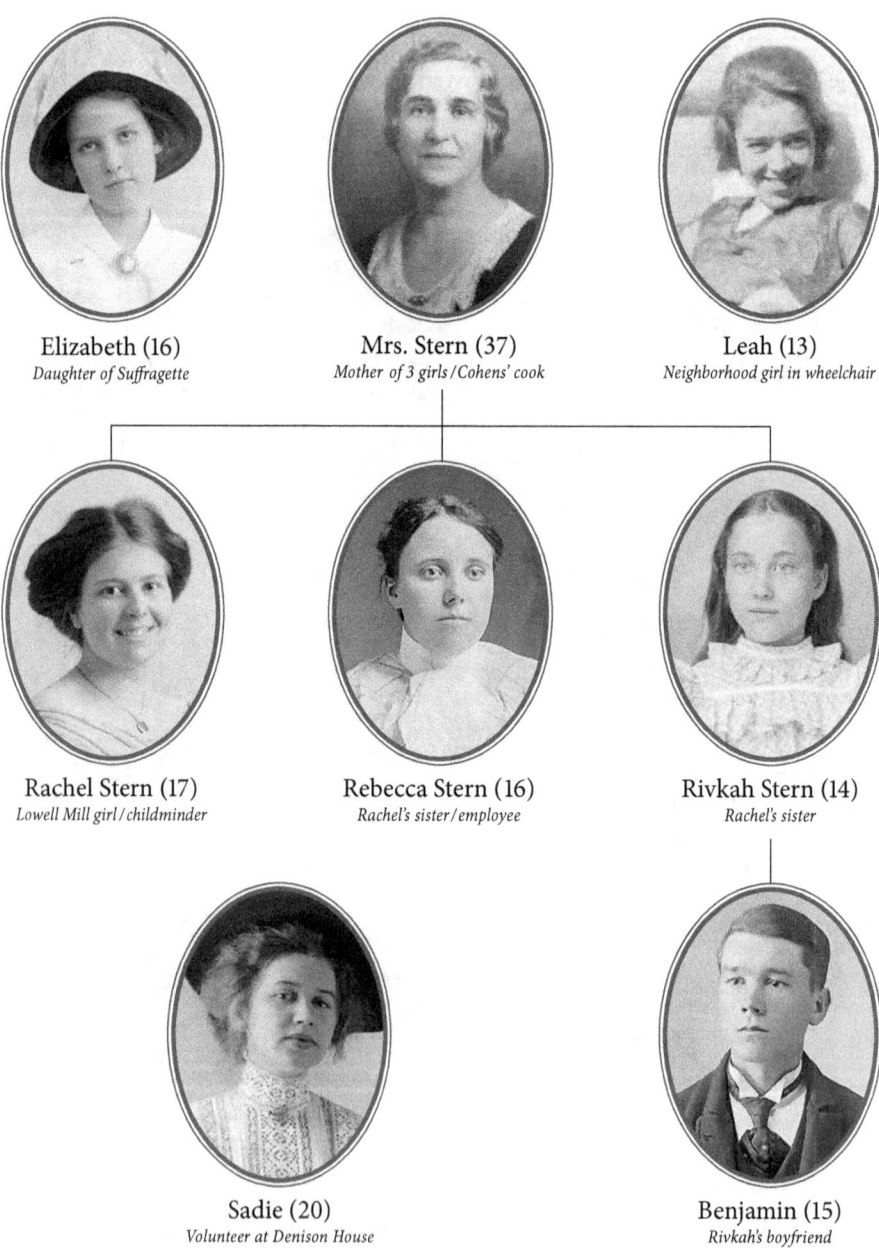

Elizabeth (16)
Daughter of Suffragette

Mrs. Stern (37)
Mother of 3 girls / Cohens' cook

Leah (13)
Neighborhood girl in wheelchair

Rachel Stern (17)
Lowell Mill girl / childminder

Rebecca Stern (16)
Rachel's sister / employee

Rivkah Stern (14)
Rachel's sister

Sadie (20)
Volunteer at Denison House

Benjamin (15)
Rivkah's boyfriend

Along with their friends, Deborah and Miriam surround others in their orbit with love, respect, support, and ways to grow.

Employees

Rebecca (printing shop)

Susan (publishing shop)

Helen (printing shop)

Marjorie (accounting)

Aaron (deliveries, then apprentice in shop)

Leah (printing shop assistant)

Mildred (printing shop assistant)

Fanny (printing shop for summer and vacations)

Rachel (babysitter)

Mrs. Stern (cook)

Episode 1 ✤ *Romance*

January 1917

When the telephone rang, Deborah stiffened; phone calls were rarely good news. Often, it was her parents calling from New York City with information about a recently deceased relative. Occasionally, it was an impatient client who couldn't wait to ask a publishing question, or someone making random calls before getting the first bill for their brand-new telephone.

Miriam waited by Deborah's side, trying to piece together the conversation from her one-sided perspective. The words "polio," "Berkowitz twins," and "frightening" sent shivers down her spine as she waited for the full story.

As Deborah hung up from speaking to her mother, Miriam noticed Deborah had broken into a sweat.

"What happened? Do Margie and Minnie have polio? I thought the polio epidemic in New York was over. And aren't they too old at ten for infantile paralysis?"

"Slow down, Miriam," Deborah said calmly, pulling aside her long skirt so she could sit on the divan. "No. The twins do not have polio, though they were exposed. Actually, all of them have been exposed since the twins played with one of their neighbors' children who was just diagnosed. The whole family is in quarantine, though no one has any symptoms."

"Was your family exposed too, living in the same building? How sick is the child? So many little ones die from polio."

"My family's fine. The neighbor's child is in the hospital, and they have no idea yet whether she'll pull through. Luckily, older children and adults rarely get sick, so let's hope Mr. and Mrs. Berkowitz's four daughters are all too old to get it."

"I'm certain Fanny is too old at fifteen, and Ethel is twelve."

"Miriam, stick with the facts, and try not to make assumptions. From what I've heard, there are occasional cases in older children or adults, though it's rare. And yes, most of the epidemic ended when the cold weather hit, yet there are still occasional cases. I've heard of some children becoming sick here in Boston. I even heard of one sick child living right here on Homestead Street. Yet let's not assume the worst."

"Let's call Mrs. B. to see how they're doing. She's always been there for us in times of trouble, so we should reach out to her." Miriam was clearly still agitated.

"You, my dear, are not reaching out to anyone in your current state. You would only increase her feeling of panic. Let's call her tomorrow when you're calmer about this."

Miriam, agreeing with Deborah's observation that she was overly emotional, made an effort to appear relaxed, even though her insides were still jumping. What about their two children, Sylvia and Ida? Sylvia's mongoloid condition and Ida's age, at only twenty months old, made them both vulnerable.

The next day, Deborah made the call, concerned that Miriam's anxiety would be obvious if she did it. She was assured that all was well at the Berkowitz home and that the family down the hall was at the hospital, hoping their younger child had been spared.

Sadly, by the end of the week, the younger sister had developed symptoms and had also been hospitalized. But the Berkowitz family, still in quarantine, said they were enjoying their time—playing games, singing, and doing art projects together. It was too cold to go outside anyway. This month was the coldest on record.

Deborah and Miriam took turns calling the Berkowitzes, cranking the long handle on the side of the wooden telephone box attached to the kitchen wall and waiting for the operator to get off her other calls to connect them. They decided it was worth the huge expense of daily phone check-ins.

❧ ❧ ❧

Deborah and Miriam had many discussions about the Berkowitz family and the stricken children. When the neighbor's younger child died, they were sad, but also frightened. Thereafter, they became hypervigilant about the health of their girls, fearing what would happen if they became ill.

"Deborah, this sudden, serious illness makes me want to talk about us," Miriam said as they approached their bedroom after having put their little girls to bed.

Surprised, Deborah asked, "Have I done something to upset you? Did I say something insensitive about the child who passed away?"

"No," said Miriam, smiling. "You've done nothing wrong. I've just been considering our life together. In this time of illness and death, I realize how happiness could suddenly be taken away from us. I want to make our lives as good as we can." Miriam hesitated for a moment, then continued, "Sometimes we're just moving through life with a focus on everyday tasks. I'd like to make certain we're putting as much effort into our relationship as we do into parenting and our business."

"Phew. I thought I'd done something awful." Deborah let out a huge sigh.

"No, my dear. There's nothing terrible going on. Though we could do better."

"In what way?"

"There's not enough romance in our relationship."

"You mean our night pleasures?"

"No. Well, yes, that too. Yet our lack of physical intimacy reflects our lack of closeness. Sometimes we just go through each day without taking the time to cherish that we have two adorable children, a successful business, and a loving relationship."

"So if I promise to satisfy you at least once per week, will that make it all better?" asked Deborah with a smirk and a playful squeeze of Miriam's waist.

"I won't complain if that happens, yet no, that's not what I meant."

"Tell me more," urged Deborah, motioning to the comfortable wingback chairs in their room. "Think back to what we were like almost seven years ago when we first met. So much has happened since then. One difference is that I'd be sitting on the edge of your chair, stroking your hair while we talked."

Miriam smiled. "Now you're getting it."

Deborah moved closer. "Okay. So, are you happier now that I'm touching you? Is it physical closeness that will make you feel more connected? Or is there something else I could do?"

"It's nice, but it's a feeling that's missing."

"Miriam, I love you with all my heart. That hasn't changed. If anything, my feelings have grown stronger as we've faced so many difficult times together. First, your father rejected us; then he died, leaving you two no time to make amends."

"Then your father also rejected us, and my mother and my grandmother passed. There's been so much loss."

"So describe what's missing." Deborah looked into Miriam's eyes, steering the conversation back to the moment.

"I want to love you with the same excitement I had when I first met you. I want the room to light up when you walk in the door. I want to miss you desperately when we're apart and to feel whole when you're by my side."

"I love you more deeply now. I treasure you in a way I was too young to understand when we first met. Back in Great Barrington for those first two summers, I was awestruck. I can even remember the lovely blue dress you were wearing when I met you, with lace on the bodice and down the long sleeves and a cinched waist, which accentuated your lovely figure. Now, I'm still in awe because you are as wonderful as I imagined you to be when I first met you. You are the kindest and strongest woman I know." Deborah ran her hands up Miriam's back, stopping at the spot on her neck that always made Miriam shudder.

"And you know just how to touch me to excite me. I love the familiarity we have." Miriam stopped for a moment, deep in thought. "I love how we work together, both at home as parents and at the shop. We've found a great rhythm."

"Then why this serious conversation about needing more romance?"

"I wish I could pinpoint what's missing. Clearly, more physical intimacy would be nice, though it's so much more than that," Miriam said.

Deborah was quiet for a moment, unsure how to progress. "Let's begin with the physical," she said, "since it's clear we both want more. I'll consider ways to add more romance."

Miriam moved her hands along Deborah's chest, stopping with a hand over her heart. "This is the center of what I want. To make your heart beat so fast that you can't ignore it."

Deborah kissed Miriam gently, brushing her lips across her cheeks, then kissing the nape of her neck.

Miriam took Deborah's hand and led her to the bed. "Thank you for taking me seriously," Miriam said.

"I love you so much, Miriam. I want to do anything I can to make you happy."

There were no more words as Deborah slowly and seductively removed all of Miriam's clothing. She unhooked Miriam's soft, peach-colored wool dress, then removed her chemise, pleased Miriam had only a loose corset covering her body. Miriam's frilly cotton drawers were easy to slip down.

Deborah took off her own dress and undergarments, dropping them on the chair. She caressed Miriam's body lightly from top to bottom, and when Miriam wanted to reciprocate, she shook her head.

Miriam remembered the very special birthday gift Deborah had once given her, when the loving was all one-sided and intense. She hoped this was to be a repeat of that thrilling experience.

Deborah nodded as she had the identical thought. She stared at Miriam's face as she caressed every bit of skin with the softness of a feather. She kissed behind Miriam's ear, then blew softly into it. As Miriam shivered, Deborah wrapped Miriam's body in the sheet and moved her attention to the other ear. Next, she whispered words of love before moving to the most sensitive area of Miriam's neck while continuing the gentle caresses. Touching every inch of skin, she stroked Miriam's shoulders, gliding along her arms and hands, then stopping to rub each finger and pull it gently. She watched Miriam smile, as she continued towards her chest. Deborah moved to Miriam's waiting breasts, licking the skin until the nipples became erect. When she placed her lips on the hard nubs, she sucked gently, listening to Miriam's breaths. Deborah stayed there for a long time.

Miriam's breathing increased; Deborah moved lower. She ran her lips along Miriam's hips, softly awakening her. As she reached the mound of soft hair, Miriam positioned herself for more contact. Deborah slowed. She softly moved the hairs, teasing Miriam's body with barely felt caresses. She moved her lips to Miriam's inner thighs, adding wetness as she licked close to her sweet spot, which was now glistening.

Deborah darted her tongue to Miriam's center of sensation. A quick lick, then hesitation before another. Then slow, deliberate strokes that soaked her lips with Miriam's wetness. She licked harder, not quicker. Miriam's breath became ragged as Deborah continued with gentle movements, gliding up and down, back and forth. She felt the area tighten, and she caressed the firmness with her tongue. She pressed her lips on Miriam's sweet spot, moving her tongue faster and harder. Miriam's breathing was loud as she arched her back and ground into Deborah's insistent mouth.

When Miriam gasped over and over, Deborah held on tight, not letting up until the final spasms stopped. They held each other tightly, lying in a tangle of arms and legs.

It was a long time before Miriam spoke. "That was a good beginning." And she smiled.

ॐ ॐ ॐ

The next evening, they sat in their wingback chairs, ready to talk. The conversation, as usual, began with their children and the printing and publishing shops.

"I was noticing today, when Sylvia was naming most items in the new picture book you brought from the library, how well she's talking. She's replaced the pointing and grunting with a name for most things," said Miriam.

"And I understand almost everything she says. It wasn't long ago when I had to ask Rachel to interpret for me. She's certainly different from other four-year-olds, but I'm pleased with her progress."

"And Ida is speaking well for a twenty-month-old. I credit Rachel for that too. We're so fortunate to have her care for our children while we work. I wonder if it's Rachel or Ida teaching Sylvia words. It should be the older sister leading, yet it's fine with me if it is the other way around."

After more discussion about their girls, they mentioned their day at the shop. Deborah was working on a complicated booklet, and Miriam finally completed the printing of a manuscript Deborah had recently edited. They discussed how well it worked to separate the publishing and printing functions, though they had done so only four months earlier.

Once they finished their daily catch-up, Miriam mentioned the cold weather and her sadness about the child who had died of polio. They talked of her family and the news from Mrs. B. that the neighbor's older girl was out of the hospital, though not walking well.

After a conversation about the pain the families must be facing, Deborah changed the topic, asking Miriam her opinion on the conflict that was raging in Europe. "Will the United States stay uninvolved? And will this war ever reach our shores?"

Miriam shook her head, saying, "I have no idea if we can stay out of it. I'm not as knowledgeable as you, probably because I have so little tolerance for aggression." She hesitated for a moment, then said, "I'd be happy to discuss warfare at another time. I'd rather discuss my need for more romance. Last night was lovely. It was a special evening, both physically and emotionally. Did I remember to say thank you?"

"You don't need to thank me. It was mutual. I thought the evening was a wonderful step in the right direction. I want to respond to your need for more intimacy, and not just the physical kind."

"I wish I could tell you exactly what I want. I just don't want us to take each other for granted," Miriam said.

"It's amazing to me that you still love me, despite how difficult I can be. I'm better than I used to be, thanks to you, yet I still sometimes react too fast and too harshly."

"Deborah, you're much gentler than when I met you, and you don't run away from your frustrations anymore."

"Thanks to you. I don't know how I'd have managed without your guidance."

"You were ready to change. I'm glad you're not so easily upset."

"So," Deborah asked, "if you are not frustrated with my harsh temperament, what is it that you need?"

"Exactly this. I want us to chat about us and how our relationship is growing. We are so focused on the house, the children, our work, the synagogue, and anything practical, that we forget to discuss being a couple."

"Well, if you are going to say such nice things to me, I'll be glad to have these conversations!" Deborah smiled.

"I can't promise it will all be smooth, though I appreciate your willingness to talk like this."

"Let's make a promise to have conversations about what we can do for each other, much like Mrs. B. suggested to us a long time ago when we were having trouble."

"Mrs. B. always has good ideas. We're fortunate to have her in our lives. We should remember to have these conversations before *Shabbos* each week." Blushing, Miriam continued, "And we should add more physical intimacy."

Deborah perked up. "I like this plan! I thought this was going to be a difficult discussion about terrible things I was doing to upset you, and instead, I'm in agreement with everything you're saying. Then let's have a special night every week when we can have a combination of talking and loving! After all, we're only twenty-three and twenty-four—much too young to act like an old married couple!"

"Deborah!"

ॐ ॐ ॐ

On their next special night, Miriam thought it would be fun to review what it was like when they first got together. "I was so confused about my feelings. I had never been so excited to see someone and so sad when we had to part. I was concerned that you'd never write to me after that first summer and that you wouldn't send me samples of your writing, as you promised."

"There was no way I was going to lose contact with you. I was deeply touched, and I couldn't even wait one day to write to you."

"The first letter I got from you arrived right after I got home. I was amazed how quickly it came and thrilled when you sent me your first article. I can remember it to this day. It was called 'Parents of Young Women.'"

"I can't believe you remember that. I really fell in love with you as we corresponded that first winter apart."

"It was the same for me. I waited anxiously for each of your letters, and I could hardly contain myself from writing back to you that same day," said Miriam.

"I worried whether you felt anything like what I was feeling, though once I saw you, I knew that you did."

"Deborah, this is just what I was talking about. I can hardly believe that we've not talked about that time in many years. We've forgotten to connect in this way. I loved our special night and can't wait for the next one."

"We may have to work at conversation topics; we can't discuss our first meeting over and over, every time. We'll need to be creative."

"It will be fun getting reacquainted with you."

Polio epidemic

Telephone

Episode 2 ❦
Mayor James Michael Curley
February 1917

"**D**id you know that yesterday was Boston's first Rat Day?" Miriam asked soon after returning from her volunteer work at Denison House.

"What are you talking about?" asked Deborah.

"The volunteers talked about it at the settlement house. There's been a serious rat problem in Boston, and the local Brahmin women decided to take on the issue. I read in the paper that they offered to pay $1.34 for each rat carcass collected on February 13."

"Wait a minute. First tell me who Brahmin women are. And then, why would they pay for dead rats? Are they going to make coats out of their fur?" Deborah laughed.

"Let me pour a cup of tea, and I'll tell you the whole story."

"We should invite Susan and Helen to hear this. I'll get them and meet you in the parlor for your incredulous tale. You'd better make tea for all of us." Deborah was pleased to include their housemates Susan and Helen, printshop employees and old friends from Barnard College.

Once the four were seated, and their tea was served, Miriam began. "Let me tell you first about the wealthy women who formed the Boston Women's Municipal League, a club of sorts. They're called Brahmins, and they meet at the Hotel Somerset, the same place we went for our first suffrage meeting."

"What does this have to do with rats?" Deborah asked impatiently.

"I'll get to it." Miriam explained, "Brahmins are an elite group of women named after the highest caste in the Indian social system."

"And what do they have to do with rats?" Deborah said, hoping Miriam would get to the point.

Miriam touched Deborah's arm gently to calm her. "This aristocratic group decided that it was up to the women of the city to help with the growing problem of rats."

"Why would they be in charge of rats?" Helen asked.

"Please let her continue," Deborah said, wanting to move this conversation forward.

"The two thousand women of this group formed the Committee on Social Hygiene, believing it was women's work to keep homes tidy and safe and free from rodents. They sent anti-rat literature to every library in the country. Here in Boston, the government responded by appointing an official city-rat catcher. The mayor, James Michael Curley, was supportive of their efforts and declared February 13 as Rat Day. These wealthy ladies offered financial support by paying a great deal of money for every dead rat."

"Ridiculous."

"No, Deborah, it was a reasonable step in ridding the city of these vermin. A man from Brighton won the contest by killing 282 rats. He made almost four hundred dollars!"

"Disgusting. And it seems impossible."

"The committee had hoped for more success than they achieved, blaming the cold weather and confusion about the date of Rat Day for the poor numbers. It may not have been entirely successful, yet it led to more public awareness. The result was actually very helpful. The Boston Board of Health offered to take over the task of ridding the city of rats from now on."

"Bravo," said Helen. "Great explanation. What are we going to do to protect ourselves from these filthy creatures?"

"A cat! I think we should get a cat!" Deborah blurted.

"I'd love to have a kitten," Miriam said, wide-eyed.

"And you should name it Jimmy," Helen suggested.

"Why Jimmy?" Miriam asked.

"After the mayor of Boston, James Michael Curley. After all, you said he supported ridding the city of these creatures."

"I like the idea, though would we really want to name our pet after an Irish Catholic man?" Miriam asked. "My father would roll over in his grave."

"What would be the Hebrew name for James?" asked Deborah.

Miriam considered the options. "I don't know any Jewish men named James. Maybe it would be Yaakov, the Hebrew name for Jacob."

Deborah laughed. "I can't imagine calling, 'Here, Yaakov. Here, Yaakov.'"

"Then Jimmy it is," Miriam said, happy to get a kitten. "Wait a minute. I don't know a lot about this mayor of ours. I want to know more about whether he has the support of the Jewish community before we name our cat after him. What do you know?" Miriam asked the others.

All around, heads shook.

"We should ask at *shul* before we name our kitten after him."

ॐ ॐ ॐ

Valentine's Day passed with lovely cards. This year, Deborah avoided mentioning the Valentine's Day card that had slipped from her pocket and alerted her father to their love for each other, causing his rejection of his daughter. Whenever she brought this up, it soured the day, and she wanted this to be a sweet holiday.

Despite the frigid temperatures, Deborah and Miriam made it to temple on Friday night. They lured many congregants into discussing something other than the second month of record-breaking, freezing-cold temperatures. They asked about the Boston mayor.

It seemed he was thought of favorably by almost everyone, based primarily on his position on immigration. This was a topic on everyone's minds these days because of the Immigration Act of 1917, federal legislation that had just passed into law. Mayor James Michael Curley, the son of Irish immigrants, fought vehemently for the rights of the foreign-born population of Boston, especially the Irish, Jews, and Italians who'd been discriminated against for years. Most of the families at the shul had been born in Eastern Europe, so they appreciated his vigilant support of immigration policies, a very personal issue for most of them.

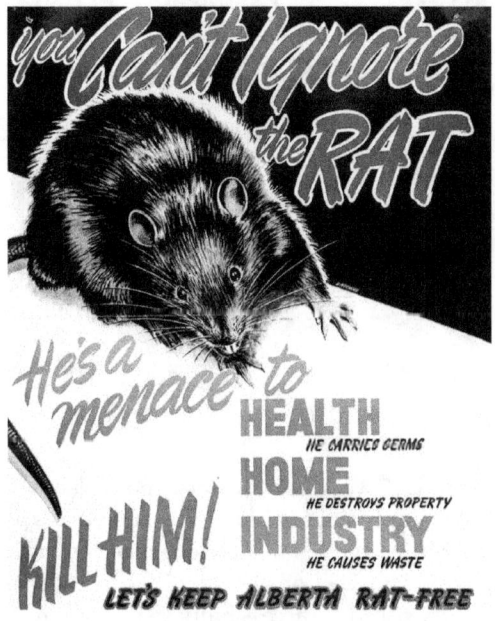

Rat Day

Deborah and Miriam, hearing the positive opinions about the mayor, decided to get a cat and name it Jimmy.

"Despite his tendency to favor the Irish?" Miriam asked.

"Yes, I still think so," Deborah said, smiling at the thought of a new family member.

❞ ❞ ❞

On Monday, Deborah headed to the library to find out more about Mayor Curley and this immigration act. With help from her librarian friend, Deborah read that this new law, the most restrictive anti-immigration law since the Chinese Exclusion Act of 1882, barred immigrants from the Asia-Pacific zone and other foreign locations. Plus, it included a new literacy requirement, making it harder for all immigrants.[1]

James Micahel Curley

Deborah returned home downtrodden and relayed the information to Miriam, Susan, and Helen over dinner. Susan and Helen's

---

[1] The Immigration Act of 1917 was discriminatory, and it placed strict quotas on those entering the country. Previously, literacy had been proposed as a prerequisite for immigrants, but this time it was suggested that anyone entering the United States had to be able to read five lines of the US Constitution. President Wilson stated this denied admission to the country based on accessibility to education, a standard he called unfair, so he vetoed the law. Both the House and Senate overrode his veto.

daughter Mildred played with the silverware and didn't participate in the conversation.

"I don't understand discrimination," Miriam responded. "Haven't all of those voting against immigration come from families with relatives from other countries?"

"Most," agreed Susan, "except for those Boston Brahmins, the elite folks whose heritage went back to the Mayflower."

"It's those Anglo-Saxons with no acceptance or appreciation of differences," Helen added.

"Anglo-Saxons?" asked Miriam.

"That refers to Protestants, mostly of English descent," Helen explained.

"What does religion have to do with this?" Miriam asked.

"Everything!" Helen and Susan responded in unison.

❧ ❧ ❧

It took several weeks to find a kitten. They named their tiny ball of gold fur Jimmy, as planned, hoping he would quickly learn that his purpose in life was to capture unwanted rodents. Miriam really didn't care about rats, since she'd never seen one, yet this playful kitty thrilled her. Their daughters were a bit rough on him, but without a single hiss or scratch, the kitten adjusted to being grabbed, sat on, and pulled around. Even though he never caught a rat, or even a mouse, Jimmy was soon an adored member of their family. Miriam was warmed by this tiny creature and spoke lovingly about the sweetness of Jimmy.

❧ ❧ ❧

Deborah returned to the library, as the discussion about the Boston mayor had piqued her curiosity. Expecting to learn more about his support of Jews, she instead learned that in 1904 he had been convicted of fraud when he took federal service exams for two men. She wondered how could someone, even someone who was quite charismatic, be elected to public office after that.

Once home, despite Miriam's lackluster interest in politics, she was willing to engage in a conversation about the mayor's despicable behavior. "I think people make religion more important than other qualities, which probably influenced the Catholics who supported him despite his illegal practices. I know my father would have supported any Jewish candidate, no matter what his policies."

"Miriam, I agree your father would have behaved in that way, and the Catholics of Boston have probably fallen into that same practice, but that's another form of prejudice."

"I never thought of it that way, but you're right. Prejudice in their favor might be just as harmful as discrimination against them."

"Let's do our best to make decisions based on a full review of a person's character, not just their religion or any single characteristic. I want to remember that when siding with women who are suffragists."[2]

Armistice Day

---

[2] James Michael Curley was one of the most colorful figures in Massachusetts history and a huge favorite of the Roman Catholic Irish Americans of Boston. Despite dropping out of school at age fifteen, he served as the forty-first, forty-third, forty-fifth, and forty-eighth mayor of Boston. He also served a single term as governor of Massachusetts, and two terms in Congress—from 1911 to 1914, and again from 1943 to 1947—his two congressional terms thirty years apart.

The Democrat was well known for his excessive spending and corruption. Curley was convicted twice for criminal behavior, and he served time in prison for mail fraud during his last term as mayor. After serving for five months, in consideration of his poor health, his sentence was commuted by President Truman.

Curley was credited with the expansion of Boston City Hospital and Boston's noteworthy public transportation system. Despite being corrupt, Curley helped a great number of people.

Episode 3 ❧ *Warhorses*

March 1917

"May I talk with you for a minute?" Rachel asked after Miriam returned from work. Rachel typically left quickly after her babysitter role ended, but today she lingered.

"Certainly. Is there something wrong with Sylvia? Or Ida?"

"They're fine, and there's really no problem at all. I just have something to ask you."

"What are you concerned about?" Miriam asked, righting herself after almost tripping over Jimmy stretched out on the floor.

"I seem to remember that you like horses."

"Yes, I do. Well, I used to. It was one of the interests Deborah and I had in common when we met. We went riding together a bit when we were in Western Massachusetts, though we haven't done that in a long time. Why do you ask?"

"Well, you see…I was wondering… Well, maybe it's not something I should bring up." Rachel bent down to pick up Jimmy, who began purring.

"Rachel, you seem nervous. What's wrong?"

"I…I…I was just wondering if you'd like to spend some time with me and some horses," said Rachel with a bit of a stammer. The cat jumped away from Rachel, leaving a tiny scratch on her arm, which she rubbed distractedly.

"I'd love to. Where do you plan to get horses? We have a car instead of a buggy now, so we aren't around horses at all."

"Well, there are horses really near here. Have you and Deborah ever taken a walk on Blue Hill Avenue and seen the stables?"

"Yes, we have. We usually walk that way on our evening strolls when it isn't cold, but everything is closed down by that time of day. I've never thought much about those horses, though I certainly smell them when we walk by."

"While I'm taking care of Sylvia, Ida, and Sarah, I sometimes take them on walks in that direction, and we've stopped by quite often lately. They're really nice people there, working with the horses."

"I'm certain they are. So what is it you want with me and these horses?"

"Well, you see, I was very touched when you took me downtown to the Parker House to have a piece of pie last year."

"I remember that well. We had a lovely afternoon together."

"Well, maybe we could go to the stables."

"Rachel. That's a lovely idea. I had a delightful time with you, and I'd planned to spend more time with you, though it never seems to happen. We're both so busy and now you have your companion, Aaron, in your life. I'm touched that you want to get together with me, though I feel bad I've not initiated something in all this time."

Rachel's blush reddened further, and she turned her face away to hide it.

"Rachel, would you really like to go to the stables, or would you rather go downtown to the Parker House again?"

"I'd really like to go to the stables with you."

"Why are you so interested in the stables?"

"You see, they've been running these stables for many years, providing horses for folks with buggies, though now there are fewer horse-drawn carriages in the city. So, lately, things have been changing at the stables."

"And…"

"And now they're preparing the horses for the cavalry."

"What are you talking about? Cavalries are men who ride horses in war, yet the fighting is in Europe, not here."

"Yes, but the soldiers will need to ride horses when they go to Europe to fight. And the army needs to train the horses and the riders. So now this little stable in our neighborhood…well, your neighborhood…is training the horses. And soon the army will be training the men to ride them in the war."

"So this is becoming a military training post?"

"Yes! Right here! And we could be part of it."

"How could we help?" asked Miriam, quite confused.

"I'm not sure. Women will be needed everywhere when we go to war, and I'm thinking we…well, maybe just I…can help with the horses. I've always loved horses, and I miss being with them. When I was a young girl, we lived on a farm with many horses."

"So where do I fit into this scheme of yours?" asked Miriam.

"I bet they'd let us help if you asked. You speak so smoothly that everyone listens to you. And I'd be afraid to ask on my own." Rachel blushed and put both hands across her mouth before continuing, "Maybe you don't like the idea at all. It was silly of me to assume you would."

"Rachel, stop dismissing your thoughts. You're wonderful with people, and I'm certain they'd listen to you. I like your plan a great deal, and I'd be happy to talk with them."

"Would you really? You don't think it's ridiculous?"

"Not at all. And I have a suggestion. Let's you and I go to the Parker House for pie on Sunday afternoon and discuss our plans."

"Oh, Miriam, you've made me so happy."

"I'm delighted," said Miriam as she hugged Rachel warmly.

෨ ෨ ෨

That evening, Miriam couldn't wait to be alone with Deborah to tell her about her talk with Rachel.

"I assume she really wants you as a friend," Deborah said.

"It seemed that way, yet I was really uncertain whether it was my friendship she was seeking, or my assistance in getting her into the stables."

"Does it really matter?"

"Not really, because I'm glad to spend time with her and also help her at the stables. Are you okay that she turned to me instead of you?" Miriam asked, concerned that Deborah may be jealous.

"Absolutely. Although while I like and admire Rachel a great deal, I can't imagine being her friend. Your temperament is much more suited to her sweet manner. No one would ever call me sweet."

"I would," said Miriam, smiling.

"I don't know why you love me so much," Deborah said, then paused. "I've no concerns about you and Rachel spending time together. I actually thought you two would become friends after you went to Parker House with her."

"I've been too focused on you, the girls, and the shop; I haven't really considered a friendship with Rachel. I already have close connections to my sister and Marjorie—we've been best friends since I was very young. And now we have several couples we see quite regularly, so I guess I just didn't have a need for another friend."

"Rachel does. She's very shy."

"Yes, I remember how difficult it was at first to start up a conversation between her and Aaron. I'm so glad that worked out. I must admit I just forgot about asking her to join me for anything, even though I see her every day."

"Please be careful not to promise her more than you have time for."

"Look at you, being the one to be sensitive to others' feelings. I've taught you well."

"Maybe I'm more sensitive than you give me credit for," Deborah said, grinning.

"I'm glad to spend time with Rachel," Miriam said. "And I'll be certain not to lead her on or have her counting on me as her new best friend."

෨ ෨ ෨

While sitting at the Parker House Hotel, waiting for the specialty of the house, Boston cream pie, Rachel talked about her love for horses.

"Do you know what these horses will be expected to do if they're sent to Europe?" asked Miriam.

"I've no idea. I assume they'll take the soldiers into battle."

"I asked Deborah that same question, and she headed straight to the Boston Public Library for answers."

"They wouldn't have books about horses in the war since we aren't in the war yet."

"Luckily, we aren't. And no, there wouldn't be books about this. Deborah has made a great connection with the librarian whose job it is to help the public answer such questions."

"What did she learn?" Rachel asked.

"It seems that horses have been very important in the war in Europe. They not only take the troops to war; they're also used to transport ammunition and other supplies. Deborah learned that there were over ten thousand men with horses when the war broke out. She was told that many horses have already died from artillery fire and because of terrible weather."

"How awful. These wonderful horses are about to risk their lives. I thought they might get overworked, but I didn't consider that so many might die," Rachel said sadly.

"The better they're trained, the better the chances are that they'll survive."

"Here is our pie! I'm so glad you invited me here again. I've been salivating about this pie ever since you mentioned coming here."

"Let's leave the ravages of war until after we enjoy our treat. And, next time, we can come back for lunch, so we can have some of their delicious Parker House rolls."

શ્ર શ્ર શ્ર

Rachel's carefully thought-out request to the men operating the stables went exactly as planned. Miriam explained they wanted to work with the horses as their contribution to the war effort, and Rachel offered a bit of information about her background with horses. Unsurprisingly, they were assigned to groom the horses and clean the stables. Despite the limited time they had, both women enjoyed their new responsibilities and the camaraderie.

"I like the orange-colored horse, Rusty, the best," Rachel said one afternoon. "Do you think they'd ever let me ride her?"

"They've never suggested we ride a horse. We just groom them and clean up after them," said Miriam, wiping the grit from her work clothing.

Then, with a giggle, Rachel asked, "Would you be willing to ask?"

"What do we have to lose? Sure, I'll ask. Though you could ask yourself."

"I'd rather not."

Miriam was certain she was just as insecure when she was younger. She wondered if she'd be able to encourage Rachel's self-reliance, in the same manner Deborah had done for Miriam. She thought about how patient Deborah had been, suggesting, rather than insisting, that Miriam take on more responsibility. Perhaps Miriam could help Rachel that way.

Two weeks later, Miriam initiated the request about riding the horses, and Rachel accompanied her. They were met with many questions about their experience, and with Miriam's encouragement, Rachel talked about her familiarity with horses.

"You did a great job persuading them that you are an accomplished horsewoman," Miriam said when they'd been granted the role of exercising the horses. It had been made clear that this was an additional task, not a replacement for their cleaning and grooming duties. The girls were thrilled to add an extra half hour to their volunteer time.

"I'll look forward to my Sunday afternoons with even more enthusiasm," Rachel said. "Thank you for helping me ask for this."

"Rachel, you would have been granted this privilege had you asked on your own. I didn't know you'd ridden in competitions."

"That was such a long time ago. I haven't ridden since my father died and we moved to Denison House when we couldn't afford to manage on our own."

"Tell me more about your childhood and your life on the farm."

They sat for a long time, an unusually animated Rachel talking about her background. Miriam asked many questions, and Rachel openly discussed how, as a child, she preferred the company of horses to that of other children. Miriam also shared stories of her childhood, building this budding friendship.

At home, Miriam talked excitedly with Deborah about the rich tales Rachel had told. Deborah listened to Miriam's enthusiasm and marveled at how easily Miriam was able to connect with others. "I'm so impressed that you know just how to bring comfort to shy people," Deborah said.

"I really like Rachel, so it was just a natural conversation."

"I don't think you realize what a gift you have. Everyone feels comfortable around you."

"You exaggerate." Miriam blushed.

"I love you so much."

かか かか かか

Just as Deborah had predicted, a friendship began between these young women. Miriam had not had a new friend in several years, and this relationship was different than her other friendships—satisfying in a way Miriam didn't know she craved. Miriam appreciated Rachel's young innocence, a reminder of how she was before she met Deborah.

With Miriam's encouragement, Rachel asked to ride Rusty. They both giggled when her request was granted. Miriam was assigned a less spirited horse, which resulted in a more relaxing experience.

Miriam and Rachel had great fun riding alongside each other around the track, their hair whipping around as they galloped. Rachel offered Miriam pointers, bringing their relationship into balance. Sundays became an important part of the week for the two friends, and Deborah cherished her time alone with their children.

As a surprise, Miriam bought matching riding hats, a gift she knew Rachel would appreciate.

Boston Cream Pie

War Horses being trained

Episode 4 ❧
WWI and the American Red Cross
April 1917

𝓟resident Woodrow Wilson and the United States Congress made a valiant effort to keep America out of the European conflict. Continued German aggression, including escalation of German submarine attacks on US merchant ships, made it impossible for the country to remain uninvolved.

In January 1917, the previously secret Zimmerman Telegram was published, and it changed many Americans' attitudes. This telegram, originating in Germany, proposed a Mexican-German alliance should America and Germany declare war against each other. The telegram stated that Germany would help return Arizona, New Mexico, and Texas to Mexico as a way to entice Mexico to join Germany against the US. Once Germany's intentions were made public in the US, public opinion against entering the war changed, and many people approved of sending troops to Europe to fight.

After three years of war overseas, President Wilson asked Congress for "a war to end all wars," hoping to make the world safe for democracy. On April 6, the United States entered World War I. A government campaign urged all eligible men to enlist and all women to take on supporting roles, citing patriotism and civic duty as everyone's responsibility. Posters asked Americans to buy Liberty Bonds to help finance the war.

More than a million young men heeded the call and prepared to leave their families, most for the first time, and women learned to take over the men's chores of their households. Some women needed to learn farming skills, others found jobs to provide income for their families, and many wives found other useful ways to assist the war effort.

❧ ❧ ❧

"What are we going to do?" Miriam asked Deborah as she read the morning newspaper.

"You mean about Passover?"

"Yes. How can we have our first Seder tonight, the first night we're at war?"

"Miriam, we can't change our Passover ritual. I'm certain Marjorie's family will still expect us at their home. We need to honor this holiday, despite the horrible war that we're now engaged in."

"Do you assume we'll continue as usual, or can we ask Marjorie to acknowledge the war during the service?" Miriam asked.

"We can't avoid talking about the war."

As they anticipated, the Seder went on, though war was on everyone's minds throughout the long evening. As they read a section of the *Haggadah*—the passages about the plagues which the Egyptian people endured long ago—Deborah likened the war to a plague that had befallen the United States. Miriam mentioned her concerns regarding Jewish soldiers being able to practice their beliefs during wartime.

By the end of the week, Miriam learned that the National Jewish Welfare Board had been founded to help Jewish soldiers deal with discrimination within the military. *War is a horror,* she mused, *but discrimination for some soldiers will only add to the pain.*

෯ ෯ ෯

Miriam and Rachel loved being at the stables together, yet everything changed after the United States joined the war. They watched soldiers arrive daily to be trained on horseback. So Miriam and Rachel were reassigned to only grooming the horses, leaving the riding to the men. The drills became more regimented, and the soldiers ran the horses through grueling exercises. Miriam flinched as she watched horses laden with heavier and heavier packs to ready them to carry ammunition and supplies. Periodically, groups of horses were shipped off to join the cavalry. Miriam and Rachel said goodbye knowing it was possible the horses and their riders would never return.

One afternoon, soon after the United States joined the Great War, their housemate Susan arrived home, bursting with news. Her girlfriend, Helen, sat in the living room with their housemates Deborah and Miriam.

"I've figured out how to help the war effort," Susan announced.

"You're already so busy. How could you possibly find time to take on another cause?" asked Helen.

"I'll find a way." Susan looked down, the smile on her face fading.

"What's this latest scheme of yours, Susan?" Deborah asked.

Susan took a deep breath and explained, "We should volunteer for the Red Cross."

"I thought they just need nurses. What could we do?" Helen asked.

"I read that the Red Cross has been caring for the wounded soldiers in France, providing comfort, and sending supplies. I also heard of a program here at home where poor women can earn money by stitching uniforms for soldiers."

"We don't sew!" said Helen, perplexed.

"That's not what I had in mind. Though I don't know exactly what we can do, I feel we need to do something for the soldiers who are risking their lives."

"I like your altruism, Susan. I agree we should do something, and we could include Mildred. At thirteen, our daughter's becoming a little self-absorbed, and I'd like to help her to notice needs beyond her own. I'm still worried about how you…okay, we…will find the time to do anything."

"I worry about our full schedules too, yet we can find a way," Miriam said. "But before we get involved in anything new, may we plan a small party for Sylvia, who is turning five on April 16?"

Deborah smiled. "Of course! Our girl's growing up so fast!"

಄ ಄ ಄

Sylvia's party was a family affair, which meant that their closest friends were invited. Deborah's best friend, Chava, and her girlfriend, Esther, arrived with a beautifully wrapped hand-knit, lightweight sweater for Sylvia, who was more intrigued with the floral wrapping paper than the sweater. Susan, Helen, and Mildred helped with the preparations, and their cook, Mrs. Stern, joined them for the cleanup. Sylvia was thrilled with the attention, and she relished the cake and small gifts. Their chosen family, which also included Marjorie and Micah, had certainly gotten large.

಄ ಄ ಄

President Wilson was appointed the honorary chairman of the Red Cross, and he put out a new call for volunteers. Susan contacted the local YMCA, which was overseeing the local Red Cross's efforts, and came home with a list of possible tasks, such as gathering personal items to send to soldiers, rolling bandages, and raising money.

The four friends talked about the options, and Mildred made the choice—collecting supplies. Organizing this project fell to Helen, who agreed to accumulate the needed materials and gather a group of friends to assemble the kits. Mildred was pleased to participate, as she valued extra time with her parents Susan and Helen. She recruited her friend Leah and several friends from school for the volunteers' work parties.

Miriam was easily involved in this project. As was typical, Deborah began with a trip to the library, where she discovered the huge impact of the French Red Cross. In the early years of the war, they opened hundreds of hospitals, creating thousands of jobs for stretcher bearers and nurses. They also opened train-station warehouses, border posts, and health centers. More importantly, they provided relief to prisoners of war. Deborah discovered that local Red Cross volunteer organizations sent food, clothing, hygiene items, and books to the internment camps in Oglethorpe, Georgia.

Following this research, Deborah was ready to participate. "I see this as an act of patriotism," she said, joining the small group who were organizing the project.

"That sounds a bit haughty," said Miriam. "Yet I'm glad you're willing to get involved. I see this as something that I can contribute to as a woman. So many young men give their lives, so it seems important I give a little of myself."

"I like to help people, too," Mildred said, clearly not understanding the discussion.

"What can I do?" asked Leah, moving towards the table in her wheelchair. Leah, their fourteen-year-old neighbor, fretted that her physical condition would limit her participation. "I can't go to people's houses to ask for supplies, yet there must be something I can do."

"Can you make a poster that asks families to donate items? I can put it up in my school," suggested Mildred.

"Great idea, Mildred. And you can both help us with sorting and packing the supplies we collect," Susan said.

"I'll find out where to send things and what kinds of items the Red Cross is trying to gather," Helen added.

"I can add pictures of those things on my poster," Leah said, pleased to have a role.

☙ ☙ ☙

After Leah's posters went up at Mildred's school, Miriam approached the Jewish temple's sisterhood and brotherhood. Rachel contacted the staff at Denison House, assuming the residents would want to help in this effort. Deborah gave all staff members at the shop some time off to participate.

Items began pouring in. The personal-hygiene supplies included soap, shampoo, and razors. Susan had heard of the importance of cleanliness, both for the soldiers to stave off infections and to keep up their morale. In addition, they collected enough books to fill a sizable bookcase.

When the group next met, Helen produced her list of places to send things. Susan was content to have initiated the project and to participate in the sorting and packing when they got together. Mildred and Leah loved having an active role, and they added much-needed humor to their gatherings with their endless questions.

"How come we're working for a group which has a cross in its name?" Leah asked. "It doesn't sound very Jewish."

"Well," said Helen, "it's *not* a Jewish organization."

"Then how come they didn't call it the American Star, or some other name which doesn't have a cross?"

"The cross became the symbol right from the beginning. It was meant to look like the Swiss flag, except in reverse."

"A cross is the same when it's backwards," said Mildred, trying to figure this out.

Careful not to giggle and embarrass Mildred, Susan explained, "The reverse of the Swiss flag, which is red with a white cross, is a white flag with a red cross."

Leah looked up from her work. "Now I get it. And I have another question. How come we're working for the YMCA? I saw papers, so I know the C stands for Christian. Some of us are Jewish, so shouldn't we be working for the YMJA?"

"Leah, you're such a smart girl," said Miriam. "There's no Jewish group doing this work, though I heard people talking at the temple about some Jews forming the YMHA, with the H standing for Hebrew. When that happens, we can work with them. Right now, it's the YMCA leading this effort."

࿈ ࿈ ࿈

Another day, Mildred arrived home from school with an announcement. "We aren't the only ones helping the Red Cross."

"Did you think we were?" asked Miriam.

"Well, I thought we were special, doing all this hard work for soldiers. Today in school, the teacher asked how many children were doing volunteer work with the Red Cross, and a whole bunch of us raised our hands. I was really glad I could raise my hand too."

"Were you disappointed you weren't the only one?"

"No, I was really proud I could help with the war. And it feels really good to do something for the soldiers."

"Did I ever tell you about the British soldier who came to visit George, a little boy at Denison House?" Deborah asked. "The soldier was a friend of George's father. He told us the Red Cross saved his life."

"How did that happen?" Rachel asked wide-eyed.

"Well, after watching some friends die in the war, he was using alcohol to drown out his sadness. The Red Cross volunteers helped him stop drinking."

"I don't remember you telling me that story. I'm proud to be a Red Cross volunteer," Leah said.

"Me too," Mildred chimed in.

Rachel discussed ways to get the young children involved too. She worked with Sylvia, Sarah, and baby Ida to decorate the paper they would use to wrap the care packages. Jimmy, always a curious kitten, played with the ribbons. The little ones took their work seriously. Sarah thought the pictures they drew would help make the soldiers happy, and Sylvia and Ida loved to draw. Hopefully, their pictures would bring an occasional smile to the face of a soldier at war who left his own small child at home.

๑ ๑ ๑

One day, Deborah's close friend Chava stopped by while they were all packing supplies. Mildred jumped up when Chava arrived wearing a Red Cross uniform and Leah, rolled towards them in her wheelchair so she too could touch the uniform.

"I joined up today," Chava said. "I've imagined doing this since we entered the war, yet I was scared."

"You joined the army?" Deborah practically screeched.

"No, I joined the Red Cross. I never considered joining the army, even though the need is huge. I heard there are only four hundred nurses in the army. I'd find it too frightening to work on the front lines as an army nurse."

"Then why'd you join the Red Cross? That seems scary too."

"Somehow, it felt just as patriotic yet less dangerous. When I heard one of my neighbors was hurt during his first week of combat, I knew

I needed to do something. I hope to work on the USS *Comfort*, a hospital ship helping soldiers hurt in conflicts overseas. It was commissioned by the navy to transport wounded soldiers to hospitals."

"Oh, Chava," Deborah said, "I don't want to see you around so much tragedy."

"Are you aware of what I see at Mass. General Hospital? I don't have a comfortable desk job. I work with patients and see a lot of illness and death. I've already seen patients injured in the war."

"I guess I never asked you much about your work," said Deborah, flustered. "You're always so cheerful. I never imagined you would have to face death at work."

"All the time. And I'll see more when more soldiers arrive from the battlefields."

"My stomach couldn't handle it," said Miriam.

Leah turned to Miriam and said, "Mine either."

"I'll do my very best to stay safe," Chava said, "and thank you all for your concern."

"I'll miss you when you're overseas." Deborah looked away, trying to compose herself.

"I'll miss all of you. Please write to me. I'll need your letters when I've had a hard day."

"Can we send you one of our soldiers' packages?" asked Leah.

"Certainly."

"We'll make you a special one. And we'll have the little children decorate your package really pretty," Leah said.

"What a lovely idea," said Miriam. "You should start saving special items for our friend Chava. And we can give her the package before she leaves. That way, we'll be certain she got it."

"I'll start saving the best things for you, Chava." Mildred hugged her.

As everyone was leaving, Deborah motioned Chava towards the back porch for a private conversation.

"Tell me how Esther reacted when you told her the news."

"I didn't surprise her!" Chava said loudly. "We discussed this repeatedly."

"Calm down, Chava. I wasn't accusing you of springing this on Esther unexpectedly. I was just asking how Esther feels about you signing up for something dangerous...and for leaving town."

"Oh, Deborah, I must be feeling upset, or I wouldn't have scolded you."

"Tell me all about it," Deborah said warmly.

They talked and cried, outlining the risks Chava would be taking. Chava admitted that Esther had initially been upset; however, once they had discussed it thoroughly, she gave her blessings. It was with Esther's approval that Chava quit her job at Mass. General and committed to being a Red Cross nurse.

Though neither of them said anything, both Deborah and Chava wondered if this was a wise decision.

࿔ ࿔ ࿔

A couple of weeks after signing on, Chava was given her assignment on the hospital ship USS *Mercy* stationed in the New York Naval Yard. Chava's first choice, the USS *Comfort*, was soon to be retired from naval service, so she'd been placed on the vessel's sister ship stationed in the New York Naval Yard.

After a tearful goodbye and promises to write, Chava departed for her service as a Red Cross nurse.

> *May 27, 1917*
> *Dear Deborah,*
> *I've done the right thing, volunteering for the Red Cross, giving service to my country. Being on this ship has already taught me lots about the value of life. Thousands of nurses have heeded the call for help, mostly through the Red Cross, like me. This war needs every one of us.*
>
> *Just this month, the War Department mobilized its nurses, sending them to hospitals in France. If I'd been assigned to the USS* Comfort, *as I'd hoped, I'd be among those being assigned to France. Although I would have valued a trip overseas in peacetime, I'm pleased to be stationed stateside instead. From what I hear, nurses in France are stationed close to the front lines, facing danger while tending soldiers with catastrophic injuries. I don't know if I'd be strong enough.*
>
> *Soldiers who survive their injuries are shipped to us, instead of to military hospitals. We're equipped to handle the most severe battle wounds. I'm impressed with the team*

of doctors and nurses on board. We are the first females ever to work on this ship, and we are treated with respect. We work well together, utilizing new operating equipment and modern laboratories to care for our critically ill soldiers.

Most of the boys are severely wounded or are fighting infections which have ravaged their bodies. We attempt to repair their injuries using every skill we were taught in nursing school, plus many untested treatments. I'm especially pleased with new ways to reduce pain, since suffering is enormous.

Esther has been writing to me with great regularity. Her letters, along with yours, have been a great comfort. At first, I sensed a bit of anger from her, though lately she's expressed her pride in my participation in this awful war. Please check on her for me and make certain she is managing adequately without me.

I often think of your friend Marjorie's husband, Micah, who suffered as these men do in the war. There are thousands of Micahs who are traumatized by what they've witnessed, which is as difficult as their physical injuries. As the men cry, I feel their tears are for their losses, not just for the physical pain they're suffering. They will never return to the lives they left behind as productive members of society. For some, I believe kind words and a loving touch can be as healing as the surgeries and medicines.

Love,

Chava

"Miriam, I'm pleased Chava wrote to us, though her words are hard to hear," admitted Deborah. "I don't want to consider other young men suffering as Micah has. Since his leg was badly damaged, he's been tormented. His life and that of his young wife, Marjorie, have been shattered. This war, actually any war, is devastating."

"I wish I could bury my head and forget what these soldiers are going through. And it's so different when it's boys we knew from school, not just nameless numbers of unknown soldiers whom we read about," Miriam added.

"I wonder how our world will be different after this war. So many young men will die or be maimed. The impact will be huge." Deborah sighed.

࿊ ࿊ ࿊

Chava's correspondence with Deborah continued with many letters back and forth.

> *November 5, 1917*
> *Dear Deborah,*
>
> *We've set sail for France. We've spent months preparing for this voyage. From this point on, boys will be brought to our ship soon after being hurt. We'll certainly witness more torment and death than we've experienced thus far.*
>
> *I feel a little guilty being on this ship, since so many nurses are at the front lines, facing much more difficult conditions. Some nurses are in the trenches, many enduring horrible weather. I just heard of the first death of a Red Cross nurse, Clara Edith Ayres of Ohio. Did your papers cover her death? She was struck down when practice rounds exploded.*
>
> *I'm pleased Esther has been spending so much time at your house. She's a wonderful girl, and I miss her terribly. I look forward to the day I'm back with her, yet I'm proud to be a Red Cross nurse serving soldiers who are giving their all for our country.*
> *Love,*
> *Chava*

When Deborah and Miriam read Chava's next letter, they became more nervous for their friend's safety.

> *December 23, 1917*
> *Dear Deborah,*
> *Life has been challenging. Caring for the sick and dying is an overwhelming task. We just heard about the sinking of several hospital ships, adding to our fears. Luckily, no US medical ships have been hit, yet German torpedoes took out at least three British destroyers and one Greek ship in recent months. They try to keep this a secret from us*

nurses, though someone with knowledge of these horrors just joined our ranks.

Facing the destruction of war has made me angry. War is senseless. Though I've learned many skills, I don't know if I can face a life of caring for the ill. Maybe I'll feel different when I return, yet I dream of finding a job where I sit at a desk, filling out papers for a living. I'll probably change my mind, especially since I know my talents will be appreciated stateside. I wonder if I'll be too bitter to continue.

I spend my days running from one ill soldier to another. To ward off infections, we change dressings as often as we can. The stench of decaying skin no longer turns my stomach.

For me, the most valuable part of this experience has been the friendships I've formed. We nurses need each other. We comfort each other and provide distractions from our cares whenever possible. Though the women come from all parts of the country, and I'll probably never see them again, they've become important to me.

Sometimes, Esther's letters are understanding and supportive. At other times, she seems jealous of my connections with these other women. I hope you'll assure her that I only love her. Her letters, along with yours, have kept me sane during these trying times. I'll not be the same person when I return. I hope I'll be tranquil enough for my sweet Esther and that she understands and loves me anyway.
Love,
Chava

When Chava arrived home unexpectedly, shortly after her last letter, her friends were relieved yet frightened by her changed temperament. Whenever Chava visited, Deborah asked her repeatedly about the reason for her return, but instead of an explanation, Chava just broke into tears. She vacillated between periods of solemnity and uncontrollable anger.

Chava admitted, "I've been sleeping little and pacing lots."

Deborah tried to comfort her friend, "Please talk to me about what you witnessed overseas, Chava. Maybe talking about it will help."

Chava was resistant, so Deborah worried more. Deborah reflected on her own mother's breakdown. She wondered if that was what was happening to Chava, fearful for her friend's mental health.

Once Chava made the decision to not return to nursing, her anxiety lessened. With Esther's attention and support, Chava gradually returned to her sweet and steady disposition. Esther was understanding of Chava's volatile moods, and it seemed their relationship would survive the damages of war.[3]

❧ ❧ ❧

At the end of the month, a soldier who lost an arm to artillery fire returned from combat. He came to the stables a broken man. Miriam and Rachel sat with him, not knowing how to react. He talked on and on about the war, especially about the horrible conditions for the horses.

"My horse was shot right out from under me. I was shot too, obviously, though it was what happened to the horses that upset me the most. They created a veterinary hospital, set right next to the hospital where I was recovering, so I went there on several occasions. I returned from my trips there quite shaken. Some horses had horrible skin conditions, and others suffered from poison-gas attacks that destroyed their lungs. The army developed gas masks for them, though most horses chomped through them, mistaking them for feed bags. The few horses who were rehabilitated were sent back to the front lines to endure more horrendous mistreatment."

Miriam and Rachel listened intently, crying silently as the soldier described his woes in detail. Later, they both wished they had not heard these tales.

---

[3] The US Navy's hospital ship *Mercy* served in the United States Navy during World War I. On November 3, 1917, the ship departed New York on the first of four round trips to France. She brought home almost two thousand casualties during the war. Two additional ships bearing the same name were commissioned in 1944 and 1986.

On December 10, 1917, the International Committee of the Red Cross was awarded the Nobel Prize for peace. By 1919, over 200 Red Cross nurses had died, mostly from combating the Spanish-influenza pandemic. During the pandemic of 2018, due to the overcrowding of hospitals, the USNS *Mercy* and the USNS *Comfort* were deployed to assist Americans fighting the disease.

Miriam was still weeping when she arrived home. As she relayed the story of the soldier and the mistreatment of the horses, Deborah attempted to soothe her by saying, "It's too painful for you. Maybe you should stop working there."

"Painful to me? It's painful for the horses and for the soldiers who lose their lives. I can't believe that you're comparing my pain to theirs."

"I didn't mean to belittle their pain. Wait. Let me try again. I'm trying to comfort you, and I'm doing it all wrong. I'm sorry that the horses and soldiers have horrible fates awaiting them. What can I do for you?"

"Just hold me and let me be upset. I'm so very sad about this war."

As Miriam cried, Deborah held her and stroked her face while whispering softly in her ear, "This war is awful. It's terrible that horses are being sacrificed, and soon, I fear, it will be our friends we'll cry for."

Miriam wiped her tears. "Thank you for understanding. I'm so glad you're here for me."

Their evening conversations, though quite intimate, were not romantic. The war had taken that away.[4]

Boston Journal

---

[4] Many horses died from being exhausted, drowning, becoming stuck in the mud, falling into shell holes, or being captured by the opposing forces. By the end of the war, more horses had been killed than men—just over 100,000 American men died, compared to more than 8,000,000 horses. Over 1,000,000 of the horses had been sent from the US.

American Red Cross

American Red Cross nurses

Episode 5 ✴ *Jewish Soldiers*

May 1917

"I have news. Aaron enlisted in the army," William announced, as the four business owners—Deborah, Miriam, Hannah, and William—gathered in the small printshop for their weekly meeting.

"I'm not surprised," Miriam said. It seemed reasonable to her that Aaron, the apprentice, had approached either William or Micah, the only other males in the office. "I figured this time was coming since many young men signed up after we declared war in April."

"There will be a draft on June 5, so he enlisted before he was drafted," William said.

Miriam thought of Margery, who would fear for her brother. "That draft will be for twenty-one- to thirty-year-olds, and he's only eighteen," Deborah said with a wrinkled brow.

"I know. But Aaron told me he wanted to serve his country."

Deborah thought about it. "And probably, as a Jew, he felt especially important to show his patriotism, to go to war for America."

"Good point. Rachel will probably be really proud of her boyfriend," said Miriam. "And also scared."

"Let's divide Aaron's deliveries so none of us are overworked," said William, being staunchly practical rather than emotional.

Meanwhile, his wife, Hannah, as usual, remained quiet and unruffled despite the serious nature of this conversation.

෯ ෯ ෯

Once they got home, Deborah and Miriam discussed Aaron's enlistment with Susan and Helen. They talked of the men they knew who might be eligible for military service. They were relieved that Deborah's father, at age forty-six, was significantly past the age to be drafted and that neither Susan's nor Helen's father was eligible. They'd be heartbroken if any of them had to leave their families to risk their health and even their lives. Mr. Berkowitz and William, both age thirty-two, were safe at the moment.

Deborah's brother, Milton, had enlisted two days after the declaration of war. He planned to be an officer due to his experience in boot camp the previous summer. Their friend Ruth's brother would soon be drafted, as would Helen's brother and several of Susan's cousins. The war was now touching the lives of their families and their community.

"I'm frightened we'll lose many young men," said Susan.

"Yes, there's already been a huge loss of life in Europe, and now we must do our part," Deborah agreed.

"How will Ruth's brother, David, do?" asked Miriam. "He's such a strange young man, never fitting in. I wonder how he'll adjust to strict military rules since he rarely lives up to what is expected of him."

"I wonder what they do with someone who doesn't follow protocol. I assume there are many boys who don't do well within a rigid structure," Deborah said.

"And how do the young Jewish men manage?" asked Miriam. "There probably won't be any services for *Shabbos*, and I doubt there's any way to keep kosher. What if they serve ham or shellfish for dinner? Will the Jewish boys just go hungry?"

"I've no idea. I assume there are no special accommodations." Deborah wondered if her brother, Milton, would soon be eating pork.[5]

❧ ❧ ❧

The next morning, while they were getting Sylvia and Ida ready for the day, Miriam almost tripped over the rambunctious kitten. As they went about their chores, Miriam said to Deborah, "There must be Jews fighting against one another. Many Jewish men serve in the German army, and now there will be American Jews fighting against them. What if a Jew faces an enemy in battle, and there are tzitzit sticking out of his uniform? Could a Jew kill another Jew? How would he manage in a battle against his brethren?"

"What a dilemma!" said Deborah while putting Ida down on the bed. "I can't understand how any man, Jewish or not, could fight another in face-to-face combat. How could they look into the eyes of another man and stick a knife into him? Maybe, when they imagine someone is the enemy, they suppress personal feelings; although, when the combat is close, it must be awful."

---

[5] The Selective Service Act, in May 1917, gave President Woodrow Wilson the right to draft into the United States military all men between twenty-one and thirty years of age. By the end of the war, the draft had provided about 2,800,000 of the almost 4,800,000 men who served. A controversial aspect of the draft dates back to the Civil War, when men were allowed to choose a substitute soldier to serve in their stead, which was advantageous for the wealthy who could hire someone to represent them. Under this new act, men could no longer do that.

"I have trouble killing a fly, so the thought of killing another human is beyond my comprehension. I'd be a horrible soldier," Miriam said.

"Yes, you would. I'm so glad women are not recruited to fight."

"Our role is to suffer at home, worrying and mourning for the men."

☙ ☙ ☙

Miriam still worried about the religious question of Jewish soldiers at war. She asked Deborah how non-Jewish soldiers would know who the Jewish boys were.

"It's quite obvious," Deborah said.

"Because of their dark hair and long noses?"

"Sometimes you're so innocent. Think about it, sweetie. These men shower together, and they must see each other relieving themselves. Sorry for my indelicate mention of this, but Jewish men are circumcised. That would be very obvious."

"I never thought of that." Miriam blushed.[6]
When they came back from synagogue on Friday night, Miriam and Deborah sat with Helen and Susan before heading to bed.

"Someone at shul mentioned something I want to ask you about," Miriam said.

"What did you hear?" inquired Helen.

"I heard that some Christian soldiers worry about having Jews in their ranks because they believe Jews would side with their fellow Jews, rather than with their own countrymen."

"You mean that a Jew would not capture or kill a German soldier who is Jewish, even if that man is the enemy?"

"I guess that's how it would go."

Susan spoke up, "I've never heard anything like that, yet when I imagine how my brother might think, I can picture him reacting that way. He's never met a Jew because he went to a church school. He's confounded by how I can live here, in a Jewish household. I bet he prays for me because he doubts you will treat me well."

"I never knew that, Susan," Deborah said, opening her eyes wide. "What does he imagine we'd do to you?"

---

[6] Jewish men are circumcised shortly after birth. In 1900, about thirty percent of American non-Jewish boys were circumcised, too, and by 1925, over half of men in the United States were circumcised. This delicate topic would not have been discussed among women.

"I have absolutely no clue. We never discussed Jews in my household, so he didn't learn prejudice at home. I bet this was a topic among his friends from school."

"Anti-Semitism exists everywhere," Deborah said, shaking her head.

"I'm sorry," Susan said. "I was just trying to answer your question."

"I don't hold this against you at all. It's just sad. I appreciate your honesty."

෨෨෨

Back in their bedroom, Miriam said, "I never thought about how Susan's and Helen's families would react to us being Jewish. Do you think that when Susan left Helen last year, part of her concern was about living in a Jewish household? We've always been accepting of them going to church."

"It wasn't the central issue for her, yet it certainly must have played into her feelings," Deborah said. "I think her concerns had more to do with her missing her family and needing to keep her life with Helen a secret from her kin."

"This is such a complicated issue," said Miriam. "And I've had another thought. Anti-Semitism may put Jews at more risk within their own troops."

"Do you mean that Jews might be killed by the Allied forces? I cannot imagine…"

"I wonder about that. Some Christian soldiers might welcome an excuse to act out against Jews."

"More to consider, especially for my brother, Milton," Deborah said while thinking upsetting thoughts as she turned out the lights.

෨෨෨

When they got home from work that night, Miriam continued the conversation. "All day, I've been reviewing our conversations about Jewish soldiers. I remembered some of the things my father told me about Jews in the Prussian Army, and I was wondering if some of the same things would happen again."

"What did he say?" Deborah asked.

"Father told me Jews didn't have equal rights. They weren't able to take government positions. He told me that thirty-thousand German Jews served in the Prussian Army, though only those who converted to Christianity were promoted to officers."

"Anti-Semitism has been rampant for many generations," Deborah said.

"What do you know about Jews who have been fighting in the German Army during this war?" said Miriam.

"Nothing, really."

"I bet your friend the librarian could tell you lots. I think you should go ask her these questions."

"Good plan," Deborah said, wondering if the librarian's answers would make her feel better or worse.

❧ ❧ ❧

The very next day, Deborah burst into the house and, without pause, told Miriam her news. "You'll be amazed with everything I learned at the library about anti-Semitism." She removed her hat and started to speak, but Miriam stopped her.

"Let me get Sylvia and Ida. Once I've gotten the girls, you can tell me everything."

Miriam walked toward the back room, where the girls were playing, and led them back to Deborah.

Deborah greeted the children and put Sylvia on her lap. The little girl began chewing on her fingers, a new habit that Deborah was trying to discourage. Deborah sang Sylvia a song to distract her, and soon they were singing nursery songs together. Ida, who was seated on Miriam's skirt, began to sing along, and they spent a lovely few minutes together.

"I guess this isn't the best time to hear about anti-Semitism," Miriam said. "Can you wait until after the girls are in bed, and I can concentrate more?"

"Sure" was all Deborah said, yet Miriam sensed her urgency to share.

"Maybe you can tell me a bit now and the rest later."

"No, I can wait. I'm practicing patience."

"And you're doing a good job of it."

Deborah shook her head and made a silly face, which Ida attempted to copy, thinking this was a game for her entertainment.

After the girls quieted, Deborah gave a shortened version of what she'd learned; her need to share had lost some urgency. She told Miriam only that Jews in Germany were chastised for not doing their part in the war effort. Many German Jews had hoped to prove their patriotism by fighting, but their involvement in the war was questioned. This attitude led increasing numbers of young German Jewish men to accept

Zionism—the belief in a Jewish state—and realize that full acceptance into German society was never going to happen.

Miriam's response was simply, "It would be amazing to have a Jewish state. I heard my father talk of Zionism with his friends from the temple brotherhood and with his study partner. It was a frequent topic among the learned men, though much of it went over my head. We'll talk about Zionism at another time. Right now, I need to pay some attention to Ida, who just messed her diaper."[7]

❧ ❧ ❧

After returning from shul on Saturday, Miriam settled Ida on her lap and said to Deborah, "Did you hear my conversation with a lady about her son's request for kosher meals when he signed up for the army?"

"No. Would they accommodate him?" asked Deborah, assuming she knew the answer.

"They said they would provide him with kosher food, yet his mother thought it was a ploy to get him to enlist. And she was right. At his first meal, he was seated with all the others and served the identical food. He refused to eat."

"He must have eaten something," Deborah said.

"He said he subsisted on mostly bread and water."

"During warfare? How could he keep up his strength? Wouldn't God be understanding in this circumstance if he were to eat *tref*?"

"I don't know about G-d's forgiveness, yet I know her son was so sickly from not eating that he ended up in the field hospital. While he was hospitalized, they fed him the foods he'd refused to keep him alive."

"Was he aware what they were feeding him?"

---

[7] Germans attempted to prove that Jews were avoiding military service, in spite of the fact that there were 12,000 Jews in the German Army at the beginning of the war. Most of them were on the front line, and almost 3,000 perished during the war. As in the Prussian War, Jews were only able to become officers in the reserves. Germans conducted a Jewish Census, though withheld its outcome because the results did not prove their point. This situation disgusted many patriotic German Jews, who'd hoped this war would prove their commitment to their homeland and would lead to their acceptance. This obviously wasn't happening.

Zionism was a response to anti-Semitism. The goal of a Jewish state in Palestine was for Jews to embrace their Jewish identity in a land of their own. They thought it would be a way to celebrate their Jewishness without discrimination. Jews found it difficult to assimilate into other cultures.

"I don't know. His mother said he was shipped back a broken soul. She tried to feed him kosher foods to bring him back to health, but he could barely eat. He told his mother about the horrible conditions in the camp, which is why he weakened so easily. Sadly, he became very frail and reclusive."

"What a horrible story," Deborah said, thinking of the unexpected tragedies of war.

Next, Miriam wondered whether Jews would be excused from duty on *Shabbos*.

Deborah laughed out loud. "There's no way they would do that. If they wouldn't serve them kosher food, why would they allow them time off from the war for *Shabbos*?"

"Well, I thought they might. It seems important that soldiers practice their beliefs."

"And," Deborah added, "if they were to demand their religious obligations be met, how would they be treated? Would it affect their safety from non-Jewish soldiers?"

"These are terrible things, yet I'm glad we can talk about this. I feel badly for the young men who have to face these issues."

"And I feel bad for all the young men having to face war, with or without the complication of being Jewish. It's a tragedy."

☙ ☙ ☙

As the war continued, Deborah talked again with her librarian friend. She relayed to Miriam that over 100,000 German Jews and over 300,000 Austrian Jews were fighting in the Great War. The German and Austrian Jewish communities enthusiastically supported the war.

"And what about American Jews?" responded Miriam.

"Almost 200,000 Jews have already served in the American Expeditionary Forces. When compared to the proportion of non-Jewish men in active duty, this number is a disproportionate number of the Jewish population in the United States."

"I would guess many Jews see this war as an opportunity to demonstrate their patriotism and become fully accepted by American society."

"I bet you're right. That's the same attitude the German Jews have, as we already discussed. Many Americans fighting in the Great War were not born here. Jews are not segregated from the general population; that practice is just for Negroes."

None of these conversations ended pleasantly. Deborah knew she would discuss this with her father when they went to the Berkshires for the weekend. Her family had just moved to their summer home, and they encouraged Deborah and Miriam to visit.

❧ ❧ ❧

As was often the case, the children's needs came first. Early in the week, Sylvia pulled on her ear repeatedly and became quite fussy, a certain sign she was developing one of her earaches. Deborah and Miriam decided a trip to visit the doctor would be necessary before they went anywhere. With Sylvia whimpering in Miriam's arms, they took the long ride to Waltham.

Deborah and Miriam arrived home from their trip to the Experimental School for Teaching and Training Idiotic Children somewhat relieved. Sylvia's beloved doctor, Dr. Kingsley, told them her condition was not serious, and he recommended they apply hot compresses to her ear. If her condition worsened or continued for over a week, they should return.[8]

Deborah and Miriam fretted over Sylvia yet were also concerned about a major shift about to take place in her care. Dr. Kingsley was pleased when the school opened its enrollment and included outpatient programs in 1915, making it available to children like Sylvia, yet things were now changing at the school in ways that the good doctor could not tolerate. He informed them that he planned to leave the school.

"I don't know how we'll manage without Dr. Kingsley to guide us," Miriam said with furrowed brow. "He's helped us with Sylvia since she was just a baby. I can't imagine trusting anyone else with decisions about her."

"Miriam, I'm worried, too, about how Sylvia will grow up strong and healthy without his direction. Her walking and talking have improved greatly, thanks to his suggestions and encouragement. But I'm actually more worried about the other information he told us regarding the school's adherence to eugenics practices."

Deborah's face tightened. "I never knew that the superintendent, Dr. Fernald, was a proponent of eugenics. How can anyone advocate

---

[8] Before the invention of antibiotics, hot compresses were the only at-home treatment for ear infections. If the infections persisted, doctors would make a tiny hole in the eardrum to allow the pus to drain out. After the infection was gone, they anticipated the hole would seal itself.

the belief in purifying the human race by ridding the world of misfits? I was shocked when Dr. Kingsley told us this man encouraged sterilization of many of those living at the school and their mothers so they'd not bear more inferior children."

"That's so upsetting. I can't imagine how Dr. Kingsley has dealt with that attitude. He's such a kind man and wise doctor."[9]

"Miriam, change is always difficult, but let's be grateful we've had Dr. Kingsley in our lives during Sylvia's formative years. She's five, and she's developed nicely. Now, she speaks in short sentences and describes many of the things around her."

"And she knows her colors and remembers the names of people. She's such a sweet girl, though she's very stubborn."

"So am I, so maybe she takes after me."

"I think she's actually even more stubborn than you, my dear Deborah."

"I don't think we can continue to receive care from a facility run by a man whose values are so different from ours," Deborah said, huffing.

Miriam's eyes swelled with tears. "I have an idea. Let's ask Dr. Kingsley where he plans to go when he leaves the school. Maybe we can follow him."

Deborah and Miriam were thrilled when a call to the clinic told them Dr. Kingsley planned to open a private practice. They signed on as his first patients.

The compresses helped ease Sylvia's discomfort somewhat, yet Miriam declared it was not wise for Sylvia to travel over the weekend. She suggested that just Deborah and Ida visit her family. Ida refused to leave Sylvia, though Miriam insisted Deborah go anyway. Deborah agreed, pleased to have some time alone with her family.

అ అ అ

---

[9] Dr. Walter Fernald, the superintendent of the Experimental School for Teaching and Training Idiotic Children, published papers about the "burden of the feeble-minded." As part of his belief in eugenics, he supported institutionalization in an effort to rid communities of those with mental retardation, selective breeding to eliminate defective genetic traits, and sterilization for anyone outside the norm, such as the school's residents. Yet he also advocated for humane care of those with intellectual disabilities. Late in life, his views shifted, and from then on, he advocated for community placement for some residents and no longer supported forced sterilization. This experimental school was renamed the Walter E. Fernald Developmental Center in 1925, a year after his death.

In Great Barrington, Massachusetts, Deborah discussed her fears for Jews in the Great War with her father. He was aware of most topics, though he knew little about the Prussian Army and the attitudes of German and Austrian soldiers. He listened intently, then informed her about the Christmas ceasefire that occurred in 1914.

"What are you talking about?" Deborah asked.

"The military has always been Christian-oriented," her father began. "Although it was unofficial, on Christmas during the first year of the war, there was a period where both sides laid down their weapons to honor the holiday. Soldiers emerged from the trenches and, in a good-will gesture, shared food and sang 'Silent Night' together. After the ceasefire, they got back to the business of killing one another."

"That is totally ridiculous. Are you sure about this?"

"I assume this is true, since I've heard it mentioned several times, though it could just be a legend. I heard the officers were disapproving and took great steps to assure that it would never occur again, sending many of the soldiers elsewhere. I'm not certain if there has been such a ceasefire again, though I've heard that since then, no shots have been fired on Christmas Eve nor on Christmas Day."

"I can't wait to tell Miriam this story," Deborah said, amazed at the power of the Christian holiday spirit.

Jewish soldiers WW1

Episode 6 ✳ *Vaudeville*

June 1917

While at Stonegate, it was especially important for Deborah to spend time with her brother, who'd soon be leaving for the navy. Deborah thought about her conversations with Miriam regarding the treatment of Jews in the service, and she wondered if Milton had thought about any of these issues.

While taking a walk together, Milton told Deborah, "I'm sure I'll be an officer because I went to boot camp. They told us that our training would make us eligible should we go to war."

Deborah took a deep breath and said softly, "Do you think you might be slighted because you are Jewish?"

"I don't think so. At boot camp, I wasn't treated any differently than the other boys. Well, now that you mention it, I was left out of some social activities, and I sometimes received fewer privileges than others. Though I never considered it was because I'm Jewish."

"I assume it was, Milton. Why else would you be ostracized? You're a bright man and a hard worker. Sometimes, I think you are unaware of the anti-Semitism all around you."

"I don't want to consider that my religion is what sets me apart from the others—" Milton stopped the conversation abruptly, upset by the possibility that he'd been discriminated against and embarrassed he'd not been aware of it. "Enough of this topic, Deborah. But I promise to write to you regularly and keep you informed of my experiences."

Deborah wondered if that would include instances of anti-Semitism, but she did not ask.

છે છે છે

On Sunday, before Deborah headed home, her sister Anna invited Deborah into her bedroom. Deborah was glad to be welcomed into this extremely feminine space, a frill in every corner, decorated by the blossoming adolescent.

"Deborah, it's been wonderful having you home for the weekend," Anna said to her big sister, "yet I've something serious to discuss with you."

"What's wrong, Anna? Does it have to do with one of your friends at school? Or maybe a boy? Or are you worried about Milton?"

"Yes, I am worried about him. But this is about you."

"Me? What have I done to upset you?"

"Well"—Anna stood to her full height and sucked in her breath—"I'd like to know why you've never invited me to Boston to visit you. You've had Fanny Berkowitz several times, and I heard you say that you're having her back again this summer. Why not me? After all, I'm seventeen, two years older than Fanny. Is there some reason you haven't invited me?"

"Oh, Anna. I'm so sorry. I'd no idea you'd want to come. You always seem so busy with your friends and your activities. I never thought you'd want to spend time with your old sister instead."

"I've been a little hurt you never considered having me. I'd love to explore the city with you and spend time with Sylvia and Ida…and Miriam too. I never got to meet Susan and Helen, and I've always wondered about Mildred. Ever since you let me read the story you wrote about her being on the Orphan Train, I've been curious to meet her and ask her about it."

"I'd love to have you. It's been a sad oversight on my part."

"Boston's such a wonderful place to be. I've only been once with Mother, Father, and Milton, and I was really young."

"That was just a couple years ago, so you weren't really so young."

"It feels like it was a very long time ago. And I've been enjoying being with you this weekend," Anna said, blushing.

"Then it's a deal. And I want you to know that we've invited Fanny because she was becoming a challenge for her parents, and we wanted to help. You've never once been a problem, so we never thought of inviting you."

"Thanks for explaining," Annie said, hugging Deborah tightly. "It's nice to know that it wasn't because you like her better."

Deborah hugged Anna even more vigorously, saying, "I'm sorry you even considered that. I love you a great deal."

They embraced for a long time; then Deborah asked, "When would you like to come?"

"I get out of school for the summer in just a couple weeks. Can I come then as a celebration for the end of school?"

"That's a wonderful idea. Let's choose a date right now."

"And there's something I'd really like to do when I'm there," Anna said firmly, making Deborah wince a bit.

"What is it?"

"I want to go to a vaudeville show."

"Vaudeville? That's not something I've ever done in Boston."

"Remember when Mother and Father took us one summer in Great Barrington? I absolutely loved it, and I've always wanted to go again. I remember every detail of the performances we saw. I especially loved the magician and the dancers."

"I remember your excitement. For me, your enthusiasm was the best part of the show."

"Can we go?"

"Absolutely. I'll do some research. Hopefully, there'll be a show when you're visiting."

"Isn't there always vaudeville in Boston?" Anna asked.

"I've no idea, though now you have me interested. Maybe we can invite Susan and Helen to join us."

"Who would watch Sylvia and Ida? And what about Mildred?"

"Look at you, acting like the adult, worrying about who would watch the children."

"I *am* an adult. I'll be graduating from high school next year. And then I'll be a college student."

"You've grown up so fast."

"Not as fast as you. Look at you. You're twenty-four, and you have two children and your own business."

"You're right. I must seem like an old lady to you."

"Not really. You can sometimes be really silly, especially when you're trying to get Sylvia to smile."

"Not silly enough, yet the children help me stay youthful. Now, I'm anxious to figure out what show we'll see and to plan the rest of your trip."

And besides, Deborah thought, *some entertainment might keep Anna's mind off the things that might be happening to Milton.*

えん えん えん

Walking through the door when she returned home to Boston, Deborah first checked on the welfare of her family. She told Miriam it was a wonderful visit, and they would have plenty to discuss that evening. Then, she mentioned Anna's upcoming trip.

"That's very sweet that she wants to visit with her sister," Miriam said.

Deborah responded, "I'm not sure it is really me she wants to see. I bet she's more interested in what Boston has to offer."

"As a young lady of seventeen, she probably doesn't understand her own motivations. Either way, it'll be nice to have her here."

Deborah looked up, then said, "I'm glad she'll be gone by the time Fanny arrives for the summer. We don't have enough beds for them both."

"We could manage the beds," Miriam said, "but it would be hard to have them visit at the same time."

"They get along, though I really want to make Anna's trip special and focus entirely on her. She was quite jealous that we invited Fanny instead of her. I actually never thought of having Anna."

Miriam shook her head. "We had Fanny here because she was such a problem to her parents, and Anna has never been a problem."

"You're right," said Deborah. "But I feel bad that she was jealous. We'll just have to make it up to her." Deborah wondered for a moment whether Anna was actually envious or whether it was a ploy to get an invitation. "Or maybe," Deborah said, "she just figured we'd work hard to make her visit noteworthy as a way to make up for favoring Fanny over her."

Deborah then changed the subject, telling Miriam about the discussion she'd had with Milton just prior to her departure. "I'm really worried about Milton. I'm concerned that he'll be in the navy during wartime, but I'm also concerned that he doesn't notice anti-Semitism, even when he's being discriminated against."

"How can he not see it?"

"He just looks beyond the prejudice that's aimed at him, making excuses as to why he's left out. Most disturbing is that he's expecting to be an officer, though I suspect he'll not be given a commission because he's Jewish."

"Did you talk with him about this?"

"Yes, but he was quite naïve."

Miriam chuckled. "That's a term I've often heard used when talking about me. It surprises me that a smart young man like him could be considered naïve."

"I hope he's not passed over and that he's not a target of discrimination. I'm really concerned."

"I don't blame you for worrying."

Sad and worried, Deborah and Miriam forced themselves to think of sunnier things. They distracted themselves by planning a visit full of adventurous outings for Anna. In addition to trips to the Swan Boats, Franklin Park Zoo, the Museum of Fine Arts, and Forest Hills Cemetery, they would get the promised tickets to a vaudeville show.

ॐ ॐ ॐ

Anna arrived full of youthful exuberance. "It's really wonderful you found so many things for us to do, especially seeing a vaudeville show. May I make a request?" Anna asked as Deborah and Miriam reviewed their plans for the week.

As they left the South Station, Miriam said, "Certainly," wondering what this young girl had in mind.

"I'd like to skip the cemetery if you don't mind. Instead, I'd love to go to a movie. I bet the movie houses in Boston are really special. I'd love to see the new Charlie Chaplin film, *The Immigrants*. It opens on June 17, and I'd love to see it in its first week, so I can tell my friends I saw it before them."

"That is a reasonable request," Deborah said.

"And do we really have to go to the Museum of Fine Arts? Mother and Father drag me to the Metropolitan quite often, and I'm not really interested in old paintings."

"Then it's off the list," Deborah said.

"Thanks."

This assertive girl is going to keep us on our toes all week.

At the house, Anna focused her attention on Jimmy, who ran to her when she beckoned him. "You didn't tell me there was a kitten here."

"Yes," Miriam said, "we really love him."

Once she put the cat down, Anna was thrilled to spend time with Sylvia and Ida, engaging them in games that got them riled up even though it was getting close to bedtime. Miriam wondered how she'd calm the girls down for sleep. But she was pleased to have so much young energy in the house.

Excited to finally meet twelve-year-old Mildred, Anna said, "Will you tell me all about the Orphan Train? It sounds so fascinating."

"I'm willing to tell you about it, but it is not a great memory," said Mildred, a bit surprised by the request. "It was a very sad time. My parents had just died in an accident, and I was really frightened. The family who chose me did not treat me well."

The smile immediately left Anna's face. "I'm sorry I asked you to relive such a horrible experience. I wasn't being very sensitive. You don't need to tell me more."

"I'd actually like to tell you the story. I've not talked about it in a very long time, and maybe, now that I'm older, it'll feel different. Why don't you come up to my bedroom, and I'll tell you everything I remember."

"That is very sweet of you, Mildred," Miriam said as she overheard the conversation and motioned for the girls to go upstairs to talk.

❧ ❧ ❧

When Deborah and Miriam took Anna downtown to ride on the Swan Boats, she said, "I love this boat with its huge wings, long neck, and that sweet swan face. And it's fun seeing the real swans and baby ducks. Thank you so much for bringing me."

"I'm so glad you're enjoying this, though please don't talk about coming here in front of Sylvia. She loves the Swan Boats, and she'll be really upset if she knew we came without her," Miriam said.

"We should have brought her."

"I would have suggested it, yet we are about to head to the movies, and she could never sit still through a whole film. She wouldn't understand the humor."

From the moment they arrived at the theater, Deborah, Miriam, and Anna were charmed by the Scollay Square treasure on Court Street—the decorative Palace Theater, which often played Charlie Chaplin films. Movie posters plastered the front of the building, including posters of the Cracker Jacks, the first live act performed in 1909 at the newly opened theater.

Each of them paid their ten cents, an extravagance saved for special outings like this one. Entering the luxurious, gilded building and passing through the auditorium doors, they looked from one decorative embellishment to another. They were enchanted by the huge lead-glass windows with balloon festoons, the plaster-cast statues along the tops of the multistory walls, the ornate ceilings, and the brass-framed stage.

While the others found their way to their plush velvet seats, Deborah went in search of the powder room. En route, a small plaque grabbed her attention. To her astonishment, she read that Thomas Edison and Alexander Graham Bell had discovered their famous inventions in the upstairs laboratory. Before heading to her seat, Deborah asked a uniformed young man about the laboratory. He introduced her to an older gentleman who was pleased to tell Deborah the history of the building. She listened in fascination until the lights blinked, signaling the beginning of the performance. The man guided her to her seat, where she was eager to tell Miriam what she learned. But Miriam shushed her, and Deborah had to hold her story.

There was an intermission during this double feature, so the theater lights came up midway through their adventure. It was then that Deborah turned to Miriam and Anna, ready to tell them everything.

Miriam tried to listen politely for a moment. With the clamor of patrons all around her, she could barely hear and couldn't pay attention to Deborah's story. Anna was totally distracted.

Deborah quieted down and eagerly anticipated the opportunity to tell them the story after the Charlie Chaplin film ended. It was not long before the silent Chaplin moving picture began. They were all entertained by *The Immigrants,* a story of the Tramp, Chaplin's feature character, crossing the Atlantic Ocean on a steamship.

"I loved the show!" exclaimed Anna as soon as they walked out.

Deborah acknowledged to herself that this was Anna's night, and her fascinating news about how Edison and Bell had perfected their inventions would have to wait.

Anna went on, "I knew right from the beginning that the Tramp was going to see again the woman he met on the boat and that he was going to fall in love with her." With delightful exuberance, she continued to comment on practically every scene in the film.

After Anna calmed, Deborah asked if anyone was interested in hearing about the inventions developed in the attic of the Palace Theater. Miriam, realizing how badly Deborah wanted to tell her story, feigned interest.

Deborah, trying to remain calm, explained that there was a laboratory in the attic of the theater; it used to be rented out to inventors. A young Thomas Edison created his first invention, an automatic vote counter, in this very location. And later, Alexander Graham Bell and

Thomas Watson first heard a human voice on their new invention, the telephone, at this same location. Everyone expressed interest, though it wasn't long before the conversation returned to Anna's discussions of the film.

Once home, Anna was careful not to rave about the Swan Boats in front of Sylvia and thoughtfully avoided talking about the movie in front of Mildred, so neither girl would be jealous that they had not been invited.

Over dinner, Anna talked about the next film she wanted to see, *Rebecca of Sunnybrook Farm*, which was based on a novel she had read. The film was due out in September, and she could hardly wait for its release. She told Mildred and the others the whole plot, probably ruining the story for those who had not already read the book. They all became interested in seeing it and the popular actress Mary Pickford. By the end of the meal, they decided to view it together, ensuring a second visit to Boston for Anna. Susan and Helen agreed to let Mildred attend, and they made plans to ask Rachel to watch the children so they could attend together. They were pleased Anna had chosen a film that appealed to everyone.

That night, Anna engaged the young children until their bedtimes; then she sat with Mildred for a long time, playing Parcheesi, a favorite board game. Deborah and Miriam talked with Susan and Helen.

In their room, Deborah announced, "Anna is a delight. She is as animated as she was as a youngster."

"I remember a conversation we had a few years ago," Miriam responded, "when we wished she'd remain enthusiastic, saying she'd be a delightful adult if she was able to retain her spark. She certainly has."

"I'm really surprised she doesn't have a boyfriend. I'm certain the boys flock to her, yet she's extremely fussy. She might be one of those girls who avoids romance until she finds the perfect companion to marry."

"I wouldn't be at all surprised. She has a good head on her shoulders. I was impressed with how careful she was to avoid making Mildred jealous that we'd gone to the movies. She's sensible and sincere." Miriam smiled.

"I'm really proud of both my siblings. She has always been a joy to be around, as has my brother. Milton's a bit more serious, though he loves a good joke. I'm worried about him becoming an officer in this war though. It scares me that he would put his life at risk. Like Anna, he has strong principles, and I am certain he'd risk his own life to protect the soldiers under him."

"I don't blame you for worrying. We just need to hope that his leadership skills will never be needed in direct combat."

"From your lips to God's ears."

Remembering Deborah's enthusiasm about the Palace Theater laboratory, Miriam asked Deborah to explain more about the inventions created in the attic of the theater.

Deborah was glad to finally have an audience. After a complete recitation of everything the gentleman at the theater had told her, Deborah seemed all worked up.

Miriam remembered other times Deborah had responded like this, and it always seemed to end with an exciting night in bed. Miriam decided to forgo sleep in favor of a night of intimacy. As they climbed under their sheets, she softly suggested something very risqué, "Can we pleasure ourselves in front of each other?"

"That's very private. I'm not certain I can do that," Deborah said.

"I bet you can figure out how to perform in front of me."

"You really are quite a devil," she said with a smile.

"I'm glad you believe I am."

Deborah felt anxious, yet she never considered turning down Miriam's proposal. Actually, she was getting aroused with the very thought of it. "I'm a bit nervous about this. I'm not certain I can do this with you watching," Deborah admitted.

"It will work best if we begin together and then finish by ourselves."

"That sounds much more reasonable."

"I don't want this to be reasonable. I want it to be tempting," Miriam said.

"I'll do my best. I've never touched myself in front of anyone," Deborah said, blushing.

"Well, I should hope not. I think it would be wonderful to learn what stimulates you the most, so I can copy some of your techniques."

"The truth is, I have only touched myself when I am already so stimulated I have to relieve the aching. When we are apart, I get worked up imagining you."

"That's very sweet, though I still want to know what you do to provide that relief," Miriam said.

"I pretend I'm you, pleasing me," Deborah said. "I try to touch myself in exactly the way you touch me. That's the only way I know how to get going."

"Then this will be interesting. Maybe you and I will both learn new things."

"Miriam, tell me what you do when you are alone, touching yourself."

"I'd rather show you than tell you. I always start by rubbing my breasts," Miriam said as she reached down to her ample bosom. "You know how sensitive they are. I squeeze them and rub them until the nipples harden, like this. I begin to pinch the nipples until they hurt a bit."

"I'm always careful not to hurt you."

"Sometimes it's pleasurable to hurt a bit."

"I'll remember that!" said Deborah.

Miriam then undressed herself until she was lying naked under the sheets.

Deborah positioned herself, pulling down the sheets and approaching Miriam's private area. She watched Miriam move her hips rhythmically as she rubbed her body. "This is stimulating," Deborah said.

"That's the point! I'm not wet, like when you touch me, so I'll lick my fingers for a bit of saliva and rub it down there."

"I never thought of doing that."

"Glad you're learning something," Miriam said as her breathing became a bit ragged.

Miriam began moving her fingers in circles as Deborah watched. Deborah could hear a sound of wetness as Miriam's circles became faster. Miriam's hips moved in similar circles. Then, suddenly, Miriam's hips stopped moving, and her fingers moved faster and faster. Deborah listened to Miriam's breathing change, sounding as if she were about to explode. She reached down to her own secret place, finding it wet and throbbing. She began to rub herself as Miriam got closer and closer to her own climax.

"No. Wait. I don't want you to be satisfied yet. I want to finish pleasuring myself and then watch you do the same," Miriam said.

Deborah moved her fingers from between her legs and watched Miriam, who had slowed the pace of her rubbing.

"Watch while I bring myself back to the point of not being able to stop," Miriam said.

Again, Miriam rubbed the sensitive area slowly at first, then gradually faster. The sounds aroused Deborah, yet she resisted touching herself. Deborah watched as Miriam increased the motion, making her circles faster and harder. Miriam reached up with one hand and stimulated her breast, tweaking her nipple hard as she increased the pace of her fingers. Miriam rubbed herself harder than Deborah had ever rubbed; she kept up the rapid pace as she panted. It took much longer than when Deborah was rubbing or sucking. Deborah wanted badly to reach out and help take Miriam over the edge, but she watched as Miriam arched her back and called out in pleasure. After short gasps, Miriam lay flat on the bed.

Deborah, who felt moisture down there, was pleased it would soon be her turn. But Miriam had other ideas. She continued to rub herself, which surprised Deborah. She thought Miriam had worn herself out, but that was not the case. As Miriam rubbed vigorously, making squishy sounds, she started to breathe heavily. She made circles with her fingers, much more quickly this time, and she was soon all worked up again. Deborah watched, her own tender parts throbbing, as Miriam brought herself to the brink of exploding. It was not long before she let out a guttural moan as she convulsed again.

Miriam lay still on the bed, relaxed. Deborah waited to see if Miriam would start again, yet was pleased when she said, "Your turn."

છ છ છ

Before Anna's short vacation ended, it came time for the promised vaudeville-theater trip. Deborah and Miriam had vacillated between several venues, finally narrowing the choices—the Orpheum Theater or B. F. Keith's. Miriam favored B. F. Keith's Theatre on Washington Street, which was built exclusively as a vaudeville-performance place.

After weighing their options, they chose to see the Fadettes of Boston, an all-woman orchestra managed by B. F. Keith; they had been headlining at first-class vaudeville theaters around the country. The ladies' band had grown to twenty women from the original six and had been entertaining crowds for many years. They performed marches, waltzes, songs, and arias to the delight of audiences everywhere. And of most importance to Miriam, they sometimes played Yiddish songs.

"I'm so excited," said Anna as they told her about their choice of places to go. "But you should have asked me where I wanted to go."

"Sorry," said Deborah with a sigh, "you're absolutely right. We should've checked with you. My apologies."

"It's all right. Next time, please let me be a part of the decision. And by the way, I would have chosen B. F. Keith's because of the Fadettes, so I'm pleased with your choice."

The night of the performance finally arrived. They climbed into a taxi—an extravagance for Deborah and Miriam, yet the normal mode of transportation for Anna, who lived in New York City, where taxi rides were common. As they got in, Deborah and Miriam left all their cares behind.

The three wore their finest outfits. For Deborah, it was the tailored skirt and blouse her mother had gifted her for her trip to speak at Barnard College. Miriam wore a soft-pink dress that she saved for special occasions. Anna's stylish outfit was of teal blue, and it had a matching wide collar, hat, and parasol. Her dress, cinched tightly at the waist, was provocative because of its short length—practically mid-calf! They made a fine showing as they were led to their seats.

"I can hardly wait," Anna said.

Anna glanced disapprovingly at a woman in a large hat, sitting directly in front of them. Miriam was pleased the woman removed it, so Anna could see the stage.

As the lights dimmed, the ladies anticipated the opening acts. Would there be a juggler, a singer, an acrobat, an elephant, clowns? None of them knew what to expect, other than the performance by the Fadette Ladies Orchestra. First, they were treated to a young boy and his father singing sweet songs to one another.

"I hope there is something funny next," whispered Anna. "They were nice, yet I want something livelier."

Miriam hoped Anna had not spoken loudly enough to be heard by those seated nearby.

Anna's wish came true, as the comedians were next—two men who told silly stories to each other, one laughing hard and the other remaining straight-faced throughout. They were followed by a performance by six dogs jumping through hoops, then an energetic singer-dancer team performing to an upbeat song. A short interlude of ballet delighted them, though Anna made faces when a slender woman belted out an aria. There was a short silent film, followed by an intermission before the Fadettes performed.

"This is even better than the vaudeville show Mother and Father took us to in Great Barrington. I really loved that show, but I was just a little girl then, so my opinions were different," Anna said as they got up to stretch.

Deborah thought to herself, though didn't dare say, *You've grown up very quickly.*

Finally, back in their seats, there was a grand introduction. "Ladies and Gentlemen, we're proud to present these world-renowned ladies, back in their hometown after headlining at vaudeville houses around the country. Please welcome the Fadettes of Boston."

Anna stared as the sophisticated women walked across the stage, lights reflecting off their sparkling dresses and off the silver of their flutes and the brass of their trombones.

Conductor Caroline Nichols, a blonde with curls pulled into an updo, and wearing a flowing dress, appeared onstage to loud cheers and clapping. She raised her arms, looked intently at her musicians, and gave the downbeat to begin. The band woke the crowd with a rousing song that everyone except Deborah and Miriam seemed to know. A bit too loudly for Miriam's sensitive ears, Anna sang along with the music.

The next piece was quiet, and as Deborah glanced over to see if Anna was making faces, she found her sister totally enthralled. For the rest of the performance, Anna moved rhythmically to each piece.

After the audience gave the Fadettes a standing ovation, they came back for an encore and played a delightful, catchy tune.

"What an amazing performance!" was the first thing Anna said while exiting the theater. "The Fadettes of Boston were the most thrilling part of the whole evening. I loved everything about the show, and I will especially remember those wonderful women. Thank you for bringing me. I will remember this forever."[10]

---

[10] Caroline B. Nichols, a violinist, was the founder and conductor of the Fadette Ladies Orchestra, naming the group after the heroine of George Sand's novel, *La Petite Fadette*. She is credited as being the first woman to make a career of conducting musical productions. In 1898, B. F. Keith booked this all-woman orchestra into vaudeville theaters across the county. By then, they had expanded from the original group of six performers to twenty accomplished musicians who headlined in first-class venues. Between 1890 and 1920, the Fadettes performed over 6,000 concerts.

BF Keith Theater

Episode 7 ❧ USS Leviathan

June 1917

Everyone's moods lightened with Anna's visit. Even the children were buoyant with Deborah's sister. No one other than Miriam noticed Deborah's sullen spirit on the day her brother reported for naval-officer duty. Miriam asked Deborah leading questions about her fears for Milton's safety during these tenuous times, and Deborah attempted to pass off her own concerns as unimportant. But Miriam was aware that the battles raging overseas brought worry for every soldier's family.

Deborah's face lit up when her first letter from Milton arrived, announcing that he was an officer! He wrote that his participation in the Plattsburg boot camp, which had expanded to train both air force and navy candidates along with the army trainees, had led to his ranking of junior lieutenant. This surprised Deborah, who'd learned that most Jews were overlooked when officers were being selected. Deborah wondered if they had overlooked Milton's religion because of his skills.

> June 3, 1917
>
> Dear Deborah,
>
> Now that I'm settled, I can tell you where I am—right here in New York Harbor! When I joined the navy, I never thought I'd be assigned to my very own city.
>
> It looks like I'll have freedom to write to you because, as an officer, I have plenty of discretionary time. Many of the others gather in the evenings to drink until they are silly, yet that behavior doesn't interest me. I'd rather stay in my bunk and study the assignments for the next day or write to you. Thus far, they've not required my attendance at religious services, so I'll also have time on Sundays, like now, while everyone goes to the onboard church. I wonder if I'm the only Jew here.
>
> The ship I'm on, the USS Leviathan, is massive. It was a German ocean liner that got caught in New York Harbor when war was declared in Europe, so it was left unattended for three years. The United States government seized it,

and recently the navy commissioned it. You'd be impressed with the vestiges of its prior lavishness. I'm taking lots of photographs with the Eastman Vest Pocket Kodak camera you bought me. I heard there are photograph-development services available to us.

I know how much you enjoy doing research, so I'm hopeful you'll gather information for me about this boat. I bet it has a fascinating history.

Our job seems to be to get this ship back in working order. When President Wilson and the United States Shipping Board seized the ship, they may not have realized it had fallen into such disrepair. It's our job to convert the ship into an armed-troops carrier, which seems an overwhelming task. We are to convert the luxurious dining hall into a mess hall, the first-class swimming pool into a baggage room, and the baggage room into the ship's prison. I'll need to inspire the enlisted men in my charge.

I hope all is well with you in Boston and with our family in New York. I have included my address. It's thrilling to get a letter during mail call, so I hope you'll write.
Love,
Milton

৵ ৵ ৵

On June 4, Susan yelled loudly, "Women's suffrage just passed in New York!"

All the adults in the house came running, excited about this news. Both Susan and Helen had damp eyes, thrilled that their dream was coming true.

A few days later, a New York-based Yiddish magazine, *Foverts*, called for essays on women's voting rights. Hoping to win the twenty-five-dollar best-essay prize, Deborah sat down to draft an article for Miriam or Hannah to translate into Yiddish. Deborah planned to write about New York districts with large Jewish populations, hoping to sway the vote there in favor of women's suffrage, but she was distracted and could not concentrate. Her mind was filled with thoughts of war and her brother, Milton; she feared this fight for women's voting rights was a lost cause. Although several states had passed women's suffrage, there was still a very long battle ahead. Deborah didn't believe women's equal say in government would ever happen. Discouraged, in the end, she gave up the opportunity to be published.

ॐ ॐ ॐ

After Milton's brief description of the USS *Leviathan*, Deborah was curious. She met with her friend, the librarian at the Boston Public Library, to find out more information, and then she sent Milton a letter to describe the ship's history.

> *June 13, 1917*
> *Dear Milton,*
> *I learned so much about the ship you are on. Built in 1900, the Germans were proud to launch the largest transat-lantic passenger liner in the world. It exceeded the size and lavishness of the Titanic, which sank in 1912. Called the SS Vanderland, it had luxury accommodations for the fortunate group of passengers in first and second class. It boasted a Ritz-Carlton main dining room and a magnifi-cent ballroom. The accommodations were adequate for four thousand travelers in third and fourth class, though it held many more.*
>
> *At the beginning of the Great War, the ship was seized by the United States government, becoming its most gigantic prisoner of war. United States Customs impounded the con-tents of luxury goods, including an eighty-piece gold coffee service designed for the German kaiser, furs, and jewels. The first-class salons had mirrored walls and carpets and chairs covered in rose-colored brocade.*
>
> *The United States named the ship the USS Leviathan, after a sea serpent noted in mythology and multiple times in the Hebrew Bible.*
> *With Love,*
> *Your sister Deborah*

ॐ ॐ ॐ

Deborah and Milton continued their correspondence with regularity. Deborah was comforted by being in constant contact with her brother, while Milton seemed to need this connection with home, sharing every detail of his life onboard the ship. Deborah also regularly communicated with her parents and Anna, telling them about Milton's military responsibilities, though censoring what she shared with them. She valued Milton's descriptions, but her family did not need to know the difficulties he faced or his discomfort as the only Jew onboard.

Leviathan at harbor

Over time, Milton shared that he was ignored much of the time by the other officers. Initially, he assumed he would eventually be welcomed by the others. But, one afternoon, Milton heard two men talking about "the Jew." One of them said, in words that were loud enough for Milton to overhear, "I'm surprised I can't see the horns that my father told me all Jews have growing on their heads."

The other man said, "I've never seen a Jewboy before. I thought they'd look different than the rest of us. I don't like that he talks to himself a lot. My father taught me never to trust them, so I'm staying away from him."

Milton felt hurt. He'd done his best to keep his religious differences to himself and had said his prayers silently. He moved his lips, but never uttered a sound, which was probably what the others interpreted as talking to himself. He never wore his *yarmulke* or *tallit* while praying and certainly never wrapped his arms in the tefillin he usually wore during morning prayers. They already thought him odd, so no need to encourage their chastisement. He worked alongside them quietly, never doing anything to call attention to himself. He was lonely, and his only real connection was with his sister through their frequent correspondence.

Deborah's mother called to inform Deborah and Miriam about a new charitable organization both she and Mrs. Berkowitz had joined. The Stage Women's War Relief had recently been established in New York City to coordinate volunteer efforts by women in the theater. They started by supplying clothing and hospital supplies to soldiers, then expanded their services to arranging performances for troops fighting in Europe.

Mrs. Levine asked, "Would you be willing to help us sell Liberty Bonds for this relief effort by printing some recruitment posters in your shop?"

"We could probably do that," Deborah said, skeptical about working for this organization rather than for suffrage.

"This group built a temporary theater right outside the New York Public Library to present entertainment to raise money for the war effort. That's how Mrs. Berkowitz and I got involved. We went to a show and were so impressed that both of us signed up that very day. We're both going to volunteer at the canteen on Broadway for American soldiers serving in New York City."

A few days later, Deborah opened a package from her mother; it contained a war-bond poster and a note suggesting that she print a lot of them to put up around Boston. Susan's and Helen's expressions soured as they eyed the poster lying on the table. Deborah noticed and asked what was wrong.

Susan huffed out a deep breath before she said, "There is a problem with this canteen. We were discussing it at our suffrage meeting. It seems that the canteens have been wonderfully helpful, but only to men. They do not serve the women who have gone there. I can't imagine supporting a group like this."

"That's not fair. Women always seem to be left out."

Helen added, "These canteens are open to both White and Colored servicemen. It is nice that they don't discriminate that way, even though women have been left out."

Deborah decided she could not produce the posters at their printing shop, and she needed to tell her mother why. She was not used to refusing to do something her mother requested of her, but it felt as if it was a moral obligation to not actively support the canteen that discriminated against women.[11]

---

[11] Established in 1917, the world-famous Stage Door Canteen began as the Little Club in New York's Times Square, an after-theater dance club. Around the same time, seven suffragettes formed the Stage Women's War Relief, dedicated to supporting the troops. At the beginning of the Great War, the Stage Door Canteen was an exciting place where servicemen were served free food and provided top-rate entertainment. Women volunteers arranged the entertainment and danced the night away with lonely men. They also sewed uniforms for soldiers and raised money through Liberty Loan drives. Stage Women's War Relief raised over $7,000,000 towards the war effort. In accordance with the nondiscrimination policy of the canteen, Negro soldiers were treated with the same respect as any other patrons.

In 1940, the *New York Times* bought the theater and converted it into a soldiers' canteen. The Stage Women's War Relief became known as the American Theatre Wing during World War II, with such notable volunteers as Lauren Bacall and the Andrews Sisters. The Stage Door Canteen's continued popularity led to a 1942 television show and a 1943 movie. The American Theater Wing eventually founded the Tony Awards for excellence in live Broadway theater.

Episode 8 ✳ *Red Emma*

August 1917

On August 10, 1917, everyone was affected by the war when Director Herbert Hoover of the US Food Administration urged citizens to limit their consumption of meat, sugar, fats, and wheat in order to properly supply soldiers with good nutrition. Grocery stores displayed Food Will Win the War posters, and there were campaigns such as Meatless Tuesdays and Wheatless Wednesdays to encourage families to do their part in the war effort.

At Miriam and Deborah's home, their cook, Mrs. Stern, took these dictates to heart. Their meals reflected the efforts of the country to help soldiers win the war. Both Deborah and Miriam were supportive of the restrictions. Mrs. Levine and Mrs. Berkowitz worked at the soldiers' canteen in New York, and they actively sold Liberty Bonds, doing whatever they could for their country. Deborah supported their activities despite the lack of canteen services for military women. As their only act of protest over this dismissive treatment of females, she and Miriam did not buy Liberty Bonds.

One evening, sitting in their bedroom, Miriam asked, "Do you remember our first suffrage event? I remember getting very excited about Emma Goldman's article on Oscar Wilde and homosexuals' rights."

"I remember that day so clearly. The whole experience was quite significant, learning about suffrage from all those interesting speakers and then meeting Margaret and Abigail, the first female couple we ever met—besides us, of course. I remember how excited you were that Emma Goldman was Jewish," Deborah recalled.

"I was pretty naïve then, more interested in her religion than her political beliefs."

"Why are you asking about that day now?"

Miriam said, "I've been following news articles about Emma Goldman since that day. She's been supporting the suffrage movement and also women's rights to limit their family size. She's been a mentor to Margaret Sanger, the woman who has been opening birth control clinics in New York."

"What's your interest in birth control?" Deborah asked, very curious.

Miriam was bristled a bit by Deborah's question. "I'm not. That's not why I brought her up. It seems Emma Goldman was recently arrested, actually arrested again. She previously spent time in jail because she distributed contraceptive devices and information, though that's not her current problem. The *Boston Globe* ran an article about her this morning, calling her an anti-war crusader and an anarchist, a word I don't understand. She was protesting America's involvement in the war when she was taken by the police."

"An anarchist is someone who believes that any form of government is unnecessary."

"Thank you. I don't know how you know about whatever I bring up."

"I guess I'm just well-read."

"And smart."

"Yes, that too!" Deborah smiled.

Miriam also grinned. "I'm so impressed with Emma Goldman. She stands up for the things she believes, takes a very strong position, then fights for that cause. I wish I could be so courageous in my beliefs and so brave."

"You do have strong opinions," Deborah said.

"Mostly about silly things that don't matter."

"I beg to differ. You are fervent about your Jewish ideals, the rights of the immigrants you volunteer with, and the suffrage movement."

"But," said Miriam, "that's exactly the point. I feel strongly, though not enough to be out on the streets fighting for workers' rights or for women's votes. All I do for the suffrage movement these days is to run off materials at the shop for Susan and Helen to distribute. That's a weak response to something I believe in so deeply."

"You do more than others, and I'm relieved you don't put yourself in harm's way. You have a family to protect and a business that needs you."

Sighing, Miriam said, "That's why I admire Emma Goldman for fighting for change."

Deborah cocked her head. "Should I be doing more to stand up for my ideals?"

"No! Please don't! I've worked hard to calm you down." Deborah smiled. "When I met you, you were ready to fight the world for your beliefs. Remember how you told off that boy who touched my arm when we first met at Ruth's party? You insisted he leave me alone because he was being inappropriate."

"I'm embarrassed you remember that incident. I was so headstrong back then."

"But, Deborah, that's why I fell in love with you. I admired your conviction. I was meek, and I looked up to you for standing firm for what you believed."

"And look at you now. My shrinking violet now is firmer than I am in standing up for her rights."

"That's where this discussion began. I'm not so strong outside of our household. I don't risk my health, or even my comfort, to stand for things as Emma Goldman does."

"Thank God. I'd hate for you to be whisked off to jail. You must leave the big protests to women stronger than either of us," Deborah said.

"Are they stronger? Wiser? Or do they get a thrill from the attention?"

"Good point. I bet Emma Goldman is excited about another arrest, another time when people will listen to her."

"This is such an engaging conversation. I love you so much. I'm so pleased we can banter ideas back and forth."

"And," Deborah said, shaking her head, "I don't run away or make a horrible fuss when your positions differ from mine."

"Yes, you used to run away whenever there was conflict."

"Or when I didn't get my way."

"Your maturity is becoming."

They embraced, then kissed gently.

Miriam, who'd ignored her own mounting desires lately, was careful not to expect too much. She gingerly kissed Deborah again.

Deborah responded with a deeper kiss as she hugged Miriam to her closely and quietly said, "Yes," as she guided Miriam to the bed.

They undressed each other in slow motion until they were naked on top of the sheets. As Deborah's hands glided along her body, Miriam held her breath, trying not to disturb the intensity of the moment. Deborah touched Miriam all over. When she reached below, her fingers found Miriam wet and ready. In a familiar yet more gentle manner than Miriam could remember, she spread Miriam's wetness. She expertly stroked her until Miriam arched her back.

Miriam reached out and touched Deborah's body gently, testing her response. She mimicked Deborah's deliberate, soft manner, increasing her quiet excitement; then she slowly and carefully massaged the tender flesh until there was a flash of relief. Miriam welcomed the intimate connection. Their loving was a healing balm amid the problems of the time.

ৰু ৰু ৰু

The next day, their birth-control discussion continued, this time at Susan's and Helen's initiation.

"Emma Goldman is an amazing woman," Susan said, reading the morning paper. "She stands so firmly for her convictions."

"We had a similar discussion yesterday," said Miriam.

"So what was your conclusion about her stance on the draft?"

"We didn't talk about the draft. We talked about her unorthodox positions, marveling at her strength of character," Deborah said.

Helen said, "I believe that war is just a bunch of hotheaded men who like to fight."

"Do you really?" asked Deborah.

"I assumed our country and President Wilson were doing the right thing. If it were not for Emma, I'd never consider there was another way," said Miriam.

"Then she has done what she set out to do—have you question warfare," said Helen.

"Since May, when the Selective Service Act was passed, Red Emma, as they're calling her, has been speaking out against the draft," said Susan. "She really is threatening the establishment. No wonder she and her companion, Alexander Berkman, were arrested. My friends in New York went to see her, and they told me she said, 'We believe in violence, and we will use violence.'"

"They got to see her?!" Miriam exclaimed with wonder, fascinated with Emma, as with any celebrity.

Helen continued, "They received the maximum sentence for conspiracy and were sent to jail in July."

"Conspiracy?" Deborah asked.

"Yes," Susan said. "Conspiracy against the draft. She got a $10,000 fine, and now they've found a new way to punish her, hitting her where it will hurt the most. The postal service has denied *Mother Earth* second-class mailing privileges; that could make it too expensive to mail."

Miriam shrugged. "What's *Mother Earth*?"

"It's the anarchist journal Emma edits. It's full of articles by activists and writers and is considered quite subversive," Helen said. "It covers such things as the labor movement, women's emancipation, and sexual freedom. It was her position on birth control that got her arrested the last time."

"And lately," Susan said, "*Mother Earth* has been calling for opposition to the United States entering the Great War and to conscription."

"Conscription?" asked Miriam.

"I know that term," said Deborah. "It's another term for the military draft."

"This really is stretching my mind. I usually just accept things I'm told," Miriam said.

"Emma Goldman will help you out of your lazy thinking," said Deborah.

Helen piped in, "She's not lazy. Just trusting. That is one of the things we love about you, Miriam."

"I don't want to be loved for being ignorant. I need to pay more attention to Emma's teachings. Maybe I'll subscribe to *Mother Earth* if it's still published."

"I hope we don't have an anarchist in the making," Deborah said, smirking. "I'll do something to help you. I'll go to the library and find out what I can about Emma Goldman."

"What a surprise!" Miriam teased.

☙ ☙ ☙

Just before dinnertime a few days later, there was a loud crash that sent them all scurrying. They discovered Deborah, annoyed though physically fine, on the floor in the front vestibule. In the corner, Susan noticed a small ball, the probable cause of the mishap. Deborah was fixing her mussed dress and ranting about toys being in the way; apparently, she was unable to directly blame the children or Jimmy. Miriam noted Deborah's excessive frustration and hoped it would be short-lived.

Right after Deborah's fall, they gathered for dinner. Deborah's mood lightened as she mentioned she'd overheard something at work that day. As the food was served, Deborah relayed a conversation she'd listened to while pretending to do her work. Turning to Helen and Susan, she said, "While their husbands were talking in Yiddish with Hannah, I heard two women saying that Emma Goldman was working to make the world a better place."

"We'd love to hear what you learned," said Susan.

"They said that Emma Goldman believes that each woman should have her own voice." Deborah looked Susan in the eyes. "I'm going to practice stating my beliefs. Though I agree with about ninety percent of what you say, Susan, sometimes you talk of the fight for women's suffrage as if it's a reality. We've not come as far as anyone had hoped, so I find your trust that women will gain the right to vote naïve and sometimes annoying."

"You are touchy tonight," Miriam said, stirring in her chair. She wondered if Deborah was about to attack Susan further.

"I speak my convictions," Susan said timidly, hoping she was not encouraging conflict.

This interaction ended without incident, as Deborah switched to sharing her discoveries from the library. Miriam sat back, watching Deborah's mood, hoping there'd be no further outbursts.

"Just a bit of background first," Deborah began. "Emma Goldman was born into a poor Jewish family in Russia; her family fled to the United States when she was young. She moved to Rochester, New York, where she worked at a factory and became involved in the labor movement. Her first protests were regarding poor working conditions, which set the stage for her willingness to fight hard for her beliefs.

"She became involved with a fellow Russian anarchist, Alexander Berkman, who was sent to prison during a violent workers' strike in Pennsylvania. Goldman went free due to a lack of evidence regarding her involvement. This was the beginning of her political activism. In 1906, she founded *Mother Earth,* becoming outspoken on working conditions and then women's sexual freedom."

When Deborah stopped to take a mouthful of dinner, Susan jumped in, "Then she got arrested for violating the Comstock Act when she sent printed materials about birth control through the mail. She was working with Margaret Sanger, the woman who invented the term 'birth control' and leads the movement. I really respect the work they're doing."

"Oh, Deborah, do continue," Helen said. "However, it's really funny that the four of us are discussing the prevention of unwanted pregnancies, something none of us will ever need."

Giggles all around the table.[12]

Deborah couldn't manage to stay silly for long since she had more information to report on Emma Goldman. "The women at the shop called her Red Emma, due to her Russian heritage and her subversive ways. She is fighting for education and against governmental control of everything, including literature and the arts. She is a rebel fighting for every cause she believes in. This brings us up to her most recent arrest and the prison term she has just started serving."

"I hope you'll keep us updated on her situation. I suspect this isn't the end of her story," said Susan.

---

[12] The Comstock Act of 1873 defined contraceptives as obscene and lewd and outlawed their transport over state lines or through the mail. This law was used to sabotage the birth-control movement.

The meal continued with political talk ceding to conversation about the children, the delicious dinner, and general chatter.[13]

ॐ ॐ ॐ

Deborah had been thinking of her brother frequently and was thrilled when another letter arrived.

> *August 22, 1917*
> *Deborah,*
> *Thanks for finding out so much about the ship I'm on.*
>
> *I must tell you that my letters are being censored. You may find holes cut out. I got away with telling you a great amount in my first letter since I mailed it on my own when I was on shore. Now, everything I write will be scrutinized.*
>
> *Although much of the ship is in terrible condition after being left unattended for three years, its earlier opulence is obvious. It looks much older than other ships built in 1900. The area where I'm living, the officers' quarters, was probably where the second-class accommodations were. I'm glad I went to boot camp and became an officer, because the enlisted and drafted men are living in the area you described as "steerage." They are crammed into a small area, not as badly as their predecessors, yet they are clearly not living in the style of us officers.*
>
> *Last week, they invited the lower-ranking officers to a reception with the captain in what must have been the first-class area. It was quite impressive. Though everything needs fixing, and it's horribly dirty, the lavish fixtures are still there. The captain showed us an old brochure he found in the back of a drawer; it had a picture of the incredible pool. The brochure made it easy to imagine how luxurious everything was when this was a seaworthy hotel. Now, it takes some imagination, because they've broke up the grand ballrooms*

---

[13] Two years later, on September 27, 1919, Emma Goldman was released from prison at the end of her sentence, yet she was immediately re-imprisoned. The head of the Justice Department's General Intelligence Committee, J. Edgar Hoover, said Goldman and her companion, Alexander Berkman, were the most frightening anarchists in the country. He wanted them removed. Goldman and Beckman, along with 250 other radicals, were deported to the new Soviet Union. Emma described it as an honor to be the first political agitator to be deported from the United States. They never returned. The last issue of *Mother Earth* was published in August 1917.

into smaller cubicles for the senior officers. There's a huge area cordoned off for carrying supplies to [CENSOR]. When I look past the boxes, I see faded brocade wall coverings and numerous dusty chandeliers full of cobwebs.

Sadly, as I left the reception, I overheard one of the other officers commenting on how "that Jewboy" must have enjoyed the event. I said nothing, but I was sad to be reminded of their attitudes.
Love,
Milton

Emma Goldman

Rationing

Episode 9 ❧ *Margaret Sanger*
September 1917

In early September, Anna returned to Boston to see the film *Rebecca of Sunnybrook Farm*. For this visit, Deborah and Miriam didn't arrange a schedule for Anna, relying on the movie as the highlight of the weekend and letting the rest fall into place. Anna said she liked the freedom to do as she pleased. Deborah wondered whether this was meant to chastise, though Miriam took her comment literally.

The weekend was filled with easy conversation and pleasant family time. Anna hinted about wanting a kitten of her own, having fallen in love with Jimmy. Deborah ignored her comments, knowing she'd never initiate something as invasive to family life as a cat without having a long conversation with her mother first.

Anna gave considerable attention to the children, acting part parent and part playmate. Anna insisted they include Sylvia on their movie trip, yet became bothered when Sylvia squirmed in her seat. Miriam removed her from the theater and walked the corridors until she settled down. Miriam didn't even mind focusing on Sylvia, rather than on the film.

It was not until the second evening of Anna's trip that the sisters discussed Milton. Deborah shared Milton's letters with Anna, as the two of them sat in the corner of the parlor.

Anna asked Deborah if it would be all right if she wrote to him aboard ship.

"Certainly," Deborah told her sister, "but I would not mention your concerns. Wish him well, and tell him about all your activities."

From the hallway, Miriam noticed tears dripping down their faces. So she left them alone to share their feelings and a loving embrace.

❧ ❧ ❧

The fall High Holidays were calm. To welcome the new year, Miriam and the children celebrated *Rosh Hashanah* with Marjorie's family, as they'd done for the past few years. Sylvia was intrigued with the many foods she had never been interested in before, probably because Ida ate everything she was offered. Her little sister was proving to be a great role model for expanding Sylvia's tastes.

Deborah had traveled with Anna to New York to be with her family for Rosh Hashanah. With Milton away, Miriam assumed it would be a difficult holiday for the family. Though it was hard for Deborah and Miriam to be apart, they both understood how important it was to be with their own loved ones.

Susan and Helen visited their families separately during the holiday week, grateful for the time off from work and the opportunity to be with their loved ones.

Helen returned from her vacation without Susan, though they had planned to travel back and forth to New York together. She began sobbing as soon as Miriam greeted her at the door, which made it difficult to get from her the story about Susan's absence. Deborah joined them when she heard the commotion at the front door, but her presence just started a new barrage of tears. Finally, they pieced together the story.

Susan had volunteered at Margaret Sanger's clinic during her visit home and was enticed with a job offer before she left. Susan was satisfied with her life in Boston, but she felt pulled by this incredible position with Sanger, which better matched her interests than working at a publishing shop. If she took the job, she could be with her family, whom she missed desperately. She decided to take the job. Helen was bereft.

A couple of weeks later, when Helen had said practically nothing about Susan, Miriam knew she had to broach the subject, so she asked, "How does Susan like her new job with Margaret Sanger?"

"All right, I guess," Helen responded in a monotone.

"What do you mean you guess? You just got a letter from her," interjected Deborah.

"She didn't say much. Maybe she's afraid to tell me how happy she is now that she's back with her family," Helen said.

"How could she be happy away from you?" Miriam asked.

"She's practically forgotten about me. This is the first letter I've received since she left," said Helen tearfully, leaving the table abruptly.

"Helen. I didn't mean to upset you," said Miriam, attempting to stop Helen. "Please talk with us."

"I can't discuss this. I'm just too upset."

"Then just sit with us, and we won't ask more questions," said Deborah, feeling bad they'd disturbed her.

Helen returned and, despite saying she couldn't talk, began a long monologue. "I know she wanted to do something meaningful with her life, and the opportunity to work with Margaret Sanger, the brave woman fighting for reproductive rights, was too tempting. Ever since hearing that Mrs. Sanger had opened a clinic for women in Brooklyn, Susan talked of little else. You were very generous with the time off you allotted us, though none of us thought this vacation would lead to her finding a new job and moving back home. I knew she missed her family, yet I hoped she'd be satisfied with visits. I can hardly believe she left me."

Miriam embraced her friend, who broke into sobs. "She didn't want to leave you. She just missed everyone in New York desperately."

"And," continued Helen through her tears, "she was distraught her family could never know she'd fallen in love with me. It pained her terribly that she couldn't discuss the most significant joy she ever experienced."

There was silence. No one knew what to say.

Deborah broke the quiet. "We certainly miss her at the shop. It's not the same without her. Micah and I are hard-pressed to run the publishing business on our own. I don't know where we'll find someone to replace her."

This upset Helen, who imagined they were going to replace Susan. She still hoped for Susan's return. The discussion caused her to leave the table in tears.

"I didn't mean to upset her even more, but we need to be practical. We've managed for several weeks without Susan, and we need to consider other options to keep the shop running well," said Deborah.

"We must be kind to Helen. She's very fragile."

"Are you saying I treated her poorly?"

"Deborah, you didn't treat her badly, though you need to be careful what you say."

"Maybe I shouldn't say anything. I always seem to say the wrong things."

"No, you don't. She's just extremely sensitive these days," Miriam said, walking the fine line of truth.

"Each day," Deborah went on, "it becomes more obvious Susan's not coming back. Do you have anyone in mind to take her place?"

Miriam was afraid to say anything lest she upset Deborah, who'd been quick to anger lately. Yet Miriam gathered her courage and said, "Unfortunately, no one. And what can we do for Mildred? That poor girl seems so lost. With Susan gone and Helen so distraught, it seems more than a sweet twelve-year-old can manage. She's been working longer hours, and I'm certain it's so she can be near Helen. I'm worried about her."

"I feel bad for Mildred, yet my attention is definitely on the business's needs. After all, it is my business, the Cohen Publishing Company, that's floundering without Susan," Deborah said firmly.

"I didn't mean to downplay the importance of Susan's absence for the office." Miriam looked down to the floor.

Deborah put her arm on Miriam's shoulder. "I'm sorry. I shouldn't take out my frustrations on you. It's kind of you to be concerned about Mildred's welfare, and it's not a battle to decide which is more important. I'll leave you to worry about Mildred while I worry about the shop."

Miriam smiled as she said, "It's a deal."

&ও ও ও

The next evening, after an especially grueling day, Deborah talked with Miriam about her newest idea. "What if we ask Fanny Berkowitz to work in the publishing shop when she's here? She's responsible and would fit in nicely."

"That sounds like a reasonable idea, though I was looking forward to her working with us in the printing shop, like she's done on her other vacations."

"I don't want us to be in competition for her; however, she's the only person I can imagine who could help us."

"Let's call her tomorrow and ask which side of the business she'd prefer," Miriam said, reminding Deborah that because Fanny was sixteen, it would just be for summers and school vacations for now. "Mrs. B. would be furious with us if we were to encourage her to work rather than finish school."

The following day, their conversation with Fanny held some surprises. Though she would be pleased to help on either side of the business, Fanny shared some significant news. She spoke quietly, so her parents couldn't hear. She had joined the United States Navy.

"That's a huge commitment," Miriam said, careful not to condemn Fanny for her decision.

"I know I did the right thing," Fanny said, though the hesitancy in her voice negated her words. "I'm just really scared what my folks will say when I tell them."

"You can practice with me if you want, so that you express exactly what you want to say. I find that practicing helps."

"No, thank you. I'll do fine."

In the end, they all agreed that Fanny would help both sides of the business during school vacations until she reported to duty.

Deborah, the practical one, needed a quicker solution to problems at the office. Knowing Fanny filled a temporary need, she persuaded Rachel's sister Rebecca to switch from the printing shop to publishing. Despite Rebecca's limited education, she was well-read and quite skilled at the necessary editing tasks. Miriam did not complain, though she too was struggling to keep up. On the whole, the business was running well, keeping all involved busy and financially rewarded.

ﰄ ﰄ ﰄ

Later in the week, once the children were tucked in for the night, Deborah and Miriam spoke with Helen.

"What do you know of Margaret Sanger's work?" asked Miriam bravely, not wanting to avoid the issue of Susan's departure, yet trying to change the focus of their discussions. Miriam felt on edge a great deal these days, wanting neither to anger Deborah nor to upset Helen. The war and worries for family and friends were taking a toll.

"I actually know quite a bit because Susan talked of her often," said Helen.

"Tell us about her," Deborah said, sitting comfortably on the divan and anticipating a long explanation.

"Margaret Sanger is a nurse," Helen began, "who fights for the rights of women to learn about what she calls birth control."

"I don't want to sound ignorant," Miriam said, "but I don't really understand the term"—she lowered her voice—"birth control."

"You aren't ignorant. It's a new term. It's a way for women to limit their family size," Helen explained.

"I still don't understand."

"I'm not certain I understand the specifics, but she's spent the past several years gathering information about how women can take charge of their own bodies and decide when and if to bear children," Helen tried to explain, but Miriam looked even more confused.

"I'll tell you what it means when we get to our room," Deborah said.

"We can be open in front of our friend," said Miriam.

"All right. It means men and women refrain from intimacy. Is that correct?" she asked Helen.

"Not exactly." Taking a deep breath, Helen said, "Women, according to Sanger, can only get pregnant during specific times of the month, so by avoiding intimacy during those times, it's easier to plan when a woman becomes pregnant."

"And who is going to get men to listen to that kind of rule?" Deborah asked with a slight smile.

After a chuckle, Helen continued, "There are also things men can wear on their privates to protect women from receiving their seed."

"That's more detail than I want," Miriam said, shaking her head and looking uncomfortable.

Despite Miriam's comment, Helen went on, explaining how Margaret's mother died young after many births and miscarriages. While working with impoverished women suffering with large families, Margaret decided to educate young women on how to avoid difficult pregnancies—or even getting pregnant at all if they were not able to care for another baby. While working in Greenwich Village, she wrote a column called "What Every Girl Should Know," and in 1914 began a monthly feminist publication called the *Woman Rebel.*

"I saw that magazine!" said Miriam. "Someone at Denison House had a copy and showed me an article by Emma Goldman."

"How exciting! I always wanted to see a copy," said Helen. After a brief pause, she continued, "There were many people who found Margaret's work scandalous, and she was found guilty of the crime of obscenity. Facing a five-year jail term, she fled to England, leaving her husband and children behind."

"She had a family?" Miriam asked. "What kind of woman leaves her husband and children?"

"Someone determined to make a difference for others," said Helen. "She returned to America in 1915, hoping she'd avoided jail time, and opened what she calls birth-control clinics. Susan works at one of these clinics." Helen got quiet, lost in thought about Susan.

Miriam thought about the new ideas Helen had shared and breathed a sigh of relief that no more details were forthcoming. For one conversation, it was an awful lot to think about.

≈ ≈ ≈

The next night at dinner, Helen brought up a related issue. "Do Jewish women think about limiting their family size? My Catholic family would find this offensive."

"I have no idea about that," Deborah answered. "I've heard 'Go forth and multiply,' and that means Jewish women must have as many children as possible. I assume it's to increase our numbers to make up for all those who've been massacred over the years."

"It's actually 'Be fruitful and multiply,'" Miriam corrected. "It's a mitzvah to procreate, and it's forbidden to 'waste seed,' a statement my parents left to my imagination, rather than explain. So I imagine it is against *Halakhah,* Jewish law, to put any limits on producing children. With my father of blessed memory gone, and no other learned men whom I'd feel comfortable asking, I suppose we'll never know."

Deborah appeared deep in thought. "So according to what you have just said, I believe Jews must disapprove of us being together, rather than your choosing a husband with whom to have a child."

"I think so, sweetie. And it certainly was not a topic I discussed with my father, yet I assume this was at the root of his rejection of me."

"I am so sorry to bring up such a difficult subject," Helen said, changing it and leaving both Miriam and Deborah to wonder about other Jewish laws that would make their situation uncomfortable for their Jewish families.

Deborah often thought of Milton during the Jewish holidays and was pleased to find a letter from him upon her return from work.

September 20, 1917
Dear Deborah,
I'm writing to you for comfort. This past week has been
tough, being the only Jew here during the High Holidays.
It was difficult; I felt alone. The anti-Semitism is obvious to
me now. Occasionally, someone will recognize my name as
Jewish, and that's usually the end of our collegial relation-
ship. Sometimes, I hear then snicker in my presence, and
I hear the jokes the soldiers tell one another. Jews seem to be
the brunt of more ridicule than any other group, though the
Irish, Italians, and Poles also take a beating.

Because of this prejudice, I pray in silence. I work my
regular shift since there is no temple, or services of any
kind. In the evening, I pull out my Shabbos prayer book
because I did not have the foresight to pack a High Holidays
prayer book. I do the best I can, chanting the holiday tunes
with the cantor's voice in my head. It feels better to write
you of this, rather than holding it inside.
Love,
Milton

This letter was very distressing. Deborah was pleased, at least, that it had arrived after Anna left, since she wouldn't want to worry her sister. Deborah shared her concerns about Milton with Miriam, who was, as always, very comforting. Deborah was more worried than ever about her brother's safety and feared he was a target.

෯ ෯ ෯

Mail began arriving more frequently for Helen. She'd dash upstairs with her newest letter from Susan in hand, obviously thrilled. In the parlor in the evenings, she updated Deborah and Miriam with news of Margaret Sanger's work, including her most recent publication, the *Birth Control Review*. Helen shared how lonely Susan had become, explaining that she was thrilled to be back with her family, yet she missed Helen more than she had anticipated.

One day, a letter came that changed everything.

September 28, 1917
Dear Helen,
My mother has been concerned about my well-being; she's
noticed how despondent I've been despite my meaningful

work. She came to my room last evening to talk with me and asked directly whether my distress had to do with missing my good friends.

I broke into tears and told her how much I've missed your friendship and how hard it was to leave Boston. She was more understanding than I ever imagined and asked me about you. As I listed your most endearing traits, she said directly, "You need to return to Helen. It is important to have such a special friend."

I was shocked! I hardly believed my ears. I was wondering if she understood the true nature of our relationship when she added, "I think it's wonderful that you have someone so special in your life."

I could barely breathe. She was giving me permission to return to you, rather than stay with the family. She understood that I have a good life in Boston with people who care for me. I'll always be grateful to her for her generosity.

So despite my important work with Margaret and the wonderful time with the rest of my family, I'll return home to you and Mildred and the publishing shop if you'll have me.

With love,
Susan

Helen came downstairs so emotional that Miriam and Deborah thought someone had died. She handed the letter to Deborah, who read it out loud to Miriam, who also broke into tears. Once everyone calmed, Deborah assured Helen that Susan would be welcomed back as part of their family and their business.

Helen headed upstairs to tell Mildred the exciting news. The sound of Mildred's happiness delighted them all.

Within the week, arrangements had been made, and Susan headed home to Boston.[14]

---

[14] Margaret Sanger created the American Birth Control League in 1921. It later became Planned Parenthood Federation of America, and she served as its president for many years. Due to her belief in eugenics and her well-known racism, in 2020, the Planned Parenthood Clinic of New York removed Margaret Sanger's name from the building dedicated to her. Statues of Margaret Sanger remain at the Smithsonian's National Portrait Gallery and on the Freedom Trail in Boston.

Margaret Sanger

Sanger Clinic, Brooklyn

Birth Control Review

Episode 10 ❦
Unintended Victims of War
October 1917

"Guess what I've been dreaming of all night?" Deborah practically shouted as Miriam arrived downstairs. She had five-year-old Sylvia in her arms, having left the baby asleep in her crib upstairs.

"What?" Miriam asked. "The Fadettes of Boston?"

"No. About the book I want to write."

"What a way to start the day. Tell me more."

"The effects of warfare on women. I thought of this in the middle of the night. And in my dreams, I even came up with a name for the book: *Unintended Victims of War*."

"Wasn't that the name of the article you wrote for the Denison House newsletter about the boy, George, whose father died on the *Lusitania*?" asked Miriam.

"What a good memory you have, my dear."

"Are you really going to include only women? Are you planning to exclude boys like George?"

"No, I will include boys and men who are affected as well. I definitely need to include soldiers who die or are harmed. Many other men we know will fight for our country, and there will be ramifications for everyone as our men go overseas in greater numbers. Warfare affects everyone, from the farmer who grows food for the servicemen, to the factory workers who produce rifles, to the women who must learn to run their husbands' businesses," Deborah said as she put Sylvia into her special chair at the breakfast table.

Just as Rachel arrived to care for the children, they heard the baby wake. Before Rachel went upstairs to retrieve her charge, Deborah shared news of her book.

Rachel's reaction was immediate and strong. "That will be a sad topic. I can't imagine one good thing that comes from war," she said sadly. "I'm especially worried with my husband, Aaron, soon serving our country."

With equal concern, Deborah said, "Maybe I can find some positive consequences as I write this book. I don't want this to be an entirely depressing story."

Miriam shook her head. "War is depressing."

Deborah stood up to emphasize her point as she continued, "Except for the women who learn skills previously only available for men. And other women will be running businesses, like we do. Women will become farmers and merchants. It will become a different culture when all the able-bodied men are called to serve."

"I'm impressed you can view war this way," said Miriam. "Maybe there'll be benefits for some women, but there will also be many who struggle when their men are killed or maimed."

"And my life will be affected if he's hurt when he goes to war," said Rachel.

"And then we'll be back to our original plan of hiring just women to run the publishing and printing shops."

"That wasn't a very caring response, Deborah. Rachel's talking about how her life will be without her husband around, and you're relating it to our pragmatic needs at the shops," said Miriam.

"Sorry, Rachel," Deborah said, shaking her head. "Sometimes I can be selfish. I'll feel very bad for you if he serves in Europe."

"*When*, not if," said Rachel as she excused herself to care for Ida.

"I'm afraid you're right," Miriam said as Rachel departed for the upper floor. Miriam focused on Sylvia's breakfast as Deborah returned to their conversation about her book.

"I'm certain I'll need lots of assistance," Deborah said, looking off into space. "Now, I'm not certain about the title. Do you have any ideas?"

"Don't rush it. I bet a lot of authors struggle over what to call their masterpieces."

"Miriam, I'm not expecting to write a masterpiece! I'm not even sure of how I'll organize it. Will it be a series of short stories or a non-fiction book? For now, I'll let it circulate in my head; I'll let you know when it takes shape."

"I'm glad to listen to you. That's one of the ways I can be most helpful," Miriam said.

"War has yet to begin for most Americans, though many men have already been drafted in preparation for our expected entry into battle. Maybe I could write about people's fears about our engagement in the conflict."

"That might be enough for a whole book."

❧ ❧ ❧

As they entered the parlor after putting the girls to bed that evening, they greeted Susan and Helen. Deborah said, "I'd like to ask you about something that Miriam and I discussed over breakfast."

"Certainly," said Helen. "Do you mind if I get us tea before we talk? We mentioned a cup on our way downstairs. May I make some for the two of you?"

"That would be lovely," said Miriam.

Once settled, Deborah inhaled the sweet aroma of her tea, then asked, "I'd love your opinions about how warfare affects those left at home because this is what I've decided to write about. You both have experiences that reach beyond those Miriam and I have."

Susan, sipping her tea, said, "I have lots of opinions, and I've actually given this topic a great deal of thought. After all, I have a brother and cousins who are approaching eighteen, the age to be called to serve. President Wilson wants the military to be all volunteers, although the number of enlistees has not been adequate, according to what I read in the paper."

Helen added, "Patriotism is at a peak, yet I wonder how many men will volunteer to put their lives at risk. I fear all of them will be drafted since we need millions of young men to serve."

"How do you think your families will be affected should your brother and cousins be drafted or volunteer?" Deborah asked.

"It will be devastating financially for my family, for without income from my brother, my parents will be hard-pressed. Since my brother finished school, they've relied on his salary to help run the household," Helen said. "And my cousins live on farms. I can't imagine how their families will manage without their boys' help."

"What will they do?" Miriam asked.

"The women will have to do everything. They're strong, except they've never taken over the farmwork. There'll be no farmhands for hire, so they'll have no choice."

"Some of the women will need to go to work," Susan said, considering options. "Businesses now seem more open to hiring women."

"They have to be," Helen said.

"And with increased needs for uniforms and rifles and other equipment for soldiers," Deborah said, "some women are being called for jobs in factories to produce these items. Many changes will happen across our whole nation."

Helen shook her head. "The scariest part of warfare is not the economic impact on our families, but the risk of death to our loved ones."

"You're right," Susan said.

"As usual, I'm focused on the practical, and you're focused on the emotional needs," Deborah said to the others. "I'm glad I have you around to keep me looking at the real costs of war. I have a lot more deliberating to do before I start writing."

Miriam shook her head. "I disagree. You should start, and we can add to it."

"You mean correct my thoughts?"

"That, too!"

☙ ☙ ☙

After Susan and Helen went upstairs, Miriam excused herself while Deborah washed the teacups gently, careful not to chip those precious family items, some from their beloved Bubbie.

Miriam knocked on Susan and Helen's door. Talking with them quietly, she said, "I hope it's a good idea for Deborah to be writing about this. She's been very tense lately."

Susan spoke first, "I understand your concern, yet it may be helpful putting her feelings on paper."

"I agree," said Helen. "Sometimes Deborah is all emotion, and sometimes she hides it behind practical problems."

"I hope you're both right. Sometimes I feel at a loss, not knowing what to say to her."

"We'll be here for you should she be difficult. Our door is always open."

"I'm so fortunate to have you two in my life…in *our* lives. I'm so glad you returned, Susan. We missed you greatly. I appreciate your offer of support. I'll probably be knocking on your door frequently."

"You're welcome anytime. We love both of you." Susan reached out to hug Miriam, who squeezed her quickly, then pulled away, fearful that Deborah might arrive upstairs and imagine quite correctly they were talking about her.

Over the next several days, Miriam watched Deborah sitting over her writing tools, seemingly frozen. No discarded paper appeared in the waste receptacle.

After that initial inactive period, Miriam watched Deborah bend over the desk for hours at a time, writing and rewriting. Miriam said nothing, knowing any comment she made might be an interruption. By now, she had learned that Deborah's artistic temperament did not allow for even the slightest break in her concentration. While Deborah wrote, Miriam tended to the children's needs, making excuses for why their other mother was unable to read them a bedtime story. All that mattered to Deborah when she was not at the shop was having quiet time to write.

After several days at her writing desk, Deborah announced, "Okay, I'm ready for you to look at this. It is far from complete, though I have a draft of the first chapter—it's actually just the first page—ready for your critical review. Please don't be too harsh."

"I love watching you when you're so focused. You go into a trance-like state. You notice nothing that goes on while you are inside your head."

"Oh, Miriam, have I ignored you? Did I miss something important? I've hardly seen the girls for days."

"Everything's fine," Miriam said, smiling and gently patting Deborah's back. "I enjoy observing your creative process. It might be nice if you spent a little extra time with Sylvia. Maybe you could put her to bed tomorrow evening. Ida's still too young to notice the difference; however, Sylvia thrives on routine, as you know, and she's noticed her regular schedule has changed."

"I'll do that. I'm sorry if I haven't done my part. I certainly didn't mean to ignore our children."

"Stop apologizing. It will be easily solved by giving both girls a little extra attention for the next couple days. It will take me that long to review what you've written."

"It isn't that long. I care a great deal about the beginning, and I want you to tell me if I'm off to a good start."

"Then it's a deal. You'll be the one putting both girls to bed tomorrow night. I'll take the night off. Maybe I'll take a luxurious bath."

"Then they'll be missing you instead of me."

"You're right. I'll wait on the bath until the girls are in bed."

"And until after you've given me your verdict?"

"I'll wait for my long bath until you're back to writing. Once you are in author mode, I'll have plenty of time to indulge myself."

"How about I indulge you in a little pleasure after your bath?"

"That sounds delightful. I'll look forward to it."

Deborah placed her writing on their desk, told Miriam it was awaiting her review, and went downstairs to pace. She trusted Miriam would give her truthful, constructive feedback.

As she walked back and forth, Deborah pondered, *Will the introduction work? Maybe I should have written the rest of the manuscript first and then come back to the introduction. Maybe I'll want to highlight things differently after I am finished; that will change the introduction.* Writing a book was going to be more challenging than she ever expected.

As Miriam approached Deborah's work, she understood the gravity of the assignment. She put a blank page and pen next to her, not wanting to mark the sheet in front of her. She hoped she liked Deborah's piece, though she knew that honesty was of utmost importance. Settling into her seat, Miriam began to read.

Unintended Victims of War

War is devastating. Some people are killed, some physically or emotionally maimed, and some grieve the loss of loved ones. War ravages whole communities.

Disfigurement or pain is life-altering for soldiers. Men who have lost their limbs, have chronic pain, or suffer from significant infirmities must abandon their familiar life. Their roles, their priorities, and their needs change. They rarely return to pleasure and hope.

Loss of skills strikes soldiers in dramatic ways, especially when they cannot return to meaningful work. What happens when a carpenter loses his arm or a cook can no longer smell? When a man can no longer tie his own shoes or complete a full sentence? The emotional effect of feeling as if you are a burden to your loved ones can be just as devastating as the physical injuries. What can a family say to their disabled loved one living in despair?

Many soldiers are plagued by horrific memories; drenched in sweat, throughout the night, they wake from dreams filled with the carnage of warfare. Sometimes, lack of hope seems worse than death itself.

Soldiers leave behind parents, siblings, aunts, cousins, friends, and teachers. Sometimes, a wife or a girlfriend mourns them. The saddest, though, are the children who wish daddy would come home. Those children must be comforted by mothers grieving the loss of their loved ones. The agony of loss is overwhelming.

With tears dripping down her cheeks, Miriam wrote some notes. She realized the enormity of the task Deborah had taken on. Miriam was proud of Deborah's choice and sensed the pain in each word as she imagined those who were suffering.

Miriam called Deborah back into the bedroom, where she offered a hug to calm the tension she sensed in Deborah's body. Deborah was not receptive; she needed words, not affection.

"Deborah, what a wonderful opening to your book. You have given lots of thought to the effects of warfare."

"Will this work? Should it be a foreword or the first chapter?"

"I'm not sure. You'll need to ask Dr. Hubbard, your mentor at Barnard College, about that."

"It will be quite a while until I contact her regarding the book."

"You could keep a list of questions and send her a note when you have enough to warrant a letter to her."

"You're so clever."

"Deborah, I'm really proud of you for taking this on and very impressed with what you wrote. You've described multiple ways that war affects people."

"Thank you. Now tell me what you found as problems."

Miriam took a deep breath and courageously explained that Deborah's beginning was well written, though it did not follow her plan to focus on the effects of war on women in particular. After saying this, Miriam waited quietly, anticipating a string of defensive comments.

Instead, Deborah said, "You are absolutely right. I talked with you about my plans and then did not follow my own directions. I'll need to rewrite the beginning."

"Thank you for remaining calm. It makes it much easier for me to critique your work."

"I'm learning. I appreciate your observations and your honesty."

"Please don't throw out what you've done. It is well written and will be useful after you've set the stage differently."

They continued to discuss the book. Miriam suggested Deborah include information in her writing about the sacrifices of the war horses. Deborah responded with appreciation for Miriam's collaborative approach to the book.

A little later, Deborah patiently put the chapter aside and decided to continue writing another night. She pulled Miriam into her arms and thanked her again.

ஓ ஓ ஓ

When Deborah and Miriam talked about the book the next night, Miriam asked, "Will you have a chapter about each of the topics you brought up—death, disfigurement, inability to rejoin the workforce when returning home, lack of industry, melancholy that persists?"

"Maybe. What do you think?"

"I agree that melancholy should be included, rather than just physical disabilities. Yet again, I think the book will be richer if it is about the effects of war on women. You should write more before I suggest changes in content or format."

"I've read that some authors write the beginning last, yet I felt I needed to outline it before I started on the content."

"This is your book, so you get to approach it any way that works for you."

"I promise not to get so lost in this project that I forget that I'm a mother and your partner before I'm an author. I'm sorry I got so caught up in writing that I ignored you all."

"No need for apologies, yet I'm pleased you've rejoined the world again, despite your desire to write. Sylvia was glad you read her a story."

They discussed reasonable ways to set limits and keep Deborah involved with her family.

"I'm glad to support you in this," Miriam said.

"Have I told you lately how much I love you?"

"You can never tell me too much. And I love you too. And maybe we can have a reward at the end of each week."

"What did you have in mind?"

"Come to bed with me now, and I'll give you an example of the reward I had in mind."

"This plan gets better all the time!"

Deborah and Miriam undressed quickly. When they climbed into bed, Deborah was enthusiastic with her kisses. It was clear to Miriam that this was not to be a slow, seductive evening, but one of unbridled passion. She spent just a moment readying herself for this change of pace and joined in with wet kisses of her own and a firm caress of Deborah's body.

Deborah wiggled into place next to Miriam, curling her body as close as possible. Miriam reached around and stroked Deborah's back until it was clear she wanted her front stroked instead. Miriam adapted easily, following Deborah's lead.

Before long, they moved to face each other, head to toe. Miriam skimmed her lips over Deborah's inner thighs, making Deborah thrash as she repositioned herself to meet Miriam's tongue. Deborah's breath came hard as Miriam found the special spot that glistened with wetness. Deborah raised her hips to meet Miriam's tongue. Miriam stroked the area with her lips, then her fingers. Two of her fingers reached deep inside, stroking rhythmically as she placed her lips on top of the fingers. She flicked her tongue, and Deborah moaned with pleasure. Faster and faster she moved, trying to keep up with Deborah's growing excitement. As everything became wet and hard, Deborah pushed against Miriam's fingers deep inside her. Miriam's lapping turned to sucking as Deborah writhed in pleasure. She called out, wanting more, no matter how satisfied she seemed. Over and over, Deborah reached a peak and started again.

When Deborah finally settled, Miriam was tired and a bit sore from the awkward position she'd been in. She stretched her back and saw Deborah staring at her with a huge smile.

"That was exhilarating," Deborah said. "Your turn."

"Give me a moment, but not too long."

Within two minutes—not long at all—Miriam was guiding Deborah's hand to her special place. It was wet and ready, and the excitement continued.

THE NEW REPUBLIC

July 6, 1918
Grace A. Hubbard

War and the Woman's College
"The only women that the authorities over here really want are the trained nurses. Where do college women come in? Yet college men started the American Ambulance."

This remark was made the second year of the war by a distinguished college woman who had just come up to Rome from Corfu where she had been aiding in the resuscitation of the Serbians after their magnificent retreat. Having already served in two wars, speaking modern Greek, and being an English citizen by marriage, she had rare things to offer and was given the rare chance that comes only to those who are ready. But she felt even then that there ought to be a place in Europe for the work of Amer̶i̶c̶a̶n̶

The New Republic

Writing

Episode 11 ❧ *Night of Terror*

November 1917

Early in the morning of November 2, Deborah's parents called to tell her the news of a horrible wreck on New York City's Brighton Beach train line the day before. She was hesitant about sharing the information with Miriam because they both had horrible memories of a similar accident in Boston.

Soon after Miriam took her seat at the breakfast table, Deborah said quietly, "Remember the horrible trolley accident on the Summer Street Bridge a year ago this week, when the train fell into the channel and fifty people died?"

"How could I forget? I had you take me by to say prayers for the dead."

"I remember your fear that we would see them pull dead bodies out of the water with the sunken train."

"I'm glad you took me away, or I'd still be having nightmares. I'm relieved they made changes so there'll never be another accident like that."

"Oh, Miriam, I'm sad to tell you there has been another one, and this one was even more deadly. A speeding train derailed, killing at least ninety people. This accident, which they're calling the Malbone Street Wreck, was the worst train disaster ever in New York and one of the deadliest accidents anywhere."

Both women shook their heads and retreated into a sad silence. They sat, handing small amounts of food to their children, until Susan, Helen, and Mildred arrived downstairs for breakfast. Deborah and Miriam hesitated telling their friends in front of Mildred, but they needed to know.

Leaving Miriam to attend to Mildred, Susan and Helen rushed to the phone to call their families to make sure no one they knew had been hurt. Helen called home first and was reassured that everyone was fine. Susan's call resulted in tears; her uncle was in the wreck and had been rushed to the hospital.

As Susan packed for her trip to New York, Helen fretted, recalling the job offer that resulted from Susan's last trip home. These memories weighed heavily on Helen. Though terribly distressed because of her uncle's accident, Susan was able to put aside her own concerns to deal with Helen's anxiety.

"I promise I'll return. I need to be with my family right now, but as soon as my uncle's health is stable, I'll be back to you and Mildred. Promise."

"I hope that's the case. I missed you greatly last time, and I don't ever want to be without you again. And I fear Mildred will be as anxious as I am."

"I'll do my best to reassure her. Please trust me. I love you, and I plan to be home as soon as possible."

Helen smiled. "It comforts me that you consider this home."

જ જ જ

Almost two weeks later, Susan was still in New York, and she had not contacted Helen. This distressed Helen greatly, as evidenced by her disinterest in the lovely meals Mrs. Stern cooked. She was even unwilling to discuss Susan's absence with Deborah, who had daily discussions with Miriam about what they should do. They both tried to engage Helen in conversation, yet they got little response.

When Helen, with a tense look on her face, approached Deborah at work, she worried she'd heard that Susan had decided not to return. But Helen said, "Deborah, I must leave right now to attend an emergency suffrage meeting at Park Square. I'm sorry to leave work early, but it can't be helped. Our friend is waiting outside to take me in her car. I can't concentrate, so I'd be no good to you anyway."

"Let me get Miriam, so she can hear what's so urgent."

"Hurry," said Helen as Deborah departed to retrieve Miriam from the printshop.

Once everyone was gathered, Helen shared the horrendous news she'd just heard from their friend. Thirty-three suffragettes had been jailed in Washington, DC, after a demonstration outside the White House. Helen, trying to control her emotions, said, "Women of the National Woman's Party had been holding peaceful demonstrations for months, hoping President Wilson would back the right for women to vote. But now this happened."

"What happened?" asked Miriam.

"They jailed the women, and word is that they've been beaten and tortured," said Helen, starting to cry. "In previous days, President Wilson was polite to the protestors and even invited them in for coffee. Maybe he became angered because they turned him down."

"I don't understand," said Miriam. "Why would they suddenly arrest and mistreat them? It doesn't sound like they provoked anyone, other than refusing coffee with the President."

"I don't know either, but I need to go. I'm not certain what I can do, but I need to be with my Boston friends and decide what steps we can take."

"Are you going to call Susan's aunt to relay the message to Susan about what's happened?"

"Not right now. She has enough to think about. I'll call when I've learned more."

"Please wake us up if you have any news, even if you return late," said Deborah. "And stay safe."

Miriam approached Helen, quietly whispering to her, "Is Elizabeth's mother in jail? Ever since she and her daughters were thrown out of their house because she was a suffragette, she has continued to fight. I know she is often one of the local women willing to be arrested for this cause. I worry that her three daughters will be left on their own to be cared for by strangers at Denison House, where they all still live."

"I didn't hear her name mentioned," answered Helen. "I think she's still here in Boston, but I'll check."

As Helen left, Deborah wished her well, then turned to Miriam, saying, "I wish the legal system was just and people understood that much conflict would be avoided if women had a say in government."

All evening, while awaiting Helen's return, Deborah and Miriam discussed the situation. They were pleased that Helen had something to take her mind off Susan's absence, but they were concerned that this added stress was not good for Helen's well-being.

It was after 10:00 p.m. when a car pulled up outside and discharged Helen into the cold night air. Deborah and Miriam, who'd waited up, greeted their exhausted friend with hugs as they brought her into the parlor. Miriam made tea, and after discovering Helen had not eaten all evening, served fruit and cheese.

"Is everyone all right? Did you find out what happened?" asked Miriam.

Helen drank a few sips, then spoke. "I heard the entire story. President Wilson opposed the federal amendment for women's suffrage, even though nine states have already given women the right to vote. Just before he was reelected, women began gathering outside the White House every day, regardless of the weather, to try to change his opinion. They wore purple, white, and gold sashes, the colors of the suffrage flag, and held signs with slogans like Mr. President, How Long Must We Wait for Liberty? and To Ask for Freedom for Women Is Not a Crime."

"I would love to have seen that," Deborah said.

Helen continued, "It seems that the demonstrations remained peaceful, though the signs the suffragettes carried became more hostile. Onlookers claimed the women were being unpatriotic.

"Then earlier this week, disgruntled men who were yelling at the demonstrators on Pennsylvania Avenue grabbed the placards from the women's hands, broke the signs, and stomped on them. The men threw lit cigarettes, stones, and trash at the women."

"How horrid," Deborah said, "and frightening."

Helen shook her head and continued, "When the women stood strong, the men kicked them and then resorted to spitting at them. They ripped down the women's banners, shaming them with disgusting insults. And the police purposely ignored the men who were attacking the women picketing. It was awful.

"For three days there were unrelenting assaults by angry mobs. The men were intimidating and violent, sending a strong message that women should know their place. The women were terrified to be arrested, fearing they would be beaten and mistreated if jailed. There was even fear they would be molested.

"This latest news is unbelievable. The police arrested six of the women who were lawfully protesting, rather than arresting those who attacked them." Helen was practically shouting by this time.

"The women were sentenced to sixty-day prison terms," she announced angrily.

"What were they were arrested for?" asked Deborah.

"For blocking traffic, when it was really the angry mobs who blocked the traffic," Helen said, sighing and collecting herself.

"They got sixty days in jail for blocking traffic?" Deborah asked, too incredulous for more words.

"Yes. It makes no sense," Helen said. "Alice Paul, the national chairman of the Congressional Union for Woman Suffrage, stayed off the picket lines to avoid arrest because she is too important to the cause."

Finally, the women all took a breath and wondered how all of this could have happened.

"There's nothing further we can do tonight," Helen said, "so we should get some sleep. I'm exhausted. Also, I wanted to be sure to tell you, Miriam, that Elizabeth's mother was not arrested. Actually, she was at the meeting tonight."

"Thank you for letting me know."

"Are you going to call Susan's aunt?"

"Tomorrow."

Between anger, worry, and indignation, not one of them slept well. In the morning, Deborah's and Miriam's worry about Helen increased. They were glad that she decided to miss work to attend a full-day suffrage meeting. She needed to be with her friends.

When they got home from work, before dinner, Deborah and Miriam invited Helen to join them in the parlor for an update. The group learned that most of the arrested women were sent to the Occoquan Workhouse in Virginia. One woman had been badly hurt, but she was going to survive. A second woman suffered terrible chest pain; she was refused treatment until the next morning. They were all waiting to hear about her condition.

"Have you told Susan?" Miriam asked.

"I haven't been able to reach her, though I did try. I think her family is spending many hours at the hospital."

"And she still hasn't called you?"

"No."

Miriam gave Helen a hug and whispered that she should call again, even if it was late.

"But the call would wake everyone on the party line. Susan's family only answers two long and two short rings, but everyone listens for their own ring."

"You're right," said Miriam, offering no other suggestions.

Just a few minutes later, the telephone rang, and Helen ran to pick it up. Watching Helen's tears, Miriam left the room and waited in the parlor for an update. The call went on longer than most calls, which were usually kept to a minimum to avoid the high long-distance rates.

Finally, Helen came into the parlor saying, "I'll pay for the call."

"I'm not worried about that, but how's Susan's uncle?"

"Improving. He was seriously hurt and will be recovering for a long time, but it looks like he'll be okay."

"What a relief. And Susan?"

Helen's eyes filled as she said, "She's coming home tomorrow. It will be wonderful to have her here. It's been very hard without her."

Deborah and Miriam were glad that Susan would return from New York, but when they got to their room that evening, Deborah spoke angrily, "I'm really upset with Susan for her lack of communication with Helen over these past two weeks."

Miriam felt protective of her friend. "Maybe there were circumstances beyond her control that made it impossible for her to call. She was staying at her uncle's home, and there's no telephone there."

"You're making excuses for her. There are phones at the hospital. She could have called. Just think what lengths you would have gone to, to reach me had I been the one who was stuck out of town."

"You're absolutely right. I would have found some way to get ahold of you. I would have sent a telegram if nothing else."

Deborah sighed deeply. "I intend to talk to Susan about this once the suffrage situation is resolved."

Miriam, who hated confrontations, asked, "What good will that do?"

"Susan needs to understand the amount of distress she caused by not communicating. I would think she'd be more sensitive to Helen, given the anguish she caused when she moved back to New York."

"It's brave of you to confront her. You are a good friend to both of them. I wish I was stronger when it comes to saying things that are difficult," Miriam said.

"I don't know if it's bravery, or if I'm being stupid, risking their anger. But I don't seem able to keep my mouth shut when someone I care about has been hurt."

"I love that about you," Miriam said, giving Deborah a firm embrace.

≈ ≈ ≈

Over the next few evenings, Helen and Susan apprised them of the suffrage situation. Helen reported that the women arrested on what they were calling the Night of Terror, finally went to trial on November 23, after nine days of torturous treatment.

"The lawyers got them freed on a technicality, claiming it was illegal for them to be jailed in Virginia since they were arrested in Washington, DC," Susan reported.

They learned that Alice Paul bravely returned to the picket lines. She was immediately arrested and given a sentence of seven months in the Occoquan Workhouse.

"Alice Paul, Lucy Burns, and Carrie Chapman Catt are my heroines, all strong women I most respect in this fight for women's suffrage," said Helen.

"But they do us no good if they're in jail," answered Susan.

"I disagree," Helen said. "They're examples to all of us of how important this cause is. They show us all that this is a fight for which we must risk our own welfare."

"Alice Paul's long sentence was probably intended to keep her off the streets, to discontinue her fight for women's voting rights. It's very unjust," Helen said.

All agreed. Later in their room, Deborah and Miriam talked further. "I'm so impressed with Susan and Helen. They've worked tirelessly for this cause," said Miriam.

"But is it worth it? Is there any chance that women will actually gain the right to vote? So far, so few states have granted us suffrage."

"I was happy when New York finally passed women's voting rights in June, the first eastern state to do so. I remember how we celebrated."

"It didn't look like Massachusetts would ever vote in favor of suffrage."

"I know. I'm so relieved it finally did. But without strong women taking on this important work, there will never be a chance for women to vote in the United States. I still have hopes it will be universally granted someday."

"Miriam, you're a dreamer. But I love you for it."[15]

ᎨᎨᎨ

Off and on that November, Deborah tried to escape the tension of the suffrage issues by writing. She found that her anger over the plight of the suffragettes fueled her imagination and helped her to write about the hardships women suffered. In addition to the Great War occurring in Europe, women sometimes felt there was a war being waged against them in the United States.

Deborah took Miriam's suggestions to heart and then asked, "Are you willing to read the new introduction I've written?"

---

[15] Called the Silent Sentinels, over 2,000 determined women organized by Harriet Stanton Blatch (Elizabeth Cady Stanton's daughter) held a vigil for over two years outside the White House gates to protest President Wilson. The President's refusal to support women's suffrage angered many, especially considering that he had been a professor at Bryn Mawr, a women's college, and he was the father of two suffragettes. Suffragists stated that Wilson had a debt to pay to women, as their sons and husbands were fighting overseas.

On the evening of November 14, thirty-three women were arrested and brutally assaulted in what was called the Night of Terror. Many of the women jailed suffered long-term damage from the abuse they received in jail. Within months, after receiving political flack for his apathy, President Wilson seemingly had a change of heart and claimed to be appalled by the treatment of these women. Many assumed that his new attitude was politically motivated; he must support this cause if he wanted to win the next election. In all, 500 Silent Sentinels were arrested, and 168 were illegally jailed. It was an emotional war on women.

"Certainly. Give me some time to review it, and I promise to offer an honest critique."

"I have faith you will. Here is my new writing. It is short, but it may set the stage better. And I'll do my best to listen to your suggestions."

> To keep food on the table, war widows and women left behind must take positions requiring skills they don't possess. Running a farm or earning a salary is foreign to most women. But they are forced to work to survive, barely able to grieve their lost or distant relatives. Most of these families are living in agony.

"You've done a wonderful job, Deborah," Miriam said softly.

The emotion in her voice comforted Deborah, who'd feared this critique.

"I liked your change in focus, though I think you dropped too much of what you wrote before. I think you should keep writing; you can go back to this after you've written more. Then you can incorporate much of your previous introduction to set the stage for your book in a way that engages your readers."

"My readers—I like that. I hope I can write a book that honors women for meeting the challenges of their altered lives with strength. The world is changing."

"Amen."

❧ ❧ ❧

Deborah's next letter from Milton provided some relief—he would not be heading to Europe to fight.

> *November 18, 1917*
> *Dear Deborah,*
> *Yesterday, we took the ship out for a trial cruise. Once out of port, we learned we were headed to [CENSOR]. All 241 of us were told to station ourselves on the upper decks, so anyone viewing us would assume we were heading overseas. We wanted our enemies to believe we were adding to the American Expeditionary Forces. I'm not certain we fooled anyone, though it was great to get out on the open seas.*
> *By the time you get this letter, we'll be back in American waters.*
> *Love,*
> *Milton*

At the end of the month, Deborah finally had the conversation with Susan she had planned. She'd practiced with Miriam what she would say so that her conversation was not just a barrage of angry words, but a well thought-out statement of love for her two friends. Sitting on the parlor chair, she said, "Susan, I want to talk with you about Helen's reaction when you were gone. I love you both, so I want to share my perspective."

"You don't need to say anything. We can take care of ourselves," Susan said with strain in her voice.

"You weren't here to witness the stress Helen displayed."

"Are you telling me that I shouldn't have gone to be with my family when my uncle was hurt?"

Deborah took a deep breath and remembered Miriam's advice that she remain calm, rather than defensive. "I agree you should have gone. I would have, had it been my uncle. Helen understood your need to be there too. But she was very concerned, given your recent move to New York to work with Margaret Sanger."

"Am I always going to be chastised for that decision?"

"Not at all. I'm not questioning your choice to be there then... or now."

"Then why are you bringing it up?" Helen said, somewhat loudly.

"Helen, let me try again. I haven't done a good job of sharing my concerns."

"Now you are concerned about us?"

"Not at all. But I am worried about Helen. She was tense and upset the whole time you were gone."

"She's fine now," said Helen, pursing her lips.

"Helen, please calm down. I just wanted to suggest that you should communicate with her when you are out of town. She was—"

Helen interrupted, "Stop telling me what to do."

Deborah, tempted to raise her voice, thought about what Miriam would do. *She would be quiet and let Helen relax.*

After a long, uncomfortable silence, Susan said, "Sorry. I shouldn't be angry at you. I know you are trying to help."

"I love you both, and it pains me when one of you is distressed. And you would have no idea how Helen was in your absence if I didn't tell you. I'm certain she didn't tell you how upset she was."

"No, she didn't."

"My aim for this discussion was to suggest that you contact her more often when you are gone. A short call, or even letters, would have allayed her fears."

"I can do that."

"That's the only thing I wanted to suggest, not to tell you that you did anything wrong."

"Thank you for being such a good friend to both of us," Helen said with a tear running down her cheek.

"Can I give you a hug?"

The two of them embraced. Deborah was proud of her intervention in this situation and of the way she'd handled herself.

As usual, Miriam was proud of Deborah. when she explained what she'd done.

Summer Street Disaster

Silent Sentinels

Episode 12 ✳ *Micah's Readjustment*

December 1917

One afternoon in early December, a catastrophe occurred at the publishing shop.

"Miriam! Call for an ambulance! Micah fell and hurt his bad leg," screamed Marjorie from the office bathroom.

Miriam ran for the telephone.

"What happened?" asked William, rushing towards the noise.

"Micah is hurt," yelled Hannah, approaching the bathroom door, afraid to go in.

After making the call, Miriam pushed her way past everyone and headed directly into the small room, throwing open the door. Micah, their friend and employee, was sprawled on the floor, his bad leg at an abnormal angle. His wife, Marjorie, also on the floor, held him as he cried out in pain. Miriam moved Micah's wheelchair out of the way and got down on the floor with the two of them. "What can I do?" she asked her best friend.

"Please call Micah's mother. She can meet us at Mass. General Hospital, where I'm certain he'll go."

Miriam left the room and made the distressing call.

The ambulance arrived relatively quickly, and they all heard Micah scream as the drivers transferred him to a gurney. Suddenly, there was no more yelling or moaning. They all assumed he'd passed out. Marjorie climbed into the back of the vehicle immediately after Micah was loaded.

Deborah was relieved that Marjorie was able to accompany her husband. She wondered if a similar emergency happened to Miriam or to her, would they be permitted to accompany one another in the ambulance? Who would they say they were to each other? The thought frightened her.

With blaring sirens, Micah was transported to the hospital. Miriam was as distraught about Marjorie as she was about Micah, so Deborah drove her to the hospital so she could support her friends.

When Deborah returned to work, she was distracted, thinking about how this event might affect Micah's future. No one was able to concentrate, so they closed the shop early.

❧ ❧ ❧

At the hospital, Miriam found Marjorie sitting in an uncomfortable chair in a waiting room, staring straight ahead. When Marjorie saw her friend, she burst into tears and stood for a comforting embrace.

Micah's parents arrived with tear-stained faces, upset that there was no word about his condition.

Soon, the doctor arrived with dire news. "First, I need to tell you that Micah's been given barbiturates to sedate him, so there is no reason for any of you to be with him," the doctor began. "Which of you is the wife?"

Marjorie stood up looking like a child, rather than the young wife that she was. She approached the doctor timidly, seemingly unsteady on her feet. Miriam rose to stand at her side and hold her upright.

"He has re-broken the femur in the same place as the original break," the doctor said. "Because the healing wasn't yet complete, and the bone is still fragile, we're unable to reattach the broken shard. We'll need to amputate the leg."

Marjorie gasped, dumbstruck.

Micah's mother let out a loud cry and begged, "Isn't there anything you can do to save my son's leg?"

"No, I'm afraid not. Yet the chance of infection will be greatly reduced once he's healed from the surgery, and that's very good news."

Miriam wanted to ask about the risks of the surgery; instead, she decided her role was to silently support Marjorie. Micah's father stood and asked the doctor Miriam's question and was given a vague answer about how all surgeries have risks and complications. This did nothing to comfort any of them. Miriam silently recited the *mi sheberach*, the Jewish prayer for healing.

While the small group sat and waited, Marjorie seemed uncomfortable initiating a discussion. Miriam took over, asking many questions about Micah's childhood. His parents were pleased to talk about their son. Marjorie slowly became fully engaged, asking about things she'd often wondered, such as whether Micah was always a fussy eater. Miriam felt proud she was bringing this small group some comfort.

It was a very long time until the group received word that the surgery was complete, the leg having been amputated below the knee. When the doctor reappeared, Marjorie took a deep breath and asked the doctor how the surgery had gone, as Miriam had prepped her to do. The doctor replied, and Miriam held Marjorie up as she faltered, once again unsteady on her feet, and whispered something into Marjorie's ear.

Haltingly, Marjorie asked, "What will his recovery entail?" Following the description of the extended recovery period, Marjorie melted into Miriam's arms, sobbing out of control until she had exhausted herself. Micah's mother offered to be there as needed, acknowledging that Marjorie was to be the primary person to provide care. Miriam complimented Marjorie on taking charge.

<p style="text-align:center">~~~</p>

Once home, Micah lay in the uncomfortable bed in the parlor of his parents' home, dealing with lots of swelling and painful dressing changes. He was exasperated by his lack of independence and the need for constant caretaking.

Micah's physical healing was steady; however, his emotional adjustment to being an amputee was slow. The doctor suggested he be fit with a wooden prosthesis once the incision had healed, but Micah refused to discuss it. When Marjorie tried to talk with him about this, she was met with annoyance, so she said nothing further.

Micah refused to read or have visitors. Marjorie spent her days tending to him, being more of a nurse than a wife. Miriam stopped by frequently to support her friend. Marjorie cried on her shoulder each time, talking of her difficulties in beginning their marriage while living with Micah's parents, but she felt stuck because she didn't believe she could care for Micah on her own.

After caring for him for six weeks, Marjorie suddenly announced, "I'm going back to work."

Micah said nothing, not even a grunt of complaint.

Marjorie started going into the office for half days, yet when it was apparent how far behind they were, she stayed longer. Many days she brought work home, partially to stave off boredom. One day, she reached a point where she couldn't stand it anymore.

"Micah, I've had enough. Your wound is healing well, but you're breaking my heart. I can't watch you ruin your life. You're more than a missing limb. So what if you can't walk independently? You can get around with crutches. You need to heal your mind."

"It isn't so easy."

"You aren't trying. You just sit there, boring me and yourself. You used to be so spirited and interesting. Now, the only thing you do is bark out commands for me. I can't take this anymore."

"Are you going to leave me?"

"No, I'm going to hang on, though you need to do something to heal yourself. I can't stand the way things are. You need to be my husband, not my patient."

"I don't know how to be different."

"I'll tell you what you need to do. You need to get up and get used to walking with your crutches. You'll have much more freedom than you used to have with your chair. And you need to get back to work. And see your friends. And be kind to me."

At this point, Marjorie broke down in tears. She had stayed strong in Micah's presence, not wanting to add to his pain, but she couldn't hold it in any longer. "I want you to be my husband," she said, sobbing. "I want you to hold me and to be intimate with me. I'm not your nursemaid. I'm your wife!"

As Marjorie started to leave the room, Micah reached out and grabbed her hand. "I'm so sorry," he said as he, too, broke into tears.

Marjorie had never seen him cry, except when the pain was so extreme that tears trickled down his face. She stood still, not knowing whether to take him into her arms or to leave him alone. But Micah's tears turned to sobs, so she couldn't resist. She sat on the edge of his bed and held him. They swayed together, both crying uncontrollably.

When he regained control, Micah mumbled, "It feels so good to hold you. I've missed touching you. I didn't imagine you'd ever want to hold me again."

"I love you," she said tenderly. "I've wanted badly to embrace you, though you keep rejecting me."

"I can never be the man you married. I'm not whole."

"I don't care if you aren't the same physically. I can love you without a leg. What I need is the tenderness and the sweetness I fell in love with. You're just a shadow of your former self. It's your soul that's not whole. I don't care about your body parts."

"I'll try to change. These past weeks, you've stood by me even though I haven't been there for you."

"First, you must get out of bed. Stand up and hug me properly."

"But…"

"No buts—I'll hold you up. You can do it. And after you've mastered the one-legged hug, you have other things to master."

"Like what?" said Micah with a bit of a smile, the first one that Marjorie had seen on his face since his accident.

"Like kisses and other unmentionables."

"I'd like to try the kisses right now."

Marjorie held him tightly as he kissed her deeply. Tears fell from their eyes.

Finally, they had a night of intimacy, and Marjorie trusted that the real healing had begun. She brought home manuscripts needing translation, and, each day, Micah asked for more. He invited friends to visit, and she heard laughter when she left the room. He was still unwilling to talk about getting a wooden leg; however, he did practice walking with his crutches. Marjorie trusted that things were better when he went outside for a walk on crutches and when he finally made the challenging trip into the office. Life returned to Micah's face when he returned to work, and Marjorie's natural sparkle returned to hers.

∾ ∾ ∾

One evening, Deborah and Miriam talked about their friends' misfortunes, wondering what it would be like for them if they faced similar challenges.

"I'd be the one to be stubborn, like Micah," said Deborah, getting undressed for the night and putting her clothing in the closet.

"I wouldn't let you. I'd make you get up and start walking."

Deborah turned to Miriam. "Yes, I bet you would. You've certainly become a resilient woman. When I first met you, you were timid, but look at you now!"

"You've created a strong woman."

"No, I haven't," said Deborah, sitting down on the bed. "You were always strong inside, just meek on the outside. Your parents taught you to be compliant."

"You're right. I was taught to do whatever they asked, and not to think on my own."

"Clearly, you had your own mind."

"I certainly did. Especially when I fell in love with you. They most assuredly wouldn't have chosen that path for me."

Deborah took Miriam's hand and pulled her upright. "I'm glad you were strong enough. Otherwise, we wouldn't be together."

The girls hugged, and Deborah asked, "Do you think Marjorie and Micah will survive this situation?"

"Honestly, I wondered if they would," Miriam said, undressing and walking across the room. Then she turned to Deborah with her finger on her lips. "May I share a secret with you? Marjorie would be so embarrassed if she knew I said anything, so you must promise to keep this quiet."

"Please tell."

"They have begun to have intimate relations again. It had been a long time. Marjorie told me she seduced Micah."

"Good for her," Deborah said, grinning.

"And there's more. She might be pregnant!"

"Wonderful! That's the best news I've heard in a long time."

"Remember, you promised not to say anything," Miriam said, looking sternly into Deborah's eyes.

"I won't...until her belly is so big that she can't get in the door."

"She'll need to announce it before then!" Miriam laughed.

All of a sudden, Deborah's face fell into a frown. "How long will Marjorie be able to work? Pregnancy is such a private matter, and I suspect that Marjorie's been taught that no self-respecting woman flaunts her condition in public. And what will happen when she takes time off after the baby is born? How will we manage?"

"Deborah, can't we spend a few minutes being happy for her before worrying about the impact her pregnancy will have on us?"

"I'll try for your sake, but I worry about our business. Someone has to."

Miriam paused for a moment, stopped putting away her things, turned, and asked harshly, "Are you implying that I don't care about the shop?"

"No, my dear. You just have so many other things on your mind. You worry about everyone. I love that you care so deeply about so many people." Deborah smiled.

"You got out of that one nicely. You made me sound less committed to the business than you, and now you've switched it around to compliment me for caring for others."

"Well, it's true that you take everyone's welfare to heart. You worry about our girls, your sister and her family, Marjorie and Micah..."

"Enough. I'm glad you appreciate that I'm a caring person, but please acknowledge that I care about the business too." Miriam stared at Deborah.

"I know you do. After all, it was your father's shop. My comment didn't mean that you don't care, though your emotions go in so many directions. My priorities are you, our girls, and the shop. And yes, my family."

Miriam, sitting on the bed again, said, "You are more caring than you see, Deborah. And yes, you are more focused on the shop than I am," she conceded. "Have you ever wondered if Rachel will have a baby? Aaron went into the service so soon after they got married; they hardly had time to get pregnant."

"Well, I hope someday Rachel will have children. It would make her so happy. I won't mention that if she does, we'll be stuck without childcare. If I do, you'll blame me for thinking about business needs, rather than being happy for her."

"I'll let you worry about replacing Rachel as well as Marjorie." Miriam smirked.

"I wish everyone in our lives had children to love. My life has been so much richer with Sylvia and Ida in it."

"I love you, Deborah."

"I love you too."

And with that, Miriam turned off the light on the bed stand.

❧ ❧ ❧

Shortly thereafter, Marjorie did announce that she was pregnant. She also confided some other wonderful news to Miriam. One of Micah's friends had recommended him as a speaker for a group of recent amputees; he'd started attending this group regularly. Marjorie wondered if her prodding had led to his decision to join.

"That's great news. Tell me what it's been like for him," Miriam said.

Marjorie spoke up loudly, "They had a speaker last week, Philip Martino, who founded United Limb and Brace, a local company specializing in artificial limbs. This man assured Micah that he could fit him with a prosthetic limb. Micah told me that one of the soldiers at the meeting raved about how much more mobile he has been since being fitted with a wooden leg from the Artificial Limb Laboratory at Walter Reed Hospital. He said that the army ensured every amputee received a modern limb."

"What about the navy?" Miriam asked, curious.

"He said that every disabled soldier is eligible, though Micah has been resistant. Yet he was quite impressed with this gentleman, and he agreed to have an evaluation. His new friends offered to take him. I'm staying out of this, but I'm extremely hopeful."

"I'm optimistic for you and for Micah."

"I assume his new attitude is because of the baby. He wants to be more mobile so he can be a better dad."

Miriam smiled at Marjorie's new, hopeful attitude. "And I am sure he will be a wonderful parent. I am so thrilled for you, Marjorie."[16]

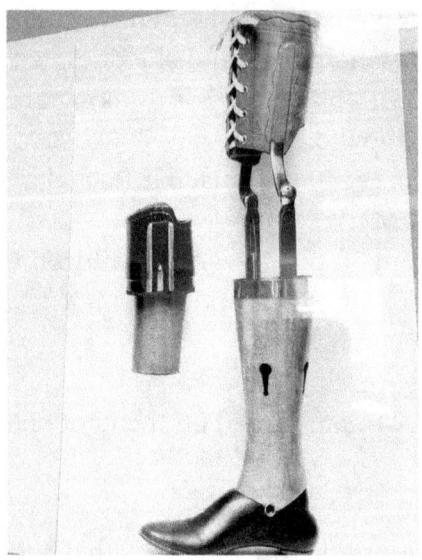

Artificial leg

United Limb and Brace

[16] Founded in 1914, United Limb and Brace Company of Boston pioneered the development of artificial limbs. Now called United Prosthetics, they are still committed to the betterment of amputees' lives.

Following World War I, the United States government provided artificial legs, hands, arms, and feet to war veterans, helping them to live productively and to return to the workforce.

Episode 13 ❧ *Yeoman (F) Fanny*
January 1918

$\mathcal{F}$anny's letter startled Miriam. This young woman had challenged her parents many times, but her newest action was her boldest yet. Miriam knew Fanny's parents would be overwhelmed with the news.

> *January 9, 1918*
> *Dear Deborah and Miriam,*
> *I know I'm due in Boston in just a few weeks to help you at the shop during my February school vacation, yet I've made a serious decision which might affect my arrival. I've joined the navy.*
>
> *A navy woman came to my school and talked to us about what girls are allowed to do to help the war effort, and I signed up on the spot. This is the first time women have been allowed in the military, and I want to be one of the first. Going to sea will be the most exciting thing I can imagine.*
>
> *I've not told my parents, yet I know they'll be very upset, especially because the navy requires four years of my time. My parents will be most concerned that I've not yet finished school. Serving my country is more important.*
>
> *I was told by the navy recruiter that we need to be eighteen, or seventeen with parental consent. I doubt my mother or father would comply, so I'll need to pretend to be eighteen on my next birthday. Once they tell me when I'll start, I'll tell my parents. Wish me luck.*
> *Love,*
> *Fanny*

Concerned, Deborah read the letter to Miriam, and they sat together on the divan, mouths agape.

"Mrs. B. values education, and she'll be furious that Fanny's dropping out of school," Deborah said.

"I doubt Fanny's interrupted education will be of more concern than her safety. It is dangerous to go to war. I remember Mrs. B. was greatly relieved to have girls when we discussed the approaching war, assuming they would be ineligible. I expect her to be terribly upset and worried."

Deborah thought for a moment, then spoke, "Do we have an obligation to tell her what Fanny has done? Our primary allegiance is to her, not to Fanny."

"Oh, I feel caught in between. Fanny may never trust us again if we tell her mother." Miriam sighed deeply. "But Mrs. B. might be angry with us if we don't tell her."

"I think we should call Mrs. B. tonight," Deborah said, knowing this was the correct decision, yet wincing at the task. She thought about how her own mother had struggled with allegiance to both her and her husband. When he disowned her when he discovered she was with Miriam, Mrs. Levine struggled intensely with loyalty to both of them. Due to the pressure she felt, she had a breakdown. Surely, this conflict would not be so intense, because it was not with her own family, but Deborah was reminded of the upsets mixed loyalties could create. Deborah did not discuss her concerns with Miriam.

That evening, after an emotional conversation with Fanny's mother, Miriam turned to Deborah. "Did we do the right thing?"

"We have the best intentions. Telling her before Fanny does, Mrs. B. has a chance to calm down and consult with her husband before reacting."

They sat quietly for a moment. "I'm glad Fanny told us first."

"But it will shatter her trust in us if she finds out we warned her mother."

"I know. But we made it very clear to Mrs. B. that she must not let Fanny know that we spoke to her about this. She won't betray our confidence."

"Young Fanny is certainly a huge challenge. She has a mind of her own, which is one of the reasons I like her so much. It makes it difficult to parent her, though."

Miriam nodded. "I agree. I've grown really fond of Fanny. I hope she'll stay out of harm's way."

≈ ≈ ≈

When the telephone rang during dinner two nights later, Deborah rose and walked over to answer it. It was Fanny, trying to hide her tears. "I was told to report to the navy office in two days, so I had to tell my folks."

Deborah wished it had been Miriam who had answered the call because Miriam always had an answer to a dilemma. Quietly, she said, "You did what was in your heart. You want to serve our country, so it was the right thing to do." Deborah did not entirely believe the words she spoke, but she knew it was too late for Fanny to retract her decision. Deborah motioned to capture Miriam's attention so she could get her suggestions about what to say, but Miriam was oblivious, deeply involved in feeding Sylvia her supper.

As the conversation continued, Deborah encouraged Fanny to come to Boston during her vacation if she had not yet been called to duty. "Maybe you can tell the navy you can't begin until the end of the school year."

Fanny was unsure if she had any say on her start date, yet she agreed to come if she hadn't shipped out.

Deborah walked back to the table and whispered to Miriam that she'd just talked with Fanny.

"I'm anxious to hear all about it, but can we talk after we put the girls to bed?"

Deborah concerned herself with tidying the dining room while Miriam took the girls upstairs. Once the children were settled, both Deborah and Miriam headed to their bedroom to talk. Deborah filled her in on the stressful conversation.

Miriam put her arm on Deborah's shoulder. "I'm really proud of how well you handled that. You did a nice job of reassuring her, and it sounds like she was more relaxed by the end of your call. Do you think we should suggest that Mrs. B. tell the navy what Fanny's real age is? That would postpone her enlistment."

"Oh, Miriam, we're already too involved in this. I think we shouldn't say anything further, except to support them all. I assume we'll hear from the Berkowitzes later tonight."

Just then, the telephone rang, and Susan answered it, after which she called the girls back downstairs.

On the phone, Mrs. B. broke down, mostly sobbing and measuring her words about Fanny's decision. With both Deborah and Mrs. B. upset, the call did not last long.

After they hung up, Deborah grimaced and said, "Mrs. B appreciated that we called her, though I sense something deeper. I think she's not just worried about Fanny; I think she's absolutely furious with her."

"I agree. She spoke so loudly I could hear some of the conversation," said Miriam, sitting on the divan.

"It wasn't her words, but her silences. I think she was fuming but trying to calm down before she said anything rash."

"What shall we do?"

Deborah paced. "Nothing. She needs time to digest that Fanny has acted rashly."

"How do you think she'll treat Fanny if she's so angry? Will she yell at her or punish her?"

"Who knows? I've never seen Mrs. B. angry. I've seen her frustrated with Fanny on many occasions, but not irate. This time, Fanny went outrageous and did something that Mrs. B. probably sees as defiant and irrational. I'm concerned."

"Fanny is defiant. I wonder if her enlistment is intended to upset her mother."

"Miriam, it's not like you to assume Fanny would deliberately act up."

"Were you ever so angry with your parents that you wanted to find ways to upset them?"

"Absolutely," Deborah answered. "I remember being furious, and sometimes it was just because my mother was being sweet, which did not feel honest. Sometimes, I wanted her to yell at me, just so I'd know she cared about me. She was always so even-tempered, so accepting, that she didn't feel real. I wanted her to care that I'd done things that were just plain wrong."

"Me, too," Miriam said softly.

"You? I thought you adored everything about your mother. Did you even know what it was to be angry, especially at your mother?"

"I hid it well. No one ever knew—actually, not until this very minute. There were times I hated my mother—sometimes, as you said, for being sweet when she should have been angry. She played her role as the perfect Jewish mother, but at times, she was not true to her own identity and feelings."

This news startled Deborah. "Maybe she didn't know how to have independent thoughts, separate from those of your father and from those found in Jewish laws and expectations."

"I think that's right. She really didn't know what it was to have her own beliefs. She was conditioned by what she was taught. It made me so angry." Remembering, Miriam huffed.

These new revelations surprised both Deborah and Miriam, and they continued talking until the phone rang again. When Deborah answered, it was not the sweet Mrs. B. she'd always known, but a very angry person.

"I can hardly believe Fanny has been so foolish!" she spat out. "I tried to be accepting and to treat her with respect. After all, I want my girls to make their own decisions and feel good about their choices. But what a foolhardy thing she's done—enlisting in the navy for four years!" Mrs. B. charged on without waiting for any response, "She's putting herself into a dangerous situation. How could we approve of such behavior? I'm so angry with her that I don't know what I'll do, how I'll be able to deal with her."

Stunned, Deborah had no response. "Can you hold on a minute while I get Miriam?" Deborah put the receiver down and quickly explained the situation to Miriam as she handed her the telephone.

"Mrs. B., Deborah wanted me to talk with you."

"No need to talk with me now. I need to calm down before I talk with anyone! We'll talk another time."

Click.

Deborah and Miriam fretted and wondered if there was anything they could do to help. Frustrated, Miriam turned to Deborah. "Why did you hand the telephone to me? You were handling things just fine."

"I didn't know what else to say. You had a much different relationship with your mother than I had with mine, and I thought you would have better ideas on how to handle this situation."

"After what I told you about my feelings about my mother, how could you think that? My mother never had ideas of her own. Your mother was more independent, and you learned from her how to deal with problems."

"You should know by now that I've never felt comfortable dealing with anger or conflict." Deborah huffed and got quiet.

Miriam broke the silence. "Clearly, we're both upset about this situation. Neither of us has seen Mrs. B.'s anger before, and I think we both feel awkward now about telling her Fanny's secret. Let's not let this situation become a problem for us."

"It wasn't a problem until you got mad at me for handing you the phone."

"I wasn't mad. I just couldn't understand why you passed this off to me. You are the stronger one."

"Oh, Miriam, I never feel like the stronger one. You deal with people so much better than me."

An hour later, Fanny called crying. She had never seen her mother so angry. It was shocking. Fanny thought her mother had been possessed by a demon; she had raised her voice so loud that the house vibrated. She was shaken because her mother had lied to her when she was being nice. Fanny could hardly talk through her tears.

Miriam was able to soothe her a bit, though it seemed the whole house was traumatized. She offered to travel to New York over the weekend to see what she could do to defuse the situation.

Fanny responded, "Would you really do that for me? I love you so much."

৯ ৯ ৯

Miriam worried about what she would say to this devastated family, so she went over multiple scenarios both in her own mind and with Deborah. She was nervous as she got on the train, and even more so as she arrived in Great Barrington to meet the Berkowitzes.

At the station, she was greeted by huge hugs from both Fanny and Mrs. B. They dabbed their noses and eyes with hankies as the tension poured out. Mrs. B. and Fanny were polite to each other, yet there was no conversation other than the most basic communication. She wondered what had gone on between them during the preceding few days.

When Miriam arrived at the Berkowitz house in Lenox, she was flooded with attention by the other three girls. Even Bridget, the governess, seemed to want a part of her.

After dinner, it was Fanny who cornered her first, taking Miriam into her bedroom for a recitation of her side of the story. "My mother was so mean. She yelled at me," Fanny said.

Miriam responded slowly, calmly, "She was pretty angry with you. Why do you think she was?"

"Because she doesn't want me to do what's good for me."

"Fanny, I doubt that's the reason for her distress. Don't you think she's worried about you being in the military?"

"Maybe, but she didn't need to scream. She never did that before."

"I know it was upsetting that she reacted that way, but I bet she's worried for your safety, plus upset that you left school."

"I don't like school. It's a waste of time. I can be doing something meaningful, but she doesn't understand that."

Miriam, acknowledging Fanny's ire, agreed that Mrs. B.'s response was excessive, but when she tried to reason with her, Fanny wouldn't listen to anything she said. Understanding what Fanny needed at the moment, Miriam just held Fanny as she cried. Once Fanny had let it all out, Miriam excused herself after she decided there was nothing further to be accomplished.

Next, Miriam took Mrs. B. aside for her turn. Immediately, there was another flood of tears. After hugging her, Miriam asked what upset her most.

"I can't believe Fanny made such a huge decision without discussing it with me first."

"It must have been hard to learn that Fanny acted independently."

"Miriam, I would have been able to reason with Fanny, but she didn't turn to me."

Miriam held Mrs. B. in much the same way Mrs. B. had held her so many times in the past. Mrs. B told Miriam she was upset that her daughter was growing up and making decisions on her own, without her mother's counsel. This transition to womanhood was hard for Mrs. B. She was grateful to vent to Miriam, and she eventually calmed down.

In a moment of introspection, Miriam wondered if she had hurt her own mother in similar ways. She went to bed with a headache and thinking of how she'd react if her own daughters were to act independently without giving her the opportunity to guide them.

The next day was a repeat of the day before, with the additional complication of Ethel, who seemed jealous of the attention Miriam was bestowing on Fanny. Ethel threw a small tantrum, one typical of a thirteen-year-old who required some attention to her needs.

But, soon, Miriam got back to the situation that had led to such conflict. She decided that the best way to deal with this situation was to bring Fanny and Mrs. B. together. It would be up to her to provide the agenda for the awkward meeting. She set guidelines: each had to take turns speaking, while the other had to listen without reacting. Miriam had no idea how she herself would respond if faced with this situation.

"I'm furious," Mrs. B. began and then looked from Miriam to Fanny. "I tried to be polite and accept your decision to join the navy, but it has broken my heart. It was awful that you didn't consult with me first—"

"I was afraid you would say no," Fanny interrupted.

"Fanny, let your mother speak; then you'll have your turn."

Mrs. B. continued, "You made a decision that puts your life at risk. I can't believe you are going to war. I thought my girls would be safe. I would be devastated if anything happened to you…if you were hurt or killed." Mrs. B. went on, tears streaming down her face as she explained she was not only angry, but also hurt that Fanny hadn't turned to her to discuss this.

Fanny cried as she listened to her mother. When it was her turn to talk, Fanny did so, also with tears freely running down her face. "I just want to serve my country. And the navy woman who came to our school made it sound so exciting that I couldn't resist signing up." Fanny stopped talking.

Miriam asked Fanny, "Why didn't you consult your parents? You mentioned that you were considering joining the service even before that woman came to your school."

Surprised, Mrs. B. looked at Miriam. It seemed to dawn on her that this was a part of Fanny she didn't know.

Turning to her mother, Fanny said, "You still treat me as a child. For once, I wanted to choose for myself."

"You're too young to make a major decision by yourself."

"I knew you'd say that—"

Miriam interrupted, "Fanny, your mother is not saying she would make the decision for you. She is saying you're too young to make the decision without her help, and that's true."

"Yes, listen to Miriam," Mrs. B. said.

"Do you hear what your mother is saying, Fanny? She wants to work with you, to help you make decisions. Many young women would do anything to have a mother who cares so much."

The discussion improved a bit from that point. Miriam explained that loving meant being there for each other, even during disagreements. Both mother and daughter cried, and after a while, they hugged one another.

Fanny ended the conversation by saying, "I love you, Mother. I don't want to hurt you. I promise, next time, I'll talk to you before making a big decision."

"And will you promise to go back to school once you've finished your military service?"

"Yes, certainly," Fanny agreed.

Even though it was late, Miriam called home to talk with Deborah; she knew how worried she'd been.

Deborah was delighted and complimented Miriam for having brought the mother and daughter together.

By the time Miriam left the next day, there was more harmony in the Berkowitz home. Fanny seemed comfortable with the results of the meeting, and Miriam had the whole trip home to think about the entire weekend.

Back home, Miriam shared with Deborah her pride at getting to the bottom of the problem—Mrs. B.'s upset over not being included in the decision. They agreed to remember this when their own daughters were maturing.

"Did you talk with your mother about every decision you made?" Miriam asked.

"I didn't make any significant decisions during my youth. Falling in love with you wasn't a decision; it was just a reality."

"Did you turn to her about your choice of friends or activities?"

"I made up my own mind about my friends. Why would I ask my mother?"

"Deborah, I'm not trying to argue with you. I'm just wondering how much you included your mother in your decisions."

"As I already said, I didn't make any significant decisions until choosing you. What about you?"

"I asked my mother or my father about everything. I assumed there was a "I assumed their was a Jewish law, *Halakhah*, about doing that, so I needed their advice." Miriam sighed.

"We certainly were brought up differently. We'll need to agree about parenting beforehand so that we can collaborate while bringing up our girls."

"I think we should teach them to ask us everything," Miriam said.

Deborah smiled, knowing that daughters rarely told their mothers everything.

ॐ ॐ ॐ

Fanny's trip to the naval headquarters worked out relatively well. Because her birthday was not until the end of June, the officer—assuming that she was turning eighteen, not seventeen—said Fanny must report to active duty immediately after her birthday.

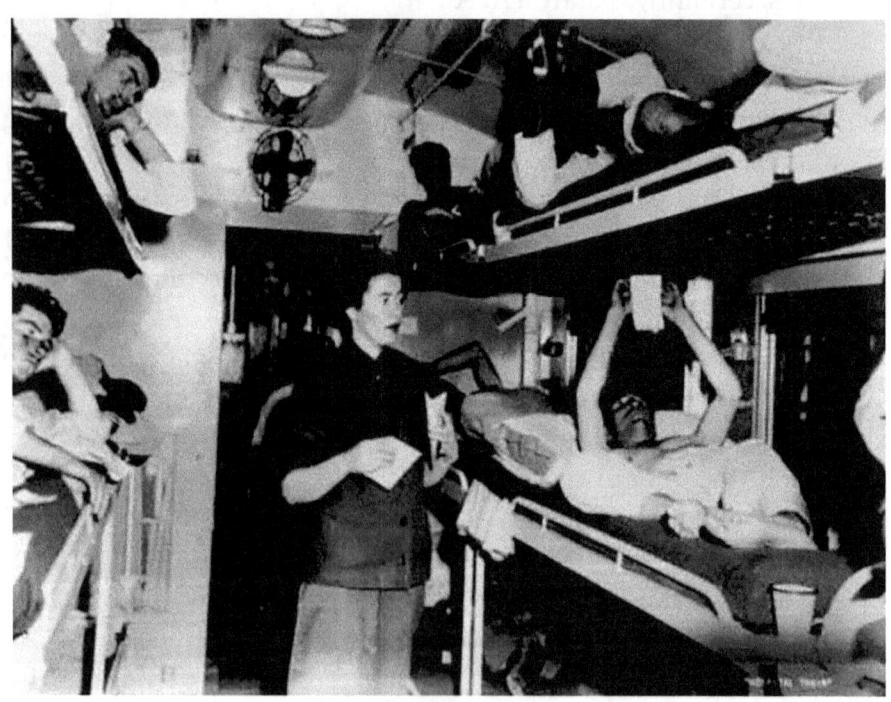

Hospital Train nurses

Fanny was very proud she'd be making $28.75 per month, the same pay as her male counterparts, and they promised her equal benefits and responsibilities as the men. Mrs. B., working very hard to be supportive, told Fanny she was proud she would be serving her country.

Fanny did come to Boston during her February school vacation, as planned. She helped out at the office, though she was more distracted than usual. When Marjorie missed some work due to her pregnancy, Fanny suggested they hire Leah to take on more responsibility. Deborah and Miriam still thought of Leah as young, though now, at fifteen, she was old enough to do meaningful work. Being in a wheelchair would not be a detriment to her assistance with bookkeeping. Marjorie, when she returned, agreed to train Leah to take over specific parts of the financial work.

During the evenings, Fanny talked endlessly with Deborah and Miriam about her upcoming military service. Miriam was proud her intervention had worked to help heal the rift between Fanny and her mother, though Deborah still felt unsettled about the whole situation. She was a bit resentful of Miriam's role, caught between Fanny and her mother, and unhappy with Fanny for her impulsive behavior. Fanny was unaware of all these reactions; she was just pleased that her mother had apologized and was being more supportive.

Navy recruitment poster

Episode 14 ❧ *Hospital Train*
February 1918

"Miriam! I got terrible news about Aaron; he's been hurt," Rachel shouted as she ran into the house one morning. Handing Miriam the letter she had received, she added, "A soldier who is caring for him wrote on his behalf, telling me of his injuries." Rachel flung off her coat and threw it on the nearest chair.

> *My dear Rachel,*
> *I was shot. My leg was blown up, and it hurts a great deal. I am on the hospital train, which is like a real hospital except there aren't many doctors. I look at my photo of you often. I love you.*
> *Aaron*

At the bottom of Aaron's letter was a separate note written by the soldier to whom Aaron had dictated his letter.

> *Mrs. Goldman.*
> *Your husband got hurt really bad, so I wrote down what he said. He came to the ambulance train when he got shot in the top of his leg. He was fighting in Cambrai, France. The train is like a hospital. We takes care of soldiers who was hurt. The train is from the British Army, so Aaron worried to talk American. But anyone who needs help can come on. He is trying to get some rest, but there's not a lot of help for the poor guys who was hurt. There are only three doctors and three nurses but 500 soldiers. It is mostly orderlies like me to care for them. We bring them food and take care of them, but most of us don't know much medical stuff, except what we learned on the train. We work very hard, but this is bad. It is very crowded, hot, and smells bad from all the sickness. And the train is bumpy, so it makes the guys hurt more. Some of the trains go to hospitals in France, but I heard this one is going to a boat to go to America. I will take good care of your husband.*
> *Private Lawrence Smith*

"Oh, Rachel. You must be devastated. I hope he's able to come home soon so he can get medical care. You can both stay with us when he returns, and we'll be glad to help you take care of him."

"Thank you." Rachel broke into sobs.

❧ ❧ ❧

On their way to work, Miriam told Deborah about Aaron.

"How badly is he hurt?" asked Deborah.

"If he was put on the hospital train, he must be bad off. I hope he makes it."

After Miriam told Deborah she had offered to let them stay at their house when Aaron got home, Deborah wondered how they would fit two more people into their home.

All week, Rachel was distracted, waiting for another letter. Finally, when she got home from working with the children one day, she received a telegram from the United States Army. She knew it could not be good news. Rachel scanned the telegram and shrieked at the top of her lungs. She rushed right back to Deborah and Miriam's house.

Flinging open the door, Rachel went directly to the parlor, knowing everyone would be gathered there after dinner. "Aaron died!" Rachel screamed out, sobbing. Her hands shaking, she held out the telegram for all to see. Miriam embraced Rachel as she cried.

Deborah got Rachel's mother from the kitchen, where she was washing the dinner dishes. Mrs. Stern burst from the kitchen and quickly ran to her daughter. They sobbed on each other's shoulders over this horrid news.

The children, bewildered by the commotion, both clung to Deborah. She whisked Sylvia and Ida upstairs, leaving Miriam to care for her friend. The children resisted being put to bed and did not calm down until Miriam joined them upstairs.

Once the children were settled, Miriam met Deborah in the bedroom, and they hugged tightly, whispering comforting words to one another. Devastating news for anyone in their extended family hurt them all.

❧ ❧ ❧

Because there was no body, there could be no funeral and no shiva. Neither Deborah nor Miriam asked questions about the disposal of bodies during war. There was no information in the newspapers about mass graves or cremation, a Jewish taboo. Rachel was too distraught to think of such practical matters. Miriam spent time with Rachel, yet she felt helpless to deal with her friend's grief.

Later in the week, Rachel received a letter.

February 12, 1918
Dear Rachel,
I am very glad I kept your address. I bet you got a telegram
from the army to tell you Aaron died, but I thought to tell
you what happened at the end. Aaron's leg got worse. They
tried to save him by amputating his leg, but the infection
was really bad. I never left him alone at the end. The last
words he said was, "Tell Rachel I love her."

I am very sorry.
Sincerely,
Private Lawrence Smith

It was a great relief for Rachel to know more about Aaron's death than just the date from the army telegram, yet her loss felt overwhelming.

ও ও ও

Soon after Aaron's death, after work, Deborah arrived home to Sylvia's greeting, "Rachel sad."

"Rachel! Did you hear that?" Deborah said in a shrill voice. "Sylvia said a sentence!"

"Deborah, she's been saying sentences for a long time, but this time she described my feelings. That's something she doesn't usually do. I'm really proud of her," said Rachel.

"Sometimes, you know our daughters better than we do." Deborah picked up Sylvia, while hugging Ida close.

"I spend many hours with your girls every day, without other distractions."

"You focus on everything they do, and you have great insight."

"Thank you, Deborah."

"Oh, I didn't mean to ignore what Sylvia said. You're so sad that even Sylvia has noticed."

"I'm sorry. I can't hold it in. Sylvia has seen me crying, and I'm definitely not as cheerful with the girls as usual. It's so difficult to believe my marriage was so short. I found the perfect boy, and I can't believe he's gone." Rachel burst into tears.

With little to say to comfort her, Deborah quietly held Rachel as she wept. Sylvia, very aware of the sadness around her, hugged them both.

ও ও ও

Miriam was glad she and Rachel had developed a friendship long before this horrible time. She wiped her friend's tears and patiently listened to the same tales about Aaron over and over. Rachel wanted to offer Rachel a distraction, so she suggested they figure out ways to contribute to the war effort.

"I've no idea what we could do, but I'd be pleased to do something meaningful to benefit others. I know I need to stop focusing on myself and my loss. Many other women have lost as much as I have," Rachel said quietly.

"I have an idea!" Miriam practically shouted. "What if we provide something for the men on the hospital trains?"

"Splendid. What could we do?"

"There must be a way we could provide a little happiness to what must be a frightful time for everyone on board."

"How about sending chocolate?" Rachel smiled slightly.

"Great idea, though I fear it would melt."

"What if we bake cookies? Maybe your Bubbie's *mohn* cookies?"

"That would be lovely, yet *mohn* cookies are fragile and would break. And we have no idea how long it will take for the packages to get there, so our cookies might be very stale. If they aren't edible, it would be worse than sending nothing."

"Other than food, how could we provide a bit of happiness for those soldiers?"

They both sat quietly.

"Jokes," Rachel said suddenly.

"What do you mean?"

"We could gather jokes and funny stories. Maybe that would make some of them smile."

Miriam nodded. "I like your idea. We could use the printing presses at the shop to make a booklet."

Rachel screwed up her face. "I'm not very funny, especially these days, so someone else will need to write the jokes."

The conversation went on for a long time. They named their booklet *Hospital Train Humor* and agreed to gather funny stories from their families and neighbors, yet no one they knew—other than Deborah's brother, Milton—was good at telling jokes. Deborah wrote to her brother and asked for a joke or two; she suggested he not ask other soldiers because their humor might be bawdy.

Deborah asked those working in the shop to each contribute a joke or funny story. The first was submitted by Leah, who shared her favorite joke. Leah proudly performed it out loud.

There was a young woman named Mayonnaise. She had a
date one evening, and her father answered the door when
her beau arrived.
  He asked, "Is Mayonnaise ready?"
  Her father replied, "No, Mayonnaise is dressing."

Everyone groaned, then accepted this silly joke for the booklet.

Leah was inspired by being the first to have a joke accepted, so she submitted a second one: "There are more crashed planes down at the bottom of the ocean than crashed submarines in the sky." Another group groan and another acceptance. Everyone wondered how this sheltered girl had a storehouse of jokes, until they remembered she had an older brother.

Miriam and Rachel developed a plan for gathering more entries. They wrote a description of the hospital trains to hand to people as they asked them to submit their favorite jokes. Miriam offered to pass out this description to folks at their temple, for them to write down their jokes and submit them later—no one would write on the Sabbath.

After reviewing the submissions from the congregants, they wondered if any Jews were funny, but Deborah reminded them there were some Jewish comedians. Her favorite was the manic comedienne, Fanny Brice, who starred in the Ziegfeld Follies. After a discussion about this funny girl from the Lower East Side, they returned to questions of whether, in this time of increased anti-Semitism, Jews were afraid to share their humor.

Rachel approached the folks at Denison House, where she and her family had lived. The residents from other countries couldn't write in English, and many foreigners didn't understand American humor, so it was the staff and a few children who submitted entries. One worker, who understood people's fear of sneezes as a direct way to spread disease, wrote a joke about finding a way to get a seat on a crowded train: One should let loose a huge *"kerchoo!"* upon entering the car. Though not funny at all, Susan rewrote it so it appeared comical, and it was voted in.

Mildred approached teachers and children at her school. One of the teachers submitted the following: "Why did the cross-eyed teacher get fired? Because she had no control over her pupils." They agreed that this was one of the best thus far, so they asked her for a second submission.

Miriam sent a note to Fanny, hoping she could get a few jokes from her navy friends. As Miriam predicted, they got mostly raw ones, probably from the men with whom Fanny served. Fanny also wanted them to include her favorite: "What's the first thing a navy wife does when she wakes up in the morning? She puts her clothes back on and goes home." They included it, despite its content. Deborah commented on how Fanny was learning things in the service she would never have learned at home.

"I love this project," said Rachel. "We've hardly started, and yet I'm already seeing more smiles than I have seen since we entered the war. Submitters are thinking about jokes instead of the horrors of war."

"And I'm pleased to see you smiling again!"

"Thank you for being my friend, Miriam. You've been wonderful to me."

"I'm glad for your friendship too. Also, this project feels more meaningful than knitting socks or rolling bandages."[17]

❧ ❧ ❧

Miriam and Rachel told people who contributed to their booklet that they hoped the jokes would lift the spirits of both the soldiers and the hardworking orderlies. That was enough to say. They didn't want to upset people with details of the horrid conditions on the trains.

Before they knew it, they had piles of material. They worked endless hours with a team of people from their homes, the shop, and the neighborhood. Sylvia and Ida scribbled little pictures, and Rachel used Mildred, Leah, and other neighborhood children to draw designs.

Once they had completed the design and layout of the project, they printed it at the shop and pasted one piece of the children's artwork on the cover of each magazine. They sent off one hundred copies to the British Army for the soldiers. Most were distributed by the lady volunteers at the railroad stations.

---

[17] Hospital trains have been in use around the world since being introduced during the Crimean War in the 1850s. England was proactive in developing these trains and completed one before the Great War. Trains were initially used to transport medical supplies and to evacuate casualties, yet when the British military realized they could also move wounded soldiers from combat zones to medical facilities, they increased production. They also built and exported hospital trains for battlefields throughout Europe. The trains were brought across the English Channel on barges, not an easy feat. According to the War Department, over 2,000 miles of new track were laid for these trains. Increasingly complex transportation networks were built by the Labour Corps, a battalion of tens of thousands of workers—from China, Egypt, India, and England—who were unfit for fighting on the front lines.

Miriam and Rachel received many notes of thanks from soldiers returning home. They were told their booklets were passed around to wounded soldiers on board the trains; they brought smiles to some of the men. This encouraged Miriam and Rachel to gather more stories and jokes for a second booklet.

The next time, they made two hundred copies, as the number of hospital trains had grown. They were pleased to spread a tiny bit of joy.[18] "I'm so proud of you, Miriam," Deborah said as they sat in their bedroom's wingback chairs.

"For what?"

"For being such a good friend to Rachel. And also for the project the two of you are doing for those on the hospital trains."

"Why, thank you, but you've helped too."

"I provided a bit of assistance, but you've helped to cheer up Rachel and to provide a bit of joy to those wounded soldiers."

"That's very sweet of you to say."

Deborah pulled Miriam into a hug. "You are one of the most caring people I've ever met. You know just how to comfort someone. When you saw Rachel in pain, you found a project that has lightened her grief. And everyone who has helped with this booklet has appreciated that they could provide some comfort to those soldiers. You've managed to bring cheer to so many."

"I wish I could do more. I know how much you've worried about your brother. I don't know how to comfort you."

---

[18] During World War I, ambulance trains were used as mobile medical centers, providing onboard surgical wards and essential medical supplies. The standard train was comprised of sixteen cars, which could accommodate at least 360 patients. There were sleeping quarters for up to fifty staff, a kitchen, staff dining cars, and a pharmacy car that doubled as an operating room. One car was designated for infectious diseases, though as the war continued and the influenza attacked more soldiers, more cars were converted for this purpose.

These hospitals on wheels evacuated thousands of soldiers and transported over 100,000 war casualties during their busiest month after the Battle of Flanders in 1914. These trains were able to connect with hospital ships to transport wounded soldiers back to Britain. By 1918, there were twenty trains in Britain and over thirty additional trains on the European continent, ready to take soldiers to ports in order to connect with ships returning to their native countries. Once American soldiers entered the war, their wounded soldiers were usually placed in facilities designed specifically for the American Expeditionary Forces, though some were sent back to the United States.

Sadly, by the end of the war, over 20,000 railway staff had lost their lives.

"But you have. There's nothing anyone can do to keep me from worrying about Milton, but you offer me understanding, a shoulder to cry on, and love that fills me. Miriam, you do more than anyone else could, and more than I'd ever imagined anyone would. I love you more each day."

"And I love you too."

Hospital Train patients

Hospital-train nurses and soldiers

Episode 15 ❧ *Karl Muck*

March 1918

Over several months, multiple letters passed between Deborah and Milton, strengthening their sibling bond. During his time on the USS *Leviathan*, Milton shared his thoughts and feelings. Comforted by his openness, Deborah admitted her tendency to be short-tempered. He sometimes had helpful suggestions for ways she could control her outbursts.

> *March 12, 1918*
>
> *Dear Deborah,*
>
> *I'm pleased to hear that my suggestions are having an impact on your moods. The tricks I've mentioned are ways I have found to keep myself steady, especially when the senior officers ruffle my feathers and affect my equilibrium. We're heading out again. Hopefully, this time we'll actually go somewhere. We've made several attempts to head to [CENSOR] but each time we came back for repairs.*
>
> *The last repairs included a new paint job. I'm not certain why they chose to paint the ship with the British-type dazzle camouflage but it looks nice and is recognizable. You'll know where I am whenever you see photos of our ship in the newspapers.*
>
> *I heard we're about to board fourteen thousand troops tomorrow for the first of many transport trips.*
>
> *Love,*
>
> *Milton*

❧ ❧ ❧

While checking the newspaper for photographs of Milton's ship, Deborah found news about yeomen (F), the enlisted women in the US Naval Reserve, like Fanny, in Boston. She was fascinated, learning about the new roles of women in the military. Though this war, as with any war, was horrible, it was exciting that women were being given opportunities previously unavailable to them.[19]

৵ ৵ ৵

The conflict in Europe and the tragedies of war filled the news. Deborah was surprised at how absorbed Miriam was with the March 26 *Boston Globe*. She even ignored Sylvia's insistent though quiet banging when she wanted a second piece of bagel.

"Do you remember seeing conductor Karl Muck at the Boston Symphony Orchestra performance we attended at Symphony Hall?"

"Yes. You gave me tickets for my birthday, or maybe it was *Hanukkah*, and we enjoyed watching him conduct," Deborah said, putting cream cheese on her bagel and handing a piece to Sylvia.

"Well, there's an article about him in today's paper. He was arrested last night," Miriam said.

"Oh my. What for?"

"I don't really understand. Government officials sometimes arrest people born in Germany, yet the paper says he's a Swiss citizen, so that doesn't seem to be the reason."

Deborah scrunched up her face. "I know there were problems with him, before, having to do with his nationality and something about him not playing an American song though it was requested repeatedly."

"I wonder how much of it is true."

"I want to find out more, so guess what I'm going to do?" Deborah asked.

"You're heading to the library to see if your friend at the information desk can help you better understand this controversy."

---

[19] The Boston Navy Yard in Charlestown, Massachusetts, officially opened its doors to 150 female civilian workers in 1917; this was a radical change in their hiring policies. The women were offered unskilled jobs at the same rate as men, $2.24 per day. This was the first time women were employed in industrial roles, and it was a direct result of men being sent overseas during the war. Initially, the women worked six-day, sixty-hour weeks, producing rope and cable in the quarter-mile facility.

On March 21, 1918, the gender barrier was broken in the navy when yeomen (F) enlistees were stationed at the Boston Navy Yard. They were assigned to clerical, administrative, and communications roles. This was an important advance for White women; no Black women were allowed in these positions. Accepting women into the US Naval Reserve paved the way for women's future roles in the military.

"You know me so well."

Miriam reached across the table with her napkin, wiping cream cheese from Sylvia's cheek. "It's not much of a mystery why you love the library. Should I be worried about this librarian friend of yours? You see her more than you see your friend Chava."

Deborah laughed. "My librarian friend, whose name is Mrs. Holt, is old. She is probably in her forties, and she's quite plump, though she has a pretty face and a wonderful laugh. She has four children and a husband she adores, so, no, you shouldn't be worried."

"Just checking."

❧ ❧ ❧

When Deborah arrived home from the library, she assembled Miriam, Susan, and Helen for tea in the parlor. She commandeered them in such a way that they guessed they were in for a lecture. The three women lifted their tea in unison, laughed at themselves, and leaned forward.

Deborah appreciated the audience and began with gusto, "Karl Muck is a talented conductor, or the Boston Symphony Orchestra would not have kept him. I'll try to recall what I learned, yet I can't promise I'll remember everything about his checkered past."

"We have low standards," Susan said. "We're just looking to be entertained."

"Let me start by saying I'm unsure whether I'm disgusted with the man or I think he's been unfairly treated. My attitude is a bit tainted by things I heard from Mrs. Holt about his difficult personality. It's hard to know whether the concerns about him are warranted."

"The story…" said Miriam.

"Dr. Karl Muck was born in Darmstadt, Germany, in 1859."

"Deborah, do you really need to start there? I want to know about the Boston Symphony Orchestra scandal."

"It is a significant part of his story that he was born in Germany. His heritage is confusing because his family moved to Switzerland when he was eight, and he became a Swiss citizen. He held a Swiss passport, though he lived most of his life in Germany."

Miriam sat back, resolved to hear the long version of his life.

"In 1906, Dr. Muck was lured to the Boston Symphony from the Royal Opera in Berlin, where he was considered one of the top three conductors in the world—and the personal favorite of Kaiser Wilhelm II, the German emperor and king of Prussia. Henry Lee Higginson, the Boston Symphony Orchestra's founder, had lived in German and was a Germanophile. Higginson wanted to create a world-class orchestra, and he wanted this famous conductor at its helm. He enticed Muck to move to Boston by allowing him to choose eighteen Germans for the orchestra."

"They hired eighteen Germans to get one conductor? Muck must be very special for Higginson to do that."

A sideways sneer reminded Miriam how Deborah hated to be interrupted.

"Muck's acceptance of this position," Deborah continued, "was a surprise to many because he was so closely tied to the kaiser. He was considered a master of music and was described as 'graceful, elegant, and aristocratic, though sometimes prickly.' From what I learned, he was quite arrogant and a challenge to the musicians, calling them in for rehearsals at all times of the day and night, and ruling with an iron hand. Muck was also a challenge to the because his repertoire included mostly German compositions."

Everyone held their comments while Deborah continued her lesson. She explained that Muck accepted the position with the Boston Symphony Orchestra despite his reluctance to move to the United States. Yet he was soon entranced by Boston's elite, and he befriended them, including Isabella Stewart Gardner, Henry Cabot Lodge, and other dignitaries. He charmed the music lovers of Boston. Yet, despite both his attachment to the area and to his job, he resigned after only two years.

"Why'd he leave?" asked Helen.

"Speculation was that he was called back to Germany by the kaiser. Yet in 1912, he returned for a second stint with the Boston orchestra. It seems he was lured back by a significant salary increase and his love of the city—and with Kaiser Wilhelm's permission.

"Everything was going well until the United States entered the Great War this year. With patriotism elevated to a fever pitch, many orchestras are playing 'The Star-Spangled Banner' to open each concert. This popular piece has been repeatedly suggested as the national anthem. The Boston Symphony didn't want to offend Muck, given his close attachment to Germany and his personal relationship with the kaiser, so he was not asked to perform it."

"I heard," said Helen, forgetting to remain quiet, "that when they never heard it played by the Boston Symphony, people questioned whether his loyalties lay with Germany or the United States."

"It's possible that he never actually refused to play it, yet wait until you hear this. I wrote down this quote from Muck when he was asked to play 'The Star-Spangled Banner.' Just a minute while I get my paper."

While Deborah rustled through several sheets of notes, Miriam repositioned herself, preparing for the continuation of this lecture.

"What an interesting dilemma," said Susan. "I knew very little about this."

"Here it is. Let me read…"

> Art is a thing by itself, and not related to any particular nation or group. Therefore, it would be a gross mistake, a violation of artistic taste and principles for such an organization as ours to play patriotic airs. Does the public think that the symphony orchestra is a military band or a ballroom orchestra?
>
> I do not know how to find he original quote, so we'll need to put "author unknown."

"That's offensive," said Miriam, huffing.

Helen gasped, and Susan's eyes bulged.

They had a long discussion about Muck's statement, with Helen appreciating what he said, which she saw as a strong statement for artists getting to choose their art, rather than having to mold it to their audiences. Susan agreed with Miriam, finding Muck's haughtiness disgusting.

Deborah shared some background information about Boston, feeling that Muck's position was tied to the general movement in the local arts community there. Symphony Hall, the Museum of Fine Arts, and the Garner Museum were trying to upscale themselves. They had established themselves near one another and far away from the crime district near the waterfront. They feared Scollay Square, with its strip clubs, would deter middle-class families from patronizing the arts. Deborah felt that Muck's statement, while elitist and highbrow, fit into a larger move towards this type of transformation of Boston.

After expressing their differing opinions, Deborah shared more, "There is a great deal of animosity growing towards Germans, and much rage is directed towards Muck. Dr. Muck created an all-German program for a concert in Providence, Rhode Island. Several women's groups requested 'The Star-Spangled Banner' be played at this performance. Higginson and others made the decision that this piece was inappropriate. Journalists at the *Providence Journal* started rumors in order to get rid of Muck. They claimed that Muck refused to play the song, though it was likely that he knew nothing of the women's demands. The newspapers called him a spy and a traitor, inciting much adverse sentiment against him. Public outrage spread quickly."

Helen added, "I read that there was an insert, in the program of his next performance in Boston, stating that 'The Star-Spangled Banner' would be played at the end of each concert."

"True," Deborah said, "and the Boston audience greeted Muck with a long standing ovation after he led the orchestra in the desired piece."

"I'm surprised they were so forgiving and that he agreed to play it, following his dismissive comments," Susan said.

"I know. But there's more," said Deborah with a smirk as Miriam shifted in her seat. "New Yorkers berated him with the intention of making the New York Philharmonic the premier orchestra, over the Boston Symphony Orchestra.

"Negative attitudes against Muck continued, due in part to his treatment of Jews and his association with the kaiser. The Bureau of Investigation kept a close eye on him, looking for suspicious behavior that tied him to Germany. The scandal continues right up until now. He was arrested a couple days ago, as you heard."

"That is what got us into this discussion in the first place," Miriam said to Susan and Helen. "I read in the paper about his arrest."

"What was he arrested for?" asked Helen.

Deborah scowled. "I find this part confusing. Many Germans were deemed suspicious by our government. They thought Muck was signaling U-boats from his Maine cottage, though they really had nothing on him. He was detained, despite being a Swiss citizen. Also, the timing of his arrest was very odd—just before a special program of Bach's 'Saint Matthew Passion,' which he had been preparing for months. The authorities pulled him from the final rehearsal. Boston police and federal agents searched Muck's home and claimed the conductor's markings in the musical score were indicative of pro-German activity. There is much speculation about his internment. My librarian friend, Mrs. Holt, has no idea what the real reason was. The end."

Miriam, Helen, and Susan applauded.

"I can hardly believe the audacity of this man, and I hardly know what to make of the police's arrest," Susan said.

"I can't tell if he is a villain, or if he is being discriminated against because of his ties to his homeland," said Helen. "People from places other than Germany would not face such intolerance."

"Even after doing the research—well, after Mrs. Holt did the research—I'm still unsure."

"That quote you read was really disgusting. It was demeaning, so I'm biased against him," Miriam said.

"And I didn't mention one more rumor. There is a question of whether he has been inappropriate with young women," Deborah said, looking directly at Miriam.

"That clinches it for me," she responded. "A scoundrel!"

"Let's not rush to conclusions, Miriam. He's been of great value to the orchestra for many years. We can't be both his admirers and his critic."

"I can be." Miriam smiled.

The discussion went on for a while with no conclusions. Muck was a complicated man, admirable in some ways and appalling in others.

❧ ❧ ❧

While returning the children's books to the library, Deborah had another meeting with Mrs. Holt and learned more about Muck. Upon her return, she gathered her housemates in the parlor and approached them with a stricken look.

"What's wrong?" Miriam asked.

"At the library, the librarian called me aside for a private conversation." The look on Deborah's face gave away her distress.

"Go on already," Miriam implored.

"It seems there is even more to the Muck story than what my friend told me last time we talked. She was afraid to offend me, so she withheld some significant information."

"Yes…?"

"Karl Muck is an anti-Semite."

This stopped the conversation. Then Deborah went on. "It seems that not only is Muck anti-Semitic, but so is the Boston Symphony

Orchestra founder, Henry Lee Higginson. They follow the beliefs of the German kaiser."

Miriam added, "But the Boston Symphony has Jews in the orchestra. When we went, I noted names in the program, like that of violinist Arthur Fiedler; Jewish poet and composer, Ernest Bloch; and others."

"But Jews in the orchestra faced discrimination."

"I'm sorry," Susan said.

"No need for apologies from you," said Miriam. "Jewish people will always be discriminated against."

When they got to their room that night, Miriam was upset.

Deborah took a deep breath. "What bothered you the most? That Muck was possibly a German spy? Or because he was anti-Semitic? Or because he was inappropriate with young girls?"

"I can't separate one horrible reason from another. And I must admit that I'm upset about Higginson and others also being anti-Semitic. I don't think I'll ever feel comfortable going to hear the orchestra again."

"I assumed you'd feel that way. I'd intended to buy tickets to hear him again, though I changed my mind after learning this."

"Deborah, I wonder how much of the world hates Jews. I know so little, being protected here in our little world of Jewish neighbors, friends, and clients."

"I'm afraid that anti-Semitism has ramped up during this war; we are less safe every day."

"I want people to unlearn their hatred, especially that which is directed towards us. I want to protect our children, though I fear that the world will never be safe for them."

"Sadly, I'm afraid you're right."[20]

---

[20] Dr. Karl Muck was arrested on the night of March 25, 1918. He was found guilty on the charge of being a dangerous enemy alien and was sent to an internment camp at Fort Oglethorpe, Georgia. It was oppressively hot, but despite the discomfort, Muck voluntarily extended his stay in the camp. He hoped that by staying, he would have a better chance of being returned to his beloved Boston to resume his post with the Boston Symphony Orchestra.

To complicate his situation further, Muck's illicit affair with twenty-year-old Rosamond Young, a student at the Boston Conservatory of Music, was exposed in the *Boston Post* soon after his return to his homeland. He was fifty-one years old at the time. His love letters to Rosamond were printed in the paper, inciting more public outrage. His friend Isabella Stewart Gardner remained loyal to him, defending him to the end.

In mid-March, Susan and Helen came downstairs one evening with a question that distracted everyone from regular conversations about Karl Muck. "Do you remember Grace Banker, our friend from Barnard College?" Susan asked Deborah and Miriam.

"Was she the girl who dragged huge books with her wherever she went?" asked Miriam.

"She's the one. Her books were incredibly large, and she always had more than one. Good memory. She was a history major."

"No," Helen said with a shake of her head, "she was a French major. Remember how she was always playing the piano and singing French songs?"

"Well," said Susan, "we may be able to ask her more about her background because she's coming to Boston in a few days. Would it be possible for her to stay with us for one night? She could sleep in Mildred's room, and Mildred can stay with us."

As this scandal became public, it was disclosed that the Bureau of Investigation offered Muck the option of pleading guilty to the crime of "dangerous enemy alien," rather than being subjected to a public trial for his lewd behavior. As a defendant in a trial for his sexual transgressions, Muck would have been humiliated and dismissed by the Boston elite. Authorities could easily prove his misconduct according to the Comstock Act of 1873, which forbade explicit sexual correspondence in the mail, so it was likely he would be found guilty. He also took Rosamond across state lines, so he would have been guilty of sexual trafficking as well. Judges Oliver Wendell Holmes and Louis Brandeis were relieved to formally find Muck guilty after years of unsuccessful investigations into his behavior.

While interned, Muck gathered several musicians, including some other members of the Boston Symphony Orchestra, into a musical ensemble. They displayed their insolence by playing German music, which had been outlawed during the war. Furious at his mistreatment, Muck committed a memorable act of rebellion against US federal authorities. Though he proclaimed he would never conduct another orchestra in the States, he led the camp orchestra in Beethoven's Eroica, Symphony no. 3 in E flat major. In an act of defiance, Muck insisted that he and all his musicians perform entirely in the nude! Later, Muck commented that the performance was "really magnificent though the heat was hard on the violin strings. Beethoven would have been proud of it" (*Karl Muck's Nude Performance of Beethoven's Eroica Symphony No. 3 in E Flat Major*, Boydell & Brewer, July 22, 2019).

Dr. Muck and his wife were deported to Germany and returned to a changed nation. He was looked upon with disfavor, though he continued to conduct. On his eightieth birthday, he received the plaque of the German eagle, an honor bestowed upon him by his good friend Adolph Hitler.

"Certainly, she can stay here," said Miriam. "But Passover is approaching, and we need to clean out our home of everything not kosher. The end of the month is a terrible time for guests."

"Miriam," Deborah said with a huff, "we can make it work. We won't leave you with all the cleaning to do yourself."

"We can help," Susan said, and Helen agreed.

Once that was settled, Miriam said, "We can offer better accommodations than having Mildred move out of her room. Your friend can stay in the room across from Mildred."

"I thought you were moving Ida into that room," said Helen.

"That is our plan for later. We are happy to have Ida in our room for now, while she's still a baby, and next she'll move into Sylvia's room. We were just speculating that someday it might make more sense for her to go to the upstairs room, rather than moving her big sister up there. I still worry about Sylvia having seizures, so I'd like her closer to us."

"She has not had a seizure in two years!" Deborah said loudly. "And she only had one."

"Yet I still worry."

"In her letter, Grace says that she's heading to Paris. She and some other girls were hired by the US Army Signal Corps. She says she'll explain it all when she sees us."

"Sounds interesting," said Deborah.

"Since graduation, she's been a telephone operator," said Susan.

Miriam commented, "That seems like such an interesting job, though I'd be afraid I'd lose track of who was calling, and I'd plug people into the wrong calls. Though I'm sure I'd enjoy listening in on everyone's conversations!"

"I bet you would," said Deborah, smiling.

Once it was arranged, Susan and Helen reminisced about Grace, remembering her as a cheerful person. Susan, who had been closer to her, said, "Even though she lived off campus, she was very involved in many student activities, and sometimes she stayed in our dormitory with her friend Suzanne. Remember the time we went to see her in that awful drama-club production about a mayor or a governor?"

"I remember. She played a judge. It was a stupid musical farce," Helen said as she raised her eyebrows.

"And she was on the Barnard baseball team," Deborah said. "We went with you once to watch her play. I wasn't at all interested; however, I rooted for her with the rest of you."

"And I remember her being very religious," said Helen. "I hope she doesn't talk a great deal about church and God."

"That won't bother us," said Miriam. "We talk a lot about being Jewish, so we should be tolerant of her beliefs. Do we bother you with our religious talk?"

"Not at all," said Susan.

~ ~ ~

A few days later, when Deborah and Susan met Grace at South Station, she was tired, having taken a train from her family's home in Passaic, New Jersey, over 200 miles away. As they drove her around Boston, showing her the sights, Grace compared the city favorably to New York City.

Arriving home in Roxbury, Grace was greeted with warm hugs from Helen. Miriam recognized her from Barnard, and it wasn't long before they were all sitting in the living room, sharing memories. Grace laughed loudly when they reminded her of her heavy history books and her French songs. She explained that she was a double major, so Susan and Helen were both correct.

"Thank you so much for letting me stay here," said Grace. "My cousin lives in Boston, and I want to see her before I go overseas."

"We're glad to see you and catch up," said Helen.

"Tell us what you've been doing since you graduated, Grace," Susan asked.

"Finding a job was difficult, so I was grateful to obtain a position as a telephone operator. Once on the job, I became skilled at training long-distance operators, which was satisfying even though it didn't use my knowledge of history or French. It was a good job for a girl with a college degree."

"Tell us what it's like," said Miriam, fascinated.

"It is interesting work, better than a factory job. There are at least twenty-five girls on our switchboard. We were given diction and elocution lessons and told to be polite to everyone, no matter how rude they are."

"What kinds of girls are on your switchboard?" asked Deborah, suddenly interested.

"All unmarried girls, of course, and no one with an accent. We all had to be a certain height in order to reach the switchboard."

"I would never have thought of that," said Helen, intrigued.

After chatting for a while, Susan asked about her new work in France.

"Although I liked my job at the American Telephone and Telegraph Company, which we called AT&T, after three years I was restless. In December, I saw an advertisement in the *New York Globe*, seeking telephone operators in France. I thought it would be a fabulous opportunity to use my French and my telephone skills, so I sent them a letter. I got impatient when I did not hear back from them, so I sent a second letter, telling them I spoke English and French, and I was thoroughly trained in telephony, the exact requirements of the job. Finally, I got an answer and they said they wanted to hire me to work for the army. I was thrilled."

"What will you be doing?" asked Miriam.

"I don't really know any details," said Grace, "except that we're to help with communication between the front lines and headquarters. I'll be reporting for duty a week from now. I don't know if they'll train us on the ship that will take us overseas, or whether we'll be trained when we reach our destination. It is all very mysterious; we don't even know exactly where we're going."

"I'm envious that you'll get to travel to Europe, though I wouldn't want to go during wartime," said Deborah. "Will they keep you out of harm's way?"

"I certainly hope so, though I'm actually a bit scared. I wanted an adventure, yet I'd not planned to have one in the middle of a war."

"You need to keep us informed about what it's like when you get to France," said Susan. "You have us interested and concerned."

"I'll be happy to correspond with you. I suspect I'll have lots of time to write letters."

Grace asked Susan and Helen how their lives had changed since they graduated from Barnard College and how they were managing in Boston. Susan and Helen had previously shared that they were now a couple and had moved to Boston after the wonderful offer from Deborah and Miriam. Grace was supportive when she learned of their

"Boston marriage," which is why they felt comfortable inviting her to stay with them.

They talked of their jobs at the publishing and printing shop and their joy at being employed together. Grace asked if they found working at the shop frustrating, as a mismatch to their education and their goals, noting the parallel to her own history, but they assured her of their satisfaction. Grace said she was thrilled to finally be using her skills in this new position. The five of them talked until Mrs. Stern called them to the dinner table.

Sylvia and Ida, who'd spent the afternoon with their Aunt Hannah and Uncle William, arrived home just in time for dinner. Grace fussed over four-year-old Sylvia and ten-month-old Ida, and also met Hannah and William and their daughter, Sarah, who was almost three years old.

Dinner conversation was mostly about the job Grace was about to take and how she was pleased to be in the army and wearing a uniform.

The rest of their time together was pleasant, and all four girls were happy Grace would write to them about her adventures overseas. They all looked forward to experiencing life in France vicariously through her.

కా కా కా

Back in their room that evening, Deborah and Miriam discussed Grace's visit.

"I'm pleased Grace is comfortable around us as couples," Deborah said.

"I assume Susan or Helen wrote to her about their relationship, or I imagine she wouldn't have been so relaxed," Miriam said.

"I always worry that people will be disgusted, or at least uneasy, especially when they are religious, as Grace is," Deborah said.

"I know you react that way even when you don't say anything. I don't even consider it; I just assume people will like us for who we are."

Deborah smiled. "That's one of the things I love about you. You trust people will accept you."

"It's probably because I never had the experience of being rejected for being a homosexual."

"Oh, Miriam, how could you forget that your own father rejected you and never forgave you before he died? And then my father did the same, as did the sisterhood women from shul."

"That seems so long ago. I guess I didn't forget; however, I've not lost any friends by being with you."

"You're just too sweet for anyone to reject you."

As soon as Grace was gone, all focus turned to cleaning the house and preparing for Passover. Though, periodically, either Deborah or Miriam brought up thoughts about Grace. They discussed her upcoming adventure and were clear that neither of them would dare to do something as bold as head overseas during wartime.

Boston Navy Yard

Boston Symphony Orchestra

Episode 16 ✳ *Influenza Epidemic*
April 1918

On April 10, Helen and Susan received their first letter from Grace, and they shared it with Deborah and Miriam over dinner.

April 1, 1918
Dear Susan and Helen,
I've been aboard a ship for several days, and I'm already overwhelmed. There are thirty-two women headed to work the switchboards with me in the Signal Corps Female Telephone Operators Unit. I don't understand why, but I've been chosen to lead the team. Although I'm honored I was offered this position, I worry that it will separate me from the other girls' companionship. I am their supervisor, and even though I'm just 25 years old, they treat me differently. I find I'm left out of the normal banter between the girls.

We've learned just a bit about the job. I can't tell you any information yet. They censor our letters.
Yours Truly,
Grace

April 4, 1918
I'm continuing the same letter because I wasn't able to mail the first part of this letter due to our perilous trip across the English Channel. We arrived in England on the RMS [CENSOR] and were set to sail on a smaller ship when a very thick fog prevented our travel. We were stuck for over three days in the channel, making us an easy target for German bombings. We stayed on the deck for two full days, ready to evacuate the boat on short notice. The girls were very strong and a great team. They are accepting of me, and all my fears were unfounded. I'm proud to be part of this group, though quite shaken by our ordeal.

Now that we've landed in France, I'm a bit unsettled. I've recently learned that the ship that brought us here struck a mine, and seventeen people on board were killed. The ship survived and several passengers were rescued, yet it's frightening to imagine this could have been us!

Tomorrow, we head to our next location, which will be too close to the fighting for us to feel safe. We'll be facilitating communications between the troops on the front line and

those officers at headquarters who will plan the next moves.
It's wonderful to have such an important role in this war,
though I had no idea when I signed up for this job that I'd
be putting my life at risk on a regular basis.
I'll write again when I'm able.
Yours Truly,
Grace[21]

❧ ❧ ❧

"I can't imagine going through what Grace has experienced," Miriam said, turning down the bed in their room.

"I'm scared for her, yet so glad it's her and not you. I don't know what I would do if you were ever in that kind of danger," said Deborah, shaking her head.

"I know what you mean. Neither of us would handle the stress of that well. I'd be crying all the time, which would not be helpful on the front lines. You'd probably be yelling at the officers, telling them to keep all your girls safe. You would be upset if anyone in your charge was hurt."

"You're right. I'm sure I'd be screaming at someone," Deborah said with a wry grin.

"In all seriousness, what would you do if something bad happened to me?"

"I don't want to imagine that. I was so scared when you got pellagra a few years ago; I couldn't eat, sleep, or think straight. I'm not very good in a crisis," Deborah admitted.

"No, you aren't. I can feel your tension, which makes it harder. Please remain calm if I'm ever hurt or gravely sick."

"Miriam, I don't want to imagine you being critically ill. I'd fall apart."

"No, you need to promise me that you'd remain strong for our girls."

"I promise. I don't want to talk about this. Can't we talk of romance, not illness and pain?"

"Intimacy is sharing the full range of emotions and experiences," Miriam said softly. "I need you to know my wishes because, otherwise, you could never carry them out."

---

[21] The RMS *Celtic*, an ocean liner for 15 years, was converted to an armed merchant cruiser to protect the British Royal Navy against enemy warships when the Great War began. Then, supposedly because of its high fuel consumption, it was converted again, this time into a troop ship charged with carrying 3,000 soldiers, plus the 33 switchboard operators.

"All right. I'll remain strong for our girls if anything ever happens to you. Now, can we talk about something else? I'd even be willing to talk about your incredibly self-centered friend, Ruth, as long as we can stop this conversation."

"Fine for now. But sharing our feelings means talking about everything, not just the good. Truly, it's the same as talking about Ruth. She was the one who gave birth to Sylvia, so she is part of our lives whether you like her or not. Sometimes we need to discuss unpleasant things."

"I love you. Isn't that enough?" Deborah looked longingly at Miriam.

"No, love includes difficult conversations, not just tales of sweetness."

"I didn't expect this. Please, can we go back to talking of how wonderful it is to love one another?"

"For now." They embraced, but there was no loving that night.

೭ ೭ ೭

Deborah returned to working on her book, which improved her mood, but she struggled to keep her focus. She'd look around, need a cup of tea, or think about something left undone at work. Although she wrote several sentences, she had nothing to share with Miriam. She'd not even come up with an improved title. After several unproductive attempts, Deborah admitted she'd lost her motivation to write about the effects of war.

But what else could she write about? She was fascinated with the story of Karl Muck and considered writing about his scandal, but never got started. She tried outlining a romance, but that fell flat too. She thought of writing a children's book called *Jimmy the Cat*, but Miriam told her that was not a project worthy of her time and creativity.

Miriam did nothing to steer Deborah in any specific direction, believing she would eventually figure it out.

೭ ೭ ೭

Arriving home from work one day, Miriam found Helen standing in the hallway, reading a letter. Miriam stopped next to her. "Is that a letter from your cousin?"

"Yes." Helen's face fell as she read.

Miriam said, "You look distressed."

"The news is depressing. My cousin said many of the soldiers on the ship to France were very sick. Though many were ill for just a few days, the disease spread unusually fast. And, like with any flu, a few of the men died."

Miriam said, "I read in the *Boston Globe* that lots of people have been getting a 'three-day fever,' as they are calling it. The paper said that almost everyone in a town in Haskell, Kansas, was ill. Some people say the illness started there."

"Haskell is a county, not a town," Susan said. "And I read that only eighteen people got sick. That's how rumors start."

"I'll not be the one to spread rumors. I'm worried about the children because it's spreading quickly through families," Miriam said, concerned.

"If anyone gets sick, you should call the doctor right away. I've heard doctors are prescribing very large doses of Bayer Aspirin to take care of the symptoms," Susan commented.

"And what I heard is that the aspirin is making people even sicker," Helen said.

"It's amazing to me that so many different stories get passed around. It's hard to decipher the truth," said Susan.

"Maybe there isn't even a flu."

"Miriam, there is an influenza outbreak each year. And this one seems to be spreading more rapidly than in any previous year, which is why everyone's talking about it."

"I hope your cousin avoids getting it, Helen. I heard that it's spreading among the soldiers very quickly. Usually, the flu affects the infirmed, but this flu seems to be attacking the young and healthy."

"I heard that too," Susan said. "Maybe that piece of the rumor is true."

"I've heard that some people get very sick, and even many people are ill for more than a week." Miriam sighed.

"The paper says the death rate from this flu is the same as other flu seasons."

Later, Miriam admitted to Deborah that she was worried about this illness. "I read that some are predicting this could be an epidemic. Do you think it could be as bad as the polio epidemic that took the life of the Berkowitzes' young neighbor?"

"I certainly hope not," Deborah said, taking a deep breath.

❧ ❧ ❧

At the dinner table with the family, Deborah said, "I've not heard from my brother since Helen's cousin wrote about the soldiers getting ill. I'm concerned because he's usually a pretty good correspondent." She'd forgotten Miriam's request that they not talk about this illness over meals.

"I hope he's all right. Maybe he got sick, so he couldn't write to you."

"That doesn't make me feel any better, Miriam."

"Sorry, I guess I was just thinking out loud."

"What are the symptoms of this influenza?" asked Susan.

"I read folks get very high fevers, muscle aches, chills, and head-aches, much like the normal flu," answered Helen.

"What makes this more dangerous than other sicknesses?" Miriam wanted to know.

"Nothing really," Helen admitted. "The only difference is that it's spreading really quickly, and many people are ill."

"And some soldiers are dying," Deborah added, taking a deep breath and worrying about her brother even more.

Finally, later in the week, a letter arrived from Helen's cousin with bad news. His friend from school had died from the grippe, as they were calling it.

"He and his friend Henry joined the army together and were trav-eling on the same ship. I assume he didn't want to worry me because he gave no details. He called it the Spanish flu, so I guess it started in Spain."

Miriam shook her head. "I'm not sure about that. I read that it started in Kansas. It is hard to keep it all straight. I'm worried about getting it from the folks at the synagogue, so I've decided not to go to services this weekend."

"Not go to synagogue? I've never heard you say that before," said Deborah, walking in during this discussion. "But there haven't been any cases in Boston, so we don't need to stay home. Why worry about something that's not even here?"

"But what if it comes here? I read that everyone gets it two days after being exposed, so we would not even know we had it until it was too late," Miriam said sadly. "I don't want to get sick and give it to our daughters."

"We still need to go to work," said Deborah.

"I hope no customers have it," said Miriam, clearly upset.

Deborah was respectful. "How can we protect ourselves and our children, other than staying home all the time?"

"I heard a few ideas. One is to wear a pouch with camphor around our necks," Miriam said and made a face in disgust at the suggestion.

"I heard some doctors are injecting camphor into people," said Susan.

"I'm not willing to try either of those treatments," said Deborah, wrinkling her nose.

"And I heard others are gargling with salt water or eating oranges," Miriam added. "And not kissing their babies. I'm willing to try anything that will protect our girls, though it would be hard not to kiss them."

"Do you really believe," asked Deborah, "that any of these remedies will protect us?"

"I've no idea, but I'll try anything," said Miriam.

Deborah managed to persuade Miriam to go to shul because there were still no reported cases of the flu in Boston. But out of fear, Miriam didn't kiss the children when she went upstairs to check on them.

The next week, Helen got another letter from her brother. She told the others, "My poor brother got the flu right after his friend Henry died. He was very ill and ran a fever of 104 for three days; they were afraid he might die too. He was very weak, but he's recovered."

Miriam shook her head quite forcefully. "This illness scares me. I have a really bad feeling about it."

ॐ ॐ ॐ

"Now, I'm really confused," said Miriam over dinner one night.

"That's nothing unusual," Deborah said, laughing.

"Don't be so mean. I'm confused because we've all heard this illness referred to as the Spanish flu, but now I read in the paper that the Spanish are calling it the French flu. People assume the Spanish are trying to avoid taking responsibility for everyone getting sick."

"From what I heard," Susan said, "the flu didn't start in Spain. It got called that because the Spanish newspapers covered it more openly than other countries, due to their belief in free press. It may have started in France or the US or China. Nothing is for certain. No one knows for sure."

"I really don't care where it began. I just care that it goes away as quickly as it started and that none of us gets it," Miriam said, holding Ida tightly.

"And now, the influenza has been reported across the globe, making it different from any other time in history," Helen said.

"I assume it's spreading because of the soldiers. They get sick and take it to wherever they're traveling," Deborah interjected.

"And I've heard," said Susan, "that one of the greatest problems is that many doctors have been shipped overseas to care for wounded soldiers, leaving few to care for the sick back home."

"Many doctors and nurses have gotten it themselves," Helen added. "It's frightening."

"This really is horrible. It might come to Boston and to us." Miriam put Ida down, then followed the toddler, who wandered off as soon as her feet hit the ground.

"I assume it will be over soon, maybe before it gets to us," Susan said hopefully.

"What will we do if it comes here?" Helen asked. "We've never seen one this virulent. And this is not even flu season."

Miriam discussed with Rachel possible ways to protect the children. Miriam was hesitant to bring up her concerns, given how easily the fragile Rachel was brought to tears since her husband died, yet this felt important. They shared beliefs about the dangers confronting them and agreed on setting some rules for added precautions. The children would not leave the house, except for short walks or down the street to Leah's.

During their conversation, Rachel told Miriam she would return to volunteering at the stables. She'd stopped by earlier in the week, and the stable hand named Roger said she and Miriam would be welcomed back at any time. Miriam declined the offer, fearful of being in places that might expose her to the flu. She wished she could discourage her shy friend Rachel, who had few activities now that her husband had perished, yet Rachel seemed set on being with the horses. But fear of this illness overrode everything for Miriam.[22]

Grace Banker

---

[22] The horrific truth was that the influenza would go on to ravage the world. To contain the illness, some cities imposed quarantines. In New York City, work shifts were staggered, so fewer people commuted to work at the same time. Other cities required people to wear masks in public. Libraries were closed, as were schools and theaters. For the next several months, the spread of disease was uppermost in everyone's mind, even though there had been relatively few deaths.

RMS Celtic

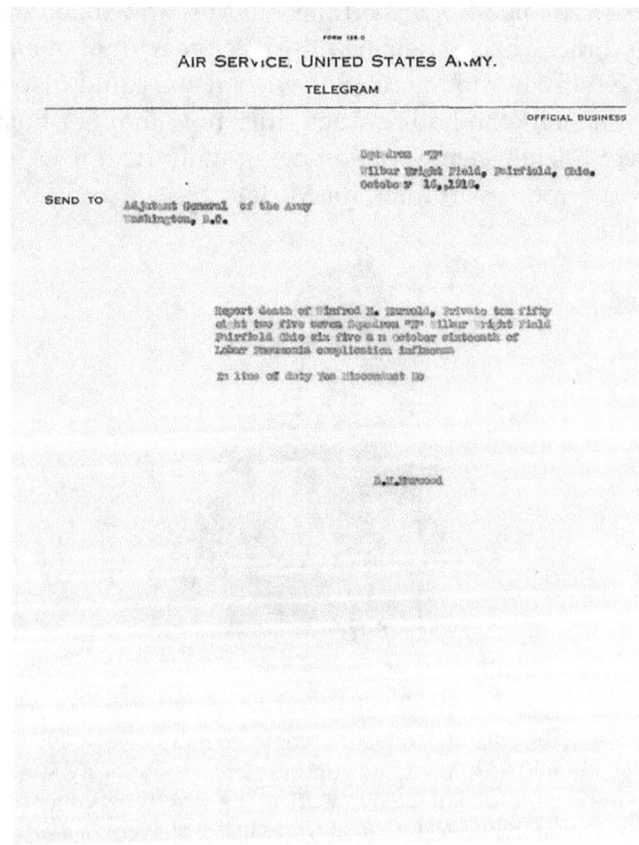

Air Force Death from flu certificate

Episode 17 ✤ *Shell Shock*

May 1918

Grace had not written them for several months, so Susan and Helen were pleased to get a letter from her. They'd worried about her safety, fearful that her lack of correspondence was because she was hurt or even dead. Miriam seemed especially concerned, mentioning occasionally that she was worried about Grace. Each time Miriam mentioned her, Deborah noted Miriam's sensitivity to other people's dilemmas.

May 1, 1918
Dear Susan and Helen,
I don't know if you will ever receive this letter since it is unclear whether I will live another day. It's also uncertain whether I will find a method to mail this.

Let me tell you a bit about what it's like for us. My alarm goes off at 2:15 a.m., and I need to rouse the two other girls on my shift. We eat a quick breakfast by candlelight (to reduce the possibility that the enemy will spot us) then report to our post. For the next few hours, we operate the communications system between soldiers on the front lines, just a couple hundred yards away, to the men at headquarters. If it were not for our assistance, there would be no way for our men to know of their next steps or for our officers to strategize. Our role is very important in this war effort.

I must go now, because I need to grab a couple of hours of rest before I'm back on duty. We serve the soldiers all day and night, so we're all very weary.

May 6, 1918 (continuation of this letter)
I'm so relieved. Our fearful days have ended. We've been moved to a lovely town, Chaumont, France. We're in a beautiful stone house with a bathtub! What a treat!

We are to help with logistics, arranging the movement of supplies from one location to another. This has nothing to do with communications, and yet we are pleased to assist in any way we can.
Yours Truly,
Grace

As was typical of her responses lately, Miriam was agitated after hearing of Grace's challenges. "Grace is so brave. I can't imagine living the army life. I could never deal with what she has faced."

Deborah hugged Miriam, assuring her that neither of them would ever face such terrifying situations, so she needn't worry so.

"You don't understand, Deborah. What she faces frightens me, but I am envious that she has more strength of character than anyone I've ever known. Sometimes I feel that my safe, secure life has much less meaning than the Graces or the Emma Goldmans of the world. I wish I were brave enough to live my life as fully as they do. I will never do good for others the way these women have. Sometimes I feel so insignificant."

"Dearest Miriam," said Deborah, embracing her, "I will always be grateful that you live a safe life, though your values are aligned with those who put themselves in harm's way. I appreciate your principles, though I'm glad you don't take risks that will make us vulnerable. I love you for your ethics and your commitment to putting your family's needs ahead of your altruistic motives."

With a deep sigh, Miriam said, "I love you so much, Deborah. We are so lucky to have found one another and to have such a lovely family."

☙ ☙ ☙

A few days after Grace's letter, Deborah arrived home from work, sorted the mail, and found an envelope addressed to Miriam.

"Here's a letter for you from Ruth. I wonder what crisis she is facing now. Her letters always describe a dilemma where she needs your help. I hope it's not about the influenza."

"You were going to change your attitude about Ruth. Maybe you shouldn't assume she's having a problem."

"She's always having a problem or complaining about something, but you're right. I try to be less critical of her, but it's my habit to berate her."

Miriam went into the back room to see Sylvia and Ida before reading the letter. After hugs, her daughters showed off the small creations they had each made from balls of what looked like horsehair and twigs pasted on paper. Miriam fussed over their artwork and asked Rachel if they'd gone to the stables to collect these craft supplies.

"Roger invited us to visit, and he let the girls brush the horses. Sylvia picked some hair off the brush and put it in her pocket, which is where I got the idea of making a collage with things the girls collected. Roger was really sweet with them and invited us to come back at any time."

"Rachel, I'm glad you and the girls had a nice time, yet I'd rather you didn't take them there. I want to avoid any possible exposure to the flu."

"I'm sorry I took them to the stables. I know you said not to go anywhere except to Leah's. This was outdoors, so I thought it would be all right."

"It's fine that you went this once, but I'd prefer that you stick to walks and Leah's house."

"I'll do as you ask, and I'll go to the stables on my own."

Miriam hoped Rachel wasn't exposing herself when there, yet she knew she couldn't restrict Rachel's free time. But it was all so worrisome.

After the girls were settled, Miriam finally had a chance to open the correspondence from Ruth.

> *May 4, 1918*
> *Dear Miriam and Deborah,*
> *I was glad for the letter you sent me a few months ago. Maybe I forgot to acknowledge it, because I never heard back from you.*
>
> *My brother, David, is not doing well. As you know, he went into the army right after the Selective Service Act passed, which required that boys his age serve.*
>
> *The day he left, I went to my parents' house to see him off. He looked very handsome in his uniform, though my mother kept talking about how much better he'd look in an officer's uniform. He paid no attention to her, though I know he heard her. David doesn't talk much, yet it was unusual that he didn't say a single word. I wished him well and gave him some of his favorite chocolate candies. My mother said they would melt all over his clothing, so she made him unpack them. I took them home rather than waste them.*
>
> *I worry about him. He never adjusts well to new situations, and he does not make friends easily—actually, he does not make friends at all. I can't imagine how he'll manage.*
> *Fondly,*
> *Ruth*

Miriam resisted writing back to Ruth, trying to break the pretense of wanting a friendship with her, but then she received a second letter.

> *May 28, 1918*
> *Dear Deborah and Miriam,*
> *Things are even worse than I predicted. We got one letter from David, saying he was shipping off to France. His handwriting seemed a bit shaky, now that I remember it. He*

*was gone for just a few weeks when my parents got a letter
from the army saying he would be coming home, telling
them where and when to pick him up, which I thought odd.
A soldier should be able to get home on his own, yet obviously he couldn't. My parents didn't mention any concerns
about him.*

*I waited at their house to greet him, not expecting our
meeting to be so upsetting. David was more nervous than
usual. When he tried to talk, he stuttered, something I never
heard him do before. He ran to the bathroom several times
that evening, and I could hear him vomiting. I was upset
when I left.*

*My parents said they heard him pacing all night, so they
called the doctor the next morning. The doctor reported to
my parents that David had "shell shock," a term I'd not
heard before. He said David was upset from observing the
destruction of war, which I assumed meant that he had seen
people killed. My father was certain David would be fine
after a few days at home. He wasn't. My mother told me she
found some papers in David's bag saying he had something
called a "disability discharge."*

*The day my mother found the papers, my father called the
army, hoping to send David back after a short rest. He was
told David was "not fit for duty." That's what they called
it. Next, my father contacted their doctor again, asking him
to write a letter to the army so that David could return.
He refused. Mother said David was an embarrassment to
the family and she didn't want her friends to know what
happened. My parents talked right in front of David about
what they would say to their friends. My heart sank.*

*David saw someone at the army office, which was the only
time he left the house. The army doctor didn't help him. I wonder
if he had a breakdown, like your mother did, Deborah.*

I'll let you know if anything changes.
Fondly,
Ruth

"What an awful situation," said Miriam. "I've not heard of others
having this thing called shell shock. Poor David."

"I'm glad to hear you're upset for David, rather than Ruth!"

"That's not nice to say, Deborah."

"I guess not. Sorry. He was always an odd boy. Remember when we first talked about the war? We wondered how a boy like David would cope with the rigid rules of the army."

"I know. Now, his reaction is more than just about the rules. I can't imagine what it would be like to watch young men get killed."

"I'd be upset even if the boys were on the other side."

"So would I. I'm so glad women aren't required to serve. I don't think we have the temperament for it."

"Obviously, neither does David."

When Miriam sat at her desk to write back to Ruth, she sighed deeply then said, "Frankly, I'm impressed that Ruth compared David's problems to your mother's breakdown. I didn't realize she'd even listened when you told her of your mother's collapse. She just went on talking about herself, as she usually does," Miriam said, moving to a wingback chair near Deborah.

"I noticed that also. Maybe she has a heart after all."

"Deborah! You are sometimes very mean when you talk about Ruth. She just showed how much she cares about her brother."

"I guess I am mean. I'm just upset she hurt you all those years ago."

"She didn't hurt me. She just disappointed me. I expected her to be a real friend since that's the way I pictured her when we were at camp together when we were younger."

"She's never been compassionate with you, like a real friend would be. She hardly ever even listened to you or asked anything about us."

"You're right. I never understood friendship, though I should have, because I always had Marjorie as a true friend. Maybe I was just nervous at camp, imagining no one would be my friend. Or maybe Ruth was different then."

"I'll never understand your motivation in befriending her."

"I don't either." Miriam sighed. "But now I feel terrible for her and for her brother."

"I guess I do too. The horrors of war that young men must have faced are awful. All that pain and suffering makes no sense."

"If only the world would let women be in charge, maybe there'd be less war."

"Or even if women could vote, maybe things would be different," Deborah said.

"That's such a sad topic. After all the work we did for women's suffrage, I'd hoped for more success by now. Do you know how many states have ratified the vote for women?" Miriam asked.

"Twelve, including New York, which finally passed women's suffrage in November."

"Will it ever happen in every state?"

Deborah smiled. "That's just as likely as having a law that will allow us to marry!"

"Right! That will never happen."

❧ ❧ ❧

The topics of the time were shell shock and the influenza. The newspapers were full of stories of people who had gotten sick or died. Most Bostonians felt confined to their homes, afraid to go out in public lest they catch the dreaded disease.

One day, the main story in the newspaper was about a young Red Sox baseball player named Babe Ruth, who had gotten ill with the influenza and had to be taken off the roster. Despite the thousands of others suffering, the newspaper made the illness of this one person seem so much more important than any of those who had died.

Over breakfast, Miriam said, "Why did the *Boston Globe* make such a fuss over this one baseball player?"

Helen responded first, "Maybe because some people feel sports are more important than anything else. My brothers would rather talk about sports than any other topic."

"Why does throwing a ball around gather so much interest," Miriam said, still stymied. "And who is this man with the strange name?"

"Even I've heard of Babe Ruth," Deborah added.

"He's a legend in my family, even though he plays ball in Boston," Susan said. "He's known as the best pitcher in the world."

Helen chuckled. "I wouldn't go that far. Maybe he's just popular because the teams are short of players because so many young men having gone to war."

"I don't agree. He's made a name for himself because he's proven his skills. I'm glad he recovered from the grippe so he can go back to the Red Sox," Susan said.

"What kind of New Yorker are you?" Helen smiled. "You've forgotten where you're from. You should be rooting for our team, the Yankees, instead of Boston. I know they're not doing great, yet you should be supporting them."

"I'll never understand sports," Miriam said.

Later that week, Miriam told Deborah, "Rachel's been going to the stables quite often lately. I hope she's keeping safe from the grippe. It makes me nervous even though she's not brought the girls since I asked her not to. I wonder if she's going there to take her mind off Aaron's death."

"Or," Deborah mused, "I wonder if it has something to do with that young man named Roger, whom she mentions frequently."

"Does she have some interest in Roger? He's a handsome young man, though what would she possibly have in common with him? What attraction could a farmhand hold for Rachel? Rachel's bright and well read, qualities not typical for young men working on a horse farm."

"Maybe he reads the same books as she does, which were the only things she and Aaron talked about when they met."

"I remember that, though Rachel's learned to discuss other things. Aaron was good for her in many ways."

"Now I'm curious. You should ask her about Roger."

"I don't want to intrude on her privacy," Miriam said.

"Isn't that what friends do? Ask each other about love interests?"

"Love? Oh my. He's just a distraction."

"Maybe."

Another day, Deborah and Miriam continued their conversation about the effects of war on soldiers. "It seems there are many boys coming home with shell shock these days," Deborah said. "I heard several girls at temple talking about their brothers or their husbands being so very different than before going to war. Some have headaches or tremors, and others have decreased hearing or sight. Only boys seriously hurt or those like David have come home so far."

Miriam asked, "What is shell shock really?"

"From what I understand, it's when men have seen disturbing things they can't get out of their heads."

"Well, maybe it is like my memories of my mother dying. I have images of her death as vivid as if it happened yesterday, even though it was about three years ago," Miriam said wistfully.

"And that wasn't even a horrible experience."

"No, it was gentle and loving. We made her passing as sweet as could be."

"So," said Deborah, "if a sweet death was so memorable, can you imagine what not being able to forget an ugly death would be like? No wonder those boys are haunted by their memories."

"I wouldn't wish that on anyone, or as Bubbie would say, '*As di bubbe volt gehat beytsim volt zi gevain mayn zaidah.*' That means, 'If my grandmother had balls, she'd be my grandfather.'"

"I never heard that phrase. What does that mean?" Deborah asked.

"It means not to make predictions or plans based on assumptions."

"That's really funny."

The next day, Miriam asked Deborah if she was still going to write a book on the effects of war and include a mention of shell shock.

"No, it wouldn't be good for me to focus on something so disturbing. I know it's wise to write during the epidemic, though I'm not motivated. Maybe I should put the whole book-writing project aside for now."

"I'll support whatever decision you make, though I'd hate to see your creative mind get sluggish."

"Thanks for saying that. I'm sure my juices will flow again when I'm ready to write."

"I'd like to make sure your other juices are flowing."

"Miriam, are you suggesting what I think you are?"

"Come to bed with me, and you'll see."[23]

꙳ ꙳ ꙳

"I'm sorry I had to leave the table for such a long call from my parents," Deborah said one evening. "It pleases me so much that my mother has a little of her old spark back. She was quite enthusiastic that the Bronx International Exposition of Science, Arts, and Industries is opening at the end of the month. That's quite a mouthful."

"What is it? It sounds stuffy."

---

[23] The term "shell shock" was difficult to define when it first came into use. The term was coined during World War I by an English psychologist who defined it as a physical ailment. It was first thought to be the result of the brain being shaken within the skull when a soldier was close to an explosion. Then it was thought to be a mental breakdown, precipitated by observing the devastation of war. Sometimes it was considered a lack of moral fiber or cowardice. The number of cases was so great that in Britain, there were nineteen hospitals dedicated to the treatment of mentally disabled soldiers suffering from shell shock.

The term "shell shock" was replaced with the term "combat stress reaction" during World War II. In the 2000s, soldiers were diagnosed with post-traumatic stress disorder, which differs from shell shock because many of the symptoms of the earlier diagnosis were physical.

"It is the world's fair!"

"Then why didn't you call it that? I heard so much about the 1915 San Francisco World's Fair, so I don't understand why I've not heard anything about this. A world's fair should be well publicized."

"Miriam, there is a war going on, and that horrible influenza has afflicted so many people."

"You're right. But luckily the grippe seems to be attacking fewer people lately, and it doesn't scare me as much."

"My parents would like us to come to New York to attend this event," said Deborah, redirecting the conversation to the issue of the world's fair. "Would you feel safe attending?"

"I would, now that the influenza cases are waning significantly. Yet I wonder if it would be fun for the children," said Miriam.

"I'll find out if there are activities for the little ones. I'll tell my parents that we'll join them if it sounds like the children will be sufficiently entertained."

"Thanks. I'll tell Susan and Helen we might be heading to New York. You'll need to get me details about the dates and what to pack."

"I bet Rachel will be pleased with a few days off to see her new boyfriend."

"I know. Things change so quickly. Not so long ago, she was mourning her husband's death. Now she is celebrating her new relationship. I'm happy for her."

Deborah made plans with her family to attend the world's fair on Thursday, May 30, opening day. It was advertised as an anniversary celebration—the settlement of the Bronx was 300 years before, and it had become an official borough of New York on that day twenty years before. The aim of the fair was to attract foreign trade and hundreds of thousands of visitors to New York. The fair was to run for five months every year, rather than as a one-time event.

Mrs. Levine sent Deborah and Miriam a brochure outlining the features of the fair, and they both became quite excited. They showed the paper to the children, who didn't know what to make of it.

"They're going to have a bathing pavilion with the largest salt-water swimming pool in the world. The children will love that," Miriam squealed in a high-pitched voice. "And one hundred twenty exhibits, a mountain with a huge waterfall, a roller coaster, and a Ferris wheel. And a miniature railway to ride on, which will be perfect for Sylvia and Ida. And a real submarine! This sounds wonderful!"

Miriam packed and repacked their valises with everyone's favorite outfits—well, Miriam's favorite outfits for each. Deborah researched information about the attractions; she was especially eager to see the pavilions of the different countries. Deborah called her sister several times, encouraging Anna to join them.

Just before they were to leave for New York, Mrs. Levine called to say the opening had been postponed for several weeks. Much of their enthusiasm waned as they wondered how such a huge project could be so delayed. They found no answers as to why, which increased their skepticism. What was happening?

Shell Shock patient

Episode 18 ✤ *World's Fair*

June 1918

Miriam was getting tired of Deborah's repeated mention of the postponed world's fair, so she was pleased when Deborah brought up a new topic one morning as they dressed for work.

"I don't understand why Rachel needs to bring her new beau to meet us."

"To meet you and her mother. Remember, I met Roger when I went to the stables with Rachel," said Miriam while dressing in her night clothing. "She wants your approval."

"How can I approve of her having a boyfriend so soon after Aaron died?"

"It's wonderful that she's moving on. Having a husband gave her confidence."

"But so soon. It feels disrespectful."

"That's why she wants our approval. She fears her mother's reaction will be like yours. Do you really want to make her feel bad?"

"No, I guess we should show support."

The following day's visit with Roger went smoothly. He was nicely dressed in a dark-sackcloth, three-piece suit, with no lingering smell of horses. Mrs. Stern was welcoming; she made a special dessert, a 1917 War Cake, with corn syrup, cloves, and nutmeg; the cake was not made with the scarce items being conserved for the soldiers—butter, eggs, or milk.

Roger sat stiffly at the table, aware that he was being scrutinized by all. He ate the cake with gusto, and his praise made Mrs. Stern blush. He was very careful not to be too familiar with Rachel in front of her mother.

Rachel wistfully thought of her father, believing he would have been proud of her choice of such a fine young fellow.

Later that evening, Deborah said to Miriam, "Roger's visit was delightful. I never saw Rachel so talkative."

"He brings out the best in her," Miriam responded, noticing that neither Deborah nor Mrs. Stern had focused on this being so soon after Rachel's husband's death.

"Rachel's young man was so engaging that I could understand how he has captured her fancy."

They agreed that the glow on Rachel's face was telling.

෫ ෫ ෫

Milton was on Deborah's mind frequently, and she wrote to him to share her feelings.

> *June 3, 1918*
> *Dear Milton,*
> *It was wonderful to hear from you and especially gratifying to have you nearby. I never imagined you'd be assigned to a ship in the New York Harbor.*
>
> *I did the library research you suggested and learned your ship was originally the SS Vaterland, a luxury liner and the pride of Germany. It was the largest ship ever built, 67 feet longer than the Titanic (which sank six years ago). Can you imagine?*
>
> *It had a magnificent first-class section that covered over 60% of the ship, though it served only 700 passengers. First-class passengers dined at their Ritz-Carlton restaurant, a twin facility to the one in New York, with linen tablecloths, sterling-silver flatware, Limoges china, and fresh flowers. How I would have loved to dine there.*
>
> *I read that the second-class and third-class accommodations were spacious, though not as elegant. The 1,600 passengers had their own gymnasium and dining rooms, yet were not allowed access to the first-class, frescoed swimming pool. It sounds so enormous!*
>
> *Another 1,700 passengers were crammed into the bow. They slept on bunk beds in cramped rooms. They were served meals on long wooden tables and had little space for recreation. The cost for those accommodations was $29.50, except for Russians, who were charged $30.75. I wonder why the rate was different for the Russians.*
>
> *We are fine here, and I hope you stay safe and well.*
> *Love,*
> *Deborah*

෫ ෫ ෫

"There's a letter from Ruth, addressed to both of us," Miriam announced. After reading, she said, "Ruth's letter is very disturbing."

"Everything she does is disturbing," said Deborah.

"Hold your tongue. You were going to be nicer about her. She has really bad news."

"Did her husband, Michael, get killed overseas?"

"Not killed, but I will let you read the letter to see what happened."

June 7, 1918

Dear Miriam and Deborah,

I'm writing to tell you that my husband is home from the war. At first, I was excited to see him. Michael surprised me by walking through the door without warning, which was a bit unnerving, yet he seemed pleased to see me. I'm going to be blunt, and you'll soon understand why.

We had intimacies. Then Michael told me he was discharged for medical reasons. He said he had the influenza but recovered. I had no reason to doubt him until he got up several times during his first night home. Initially, I thought he was just getting over his disease, yet when he got up for the fourth time to relieve himself, I asked him to tell me what was wrong. It was then that he told me that he had gonorrhea, not the flu. At first, I didn't understand what he was saying. He had to explain that he had a venereal disease.

I became incredibly distraught, imagining he got sick from a French prostitute. He told me he got ill from one of the other soldiers, not from a French girl. This worried me just as much until he explained. He said one of his friends got an infection from a lady and had pus sores on his private part. This friend was being sent home because of this, and Michael was envious. Michael said it would be better to get a venereal disease than to get killed in combat.

The men had learned a trick, a way to get out of the army. Michael said he rubbed some of his friend's puss on a matchstick and transferred it to his own private parts, so he would get infected too. That way, he could get out of the service. I wasn't sure if I believed him.

>   *Then I became really upset when I realized Michael had*
> *just had intimacies with me, and he probably passed it on*
> *to me too! I can't believe he did that. Selfishly, Michael only*
> *paid attention to his own needs. Like always.*
>
>   *I hardly know what to do. I sent him to sleep in the other*
> *room, and I may never let him back into my bed. I have heard*
> *it might make me sterile. I have begun to feel itchy down*
> *there, but I'm scared to go to the doctor. What would he say?*
>
>   *I'm feeling very alone. But I needed to tell someone this*
> *awful story.*
> *Ruth*

Deborah shook her head after reading the letter. "Oh my. What a horrible situation. I hope Ruth is not sick, though it sounds like that uncaring husband of hers may have infected her."

"I feel bad for her. I knew he was a scoundrel, yet he's actually worse than I thought."

Miriam wished she could think of a different topic; she would rather hear about Deborah's obsessive interest in the delays of the world's fair. But Ruth's news stayed with her, and she could not even sleep that night.

❧ ❧ ❧

Miriam wrote to Ruth, encouraging her to go to the doctor despite her shame. Through subsequent letters, Miriam learned that Michael had indeed infected Ruth, and the doctor informed Ruth that she would probably never have more children. He put her on a strict regimen of mercury and arsenic, the same chemicals used to treat syphilis. The drugs caused nausea and vomiting—a terrible reminder of Michael's indiscretion.

Ruth banished Michael permanently to the other bedroom and refused to be intimate with him ever again. He often headed out at night, probably passing his disease on to some other unsuspecting woman.

Ruth asked in multiple letters if she could come to Boston to visit Miriam and Deborah.

While Miriam found it difficult to lie or to be uncaring, she said no, using the excuse that all their beds were full.

When Ruth offered to stay in a nearby hotel, Miriam had to tell her directly that she couldn't visit. Miriam lost several nights' sleep, feeling awful that she had abandoned her old friend in her time of need, but

Deborah persuaded her that this was the best decision for all of them. Deborah and Miriam had the children to think of—Deborah feared Ruth could pass her illness on to them—and she had no desire to see her anyway.

It seemed to Deborah that Miriam had finally let go of her responsibility to Ruth. They had more than compensated Ruth for giving them Sylvia, the child they so desperately adored, the child Ruth wanted to abandon. Deborah finally persuaded Miriam she did not need to feel beholden to Ruth for the rest of her life. Miriam had been more than kind and understanding for years, even when Ruth remained self-absorbed. Hers was a debt fully paid.

Fanny Berkowitz was sworn in as a navy yeoman on June 12, 1918. Though she hoped to be sent overseas, she quickly learned that most of the twelve thousand women who had signed up were to be kept stateside. It was mostly nurses who were sent abroad. Fanny had fantasized about being a strong, independent woman in the navy, but she was disappointed with the outcome.

> *June 16, 1918*
>
> *Dear Deborah and Miriam,*
>
> *I am a yeoman (F). That is what they call us girls who joined the Navy.*
>
> *They stationed me at the Naval Aircraft Factory in Philadelphia, Pennsylvania. I had hoped to be on a ship, but that didn't happen. So much for choosing the Navy over the Army.*
>
> *To get here, they squeezed us into a very crowded train, and I'm sure that's why so many of the girls got sick. By the time we arrived, many of the girls started showing symptoms of the influenza. Somehow, I avoided getting it.*
>
> *When I first got here, I was sure I'd made a terrible mistake. The base has a huge number of buildings, and I got scared that I'd never find my way around. I got assigned to a bunk and was given clothing and supplies. The only good news is that I have a Jewish bunkmate. Her name is Rina, and she's as nervous as me about being here. It's good to have a friend.*
>
> *Rina and I are totally disgusted with the food. We have to eat, or we get in trouble (they call it demerits) but I don't*

look forward to meals. But I must tell you that I like my new haircut. Rina says it's cute. She looks adorable in her haircut too. But the uniforms are awful, totally shapeless, probably so the men won't notice us. Next week we get our dress uniforms, and I bet we'll look really nice in those. Rina has a cousin in the army who loves her dress uniform, and I am hoping we'll feel the same way. I will send you a photograph if I ever get ahold of a camera.

Have you talked with my mother and father? How are they? And how are my sisters managing without me? I bet Ethel already moved into my room and is enjoying being the oldest sister.

I need to go now. Rina is waiting for me to take a walk. Please write. It is really exciting to get letters here. They call out our names, and we step forward in line to collect our mail.

Love,

Fanny

Deborah and Miriam were surprised to get another letter just a couple of days later. They assumed that Fanny was homesick.

June 18, 1918

Dear Deborah and Miriam,

Rina and I are adjusting okay. They told us that this is a new facility, and we should be proud to be the first group here. They manufacture biplanes, small seaplanes supported by pontoon floats. I think that's the closest we'll get to the water.

Like the other recruits (that's what they call us), Rina and I were hoping to be truck drivers, mechanics, or radio operators, skilled jobs done by men before they shipped off to Europe. Instead, we reported to a massive building filled with finished planes and half-built planes. I was tremendously disappointed when I learned that I was to be a secretary, stuck in the clerical role that girls always get. I was given a desk in a quiet office, and I look with envy at the women operating manufacturing equipment or driving trucks, the jobs I'd like to do. Rina will test equipment, a much more appealing job, so I am a little jealous. Rina says

that she'll ask her commanding officer if I can come work
with her, but we doubt he'll listen to her.
Love, Fanny

Deborah looked at Miriam once she was done reading the letter
and said, "Well, we know more about Rina than anything else!"
"I noticed."

≈ ≈ ≈

Deborah and Miriam decided to take turns writing to Fanny at least
once each week. They asked Mildred and Leah to write letters and
requested that Rachel instruct the girls to make pictures to include in
the envelopes. They also decided to check in with Mrs. B. quite regularly, understanding that parenting a teenager was sometimes more
difficult than caring for a young child.

Deborah thought back to the first article she had published, called
"Parenting a Young Woman." She had written it when she was about
Fanny's age, so rereading it aided her in understanding that Fanny
viewed herself as a mature adult. This helped when they got yet another
letter from Fanny.

June 25, 1918
Dear Deborah and Miriam,
I have exciting news. My assignment was changed. I don't
think it was because I was doing a poor job as a secre-
tary, nor did they listen to Rina's suggestion that I work
with her. It was more because there was a girl working on
the biplanes who got the grippe and had to be replaced.
I thanked the officer who gave me my new job, but I don't
think he cared whether I was pleased or not. They just see
it as a job. Once I start my new job, I'll let you know what
I am doing.
Although I won't be working with Rina, I will be on the
floor with her. Now it will be easier to go to lunch together.
Love,
Fanny

Miriam turned to Deborah and asked, "Did I talk about you this
much when I was busy falling in love with you?"
"I don't know. But you talked this much about Sadie when you
were infatuated with her."

"Deborah! I did not. And I was not infatuated with her."

"You were too. But let's drop that subject since I won. I have you all to myself!"

"So," Miriam said, "do you think Fanny could be like us?"

"Time will tell."

❧ ❧ ❧

On June 29, after a full month's delay, the world's fair opened. Deborah's family traveled to the Bronx on the new opening day, a little less excited than they would have been if it had opened on schedule. Her mother had hesitated about attending the fair, yet Deborah persuaded her to join the family, noting her disposition had been solemn of late. Deborah observed her mother during their visit, fearful she was more prone to sullenness following her mental collapse four years earlier.

The group put on their special outfits and traveled as a group of seven: Deborah's parents; her sister, Anna; and the four of them. They decided to take the car on the new automobile boulevard, rather than the new railway, surface lines, or elevated trains, all built to take crowds directly to the exhibition. After a slow trip down an extremely crowded road, they entered the fairgrounds located on the Waldorf Astor estate just south of Bronx Park. After parking in the huge lot, they walked for a long while, their eyes fixed on the gates ahead.

As they entered, they were dazzled by a huge roller coaster. They heard screaming riders soaring above as they navigated between throngs of excited guests. They entered the grounds enchanted, though surprised there were far fewer than the one hundred buildings described in the advertisements.

They traveled down the grand esplanade, alternating who pushed Sylvia in a stroller and who carried Ida. Mrs. Levine noted that it barely resembled the drawings in the promotional materials and was concerned it might disappoint her enthusiastic family. They headed first to the food area, drawn by the smell of popcorn and a brand-new food called hot dogs. They looked like sausages, which they knew were made of pork, so they were reluctant to try them. Mr. Levine gave each of them several coins and told them to choose their own treats. Both the children chose ice-cream cones like those introduced at the 1904

World's Fair. Everyone sampled different items, sharing tastes with one another.[24]

After their treats, they searched for the international pavilions to explore the cultural displays promoted on the brochure. When they got there, Deborah said, "Look at the extremely long lines at the Brazilian pavilion. I don't want to wait so long to get in. Do you see any other countries represented?"

No one spotted any. Deborah complained, "What happened to the other international pavilions we were promised in the brochure. That's what I really wanted to see. I don't know if I would have wanted to come if I knew that only Brazil had an exhibition. This is not really a world's fair."

Miriam directed everyone's attention to the clowns on the path, wanting their girls to have a nice experience despite it being a disappointment for the adults.

The group had planned to forgo the bathing pavilion because it would mean changes of clothing for everyone, but they questioned their decision when they saw throngs of people heading that way. This area, the largest saltwater pool in the world, astoundingly had a capacity of 4,500 bathers. Deborah and Miriam whispered to one another that they would return with the girls—the pool area their sole destination—and make a day of it. They wanted to see the beach within the city. The children did not know what was inside the huge pavilion; only Anna expressed displeasure that they were not going there.

Next, the group followed a map to find the *Holland*, the first submarine commissioned by the navy. Being neither large nor glamorous, it was less exciting than they expected. They walked around the sausage-shaped boat hanging from an apparatus on a pier, disappointed they could neither view the inside nor see it submerge.

The main attraction of the fair, other than the expansive swimming area, was the amusement park. Anna wanted to soar high on the Ferris wheel and ride on the dramatic roller coaster, which loomed above, but no one wanted to join her. Mr. Levine offered to come back

---

[24] In 1916, Nathan Handwerker, a polish immigrant, opened his first hot-dog stand on Coney Island. Though the all-beef franks had no pork or horsemeat, they were not made under rabbinic supervision, and therefore were not considered kosher. To prevent loss of business, Nathan coined the term "kosher style" to describe his dogs.

with her and some of her friends on another occasion, with the purpose of exploring the amusement park.

Throughout the day, Deborah kept an eye on her mother, making certain she was engaged. Although she didn't have a rosy disposition, she was adequately talkative and showed relaxed interest in the activities. She didn't make suggestions, as she normally did, yet Deborah was satisfied with her involvement.

Ida was animated, obviously stimulated by all the sights and sounds. She pointed to colorful items, often naming them something which had nothing to do with the real title. Sylvia caught on, mimicking Ida's labels as best she could, making it into a delightful game.

There were many free attractions, such as a comedy circus, the Whirling Geisha Girls, performances by the world's greatest high-diver, and a Monkey Cabaret. After two shows, the children were verging on cranky, so they all headed towards the car, leaving other events for another time. As they traveled the crowded paths, several of them smelled the tantalizing aromas. Mr. Levine was easily persuaded to stop for another round of snacks before leaving the park.

In the car, the children were exuberant, probably due to the sweet snacks they had just consumed. Repeatedly, Sylvia said, "Corn." Deborah couldn't distinguish whether she was excited about the corn served on the cob or the tub of popcorn heavily ladened with butter and salt. She promised to serve both to her again, knowing they would easily figure out the correct food through trial and error.

After a long and exciting day, neither of the children could settle down when back at the Levines' home. Deborah and Miriam replaced their usual bedtime story with discussions about everything new or different they had seen. Ida enthusiastically put her funny names to things she had seen, and Sylvia copied her words. Deborah and Miriam were pleased with their girls' delight, declaring it a perfect adventure despite the limited attractions. Neither worried about the children getting to sleep because they could nap on the long trip back to Boston.

Once home, both girls nodded off quickly, and shortly the adults headed to bed. When they got to their room—Deborah's old bedroom in the Levines' home—Miriam quickly changed into her night dress, yet Deborah lingered.

"What a fun time. I know we're both tired, but could you stay awake long enough for a little pleasure. It seems the day has stimulated me," Deborah said.

"I'll do my best, though I can't make promises."

"Then you should pleasure me first. That way, if you fall asleep, you'll be the one to miss out."

"Maybe the promise of delicious attention from you will keep me awake."

Deborah was excited, so her turn was quick. Deborah recovered swiftly and turned to touch Miriam. Miriam was more stimulated than Deborah expected, so it was a short time before they were both content and sound asleep.

∿ ∿ ∿

The next day, arriving home in Boston by car after dinner, Deborah and Miriam proceeded directly upstairs to settle the girls in their beds. Once the children were sleeping, they relayed enthusiastic stories of the fair to Susan, Helen, and Mildred.

Deborah grabbed the stack of newspapers from the days they'd missed and said, "I'm not surprised the paper describes the world's fair as a disappointment."

Miriam said, "It wasn't what any of us expected, but we had a lovely time."

"You always focus on the positive. That's why I love you."

Deborah and Miriam decided not to return to the bathing pavilion due to the crowds, though Anna took her father up on his offer to take her and her friends to the amusement park.[25]

---

[25] The 1918 World's Fair was labeled a failure by the press, though it was ultimately a financial success due to the large number of attendees enticed by a spectacular publicity campaign in the city's newspapers. Many folks were drawn to the swimming pool and the amusement park. Although the venue was supposed to be open each summer, after its first year, it was repurposed as an amusement park. To bolster reviews, the fair was renamed Starlight Park. The exhibition hall became an ice-skating rink and a dance hall, and more amusements were added. In 1926, in its heyday, there were 150 concessions and 26 rides, as well as the famous saltwater pool. Summer events included free opera performances and Saturday-night, big-band jazz concerts.

Starlight Park continued to operate until 1932, when a fire ravaged much of it. The surviving pool, sports fields, and picnic areas continued to attract visitors. The

At the end of the month, Deborah was pleased to receive a response from Milton.

> *June 25, 1918*
> *Deborah,*
> *Thanks for finding out so much about this ship.*
>
> *I must tell you that my letters are being censored. You may find holes cut out or words blackened. I got away with telling you a lot in my first letter, because I mailed it on my own when I was on shore leave. Now everything I write will be scrutinized.*
>
> *Although much of the ship is in horrible condition, its earlier opulence is still obvious. The area where I'm living, the officer's quarters, was likely the second-class accommodations. I'm glad I went to boot camp to become an officer because the enlisted and drafted men are in the area you described as steerage. They are crammed in, not as crowded as their predecessors but not living as spaciously as we officers are.*
>
> *Last week, the captain invited the junior officers to a reception in what must have been the first-class area. What I saw was impressive. Though everything needs fixing, and it's horribly dirty, the lavish fixtures are still there. The captain showed us an old brochure he found in the back of a drawer; it had a picture of the incredible pool. The brochure made it easy to imagine how luxurious everything was when this was a seaworthy hotel. Now, it takes some imagination because they've broken up the grand rooms into smaller compartments for the senior officers. There's a huge area cordoned off for carrying supplies to [CENSOR].*

---

largest building, the coliseum, was rented out for vaudeville acts and political rallies, including those of the Communist party. Despite all efforts to stay afloat, Starlight Park went bankrupt in 1940. The United States Army took over the coliseum during World War II, but after another fire, it was condemned, and the space was used as a bus depot.

After a 2017 renovation, the New York Parks System announced: "A new gem of the Bronx River, Starlight Park, has opened as a reclaimed, reconstructed, and expanded park. This 13-acre park now features a synthetic-turf, multipurpose field, a picnic area, two new playgrounds with spray showers, basketball courts, multiuse pathways, and floating docks." More than three-quarters of a mile of new greenway was built to connect Starlight Park with other parks.

*When I look past the boxes, I see faded brocade wall cover-
ings and numerous dusty chandeliers full of cobwebs.*
Love,
Milton

Letters from Fanny continued arriving with great regularity.
June 26, 1918

Dear Deborah and Miriam,
*I have begun my new job, and I am really pleased. It is
thrilling to climb into the cockpit to install the seat. Occasionally I sit in it and imagine the excitement of flying over
the ocean.*

*I am learning so much. The biplane has one pilot and
no passengers. It is built with two wings above each other,
the lower one is smaller, making it easier to maneuver the
aircraft. It has a small engine and flies slowly. I don't really
understand much else, but I really like working on it. Maybe
someday I'll learn to fly.*

*Rina is really excited at having me work nearby on the
planes. She knows I am happier and that makes her happy too.*
Love,
Fanny

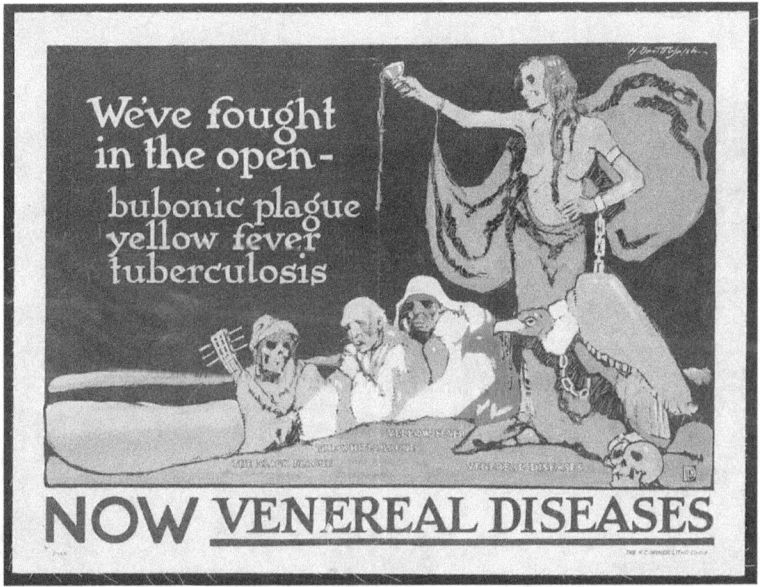

Venereal Disease

Bronx Exposition

Naval Aircraft Factory float

Episode 19 ❧ *Unnatural Acts*

July 1918

As she came down to breakfast, Miriam asked Deborah, "What are we going to do this evening during celebrations for July 4? Last year, Sylvia got really scared with all the noise, though I have no idea how to protect her from hearing it tonight."

"The fireworks happen every year, so she'll just have to get used to it," Deborah said.

"What an insensitive answer."

"You're right. I'm sorry. I was deeply engrossed in a story in the newspaper, yet that gives me no right to treat you like that. I'll put the paper aside to discuss this with you."

Miriam reminded Deborah that Massachusetts was one of the first states to recognize Independence Day as a holiday and one of the first to incorporate fireworks in their celebration. She took a deep gulp of air while thinking that there was no way to keep Sylvia out of earshot of the explosive sounds. With no obvious solutions, she turned the discussion back to the newspaper article Deborah was reading.

Deborah said, "I read that there's been a great deal of violence against Negroes in Saint Louis. Yesterday there was a huge massacre, and at least fifty people have died."

"No wonder you were distracted. Sadly, I don't even know where Saint Louis is."

"Missouri. I didn't know how troubled I was until I reacted so coldly to you. I read that Saint Louis has been having race issues since May, with extensive vandalism; Whites have burned buildings throughout the Negro parts of the city. Yesterday's riot was the worst labor-related violence in history."

"What do they mean by labor-related violence?"

Susan and Helen joined them at the breakfast table and answered Miriam's question. They understood union violence because they both had relatives in unions. Susan's cousin had been shunned for being a union member, and Helen's uncle was a labor organizer, focused on preventing labor replacements during strikes. This was all new to Deborah and Miriam.

Deborah said, "You two seem to know more about this than I do. Please share what you know."

Though Susan and Helen had only minimal knowledge about the race issues, they knew that organized labor groups had bargaining power. They explained that unions negotiated for shorter workdays and improved working conditions.

Miriam asked, "Do you think violence could happen here?"

"I hope not," Helen said. "Though there have been a number of local protests for pay increases and safer working conditions."

Susan added, "Such as the strikes after the Triangle Shirtwaist Factory fire, which caused the deaths of so many young girls. The terrible working conditions prompted walkouts and unions organizing all over the country."

"It's sad that it took so many deaths to highlight the matter." Miriam left the conversation when Ida made noises that signified a necessary change of diaper.

Deborah continued to talk of the violence that had occurred, and she wondered why Negroes were so often targeted. No one had answers.[26]

Miriam returned from tending to Ida just as Rachel entered the room. Unaware of their prior discussion, Rachel mentioned Sylvia's fear of firecracker noises. She asked, "May Roger and I take Sylvia and Ida to his house, which is farther from the celebrations? There will be less noise there."

Deborah thanked Rachel for the idea, but said they'd need to discuss it. Privately in the kitchen, Deborah talked of her insecurities. "We don't know much about this man, his neighborhood, or how the children would fare in his care," she said. "And the children would be out past their bedtime, and they'd be driven home on the dark streets by a man who is practically a stranger."

Miriam, who was less concerned, said, "I trust they will be safe with Rachel, who would never let harm come to them. Let's ask her how they plan to entertain the children."

---

[26] The issue behind the East Saint Louis Race Riot and others, such as the large one in Tulsa, Oklahoma, was race. The mood in Saint Louis was tense, as folks were strained by economic struggles. White soldiers returning from war were upset that Blacks, who were moving to the North in great numbers during the Great Migration, were taking their jobs. Both Whites and Blacks were fighting for the same positions and for economic survival. Hundreds of Blacks were killed in these riots.

Deborah held her tongue, attempting to quell her anxiety about this situation.

Rachel spoke calmly, talking of art projects and special snacks they would make with the children, calming the worried mothers' concerns about their girls. After Rachel spoke of Roger's impeccable driving record, Deborah reluctantly agreed.

Several times that day at work, Deborah nervously talked with Miriam regarding her concerns about the arrangements for the evening. "Do you think the children will be scared being with Roger?"

"No, they already know him from visiting the stables."

"What if they miss us?"

"Deborah, they'll be with Rachel, whom they adore, so they probably won't even think of us."

Their conversation then turned to their amazement that Rachel had a beau. They hoped this was a good situation for her, and that Roger wasn't taking advantage of Rachel's vulnerability so soon after losing her husband. Yet they were glad to see her smile again. They talked of how they would never recover so quickly if they lost one another, and they hoped that painful situation would never happen to either of them. After sending Sylvia and Ida on their adventure with Rachel and Roger, Deborah and Miriam took advantage of the rare experience of having an evening alone. Preferring uninterrupted time together, they decided to forgo the festivities throughout the city. They shyly wished Susan, Helen, and Mildred a nice evening, embarrassed that their plans might be obvious.

Immediately after their friends left, Deborah pulled Miriam into a tight embrace. Their kisses soon became passionate, and before they realized it, they were both worked into a frenzy.

"Let me love you right here in the parlor," Deborah whispered.

Miriam giggled as she pulled her dress down from her shoulders, exposing her breasts. She looked around as if some stranger might be looking at them, though she was soon caught up in the passion Deborah was already feeling. They lay on the long camelback couch, barely fitting their two bodies onto the narrow width. Gradually, they peeled off their clothing until they were naked, right in the middle of the parlor. Neither had ever imagined making love there, which only added to the excitement.

Deborah rolled off the couch and positioned herself between Miriam's legs, facing the beautiful sight of Miriam's nakedness. They had not taken the time to turn off the lights, so she had a full view of Miriam. Just a few licks of Miriam's private parts, and they were fully engaged in making love. Deborah moved her lips and tongue rapidly as Miriam called out loudly.

Deborah rolled on to the lush carpet, inviting Miriam to join her. They turned towards each other's pleasure spots, and as Miriam joined Deborah in lapping up the flowing juices, they both writhed in pleasure. Neither were ready to stop, and they reached the peak of climax over and over.

They repositioned themselves so they were lying face-to-face, licking their tasty lips, wet from each other's excitement. Suddenly they realized they were naked on the parlor floor and could be caught. They hastily grabbed their clothes and rushed upstairs.

Although they intended to fall asleep after such intense satisfaction, once in bed, they began again. The excitement of forbidden love in the parlor in an empty house fueled their passion. The sounds of the fireworks cracking in the distance added to the thrill of the evening.

They fell partially asleep, waking each time a new boom startled one of them. Once the fireworks concluded, they dressed, ready for their girls to return. This had been a memorable Fourth of July celebration.

∾ ∾ ∾

The next day, as everyone discussed the fun activities of July 4, Deborah and Miriam averted their eyes and avoided each other's glances. Inside, they were smiling.

At the end of the day, Roger came to pick up Rachel. "Miriam and Deborah, thank you so much for letting me celebrate the holiday with Sylvia and Ida. I miss being around children, so it was a treat for me."

"I'm glad you enjoyed them. When have you spent time with children?" Miriam asked.

"I lived with my aunt and her young children before moving here to attend college and live with my ailing grandmother."

Deborah and Miriam listened intently, noticing the children squealed when they caught glimpses of him. He pulled them both into his arms at once as they delighted in his attention.

Deborah whispered to Miriam, "I guess I shouldn't have been so worried about him."

Miriam smiled in response.

❧ ❧ ❧

Nestled in their wingback chairs that evening, Deborah said, "Rachel found an impressive young man."

Miriam nodded. "A college student who likes children. How nice."

"I worried that she was jumping into another relationship too quickly, yet now I can see why she's so enamored with Roger. He might be as sweet as she is."

"I agree."

After a short pause, Deborah brought up the race riots again. "Yesterday's disturbance in Saint Louis distressed me. It sounds like a war in our homeland. I've no understanding of why there's so much hatred towards Negroes."

"I don't understand either. The only Colored people I've met are the Southerners at Denison House, and they're all very nice people. I'm so glad I've gotten to meet folks of different backgrounds at my volunteer work," Miriam said.

"I remember meeting with that little girl, Cleo, who was living there. She told me about her life when her father was a sharecropper in the South. Then I read about the riots and realized that the hatred is much more extensive than I thought."

"We shouldn't be surprised by discrimination. After all, we're Jewish, a group that's faced prejudice for centuries."

"That doesn't make it right."

❧ ❧ ❧

Arriving home from work a week later, Deborah opened and read another letter from Fanny. "There's reason to be concerned about Fanny's safety."

Miriam's eyebrows raised. "Is she being sent somewhere near combat? Women are usually kept away from the front lines unless they're nurses, which she isn't. I thought Fanny was at the Naval Aircraft Factory in Pennsylvania. Oh no, has she gotten the influenza that traveled through Philadelphia?"

"Calm your thoughts, Miriam. No, she isn't on the front lines, and she hasn't gotten the grippe. The risks to her are because of her acquaintance with Rina."

"Oh no, have they been caught together? I wouldn't be surprised at all if they were now a couple like us. Yet Fanny might not know enough to protect herself from criticism for being with a girl."

Deborah shook her head. "You don't have much faith in the dear gal. Yes, it appears they are together. She knows enough to be careful; however, someone may have told on her. She doesn't know what will become of her because of what they called unnatural behavior."

"Unnatural behavior? Is that what they call two women together? Can she be thrown out of the navy? That's awful."

"Slow down. I don't have any answers for you. And she's not even certain that she's been found out. Here, read her letter."

> *July 6, 1918*
> *Dear Deborah and Miriam,*
> *I'm beside myself with anguish. Over the July 4 holiday, Rina and I had some time off together and went into the city to celebrate. I'm certain you've figured out by now that Rina and I care for each other a great deal; we're really smitten.*
>
> *We took a room at the downtown St. James Hotel so we could enjoy the festivities the city offered for Uncle Sam's birthday. The Naval Aircraft Factory is planning a huge float for the parade in downtown Philadelphia in September, but not for this holiday.*
>
> *Rina and I, as usual, were very careful, and our behavior was beyond reproach. I must admit, though, that we had a bit too much to drink, and we were a little tipsy when we headed back to our room. We didn't notice a group of naval officers leaving the hotel bar as we walked through the lobby. We were leaning on one another, and Rina may have planted a small, innocent kiss on my ear as we held each other upright. One of the officers walked up to us and offered to help us get a taxicab back to the naval base. Rina giggled and told him we were staying at the hotel.*
>
> *The officer said nothing, but the look on his face gave away his astonishment. He went back to the others, and I have no idea what he said to them. I don't even know if he reported us, or whether we'll be called in for our behavior.*

I'm really scared. Can they throw us out of the navy? Can
they put us in jail? Could this be the end of our careers?
What might happen to us?
Love, Fanny

"Now what?" Miriam asked after Deborah had finished reading.

"What might happen if they were reported? I don't know. What would they do to two women together, and would a kiss be considered offensive behavior? I doubt it."

"Well, that's a change of heart for someone who almost threw me out of her life because of one small kiss. Did you forget that?" Miriam said.

"I would never forget that, nor would I forgive you for kissing Sadie. You almost ruined our relationship because of your attraction to her."

Miriam blushed. "I'm ashamed at what I did, but that's not the topic right now. Fanny is."

"Oh my, how convenient to change the subject back to Fanny when I mention your infidelity with Sadie."

"I wasn't unfaithful. It was just one kiss, and I pushed her away," Miriam said as she stood her ground.

"I hope it was just one kiss. Yet I agree. We should get back to the discussion at hand."

"What if they throw Fanny out of the navy? Or worse, what if they charge her with indecent behavior?"

"I'll get as much information as I can."

"And where do you plan to go to get the information? Are you going to tell Mrs. Holt, your friend the librarian, that you and your niece are both lesbians, and you want to know what would happen if they were caught? Maybe she wouldn't help you anymore if she thought you a pervert."

"Miriam, I can't believe you said that. No, she would not treat us or Fanny that way. She's surprisingly accepting of the way we live."

"She knows about us? You told her?" Miriam stared directly into Deborah's eyes.

"I didn't exactly tell her, though she knows we live together, and we have two daughters and no husbands. I assume she's made some reasonable deductions."

"Very interesting. You say I've nothing to worry about regarding this librarian; however, somehow she knows your most intimate secrets."

202

"How did this conversation get on this track? I thought we were discussing Fanny," Deborah asked.

"I'll drop the subject for now. Though, as you always say, we'll get back to this at another time."

๑ ๑ ๑

Miriam wrote back to Fanny, offering her support yet providing no suggestions. She worried about Fanny's well-being but felt helpless to solve her problem.

Deborah, as planned, turned to Mrs. Holt. "Miriam, I just got back from the Boston Public Library. I learned about the Articles of War of 1916. I'll read to you from my notes: 'Intent to commit sodomy is an offense punishable by five years in prison.'"

"What is sodomy?" Miriam asked while folding the children's laundry.

"I didn't know what it was until the librarian tried to explain. It has something to do with 'unnatural acts.' That term covers intimacy with someone of the same sex or with animals."

"Animals? Ewwwww. I don't want to learn about that." Miriam snickered.

"Me either."

Miriam asked, "Does that mean that Fanny could go to jail?"

"I guess so, though it's unlikely. Mrs. Holt said rules about homosexual behavior typically just apply to men. The military believes there's no such thing as immoral women who seek each other out sexually."

"That is good news for Fanny."

"Yes, it is, yet I find it amazing there's no acknowledgment that women are capable of loving one another or that women have any sexual urges. Men assume us chaste, except when they want us in bed."

"This discussion goes far beyond my understanding. I don't understand men at all, and I'd rather they keep their minds off us women," Miriam said.

"Agreed, though in this instance, it may prove beneficial for young Fanny."

"I wouldn't want to see her chastised or jailed. And I can't imagine what she'd say to her mother if she were thrown out of the navy," Miriam said, concerned.

"She's hasn't told her parents about her relationship with Rina?" Deborah asked.

"I hadn't considered that until just now. I have no idea. The Berkowitzes have been incredibly accepting of us, so I doubt they'd reject Fanny."

"I wonder about that," said Deborah, looking quizzical. "It is one thing to approve of us, but an entirely different matter to approve of their own daughter as a lesbian."

"Might they blame us for leading her astray?" Miriam asked.

"Goodness, I hope not. Though maybe. Although we never encouraged her, maybe watching how well our lives work made it seem a possibility."

"I never had a conversation with Fanny about us being together. Did you?"

"No, though it is obvious to anyone living with us, as she has. I wonder if we should bring this up with Mrs. B.," Deborah said.

"I don't want to tell her that her daughter is a lesbian. If it comes up in conversation, however, I'd be happy to discuss it."

"Miriam, sometimes you are so innocent. I can't imagine this ever coming up in conversation. We've never really talked about this topic with Mrs. B., except when our parents first rejected us. She supported us then."

"We were certainly unsettled. We didn't have any words yet to describe our relationship, though it was obvious we were in love."

"And we still are," said Deborah with a smile. She grabbed Miriam tightly and kissed her passionately. "Want some loving now?"

"We have so much to do. And the children are still awake."

"Excuses, excuses. Later this evening, I plan to entice you to change your mind."

"Is that a promise?"

&∼ &∼ &∼

Deborah and Miriam were relieved to receive another letter from Fanny, who stated that no trouble had come from her July 4 fears, though she was annoyed with Rina for her moment of indiscretion. Fanny threatened to never drink again if her girlfriend couldn't behave appropriately. That comment made Miriam wonder if these two young women had taken to drinking regularly.[27]

∾ ∾ ∾

A week later, a letter from Grace arrived. Susan opened it first and gathered Helen, Deborah, and Miriam to hear Grace's exciting news.

> *July 15, 1918*
> *Susan and Helen,*
> *I've just been awarded a Distinguished Service Medal!!!*
> *This is a military honor bestowed by the United States*
> *Army, and I am overwhelmed. President Wilson honored*
> *me with this, even though I am not actually considered a*
> *member of the armed forces. I have never felt so much pride!*
> *The citation says:*
>
>> The President of the United States of America, authorized by Act of Congress, July 9, 1918, takes pleasure in presenting the Army Distinguished Service Medal to Chief Operator Grace D. Banker, United States Army, for exceptionally meritorious and distinguished services to the Government of the United States, in a duty of great responsibility during World War I. Chief Operator Banker served with exceptional ability as Chief Operator in the Signal Corps exchange at General Headquarters, American Expeditionary Forces, and later in a similar capacity at 1st Army Headquarters. By untiring devotion to her exacting duties under trying conditions, she did much to assure the success of the telephone service during the operations of the 1st Army against the St. Michel salient and to the north of Verdun.
>
> *Isn't this exciting?*
> *Yours Truly,*
> *Grace*

---

[27] The Articles of War of 1916 included Article 93, the first ban on male homosexuals serving in the military. Effeminate men were excluded from serving and "sexual psychopaths," the military term for homosexuals, were discharged. In enforcing this article, there was little consistency between military branches, yet those caught "in the act" were usually court-martialed, given a two-year prison sentence, and dishonorable discharge.

The four of them were excited, proud for their friend, and pleased she'd been acknowledged for her service. Yet, closer to home, they were preoccupied with a staffing issue for their business. They called Mrs. B. to discuss Marjorie's pregnancy and to get her opinion regarding whether they should allow her to keep working. Marjorie, in her fifth month, was feeling well, and there were no stairs in the office to inhibit the safety of a woman in her condition. Marjorie needed more time to train Leah, who was going to take over for her after the baby was born.

Marjorie's belly was swelling more each day, and she could no longer hide it. People did not look with favor upon pregnant women out in public, never mind a pregnant employee. They agreed to sequester Marjorie in the back room, so customers would not see her, though an even more troublesome problem involved Marjorie's clothing. Deborah worried she would pop right out of her work dress one day.

Mrs. B. had an opinion and a potential solution. "I think you should let Marjorie work as long as she wants. You're probably wise to drive her in early and have her stay in the back office, so customers won't complain. Yet I have an idea about her clothing. My friend has a cousin who's making quite a name for herself by sewing clothing for women in her state. Her cousin, Lena Maslin, is quite a seamstress and is selling clothing for expectant mothers in a shop in Chicago and also through the mail. I'd be willing to order a dress for Marjorie to wear."

"You're such a dear. How do you always have a solution for every problem?" Miriam said.

"I'm just fortunate to know about this company from my friend. They've advertised in the *New York Herald* for several years, breaking with the tradition of keeping pregnancies hidden from the public. I'll send you one of their catalogs, and you can have Marjorie pick out a dress."

"That's very sweet of you, Mrs. B. It's interesting to order clothing from a catalog. I guess it's like ordering home supplies from Sears, Roebuck," Deborah said.

"There's actually a funny story that goes along with the company name. Her cousin Lena was married to a Mr. Bryant, who died several years ago. When she went to get a bank loan to expand her business, they misread her name on the loan application. She kept the mistaken name for her business. Instead of Lena Bryant, the company was named Lane Bryant. Her second husband, Albert Maslin, is quite a businessman, and he helped her expand sales. The day of her first advertisement for maternity clothing, she sold all her stock, so he suggested selling through a catalog, a creative idea."

Miriam smiled. "I'm certain Marjorie will be pleased to have something to wear that won't squeeze her so tightly. Each day, she must be more uncomfortable in her current clothes. And thanks for your help with our decision about keeping her at work. This might be the most outrageous thing we've done in the office. I hope no one's upset."[28]

Lesbians   Communications

---

[28] Lena Himmelstein, a sixteen-year-old Jewish orphan from Lithuania, arrived alone in New York. She married David Bryant, a Russian immigrant, who left her a widow with a newborn and a small business to run as a seamstress. Her second husband, Albert Maslin, with whom she had two more sons, helped her expand the business.

Pregnant women were rarely seen in public until the Bryant dresses Lena produced made that possible. Their dresses were the first commercially made maternity clothes. Their popularity allowed the Maslins to open several stores and to increase their merchandise to include plus-sized garments, another market that had never been tapped.

After Albert's death, Lena provided something unheard of at the time—employee benefits, which included health insurance, disability insurance, pensions, and profit sharing. Following World War II, Lane Bryant stores became distribution centers for needy families, including Holocaust survivors. By 1923, company sales reached $5,000,000 annually. Lane Bryant, Inc. became the largest plus-size retailer in the United States. It remains in business to this day.

Episode 20 ✳ *Second Wave of Flu*
August 1918

"The headline story of the *Boston Globe* really scares me," Miriam said one morning in mid-August.

"Let me see," Deborah said, reaching across the breakfast table and grabbing at the paper.

"I'm reading, Deborah. Let me finish, please!"

"All right. Tell me what's upset you."

"Lately, the news has been so positive. The grippe has almost disappeared, and all of Boston seems excited that the Red Sox will soon be in their fifth World Series."

"Yes…"

"Well, we've been too optimistic. The influenza is back and is worse than before. Many folks at the docks have become sick." Miriam sighed.

"What docks?"

"The Boston docks—Commonwealth Pier, not far from our shop. There's a new, more virulent strain of the influenza. This one is killing many people…and very fast."

"That's awful! And you predicted this."

"I never expected Boston to be the center of this disease. It seems the new virus started here, affecting many of the twenty thousand soldiers stationed in Boston and spreading to the soldiers at Fort Devens."

"Fort Devens?" asked Deborah. "Isn't that thirty miles away?"

"Yes, though some of the soldiers who were sick at the docks probably brought it there. Within two weeks, there were two hundred sick soldiers and at least two dozen dead at the army installation."

"What are they doing to stop the spread?"

Miriam sighed as she read more. "They moved twenty-five hundred healthy soldiers to Framingham, an hour away. They stopped two hundred soldiers bound for the South, hoping to keep them from spreading it. It's not worked. The paper says that civilians are starting to get it."

"I'm not surprised. It was probably impossible to keep the soldiers locked away."[29]

❧ ❧ ❧

---

[29] Within a few weeks, the second wave of influenza in Boston reached epidemic proportions. The public health commissioner urged everyone to stay at home and avoid crowds. There were disagreements regarding whether to close the schools, with some people arguing the children would be safer at school where nurses could monitor them.

Mildred was crying as she ran into the house. "Leah has the influenza."

"Oh no, have you been exposed?" asked Miriam.

"I don't know. Will she die?" thirteen-year-old Mildred asked.

"You wait right here while I get Susan or Helen."

"How do you feel?" asked Helen as she entered the room.

"I'm fine, but my friend Leah is sick. Will she die?"

"I certainly hope not. When were you with her last?"

"I didn't see her yesterday because her little brother was sick, so her mother wouldn't let me into their house. And she didn't come to work at the printing shop because she wasn't feeling well."

"That's a relief. We need to protect everyone from you in case you were exposed. Come upstairs. You need to stay in your room until we're certain you didn't get it. Sick people need to quarantine."

"You won't come upstairs with me?" cried Mildred. "I don't want to be alone."

"I'll come up, yet no one else will," Helen explained.

"Not even Susan?"

"For now, no one. We must keep you isolated from everyone."

"I'll starve to death."

"No, honey," said Miriam, "I'll make certain you get food. We'll bring it up to your room."

"You can't come upstairs."

"No, I can't. I'll send it up with Susan, who can drop it outside your door. Now scoot upstairs."

Mildred started towards her room, but Miriam stopped her. "How's the rest of Leah's family?"

Mildred didn't know because she wasn't allowed inside.

Miriam took in a very big gulp of air. "Now go upstairs. We'll keep you and everyone else safe."

"I'm scared about Leah, and I hope I won't die."

"No, Mildred, you won't die." Miriam hoped her words were true.

Susan joined them a few minutes later, and Helen caught her up on the situation. "I will stay in the other bedroom on the third floor to be near Mildred. You can come up to deliver food and to empty their chamber pots."

"Your decision's a good one," Miriam said. "You need to keep her away from everyone, especially the other children, until we know if she is sick."

"This could happen to any of us. Although Leah was not at work yesterday, she was there the day before, and maybe she was already sick," Susan said.

"This is such a scary disease," said Miriam, a sentence she had repeated often this week. "I'll go to Leah's house to see if they need anything."

"Be careful. Don't get sick," Susan warned.

"I'll stay outside and talk through the open window."

Deborah arrived home while Miriam was next door. After Susan explained what happened, Deborah said, "I'm upset she went next door where she might expose herself."

"She promised to stay a safe distance away and just talk to them from outside. She's a good friend and neighbor."

"Yes, that's just like my Miriam, always worrying about someone else. That's one of the things I love about her."

Miriam arrived home sobbing. "Their little baby just died. Neither Leah nor her brother are deathly ill, although the baby caught it and quickly turned blue and died. They want me to get the doctor, yet I doubt he'll go into the house. They need an undertaker."

"The doctor won't go inside? That's horrible," Deborah said forcefully.

"He's old, and it's the old and the young who die first."

"That's not what I heard about this illness. Though that is usually the case, the largest group of sick people with this disease are healthy, young soldiers. This influenza seems to attack anyone," said Deborah.

"Then maybe the doctor will go in, after all. Or maybe the public-health nurse. I'll walk down the street and see if she's visiting the family a few houses away, as she's been doing the last couple of days."

"Maybe that's how Leah got it. It has come into our neighborhood." Deborah shook her head and said, "I don't want you leaving the house. The telephone is a better way to communicate. We'll spend the money to make phone calls instead of risking our lives."

"Good plan. After I call the doctor, I'll call Hannah and William. I'll tell them that none of us will be at work for a few days, and we think they should close the office due to the increase in cases of the grippe."

"And after Hannah, please call Marjorie to tell her that she and Micah shouldn't go out, especially in Marjorie's delicate condition. She can also tell Rachel not to come here and her sister, Rebecca, not to go to the office."

"This is all so complicated. I really hope we can stay safe."

"But Rachel already arrived," Deborah said, noticing their baby-sitter coming up the walk. "It's very early for her. I'll talk with her outside and tell her the situation. You make your phone calls, and then we should all stay home for a couple of days and hope the rest of us don't catch it."

After talking with Rachel, who stood several feet away, Deborah had more news. "Because she does not have a telephone, Rachel came to tell us she couldn't be with us for a few days. Roger may have been exposed to the influenza from someone at the stables. Though not feeling sick, he's taking precautions and not leaving his house. Rachel, likewise, has decided to stay away until it's clear they aren't ill."

"I hope they don't have it. Roger's been playing with the girls when he picks up Rachel each afternoon. It's lovely that she's seeing so much of him, yet it's another avenue for this disease to enter our home."

Deborah sent Rachel home, along with her mother, who had just arrived to prepare breakfast. Miriam offered to cook for the family for the next few days. Deborah said she'd watch Sylvia and Ida. Susan and Helen dusted the house and did laundry for all. Sylvia was pleased that the whole family was home, but she sensed the anxiety all around her. Everyone talked repeatedly about their hopes that no one else caught the influenza.

Without Mrs. Stern to go to the kosher market, the group had to figure out how to get food. They all agreed to eat whatever they could get safely. After they planned meals based on foods which wouldn't spoil, Deborah went to the outside stalls to pick up some items. Upon Deborah's return, everyone helped with the groceries because she'd gathered more than on a typical grocery trip.

Miriam noticed Deborah's countenance had dimmed, but she waited until the task was complete before asking what happened.

Deborah said, "I'm not surprised you noticed my mood shift. It was quite overwhelming to be out there in the community. I was quite scared to be around other people. Also, I noticed different merchants manning the stalls, so I assumed the virus had struck some of the people we know. Then I learned the fishmonger died."

"This illness is taking many wonderful people."

࿊ ࿊ ࿊

After three healthy days at home, Deborah declared that their household was safe. Mildred was allowed downstairs, though she couldn't see Leah.

None of them knew how she was because the family had no phone. Mildred was very worried about her friend and couldn't be consoled.

Finally, Susan went down the street and came back with good news. Leah and her brother were feeling better, and no one else had contracted the dreaded influenza. They were all incredibly sad about the baby's death. Mildred asked repeatedly when she could see her friend, but no one had an answer.

The shop remained closed, as did most businesses in Boston. The government closed the Museum of Fine Arts, the Boston Public Library, bars, barbershops, and theaters. Schools remained open until the flu was contracted by fifty children and attendance had dropped by 40 percent. After four children died, the Boston School Committee finally closed the schools.

"Lieutenant Governor Calvin Coolidge has taken such an active role in keeping us safe, despite the schools' reopening," said Deborah.

"He sees this as a serious health crisis, and he's encouraging people to be very careful," Miriam agreed.

"And," Deborah added, "there are now fines against coughing, spitting, and kissing in public. And the funny one—a fine for being a big talker, meaning someone who talks loudly."

"That's funny. I would guess that loud talking is assumed to cause more spitting. I don't understand why there's no rule about wearing masks. I thought they help people keep from spreading the grippe."

"I've read many articles in the *Globe* about masks. Some people believe they help. Others don't. Even the politicians are divided."

"Sometimes I don't understand politics. It seems to get in the way of good sense," said Miriam.

"And I just read they're considering allowing businesses to reopen. If there's one more day of under one hundred deaths, they've decided it will be safe to open things back up."

"Two days out of three with under one hundred deaths does not seem to be a good guideline."

"I agree. We should keep the shop closed a while longer." Deborah offered to call Hannah and William and discuss this with them, though she had no intention of going back to work yet, even if they did. Luckily, they agreed to at least another week of closure.

Deborah was sad to lose business, but she was enjoying this break from the intensity of work even though she worried about how they would ever catch up. Everything had slowed down due to the illness which was wreaking havoc with their city.

Eventually, Rachel and Mrs. Stern returned to work, which made things appear close to normal.

"This has been a tough time," Miriam said before bed one night. "It's been hard isolating ourselves from everyone. I miss my sister and our friends, and I miss going to shul. I also worry about the people at Denison House. I've not been there for weeks, so I have no idea how they're doing and whether the influenza has hit them hard."

"I feel sad for others who don't have what we have," Deborah said. "We have enough food and a good home, and our daughters and friends are with us during this quarantine."

"You're right. I shouldn't complain. I've been feeling bad for myself, and that's really selfish."

"It's a pretty common reaction, I assume. It is difficult to give up our normal lives, even if just for a limited time. Yet I feel that we're doing everything we can to avoid this dreaded disease."

"I'm so glad I have you in my life. I can't imagine being isolated with anyone but you. I love you, Deborah."

"And I love you, my Miriam. We always manage to get through these difficult times."

All the adults gathered while awaiting dinner. Discussing the influenza was their most common pastime.

"Remember how I told you that people who were taking large doses of Bayer Aspirin were getting sicker?" Miriam asked Deborah over dinner one evening.

"I remember that vaguely. Why?"

"Well, I just heard another rumor about Bayer Aspirin. This time I read that some people believe the Bayer company is putting the virus into its medication to make people sick."

"Why would they do that?" asked Deborah, completely baffled.

"The rumor is that Bayer is a German company, and folks want to blame Germany for everything. People come up with the most incredible tales."

"I have another German tale," said Susan.

"I can't wait to hear," Deborah stated, expecting something unreasonable.

"I heard that two vials of the virus were carried into Boston Harbor by a ship that some suspect came from Germany. They planned to take the vials into highly populated areas like the sites of war-bond rallies or movie theaters."

"Such ridiculous stories," Helen said. "Who thinks up such outlandish things?"

"I assume," said Deborah, "that everyone is going crazy because of fear. I heard that off the coast of Cape Cod, German U-boats sank ships; those rumors increased everyone's fear."

"And also," Helen interjected, "folks are crazy from sadness, having lost so many friends and family members to war and disease. It's a terrible time."

They all nodded, unsure where the rumors had come from, yet in agreement these unprecedented conditions were affecting everyone.

Meanwhile, the printing business remained closed, and everyone stayed home.

෴ ෴ ෴

Discussions continued as predictions grew more dire each day.

"This illness seems to be sweeping the world," Deborah said as she read the morning paper. Each day, the news included descriptions of how other countries were suffering from this illness. "We are not alone in our rising infection rate."

Miriam's response was unsurprising. "I'm worried about what is happening here. I read that burying the dead is a serious problem because there are so many. Cold-storage buildings have been used as temporary morgues and packing crates as coffins. Funeral parlors are overwhelmed; five hundred corpses are awaiting burial. The worst part is that some people have to dig graves for their own family members. It's horrifying."

"I don't think there is a *worst* part. It's all pretty terrible."[30]

---

[30] The second wave of the virus was highly contagious. Victims died within hours or days of developing symptoms. Their skin turned blue as their lungs filled with fluid, causing them to suffocate. By mid-September a proclamation called for everyone with medical training to report for duty since many health professionals were sick or on active military duty. Over half of Boston's nurses contracted the illness, and within a few weeks, thousands in the Boston area were infected. It was a bleak situation. By late September, there were approximately 150,000 cases of influenza in Massachusetts. The

only way to track new cases was by residents of the city calling in or sending letters to let officials know who was sick. According to this reported information, about 850 Bostonians had died. No one knew what the real numbers were.

Finally, on September 25, the Boston public schools were converted into emergency hospitals. Patients filled every available hospital bed. Churches, temples, and theaters were closed. Camp Devens, an army base, was filled with the first group of soldiers who contracted the grippe. They repurposed a building on-site as a hospital for 2,000 afflicted with the flu, yet they had 6,000 sick men. There were one hundred deaths per day.

In October, the Boston Health Department mandated that everyone report all those sick with influenza, and folks were shocked to learn 3,500 Bostonians had perished. They placed signs around the city, telling people that coughing, sneezing, and talking in crowds was increasing the number of sick people. The city restricted business hours, hoping to reduce the number of people on public transportation, though this didn't help. Businesses returned to their normal schedules, and warnings went unheeded. Huge crowds of bored people returned to theaters when they reopened, sometimes for standing-room-only tickets. By the end of October, almost 5,000 Bostonians had perished, making Boston one of the worst-hit cities. October 2018 was the month with the highest fatality rate.

Things were out of hand. Between September and November, this second wave of the influenza peaked, resulting in the greatest number of deaths during this pandemic. Most hospital beds were filled by influenza patients, and there was a serious lack of doctors and nurses. Even some private homes were converted into makeshift hospitals, some staffed by medical students. Lieutenant Governor Coolidge wrote to President Wilson, asking for help in obtaining medical care from other states. These two men, along with Boston Mayor Andrew Peters, were influential in helping Massachusetts gain control over the epidemic.

By Thanksgiving there was a rise in influenza cases as people gathered to celebrate the end of the war. As Boston's epidemic was waning, a navy ship from Boston docked in Philadelphia, bringing the first case to that city. The next day, 600 sailors were diagnosed with the flu. To celebrate the end of the war, Philadelphia ignored the new cases and held a victory parade on September 12, with a crowd of over 200,000 people. By the next week, 2,600 had died. Over the next month, hundreds of thousands of Philadelphia residents became sick, and almost 11,000 died. Philadelphia had become the center of illness.

It was three weeks before Pittsburgh had any cases of the virus, and Saint Louis, which canceled its end-of-war parade, experienced under 700 deaths.

The influenza traveled to places outside of Boston and Pennsylvania. Ford Motor Company in Michigan claimed that over 1,000 of its workers were sick, and one-fourth of the prisoners at San Quentin State Prison in California were ill. Chicago and many other cities closed theaters and schools and prohibited public gatherings. San

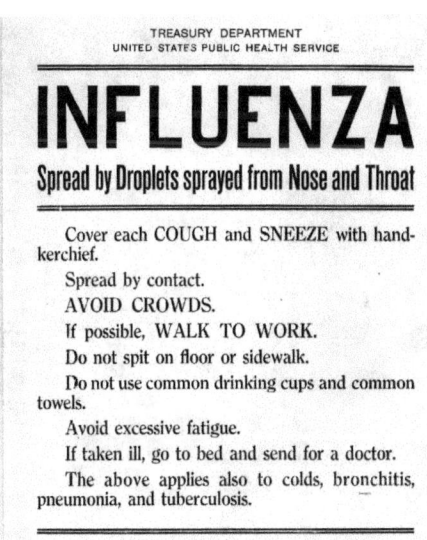

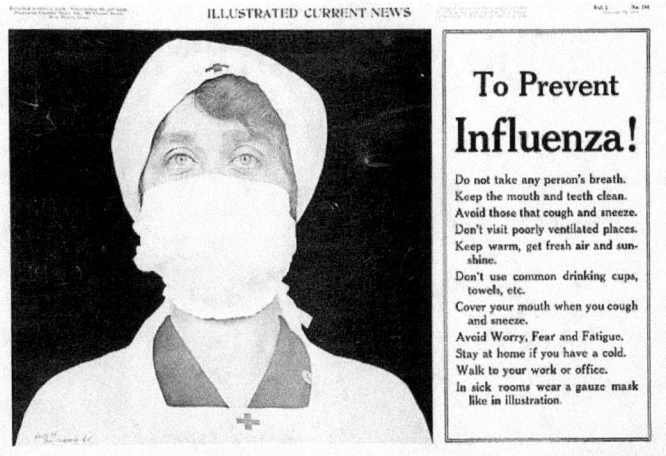

Francisco's Board of Health required any person serving the public to wear a mask, and New York City reported a 40-percent decline in shipyard productivity.

One unusual aspect of this flu was that it struck down many previously healthy, young people, such as servicemen and those usually resistant to this type of infectious illness. Forty percent of the US Navy and over thirty percent of the US Army became ill. Very few locations remained unscathed; 84,000 American soldiers traveled overseas, carrying the flu with them. Spain, which was initially blamed for the flu, saw 8,000,000 infected, including King Alfonso XIII. The British Army had to put off attacks because with so many sick, it was hard to fight. Half of British troops and 75 percent of the French military were infected. China seemed less affected than other countries, which led some to believe that it had been the country of origin. The draft was canceled, and in 1918, the average life expectancy in America plummeted by a dozen years.

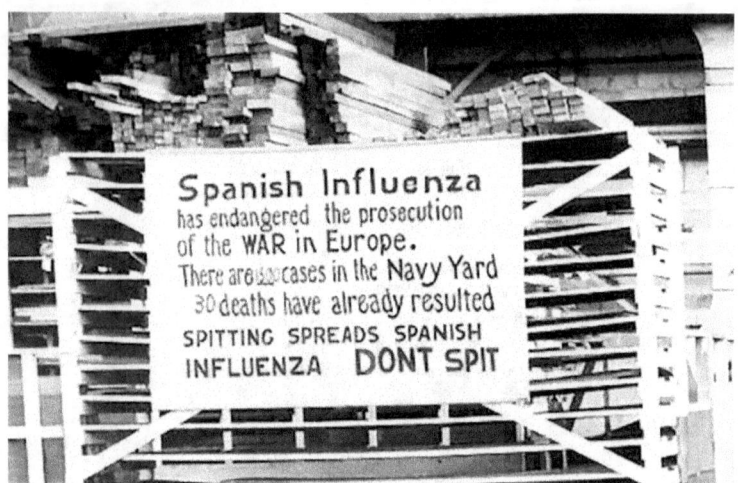

Spanish Influenza Navy Yard

1918 Influenza Poster

Episode 21 ❧ *Women's Land Army*
September 1918

Due to fears of the influenza, Deborah did not travel for the High Holidays. She worried about catching the disease from train travelers. Susan and Helen also decided to remain in Roxbury rather than visit their families. Marjorie decided not to return to work, protecting her unborn child from the dreaded illness. Both Leah and Mildred were banned from the office despite their pleas. Worries about catching the flu were affecting every aspect of life.

Miriam was worried about being in shul for many hours, yet she could not imagine missing Rosh Hashanah services. She and Deborah attended, though the parishioners in attendance were much fewer than usual. They wore masks, sat with people they knew who were being careful about exposure, and went outside for breaks quite often. They left the children at home with Rachel and used the girls as an excuse to leave services early.

They treated Yom Kippur similarly, with reduced hours in temple and frequent breaks in the fresh air. Though they had never before been alone for this meal, they did not gather with others to break the fast at the end of the holiday. Everything felt very different, and they wondered when normal life would return.

❧ ❧ ❧

On September 12, Susan and Helen came downstairs early to read the morning paper. Even though the paper was of reduced size, they knew it would contain the results of the final game of the World Series, the Boston Red Sox versus the Chicago Cubs. Each morning over the past week, they had rushed to read about the previous day's game. The scores were impossibly low because over two hundred professional baseball players were at war, and the stands were relatively empty because many people feared gathering during the epidemic.

"We won!" Susan yelled, bringing everyone quickly to breakfast. "We beat the Cubs!"

Helen smiled broadly, and the others feigned interest. "This whole series was unusual. There were only nine runs for all the games, combined, and no home runs."

"And this was a five-out-of-five win," Susan exclaimed.

"What does that mean?" asked Miriam.

"It means that the Red Sox have won all five times they've played in a World Series. An impressive record."

"Great," Deborah said, clearly not caring about baseball.

❧ ❧ ❧

"My sister just got home from her summer job as a farmerette," Esther said as she and Chava sat in the parlor with their friends on a crisp fall Sunday afternoon. These were the only friends Deborah and Miriam allowed to visit during this time of illness.

"A what?" Deborah asked, wrapping her shawl around her shoulders.

"A farmerette. I'm certain I told you of my sister's experience."

"No," Deborah snipped. "Do the rest of you know what she's talking about?"

Miriam, Susan, and Helen shook their heads.

Chava, a bit defensive of her girlfriend, said, "I'm sure she explained this to you."

"I've never heard the term," Deborah said, staring at Chava.

"What about the Women's Land Army? Do you remember hearing of that?" Chava asked.

"No. Another term I never heard of."

"Deborah, stop and let her speak," Miriam said.

Deborah sat back, folding her hands in her lap and imitating a well-behaved schoolgirl awaiting her lessons. Miriam shook her head.

"Do you want the short version?" Esther asked.

Miriam looked at Deborah, who was quietly twiddling her thumbs.

Susan spoke up, "I'm very interested. I've heard something of the Women's Land Army, and I'd love to hear all about it."

Esther sat up and began, "Last spring, after her junior year, my sister, Naomi, enrolled in a special program offered by Smith College. Her college, along with several other girls' schools, wanted to help alleviate the impending food shortage when farmers went off to war. Women were suddenly tasked with running their family's farms despite their limited experience with planting and harvesting crops."

As they sat back, Esther explained that her sister had reported to a training program in Chicopee, Massachusetts, where she and eleven other girls were given uniforms and put to work. There, they were taught how to prepare the soil for the summer crops and how to milk cows. They also learned about the challenges of weather, pests, and heavy equipment.

"They did this dirty work in uniforms?" Miriam asked.

"Their uniforms were coveralls, not dresses."

"They had to wear pants?" Miriam said, shocked.

"Yes, farmwork is difficult and very messy," Esther said. "My sister said she never worked so hard."

"Where did she live?" Miriam asked.

"Local families took in the farmerettes as a way to contribute to the war effort."

"I want to hear more about what they did," Deborah interjected. "I'm not really interested in what they wore or where they stayed."

"Deborah, some of us are interested in those details. You need to be patient and listen to the whole story." Miriam sighed deeply, then turned her attention back to Esther. "What if we invite Naomi to tell us about her experience?"

"That's a good plan," Helen said.

"Is it wise to have her here? Has she kept safe?" asked Deborah.

Esther explained that her sister had not gone anywhere since getting home. If she had been exposed to the grippe while on the farm, she would have been sick by now. Deborah was soothed, and they agreed to have her to dinner the next Sunday if she promised to stay away from others until then.

"And I'm going to the library to learn more facts about this program," Deborah announced, pleased the library was open.

"Please keep safe when you go there, Deborah. I'll look forward to your lecture," Miriam said.

Everyone smiled.[31]

❧ ❧ ❧

---

[31] When the war broke out in Europe, Britain acknowledged that there were few men to run farms after many were recruited into the service and others moved to better-paying positions in the defense industry. Training programs were established to equip young women to do agricultural work. Most of the farmerettes, as they were called, were educated and from wealthy families. Girls with farm experience were sent directly to farms, and the rest were subjected to physical assessments and medical exams. If accepted for a rigorous four-week training period, they were assigned to a farm. Over 10,000 college students, teachers, and secretaries were recruited to attend agricultural camps.

After her library visit, Deborah gathered her friends in the parlor; she withheld information from everyone, including Miriam, until they were seated.

"The most fascinating thing I found when I was searching for information about the Women's Land Army was from an article written by Professor Hubbard in the *New Republic,* a magazine I'd never read before."

"Is she the professor from Barnard College who's been helping you get your articles published?" Helen asked.

"The very same," Deborah said with wide eyes. "I'm impressed with Dr. Hubbard's article outlining the efforts of the women's colleges during the war. She compared this program to that of the young men volunteering for the US Ambulance Corps. She cites Barnard College as one of the most influential schools in the training for women."

"I'm impressed with our school's efforts," Susan said as Helen nodded in agreement.

"Dr. Hubbard wrote of many programs, such as the summer training camp for nurses, developed by the Vassar alumnae. Let me read you what she wrote: 'Never in the world has any woman been so wanted as the trained nurse is wanted now.'"

"I'm proud to be a nurse," Chava said, smiling broadly.

"Your professor is certainly an interesting woman," said Susan.

"I'm really proud to know her."

Helen interrupted, "Can you tell us what you learned about the Women's Land Army program at Smith College, where Naomi is a student. I want to learn more before she talks with us."

Deborah began, "Well, Smith created one of the most daring of all the programs. In addition to the Women's Land Army program, Smith started a training school in psychiatric social work. The students work at Boston Psychopathic Hospital, the same place they wanted to send my mother when she had her breakdown." Deborah took in a deep breath before she resumed, "They created a team of social workers to assist shell-shocked soldiers."

"What's shell shock?" Susan asked, embarrassed not to know the term.

"Nervous disorders that come about as a result of war."

"Like Ruth's brother, David," commented Miriam.

"Yes, exactly. Dr. Hubbard believes this program will help with the rehabilitation of disabled soldiers."

"I'm still more interested in the Women's Land Army than the other programs that Dr. Hubbard wrote about. That's what started this discussion," Helen said.

"You don't want to hear the rest of what I learned?" Deborah asked.

"Deborah," Miriam interrupted, "maybe we can discuss it on our own."

And with that, Deborah stomped off.

"Sorry," said Miriam, "she can be so temperamental. I'd better go calm her down."

"Not your fault, Miriam. I'm sorry I upset her."

"I'm glad you spoke up. I felt the same way."

As soon as Miriam approached, Deborah apologized. "I don't know why I get like that. They were asking something reasonable. I shouldn't be so irritable."

"You're just eager to share. I don't blame you for being excited to find an article written by Dr. Hubbard."

"I'd better go apologize."

"That would be nice. Thank you for informing us about the Women's Land Army so that we are prepared for Naomi's visit on Sunday."[32]

                      ॐ ॐ ॐ

On Sunday, Naomi arrived with Chava and Esther. Privately, Deborah promised Miriam she wouldn't be difficult.

"It was a fabulous summer," began Naomi. "I arrived at the farm in Chicopee, where I was to be trained along with two farmerettes from Smith College. I'd not met them before. And there were ten girls from other colleges. I was really nervous because this was my first time away from home. And I'd never slept in a strange bed or eaten food that was made by someone other than my family or my school. Well, I guess I had eaten at my friends' homes, though this felt different since they were all strangers.

---

[32] Grace A. Hubbard's article in the New Republic magazine, "War and the Woman's College," went into great detail about the great impact of college women during World War I. The colleges directed women's enthusiasm and intelligence into serving the emerging needs of this country.

Hubbard wrote of Wellesley College as the first institution to form the Women's Land Army of America; the college program trained women in agricultural work. She described a professor from Smith College who created a reconstruction unit based loosely on the directives of President Lincoln after the Civil War. Units were created at Vassar, Bryn Mawr, and Barnard College, all of which sent young women to France beginning in 1917.

"When I got there, they asked me lots of questions and looked me up and down to figure out what size denim coveralls would fit me. I could hardly believe I was paying for those ugly, scratchy uniforms. They took my money and told me to choose a bed in the upstairs room. There were six of us sleeping in the same room, with very little privacy, so I wondered how I'd get dressed. I had to develop a plan quickly since they expected us to arrive for dinner in our uniforms, even though we wouldn't start working until the next day. I learned to stand with my back to everyone and to pull my clothes out from under my sweater, leaving me less exposed. I didn't look up to see if anyone was watching me, though I suspect they were busy covering themselves.

"Then I discovered there was one bathroom for the twelve of us. It was small, and there was no tub. I later learned that the bathtub was downstairs in the kitchen so the farmwife could control the use of water; she prepared one hot bath for everyone. She poured in hot water for each girl, but we all bathed in the same dirty water. We had no privacy at all, so I wondered if I'd ever be clean all summer.

"Dinner was really good, with fresh food from the farm. I ate a lot, yet I later understood why the others ate less. There were no indoor toilets on this farm. The one-hole outhouse meant that twelve of us had to wait a long time for our turn to relieve ourselves. And no one appreciated the pungent smell."

Deborah bit her tongue, dug her fingernails deep into her palms, and did what she could to distract herself during Naomi's too-detailed description of her experience.

"One of the hardest tasks was to dig long, straight ditches in which to plant seeds. Mine were not straight, and I had great difficulty cutting out roots in soil that had not been tilled before. On the very first day, we all had blisters on our hands and feet, and muscles that ached all evening.

"And the other part that was hard was getting along with the other girls. The Smith College girls were nice; however, some of the others were loud or demanding. One girl arrived with only high-heeled shoes, even though we had been told to bring boys' boots to wear in the fields. The first time she wore them, she stepped into a steaming pile of dung, and we all laughed. This same girl was quite a snob, believing the work we were required to do was below her. And another girl was always teasing the farm boys who were too young for military service. Well, I assume it was just teasing.

"And we were hot all the time, and because we took infrequent baths, some of the girls were less than fragrant. I learned to take baths with dirty water in front of the others, though I never got used to it. I longed for a luxurious private bath.

"I liked working in the fields, being in the fresh air all day. It was hard for us to use the men's tools, so we were pleased when they brought us farm equipment to fit our smaller hands. Girls at Wellesley College made the tools especially for us. We learned basic chores, like how to bale the hay, which was hard work. You should have seen those snobby girls with their hair full of dried grass!"

Naomi's description of her summer went on and on with no break in her story and no opportunity to ask questions. Deborah remained quiet, yet Miriam eventually interrupted to offer more tea. When Sylvia woke from her nap, they had a perfect excuse to stop. They were happy to thank Naomi for the information and send her on her way.

"That was exhausting," Deborah said when Naomi left.

"Much of it was interesting," Helen said. "Though she did go on and on. I wonder why a young college woman would willingly live under such conditions."

As they retired to their own bedrooms, the two couples continued the conversation, marveling at the new roles that women had assumed during wartime. It seemed a very good thing.[33]

≫ ≫ ≫

Over dinner the day after Naomi's visit, the work of the college girls was still on everyone's minds.

Miriam said, "I feel so helpless, watching men we know go overseas, with us just sitting here doing nothing. I'm glad Rachel got me involved in preparing horses to be sent overseas, yet we should look for something else that's productive."

"What about the joke book that Susan got us involved in? That counts," Deborah said.

---

[33] The Smith College Relief Unit was organized by Harriet Boyd Hawes, a nurse from Boston, who gathered fourteen students and alumnae from Smith College and several other women's colleges. They traveled to France, where they built a library, a school, and a hospital and sold household goods. Also, they planted fruit trees, vegetables, and wheat.

Susan took a deep breath. "I'm still interested in putting my efforts toward suffrage. I don't have enough time to work towards more causes. I believe we're getting close to gaining the vote for women."

"I agree," said Helen. "The war upsets me, and the women's vote excites me. That's where I choose to put my energy."

Deborah and Miriam wanted to do more, though they had limited time and energy. They decided to put aside their interest in the Women's Land Army to focus on their business. Any extra time would be devoted to helping Susan and Helen in their efforts to gain women's right to vote.

ॐ ॐ ॐ

Rosh Hashanah began on September 17. They traveled to New York to spend the first days with Deborah's family, who were feeling the absence of Milton. They'd never celebrated the holiday without him. Deborah hoped he'd have some way to pray during this important holiday. They headed home midweek and spent Yom Kippur with Marjorie's family, as had become their custom.

ॐ ॐ ॐ

The four women in the house passed the *Boston Globe* back and forth to one another over breakfast, learning about the monumental speech President Wilson had delivered to the Senate on September 30.

Excitedly, Helen said, "In his talk, the president encouraged giving women the right to vote. The House of Representatives has already voted in favor of the nineteenth amendment, but the Senate has not yet voted on the bill."

"Though Wilson was not a supporter of women voting," Susan said, "his attitude seemed to shift after the horrible treatment of the suffragists following the Night of Terror. I'm glad that awful event had a positive effect."

"I assume Wilson's changed position," said Helen, "was less because of the cruel and unwarranted treatment of those women than because he realized his political future was at risk. His Democratic Party would lose if they did not support women's suffrage."

"I hope his words will make a significant difference towards suffrage," Miriam added.

Nodding, they all took in deep breaths and continued eating breakfast, each hoping change was coming.

They were crushed when, despite the President's impassioned speech, the bill did not pass the Senate.[34]

The month ended with a disturbing letter from Grace overseas.

> *September 25, 1918*
>
> *Dear Susan and Helen,*
>
> *I'm sorry to have been a poor correspondent. My life has been quite overwhelming, and I have been frightened. Luckily, I've survived unharmed thus far.*
>
> *The most difficult part of this assignment began on August 25 when I was assigned to the war's front line, and I had to select five girls to assist me. What a horrible decision that was! We were equipped with helmets and gas masks, and moved into the Advance Section, about ten miles from the front lines. We were at risk for air raids, though luckily too far from the spray of bullets.*
>
> *I'm fearful still, even though we've been reassigned to safer quarters. The slightest noise startles me, and I often find myself shaking for no apparent reason.*
>
> *After the worst of this assignment was over, and the six of us were returned to the rest of our group, I discovered something surprising. The girls I did not choose were envious of the ones I had selected, even though it was an extremely dangerous assignment. Their dedication to this war effort amazes me, and I am grateful to be working with them.*
>
> *Now that I am finally done with my assignment, I can tell you details about my time in France. It was difficult for me to withhold information from my friends and family at a time I was desperate for a connection with home, yet I had no choice.*
>
> *Yours Truly,*
>
> *Grace*

---

[34] In his address to the Senate about the Nineteenth Amendment, President Woodrow Wilson called women's suffrage a "vitally necessary war measure." He acknowledged that women suffered when their menfolk went to war and that the nation benefited greatly from the women's contribution to the war effort on the home front. The President's speech included the following: "We have made partners of the women in this war... Shall we admit them only to a partnership of suffering and sacrifice and toil, and not to a partnership of privilege and right? This war could not have been fought... if it had not been for the services of the women—services rendered in every sphere... I know how much stronger that heart will beat if you do this just thing and show our women that you trust them as much as you, in fact and of necessity, depend upon them" (The American Presidency Project).

That night, preparing for bed, Deborah and Miriam talked about Grace's experience. "I couldn't be so brave," said Miriam, repeating the words she stated every time they heard from Grace.

"She didn't have options," Deborah said. "Once she was there, she had to do as she was told. It sounds like she had one harrowing experience after another. I wonder how she'll do returning to civilian life. It sounds like she is still quite rattled by her experience."

"I'm glad that you'll never need to be in harm's way. I couldn't stand it if I had to worry about you every day," Miriam said.

"I feel the same way. I love you."

They talked on in a more intimate manner about their own worries. Miriam worried that Deborah might return to running away when upset, but Deborah assured her it would not happen; she was determined to be better. Deborah was concerned that Miriam would get so caught up in caring for the children that she would forget about Deborah's needs.

"Has that ever happened?" Miriam asked.

"No, not really. I know it is not a reasonable fear, though sometimes I feel less important to you than the girls are."

Miriam held her close and promised that would never be the case. No matter how immediate the children's needs were, she would always have Deborah's welfare at the center of her concerns. Deborah felt embarrassed by her insecurity, but Miriam assured her and stroked Deborah's body with great tenderness.

It was not long before they were thoroughly engaged in loving each other.

Farmerettes

Episode 22 ❧ *The Great Migration*
October 1918

"Have you noticed that lately Roger is driving Rachel to work in the morning, in addition to picking her up in the evening?" Deborah asked.

"Yes," Miriam said, "I've been wondering if he is picking her up early, or whether they've spent the night together."

"I think that might be the case. I'd be astonished and think he's taking advantage of her if I didn't know Rachel was a widow."

"Saving herself for marriage seemed important before, yet maybe it doesn't have the same significance now." Deborah's face tightened as she thought more about this. "She's already learned the joys of being a couple, so I bet she missed it."

"I would if you died."

"Miriam, what a horrible thought. I don't know why you're so obsessed with death."

"Maybe because I've faced so much loss in the past few years. My response to loss is to worry about my own death—and yours."

"I'd be devastated if I faced the same losses you have," Deborah said.

"I concentrate on keeping myself, you, and the girls safe. These are frightening times with the influenza taking so many healthy people. I'd rather be overly cautious."

"I'm glad."

❧ ❧ ❧

"I've noticed something recently," Deborah said over dinner, suddenly hoping Susan and Helen wouldn't bring up Rachel's new behavior.

"What?"

Deborah continued, "Have any of you been aware of the increased number of Negroes in Boston lately?"

"Yes, I've seen many more Colored families at Denison House," said Miriam, pleased to have returned to her weekly volunteer work.

"And there are more at the grocery store…and, actually, at all the stores," Helen said.

"And I've noticed several new Negro families at church," said Susan.

"Why?" asked Mildred, always the most curious.

"That is a really good question, Mildred," Susan said with a smile and a pat on her shoulder. "Things are changing in the South. Lots of Negro folks have come here for jobs. Many of them worked in the fields as sharecroppers, though now that our men have gone off to war, there are many more jobs open to them."

"Why didn't they take those jobs before?"

"How do we explain prejudice to a twelve-year-old?" Susan asked.

Helen shook her head. "Like you would to an adult. Mildred is a smart girl, and I want to support her in learning about the world."

They described the unfair labor practices in the South, the prejudicial treatment of Negroes, and the new opportunities for Negroes in urban cities. They explained that the Negroes' movement North was not only due to jobs vacated by men going to war, but also due to farm failures in the South. They explained Negroes were forced to find new employment after the crop devastation wreaked by the boll weevil, a beetle that feeds on the cotton plants' buds and flowers.

Mildred asked many questions. "Why do you sometimes call them Colored and sometimes Negro? Does their name have to do with if they're dark or light?"

They answered her as best they could, but not even they knew the answer to her question about names and skin color.

Mildred also wanted to understand the basic premise about why Negroes were considered lesser beings by many. She became upset when told of the routine prejudicial mistreatment of Negroes and vowed to change things when she grew up.[35]

ҩ ҩ ҩ

---

[35] After the Civil War, racial oppression was made worse by Jim Crow laws, which forced segregation of public facilities and public transportation. Negroes were denied the right to vote, hold jobs, or get an education, even after the passage of the Thirteenth Amendment, which outlawed slavery in the United States. President Woodrow Wilson furthered the impact of discrimination by initiating the segregation of federal workplaces in 1913. The segregation of people by color was adopted in the South, the Midwest, the West, and even in New England. Sundown towns required Blacks to leave town before dark, or they would be shot or lynched. In the South, prejudice was obvious, though Blacks were discriminated against throughout the country. State legislatures worked to disenfranchise Blacks, limiting their voting rights and removing any opportunity for political and economic gains. Jim Crow laws were enforced until 1965.

Mildred soon decided she could not wait to grow up to make changes. She was given permission by Susan and Helen to invite a Negro child to dinner. The women assumed none would accept her offer, given the awkwardness of a social connection between the races. As expected, one Colored child after another refused her after going home to ask their parents' permission to visit a White child at home. Mildred was disheartened.

One night, Deborah and Miriam talked with Susan and Helen after Mildred went to bed; they were trying to determine what kind of parents would allow a Colored child to dine with a White family. It was such an unusual situation. Might they be impoverished? Or maybe they were new to the area and desperate for any connection for their child. Or perhaps they'd worked with White people without feeling the social stigma most Negro families feared.

≈ ≈ ≈

On Sunday, Susan and Helen arrived home from church with an unusual request. Their pastor had asked if they'd be willing to host a visit with a new reverend who had just moved to town. His wife was a suffragette, and the pastor thought Susan's and Helen's liberal leanings would make them a good match. The pastor was quite taken with this newly relocated reverend and hoped to help him make connections with like-minded parishioners. The one caveat to this situation

---

Late in the 1910s people of color enjoyed a new status as their labor was needed in both the South and the North. Negroes were forced to take unskilled and dangerous jobs, such as in munitions factories, though some Negroes were able to take positions that had never been available to them before. Colored families migrated to the North or West in search of better opportunities and less racial tension.

As Negroes moved into urban areas, they segregated themselves into ghettos, finding more comfort in being with others like themselves. They were often looked down upon by Northerners for their country ways, and unfair practices followed them wherever they moved.

One major issue Negroes faced was the prejudicial attitudes of the police. Unfortunately, there were many stereotypical racist beliefs held by White officers, not the least of which was the belief that Colored men were more apt to commit criminal acts. Ostensibly to protect Whites, the police subjected Negroes to a preponderance of brutality in the form of beatings, verbal assaults, and even killings. Most Whites remained unaware of this.

was that the reverend was a Negro. Susan and Helen talked about this situation all the way home, wondering why the reverend had chosen their church, rather than one with a Colored congregation.

Mildred listened in with great excitement, overjoyed with the thought of having a Negro in their home. Susan, however, was aware how awkward it might be to socialize with a Colored man. But as they expected, Miriam assured them he would be welcomed, and Deborah agreed.

The big challenge was deciding when he could visit. Saturday was their *Shabbos*, and Sunday was his church day. On a weekday, they'd need to invite him after work hours, but before the girls' bedtime. Because of the timing, Miriam suggested they invite him for dinner on a weekday, early enough so the children would be awake. They were all surprised when the reverend said yes and agreed on the next day.

Mrs. Stern prepared a lovely dinner with no typically Jewish foods for "the gentleman" from Susan and Helen's church. Miriam speculated how the pastor would react when they recited the *Birkat Hamazon*, the Hebrew Grace After Meals. She wondered if anyone had explained to him that he was coming to a Jewish household, something Susan, Helen, and Mildred had adjusted to easily, but Miriam speculated that it might be uncomfortable for a Colored person. And would the reverend be at ease in an all-women household?

The next evening, looking forward to meeting a Negro man, Mildred excitedly answered the doorbell. Miriam rushed to greet the guest, hoping to counterbalance Mildred's exuberance. To their surprise, Susan and Helen's pastor and his wife were at the doorstep, accompanying the new reverend and his wife.

The whole group came inside, and it was obvious that they'd all come for dinner. "I'd like you to meet Reverend Brown and his wife," the pastor said casually. "We appreciate this lovely invitation."

Miriam greeted them warmly and led them into the parlor to meet Deborah, Susan, and Helen, who'd come downstairs to welcome the reverend. Susan and Helen seemed perplexed at how they could have misinterpreted the situation; they had been expecting only one person.

The visitors probably took note of the astonished faces, yet out of politeness, no one said anything. When Deborah invited them to sit in the parlor, they seemed hesitant and uncomfortable with this unusual social situation.

Miriam snuck into the kitchen to inform Mrs. Stern there would be a large group for dinner. Initially rattled because she'd cooked just enough chicken for the intended group, she began searching for additional food. She sent Miriam to the root cellar to bring up potatoes to stretch the meal, and Miriam agreed to help with the preparations.

Deborah sent Mildred into the kitchen to find out how they were managing the expanded-guest-list situation. Mildred found both Mrs. Stern and Miriam peeling potatoes while the awaiting pot on the stove boiled furiously. Mildred watched as Mrs. Stern shifted to cutting the chicken into smaller pieces and peeling carrots intended for another night's dinner.

Mildred reentered the parlor, explaining that dinner would be slightly delayed. Susan caught on immediately and offered to set up an extra table to accommodate the additional guests. Susan and Helen rearranged the room, glad to have a task because they were unsure of how to initiate a conversation with the group who were sitting awkwardly in the parlor.

Miriam was surprised by the silence that filled the parlor. When she asked Mrs. Brown why they had chosen to move to Boston, Mrs. Brown lowered her head and turned towards her husband. They'd all assumed the suffragette would be independent and vocal, but that did not appear to be the situation.

The Black reverend spoke, "I've heard of several famous Negroes from Boston, including the educator and author Booker T. Washington and the writer W.E.B. Du Bois."

"And don't forget about the civil-rights leader Josephine St. Pierre Ruffin, a suffragette," his wife said, speaking up once her husband had his turn. "She worked tirelessly to encourage Boston Negroes to support the right for women to vote. Mrs. Ruffin was also editor of the *Woman's Era*, the magazine which led to the women's club movement for Negro women. Boston was also home to the Massachusetts Anti-Slavery Society, and we can't forget to mention Boston's *Colored American Magazine*."

"Yes, dear. I assume that Boston will be more accepting of educated Negroes than any place we've lived in the South."

After assuring them that they'd find more comfort in Boston, Susan asked questions about his church and his role as a pastor. Helen hoped this church talk would not be uncomfortable for Deborah and Miriam.

But Miriam joined the conversation, "I don't know if you were told Deborah and I are Jewish." Timidly she asked, "Would you be comfortable with hearing the Hebrew grace before we eat?"

The pastor's wife's face lit up. "Certainly. My sister's employers in Birmingham, Alabama, were Jewish. My sister started out as a maid, but ended up running their whole household. She became unconventionally close to the woman of the house, who invited our extended family for a special meal at their house."

When dinner arrived, the conversation flowed more easily. Reverend Brown described the struggles they'd faced when relocating to Boston. "We were often treated as servants during our trip, confusing people when we asked for lodging or food for ourselves. We were often relegated to small quarters and served separate from other diners."

"I was disheartened when they expected me to clean up after the meal," his wife said, frowning. "They were polite yet uncomfortable with us."

Mildred listened to the conversation and became both fascinated and upset at hearing about the prejudice they'd faced on their trip. She accepted a smaller piece of cake than usual, understanding the two-layer chocolate cake she'd been admiring all day had to feed the whole crowd. She was willing to sacrifice that little pleasure for their guests.

After the company departed, Miriam went into the kitchen. "Thank you, Mrs. Stern, for the wonderful job you did putting together the lovely meal on short notice."

Miriam was shocked when she heard Mrs. Stern mumble under her breath, "All that work for *Schvartzes*," a derogatory Yiddish term for Negroes.

"Mrs. Stern, we never use a term like that in our house, so I'd appreciate it if you would refrain from saying that." Miriam's face flushed as she took a huge breath and continued, "This was a lovely couple in our parlor, one with good breeding and strong Christian values. I hope you will have it in your heart to welcome them, as you would with any guest, should they come again."

Mrs. Stern said nothing, leaving Miriam to wonder.

When they got to their room, Miriam hesitated before telling Deborah about the despicable comment she had heard from Mrs. Stern; she was worried that Deborah would not be forgiving. She actually wondered if she, herself, would ever be able to see Mrs. Stern in the same way again. She decided to admit she was upset.

Deborah was forgiving and understanding; she felt Mrs. Stern had been brought up with that discriminatory attitude. The best they could do was guide her towards seeing Colored people as equals. They agreed to never tell Mildred of this.

The next morning, Susan and Helen talked with Mildred about the rarity of Negro and White families socializing. At Mildred's insistence, they agreed to have Reverend and Mrs. Brown back another time, hopefully with their children. Mildred was overjoyed, yet Susan and Helen wondered if the couple would really bring their daughters to visit.

When Susan suggested that Mildred stop inviting other Negro children, Mildred wondered why, because this first interracial gathering had gone so well. Susan's explanation about the awkwardness of having Negroes as friends saddened the young girl. They came to a compromise—instead of bringing them to the house, Mildred could take any of her new Black friends to the corner store for a special treat. Mildred thought this an adequate solution since treats like candy were rare. Now, in addition to her altruistic motives, there was the promise of a sweet treat.

To Mildred's distress, when she and a new Colored friend went to the corner store a day later, the Negro girl was not served. The store owner ordered her to wait outside. Mildred asked her friend about her favorite candy and apologized when later handing it to her. Near to tears, she decided not to subject another Negro child to such offensive behavior.

Mildred continued her personal efforts to befriend Negro children. She went to Denison House with Miriam twice, talking exclusively with children with dark skin. She walked their neighborhood, looking into the windows of homes, hoping to find Negroes living nearby. Because theirs was mostly a Jewish neighborhood, rather than a Negro ghetto, she found none.

❧ ❧ ❧

Mildred begged Deborah to take her back to the library to study more about the plight of Negroes. Scouring the papers, she learned of race riots and became incensed. She was especially upset when reading of an incident in the Tenderloin section of New York City in 1900 between a Colored man and a White undercover police officer. The Negro was slaughtered after being accused of a crime he did not commit. The plan to prosecute the White officer led to a riot between Negroes and an angry Irish mob. Colored men and women were arrested in disproportionate numbers to the White aggressors. Mildred's school report on this incident was met with disdain by her teacher, who could not understand why a sweet White girl would study such an event.

Mildred's teacher's response angered her so much that she compiled a lengthy report for her class about the riots in this country. She read it out loud to Leah before presenting it to her fellow students. Leah clapped, proud of her friend. Susan hesitantly described what a rape was when Mildred probed for a definition of this unfamiliar word. Then, when Mildred was finished with the report, she handed it to Susan for her approval.

Susan stopped reading to say, "Mildred, this is really disturbing. Where did you get all this information? It hardly seems possible this is all real. Why would people riot because someone won a boxing match?"

"I don't know why they would. But that's what the papers said. I got this all at the library."

"I think this is more than enough. I don't think you should add the rest of the report. It's hard to absorb this much information."

"But, Susan, this is all real. And most of this was in the back pages of the newspapers. I think they were trying to hide it, so people wouldn't know how bad things are."

"I'm not sure I wanted to know all this."

"There's lots more. Please read the rest. I want to tell what happened, but I don't want anyone to stop reading, like you have."

"I'll read the rest, and then we'll share it with Helen. Maybe the three of us can decide how much to include." She continued reading.

When Helen read the report, she first talked to Mildred about plagiarism because much of the report sounded as if it had been lifted directly from the pages of a newspaper. After dealing with that issue, the three of them worked together to put the report into Mildred's own words. They shortened many of the descriptions, but at Mildred's insistence, they did not leave out any of the riots, for which both Susan and Helen had advocated.

"No, I want to keep it all there. I want people to be shocked, as you were."

Mildred suggested they invite Reverend Brown and his wife to dinner again to discuss the race riots. Susan was concerned about discussing such a difficult topic with someone who would be even more incensed than Mildred, but Mildred went ahead and approached the reverend at church.

"Mildred, you can't invite people to dinner at our home without checking with us first, and certainly with Deborah and Miriam," Susan said sternly, trying to keep frustration out of her tone.

"Why not? It's our house too."

"It isn't really our house. Miriam's family owned the house, and now it's Deborah and Miriam's."

"That's not fair. Do you have to ask them before we do anything? We should be able to invite our own guests."

"Mildred, it doesn't work like that."

"Well, I invited them. Am I in trouble?"

"No, you're not in trouble," Helen said, "but we still need to ask Deborah and Miriam."

To Mildred's delight, Miriam agreed to this arrangement without asking Deborah. Mildred asked if their children could come too, yet she was told that it would be awkward to have the whole family visit. The second visit of Reverend and Mrs. Brown was scheduled for later that same week. Mrs. Stern cooked a lovely dinner without comments, despite knowing who the invited guests were.

Mildred wanted to tell the reverend the reason for his invitation as soon as they sat down, but Helen insisted that Mildred wait to share her report until dinner was over.

Deborah and Miriam invited the reverend's wife into the parlor, leaving Mildred, Susan, and Helen at the table while Reverend Brown read Mildred's report.

"Yes," agreed the reverend, "discrimination against Negroes has been rampant in this country for years, but things have escalated of late."

Mildred's question, "Why?" was met with a lengthy discussion, which seemed beyond her understanding. When Helen noticed Mildred's eyes glazing over, she insisted that it was Mildred's bedtime and put an end to the conversation.

For days after this, Mildred talked of the riots and of her new friend, the reverend. Susan and Helen were certain there would be another invitation and further conversation in their near future.

Mildred's Report on Race Riots
1903 Evansville Race Riot

This was the worst racial incident in this city in Indiana. White people stormed the jail. They lynched 16 Negroes, and 200 White militiamen killed 12 people.

1906 Atlanta Massacre

For two days, a White mob killed 23 Negroes. They hung some from lampposts and shot, beat, or stabbed others.

1908, Springfield, Illinois

There was a huge mob; 5,000 Whites rioted because they said that Negroes raped two girls.

1910 Johnson-Jeffries Race Riots

The Negro boxer Jack Johnson beat the White boxer James Jeffries. Whites all over the country attacked Colored men because of this.

1917 East St. Louis Riots

Lots of riots happened in Illinois. Some papers said White Americans murdered 40 Negroes, but other papers said it was 250; 3,000 White men marched down the main street. They attacked Colored men and ruined businesses. Lots of houses were destroyed, so there were 6,000 people without homes.

1917 Chester, Pennsylvania, Race Riot

This was because so many Negroes moved North to get jobs. White men didn't want them to take jobs that they wanted for themselves.

1917 Camp Logan Mutiny

There was a unit of Black soldiers who came to guard Camp Logan in Houston, Texas. The police department was all White men, and they arrested some Black soldiers for no good reason. So 156 Negro soldiers rioted. Five policemen got killed, and 11 people who weren't soldiers or policemen got killed too.

❧ ❧ ❧

During this time, there was a great deal of civil unrest regarding issues like unfair labor practices, yet Mildred's focus was entirely on racial discrimination. She was determined to be a voice for the Negroes who were being victimized in this country. Susan and Helen wondered if her devotion to the rights of Negroes resulted from the cruel treatment she had received as an orphaned child. They assumed this was not a passing phase, but probably the beginning of a lifelong fight against prejudice. Their own efforts remained toward women's suffrage, though they supported Mildred in her strong belief in the importance of racial justice.

Evening after evening, Deborah and Miriam discussed Mildred's obsession. "I'm impressed with Mildred's fortitude. I hope someday she'll find a way to make an impact on racial disparities," Miriam said.

"I hope so too. I marvel at Susan's and Helen's support, which is always helpful, though never overbearing," said Deborah.

Miriam nodded. "I think about our children and hope that someday Ida will find a passion, as Mildred has. She's still a baby, too young to show any direction in her life, yet she's already displaying signs of compassion towards her sister."

"Sylvia will probably never have the ability nor the language to pursue any social causes, yet we can guide her to have healthy values."

"That will include treating others with respect," Miriam said.

Mildred's realizations about racial tensions paled when compared to their next news.

❧ ❧ ❧

Later in the month, Deborah received disturbing correspondence from her brother.

> *October 20, 1918*
> *Dear Deborah,*
> *We arrived in France, weary, but glad to be on solid ground. We started our voyage with 2,000 crew and 9,000 troops, yet not everyone made it. We've been hit with a horrible outbreak of the influenza, which has taken over the ship. We're fortunate that in addition to the troops, there were two medical units being transferred. I don't know how we would have managed without them.*

We converted many compartments into sick bays, but that wasn't enough. I don't want to be too detailed. Suffice it to say that some soldiers died on deck before they could be transported to sick quarters. I've never seen an illness like this. It sometimes turns deadly in just a few hours.

By our third day at sea, even the colonel in charge of the medical units was ill. I've heard it said that it's because we're packed in so tight that this disease is spreading so quickly. We've been working 24-hour shifts, moving the ill and dying patients to the sick areas, thus exposing ourselves to this illness.

I'm sad to report that there are only 966 of us left alive, less than a tenth of those aboard when we set sail. Maybe we'll disembark quickly, and I'll be able to mail this letter. I sincerely hope I'll be one of the lucky ones not to get this illness. I'll keep you updated on my health and whereabouts. I pray that you'll see me again.

I love you, my sweet sister.

Milton

After Deborah received this letter, she became very anxious. She noticed there were no holes cut in this most recent correspondence, undoubtedly because the censors were dealing with essential needs, were ill, or had died.

Deborah and Miriam repeatedly discussed Milton and the horrible illness that had taken so many lives. "I'd be so afraid if this illness came to us," Miriam said. "I would especially fear for our children."

"The illness that Milton wrote of is unlike anything that's befallen us here. It was young, healthy soldiers who died, and so many of them. And they died so quickly. I'm anxious to hear from Milton to make sure he's not fallen ill."

❧ ❧ ❧

Deborah waited for correspondence to tell her of her brother's health, frustrated to find nothing in her daily mail checks.

Instead of a letter from Milton, she got the dreaded telephone phone call from her parents. Her father called after receiving the official notice of his son's death, conveying news that he'd been buried at sea.

Deborah cried uncontrollably when they informed her that Milton had died from the Spanish influenza on October 22, just a couple of days after his last letter to her.

Miriam came running when she heard Deborah sobbing. Deborah couldn't control herself enough to tell Miriam what had happened, though Miriam guessed the reason and just held her. She took the phone from Deborah's hand and softly said to Deborah's father, "I'll have Deborah call you back when she's calmer."

They stayed in the kitchen, next to the phone, for a very long time. When Deborah's tears lessened, Miriam escorted her to the parlor, finding that Susan and Helen had taken over care of Sylvia and Ida after hearing her sobs.

Sylvia approached Deborah timidly and stroked her face. Ida cuddled in Miriam's arms, unused to the show of emotion. Once both their mothers comforted them, Susan and Helen quietly whisked the children away so Deborah and Miriam would have some time alone.

"He was so young, just twenty," said Deborah as she burst into tears again.

"And such a lovely young man," Miriam said, wiping Deborah's tears and handing her another hanky, which Susan had retrieved from the hall dresser.

They talked of Milton, his funny sense of humor, his kind heart, and his brave enlistment in this horrible war. After a half hour, Miriam suggested Deborah call her parents back.

Before making the call, Deborah half whispered, "There will be no body, so there can be no funeral tomorrow and no burial."

During the telephone call, Deborah's parents asked her to get on the next train to New York. Miriam said she would follow once she had packed up the girls, yet Deborah insisted they travel together as a family. Miriam searched the drawer in the kitchen for the train's timetable. After she went into the back room to tell Susan and Helen they'd be leaving for New York in the morning, Miriam headed upstairs to pack their bags.

Deborah joined Miriam, though she was too distracted to help with the packing. "They're going to have a funeral tomorrow even though there's no body to bury."

"According to *halakah*, there can be no funeral without a body, yet there can be a shiva."

"I'm going to honor my parents' decision, whether it fits Jewish law or not," said Deborah sternly.

"Certainly," said Miriam, hoping not to upset Deborah further. She was aware how devastating this situation would have been to her own family, who would not have had a burial without a body.

They left on the first train the next morning, aware that the funeral would not be held until they arrived.

≈ ≈ ≈

On the train, and in the days that followed, they spoke quite often of the shocking disease that had taken Milton. "I'm so afraid of this illness," Miriam said. "I fear you or the girls could get this sickness and die."

"We know so little, except that it takes people quickly," Deborah replied.

"Might it come here to Boston when the soldiers return?" Miriam asked rhetorically. "Or maybe it started in Boston."

Deborah had no answers.

≈ ≈ ≈

When Deborah arrived at her family's New York home, the first thing she did was hug her sister Anna, who was inconsolable. Deborah's parents could not pull themselves out of their own grief to attend to anyone but themselves.

That afternoon, they sat together in the front row of the temple, listening to the service through their tears. The rows of the shul were filled to capacity with extended family and friends gathered to send Milton off to his final resting place. The service was traditional, the mournful chanting hardly comforting. During the entire funeral and at the burial at the cemetery, Anna clung to Deborah.

After Milton's funeral, Deborah and Miriam stayed in New York to sit shiva all week. Most of the mourners knew Deborah had a family, and many had met Miriam over the years, but few had met their children. Everyone made a fuss over them as if theirs was a typical family. Miriam was certain they'd be the topic of many dinner-table conversations. Because Deborah did not seem concerned, Miriam said nothing.

Deborah and Miriam arrived home to record-setting temperatures in Boston; it reached an astounding temperature of 79 degrees on October 29.

Reverend Brown

October 20, 1918
Dear Deborah,
We arrived in France,
weary, but glad to
be on solid ground.
We've been hit
with a horrible
outbreak of the
influenza, which
has taken over the
ship. We're fortunate
that in addition to
the troops, there were

Milton's letter

Temple Mishan Tefila Memorial Park

Episode 23 ❦ *Armistice*

November 1918

Once Deborah, Miriam, and the girls arrived home from New York, they returned to their pattern of regular discussions in the wingback chairs. There was little content to their talks, other than Milton's death. Miriam could not have been a more loving or solicitous partner through this difficult time, as Deborah was sure to tell her at every opportunity.

Susan and Helen cared for the children whenever they sensed Deborah and Miriam needed some time alone, and they consoled Deborah whenever she brought up Milton's name. In their room, they talked of what it would be like had one of their siblings died.

❧ ❧ ❧

On November 7, Susan opened the newspaper—"Suffrage Passed in New York." Though thrilled inside, she dared not show excitement in this house of mourning.

Helen said, in an equally calm manner, "Of course, there is a long way to go for the entire nation to approve the vote." They did not discuss this further at the breakfast table; instead, later, they broke into excited chatter in their own rooms.

❧ ❧ ❧

During this time, Susan and Helen were appreciative of Mildred's continued focus on racial equality. The thirteen-year-old struggled through several books about the abolition movement, which Susan got at the library, since such a trip there was beyond Deborah's ability at the moment. Mildred studied the extensive efforts required to end slavery, which had been officially outlawed with the passage of the Thirteenth Amendment in 1865. In the books Susan chose, Mildred read about the suffrage leaders Susan B. Anthony, Lucretia Mott, and Lucy Stone, whose social activism began with their fight for equality for Negroes.

Mildred's next school report for her sixth-grade class was about Lucy Stone, Massachusetts's own abolitionist turned suffragette. She handed her completed paper to Susan, who approved of her research and her writing, pleased that her lesson about plagiarism had been effective.

Lucy Stone

Lucy Stone was born in 1818 in West Brookfield, Massachusetts. She was the first American woman to earn a college degree. She graduated from Oberlin College in 1847. They asked her to write the commencement speech, but she refused because it would be read by a man.

Lucy Stone fought for slaves long before she fought for women. She supported the 15th Amendment, which granted Negro men the right to vote. She was hired by the American Anti-Slavery Society to write speeches, and she got to travel across the country to give the speeches herself.

Afterwards, Lucy Stone began to fight for women's suffrage. She was an organizer of the first National Women's Rights Convention in 1850 in Worcester, Massachusetts. She got to give her own speech there. Lucy was the one to tell Susan B. Anthony to fight for women's rights. She wouldn't use her husband's name, Henry Blackwell, even though she was married. Lucy Stone and her husband edited the *Woman's Journal*, a magazine about women's rights, published in Boston. She died in 1893 and was buried in Boston.

Mildred read many articles from *Woman's Journal* magazines, which were piled in a corner of Susan and Helen's room. Both mothers were enthused with their budding abolitionist.

When Helen informed Mildred that Lucy Stone was buried at Forest Hills Cemetery, just blocks from where they lived, Mildred insisted on a visit. Helen took her to find Lucy's grave the very next day. Arriving at the cemetery, they discovered there was no grave— Lucy was the first cremation to occur at this location. Mildred needed to change her report to reflect this.

With a crude map in hand, Helen and Mildred tried to follow major paths en route to the crematorium. They were distracted by dramatic crypts, a serene lake, and beautifully landscaped slopes as they retraced their steps multiple times to get back on course. They finally found the large stone and granite building with distinctive columns—the crematory. Inside, they were guided into a back room, where Mildred's eyes bulged upon viewing the urn for Lucy Stone Blackwell, her heroine. Both Mildred and Helen were speechless.

∼ ∼ ∼

"Deborah, there is a phone call for you from your father," Hannah announced just after lunchtime on Thursday.

"My father rarely calls me at work. I wonder if he's heard something about Milton," Deborah said to Miriam, passing her desk on the way to the telephone. Her face flushed as she remembered Milton had perished, and there were to be no more updates.

Miriam followed Deborah, wanting to be by her side if there was more bad news.

"The war is over!" shouted Deborah so that everyone in both offices could hear.

"Wonderful!" Miriam said calmly, followed by shouts from everyone else. "November 7 will always be remembered as the end of this horrible war."

"I want to talk to you, Father, but I can hardly hear you," Deborah said loudly into the phone. "I'll call you later when all the excitement here has died down."

After hanging up, Deborah realized there was commotion outside their office on Newspaper Row. She opened the door to hear folks screaming, bells chiming, and horns honking. Practically every shop person had emptied onto the streets, despite the recent caution due to the influenza epidemic. People seemed to have forgotten their health concerns as they streamed outside to celebrate.

"Please shut the door," yelled Hannah, uncomfortable with the cacophony of sounds.

Miriam asked, "Will they send the soldiers home right away?"

No one had answers; however, question after question was posed.

Miriam was the most emotional of all, tears streaming down her face. She quietly said to Deborah, "Finally an end to all the death and destruction. I hardly know anyone who's not lost a friend or relative to this horrible war. It all seems so senseless now that it's over. So many were maimed or died. Was it worth so much loss of life?"

Deborah wiped the pleasure from her face as she comforted Miriam. "Many young men lost their lives, including my brother. I agree that nothing seems worth their deaths."

"And so many more deaths occurred in France and Germany and everywhere else the conflict was fought. Many historical buildings and sometimes whole towns were annihilated. How can people be celebrating? I'm relieved there's an end to this needless fighting, yet I'm certain it has done more harm than good. I don't understand war at all."

Deborah held Miriam, wishing she could be shouting her relief that the war had finally ended. Miriam could not comprehend the pleasure Deborah was experiencing in spite of the significant destruction of war.

"And how," Miriam continued, "can they all forget the influenza that has caused them to stay away from public gatherings? As I peeked out the window, I noticed there are few folks wearing masks while celebrating in the streets. Have they all forgotten themselves? Maybe they won't die from bombs or bullets, yet the influenza is just as deadly."

Deborah sat with Miriam, who talked of the horrors of war and of the epidemic, which were both killing so many people. Deborah's nerves were on edge at the mention of her brother several times. Sitting alone in her office, she thought, *If only the war had ended earlier, my brother would never had been in the service and would never have gotten the influenza.*

William and Hannah concurred in shutting the business for the day. Everyone needed to celebrate…or to mourn, as Deborah and Miriam were doing. Deborah appreciated a day to be alone with her thoughts.

The staff left, and everyone returned to their families. Only Micah and Marjorie remained, for there was no way to get Micah's wheelchair through the streets in which throngs of people were gathering. William offered to pick up Micah and Marjorie as soon as things quieted.

Deborah and Miriam arrived home to find Rachel anxiously awaiting news. Even on their quiet residential street, there was commotion outside. Rachel kept the children safely inside, opening the windows—glad for the relatively mild 57-degree temperature outside—to hear cries of "Germany surrendered." She was pleased to celebrate with Deborah, Miriam, Susan, and Helen over cups of tea. The children were gleeful, stimulated by the excitement and pleased to have everyone at home.

After listening to over an hour of revelry on the street, Deborah heard the back door open. William had arrived with Micah and Marjorie.

"The streets are still crowded with merrymakers," William said. "I do not know if they are drunk from drink or excitement, but they seem to have no regard for anyone. My trip here took a long time for I feared for Micah's safety in the wheelchair. I did not dare take him any farther, so he's right outside your house."

Miriam spoke up, "Is there some way to get him home safely?"

They decided to enlist the help of some neighbors to carry Micah to the car. The bigger problem was how to get him into his house without the wheelchair if they left it behind. They all turned to William, their proven problem solver.

"I can strap the chair onto my truck, and if I drive slowly, avoiding the major streets, I think I can get them home safely. Once at his home, I can transfer Micah to his chair with the help of just one person."

William's plan worked, with Deborah being his assistant for the transfer. It was over two hours before he returned to drop off Deborah and pick up his daughter, Sarah, who'd remained in Rachel's care. Everyone was exhausted.

When the telephone rang at work late in the afternoon, Deborah ran to pick it up, assuming correctly that it was her father again. Miriam could not read the expression on Deborah's face as she listened intently to Mr. Levine. As she got off the phone, Deborah said, "My father told me all of New York City came to a halt. Mayor Hylan called for a public holiday, shutting all businesses. People celebrated wildly, hopeful their loved ones would soon be home. People danced in the streets with newspapers, brandishing the headline 'Germany Surrenders,' and shredded telephone books were thrown from tall buildings, littering the streets. In the middle of Times Square, the well-known singer Enrico Caruso sang 'The Star-Spangled Banner' from the second floor of the Knickerbocker Hotel."

"That's where Ruth and Michael got married," Miriam said.

It amazed Deborah that Miriam could not feel the excitement. *If anyone should be mournful,* she thought, *it should be me, over my lost brother.* Yet Deborah felt joyful.

The end of the war was paramount in everyone's mind. Micah, who grasped politics better than anyone else, initiated a conversation among the employees who'd gathered for this monumental occurrence. "Germany was so strong at the beginning of 1918; it seemed they were winning the war. Russia had already left the conflict, which made Germany's position stronger."

"Do you think the Germans surrendered because America joined the war?" asked Miriam.

"That could be the case," Micah said. "Germany knew America was a powerful nation, and American troops were not exhausted from years of fighting, as the Europeans were. Germany went on the offensive, pushing Britain and its allies back. Then, in August, the British and French launched a counterattack called the Hundred-Day Offensive, which was a series of attacks on the Western front."

"What I read," said Helen, "was that there were over one million American soldiers in France by April, totally overwhelming the Germans and their allies."

Micah responded, "Germans back at home were suffering from food shortages and illness; those conditions prompted rebellions that weakened Germany's resolve."

Miriam added, "I'm just pleased it is finally over."

❧ ❧ ❧

On November 8, Susan was the first to open the *Boston Globe*, expecting to read articles about the end of the Great War. Dazed, she read the headlines loudly to those at breakfast, "REPORTED SIGNING OF ARMISTICE A FAKE. NATION HOAXED INTO WILD CELEBRATION. GERMANS DELAYED ON WAY TO PARLEY."

"Hoax," "misinformation," and "untrue" were words Miriam heard, yet she could hardly believe them.

Reading on, Susan said, "The war is not over. There was a misunderstanding. The fighting has not stopped."

"Everyone is celebrating," Miriam said, unsure. "So many people believe the war ended."

"It seems," Susan said as she scanned the article, "that a message was misunderstood, and the war is still raging."

"Were Boston and New York the only cities to receive this misinformation?" Deborah asked.

"No, there were celebrations throughout the country."

Deborah read over Susan's shoulder until Susan handed the paper to her.

శ్రీ శ్రీ శ్రీ

A few days later, the papers stated that Kaiser Wilhelm, Germany's ruler, had stepped down from office. People were skeptical, given the misinformation previously printed. This time the news was accurate, and on November 11—at the eleventh hour of the eleventh month—the war was over. Germany signed an armistice, an agreement for peace, ending the war.

Deborah's father called again, telling them of the wild excitement on the streets of New York. People abandoned their cars and their work, filling the streets. Sirens blared throughout the city, and a searchlight on the tower of the New York Times building shot a ray of light across the city until daylight. The partying continued all night.

Again, to Miriam's distress, people forgot their disease precautions. Bostonians packed the streets, ending the citywide prohibition on public gatherings. Many people had been in mourning because almost 5,000 of their friends and relatives had died during the epidemic, yet they woke from their numbness for this night of merriment.

Deborah and Miriam, along with the rest of their extended family, still feared the virus that had killed so many, so they stayed inside, listening through their windows to the festivities that they feared would cause sickness and death.

Miriam was not the only one to be saddened during this time, though it seemed that most people, even those who'd lost a loved one, were cheering. Miriam focused on the destruction of precious cities and the lives lost, though she was relieved the war had ended.[36]

శ్రీ శ్రీ శ్రీ

---

[36] The newspapers covered the November 11 end-of-war celebrations in every city around the world. In London, Big Ben, which had been silenced since the war began, rang out joyfully, and throngs of people stood side by side to fill Trafalgar Square and the area around Buckingham Palace. Churches in France were filled with jubilant parishioners, and the French national flag waved in buildings across the country. France had suffered heavy losses, yet everyone focused on the end of the horrific war. Soldiers filed onto the streets in many cities, sometimes in the tanks that were no longer weapons of war. They were cheered by the crowds. Bands played as jubilant partygoers crowded the roads. Papers carried pictures of people gathering in celebration everywhere.

November 12, 1918
Dear Deborah and Miriam,
The armistice was just signed. That means that the war
is over. I don't know what that means for those of us who
signed up for four years. Will they make us stay that long,
now that the war is ending?

Things have changed with me and Rina. When we heard
that the war had ended, we got really concerned that we
might be separated. What if they close the Naval Aircraft
Factory? Or what if they need fewer people and send one of
us somewhere else? Or what if we're no longer in the navy
because they don't need us at all?

Rina and I got really scared about being apart. She's the
most important person in my life, and she told me that I'm
the most important to her too. I don't know exactly how to
tell you, even though I'm sure you'll understand, I think we
love each other, though we've not said those words yet. We
figured out that we really want to be with each other. So,
now, I guess we're like you two. We see ourselves as being
together always, now that we've admitted being sweet on
each other. I don't want to tell you the details, though I'm
certain you can figure it out. We got leave last weekend,
and we went to a hotel in Philadelphia and spent the whole
weekend there. So things are different with us now.
Love,
Fanny

"I'm not surprised about Fanny. Are you?" asked Miriam.

"Not at all," Deborah said with a smile. "She couldn't stop talking about Rina, letter after letter. I wonder how Mrs. B. will feel. She's always been accepting of us, yet this is her own daughter. It'll be interesting to see how she reacts."

In more than four years of fighting, over 8,000,000 soldiers had given their lives, including more than 100,000 Americans and 7,000,000 civilians. Many who survived physically suffered from mental trauma. This War to End All Wars, as it was called, caused devastation to many individuals, families, and cities. It would take years to rebuild.

The Germans did not celebrate.

"I doubt she'd ever considered Fanny could be like us," Miriam said as though she were asking a question. "I doubt she'd even consider it a possibility."

"How could she not guess, given Fanny's behavior and knowing we're together?"

Miriam had no answer. She imagined Mrs. B. turning to them and asking how they felt when they suddenly realized her daughter was in love with a girl.

Deborah's thoughts were about how they'd never discussed these issues with Mrs. B. Out loud to Miriam, she said, "I'll do anything I can for Fanny should Mrs. B. ever question the obvious."

Miriam shook her head repeatedly.

∾ ∾ ∾

Throughout the month, everyone focused on the end of the war, while Deborah thought obsessively about her brother's death. Mildred, oblivious to the significance of these occurrences, asked repeatedly for further interactions with Reverend Brown and his family. Susan and Helen explained that Deborah's sorrow over having lost her brother prevented any social activities at their home for the time being.

Mildred fretted, worried that the minister and his wife would feel slighted. To reassure her, Susan arranged a gathering after church one Sunday. Mildred was excited about planning a short walk, followed by a picnic, a solution they'd previously discussed. Mrs. Brown insisted on providing the food for this gathering and sent her condolences to Deborah and Miriam.

When Sunday arrived, Mildred was elated. She'd seen the reverend's daughters at church and was thrilled to finally play with them. The ten- and twelve-year-olds displayed no awkwardness when Mildred approached them with enthusiasm. The three girls wandered off on their own, while the adults set out the picnic lunch on a blanket in a shaded area of a nearby park. Susan glanced over and saw Mildred fingering the braids standing out from the scalp of both girls. She was not surprised when Mildred asked to have her hair braided. Susan agreed they could braid a small section of Mildred's hair.

After the delightful meal, and a cleaning of everyone's hands in a stream near their picnic spot, Mildred sat still while two thin braids were tied on the sides of her head. She pulled on them throughout the rest of the afternoon.

When they got home, Susan and Helen discussed the successful afternoon, yet wondered what they would do about Mildred's new hairstyle. "Can we let her go to school with the cornrows?" Helen wondered. "How will the other girls react to her?"

"I think Mildred will explain how she got them, and I suspect that will open some interesting discussions," said Susan.

"Our girl is certainly an advocate for Negroes."

Susan pondered, "I wonder if her experience on the Orphan Train had an impact on her attitudes. She certainly met a wide range of people during that experience."

"There were no Negro children on the Orphan Trains. They were mostly young Irish girls and boys who were carted across the country to find new families."

"I know that, but I wonder whether it led to her sensitivity about the downtrodden. It seems her values are deeply embedded, and I assume that experience affected her greatly."

Helen sighed. "No matter what the reason, Mildred certainly has turned her strong character towards helping those less fortunate than her. I'm proud of her."

"So am I."

As expected, Mildred wore her tiny braids to school and came home with stories of how she'd been teased. She had used the opportunity to educate the other children about how Colored children are more similar than different from them.

દે૦ દે૦ દે૦

The end of the month brought more excitement. The telephone rang late in the night of November 16. It scared Deborah, who ran downstairs to answer the call, because when the phone rang in the middle of the night, it was always bad news.

Miriam followed, her heart racing, and listened to Deborah for a moment. She quickly caught on when she saw a smile form on Deborah's face.

"We'll be over shortly to pick you up and drive you to the hospital."

"It's time for Marjorie's baby!" Miriam said loudly, despite it being the middle of the night.

"Yes, Micah said to hurry."

As the two of them headed upstairs to change into outdoor clothing, Helen entered the hall, having heard the telephone ring and Miriam's poorly muffled scream. Deborah explained they would be leaving shortly and asked Helen to assist the children in the morning. They'd probably not return in time to get them settled.

Everything went smoothly, and baby Ezra came into the world at 4:17 a.m. Marjorie and Ezra were sent home from the hospital after just two days because the hospitals were crowded with many of those sick with the grippe. This was much earlier than most women were released after having babies. Marjorie's mother and Micah's mother were called into service to take care of the baby, a task they both relished. Both Marjorie's and Micah's parents were overjoyed to be first-time grandparents.

Micah was relieved that Marjorie had made it through her pregnancy without contracting the dreaded virus. They knew several women who had contracted the influenza and lost their babies.[37]

৵ ৵ ৵

Another letter arrived from Fanny. Miriam opened it carefully, certain it contained an update about whether Fanny had been discharged.

> *November 20, 1918*
> *Dear Deborah and Miriam,*
> *Now that the war has ended, we are all waiting to see what*
> *will happen. We still don't know if we'll be reassigned or if*
> *they'll make us live out our four-year commitment to the navy.*

---

[37] During this outbreak of the Spanish flu, 50 percent of the pregnant women who contracted the influenza perished, and the fetal mortality rate was uncommonly high. Massachusetts had one of the highest death rates. The trend during this period was towards hospital births, rather than home births, because hospitals could offer painless childbirth. As recently as 1900, almost all babies were born at home, with the assistance of a doctor for middle-class families or a midwife for those who could not afford a physician. Twilight sleep, first developed in Germany to allow a woman to sleep through childbirth, became a popular alternative to painful birthing. The first maternity hospital was founded in 1914, in Boston, by Dr. Eliza Taylor Ransom, a suffragette. That same year, feminists in Manhattan formed the National Twilight Sleep Association.

Rina and I heard talk that they were closing the Naval Aircraft Factory, and we'd be getting new assignments. It seems that was just a rumor. It looks like the factory will stay open, and some of us will remain to continue to provide planes for the navy. I wish we knew if we'll be the ones staying.

Rina and I have begun to think about what we'll do once we are out of the navy. We need to be together, yet we don't know where we'll live or what we'll do. I left school, as Rina did, and neither of us expects that the skills we've learned working on airplanes will help us get other jobs.

Maybe I could come work for you. You always tell me that I'm valuable at the office, and we'd love to live in Boston. What could Rina do? And where would we live if they dismiss us from our jobs?

I'm really glad the war is over.

Love,

Fanny

"What do you think?" Miriam asked quizzically.

"She is a great benefit to us when she's here," Deborah said.

"But we've not even met Rina. It's hard to know how she'd fit into our business."

"Let's wait before making any offers."

෩ ෩ ෩

As was becoming a usual pattern, Deborah went to New York to be with her family for Thanksgiving, and Miriam celebrated with Marjorie's family. Marjorie and Micah's new infant added great excitement.

When Miriam walked into Marjorie's family home with Sylvia and Ida, she was entranced by the aromas. "Thanksgiving always smells wonderful, though this year is even more luscious than usual."

Marjorie smiled as she handed baby Ezra to Miriam in exchange for Ida. "It's amazing that you can smell the difference. For the turkey and stuffing, we have a new secret ingredient that has us all excited."

"What is it?"

"A new shop opened downtown, not far from their manufacturing plant on the waterfront, to sell this incredible mixture called Bell's Seasoning. It's a mixture of thyme, sage, marjoram, rosemary, black pepper, and its secret ingredient—nutmeg. The aroma pulled me inside; I had to try it. Now, you can see why I was so entranced by the distinctive smell."

This new seasoning was a great hit, and they agreed to include it each Thanksgiving.

❧ ❧ ❧

After another long wait for news from Grace Banker, they finally received word.

> *November 29, 1918*
> *Dear Susan and Helen,*
> *I'm in Paris now. We have been assigned to live at the temporary residence of President Woodrow Wilson, a great honor. I must tell you that after all those months on the war front, I find this a bit boring. I cannot believe I miss the excitement of war.*
> *I've just accepted an offer to move to the Army of Occupation in Koblenz, Germany. I have no idea what's ahead.*
> *Sadly, my girls and I were never discharged like other soldiers, so it is unlikely we will get military benefits. I don't understand this because we were told we were hired by the army, we wore uniforms, and we were treated as the other females.*
> *Yours Truly,*
> *Grace*

Deborah and Miriam talked with Susan and Helen about Grace's news. None of them had any idea what this meant for her, but they were relieved she'd be safe now that the war was over. But what was she doing there after the armistice had been signed?

Armistice celebration

Armistice Boston

Episode 24 ❧ *Hanukkah Sensations*
December 1918

Miriam insisted on regular visits to see baby Ezra. Deborah hoped this would satisfy Miriam's endless desire to be around infants, rather than stimulate her hopes of having another child. Miriam spoke to Deborah's unspoken concern after they got home one evening.

"I love cuddling with Ezra and then being able to come home afterwards. Remember how exhausting it was to be new parents? Marjorie and Micah looked overjoyed yet also deprived of sleep. I would not want to go through those endless nights again. I don't understand how women manage who have large broods."

"I think that's why Margaret Sanger's birth-control clinics are so popular," Deborah said with a smile.

"Could we take the baby for a little while, just to give them some relief?"

"I doubt they'd let Ezra leave their sight for even a few minutes. Maybe we could offer to spend some time at their home while they take a nap or do chores, though I suspect that Marjorie's parents are already doing that for them."

Miriam, changing the subject, said, "It's too bad Micah hasn't agreed to get a prosthetic leg. He'd be able to handle the baby so much better than on crutches."

"I agree. Disabled soldiers must all have great difficulty managing their children."

Miriam sighed deeply. "Deborah, do you think they will continue to live there, in that little room the brotherhood men made for them? We're paying Micah enough now that they could afford a small place of their own."

"I suspect that's already on their minds, though, right now, having Marjorie's family nearby is a wonderful benefit. Maybe they'll move after Ezra is a little older."

"I hate to think of the baby growing up. I love him as a newborn." Deborah smiled. "And he has that new-baby smell."

"I hope you're not getting any ideas about having another baby."

"Don't worry about that," Deborah replied with a wry smile. "I've been worried about you getting baby urges again."

"No possibility."

ॐ ॐ ॐ

Mildred was in tears as she and Deborah arrived home from the library. She ran upstairs to her room, shutting the door behind her. Deborah, who'd finally returned to regular outings to the library, had invited Mildred to join her that day. Deborah went immediately to find Susan, who was relaxing in the parlor, to inform her about the incident that upset Mildred.

"Mildred read a story about Mary Turner, a young Negro woman from Georgia who was lynched when she spoke out about her husband's murder. The victim was eight months pregnant. Mildred became extremely upset."

"Why did you let her read about this horrible situation?" Susan scolded.

"She was reading on her own while I was talking with my friend, the librarian. Suddenly she was in tears."

"If you take her to the library with you, you must monitor her more carefully," Susan said sternly as she hurried upstairs to comfort Mildred.

"Then you take her," Deborah called up the stairs.

This was the first time harsh words had been spoken between these friends, and it immediately got Miriam's attention when she overheard the last part of the exchange. "What happened?" she asked.

"Susan is furious with me because I let Mildred read something upsetting at the library. I didn't know I was to watch her every second, like I would if she were a young child. She's almost fourteen, old enough to read what she wants."

"What did she read?" Helen asked before automatically defending Susan.

"It was the story of Mary Turner, a young, pregnant Negro who was lynched in May. What made it so gruesome is that the crowds watched as they tied her up and cut the unborn child from her belly."

"Poor Mildred," Miriam said, shuddering.

"Poor Mildred? Poor Mary Turner!" Deborah practically shouted.

Overhearing this, Helen went upstairs to comfort Mildred, leaving Miriam to deal with Deborah.

"I'm very sorry Mildred read about this incident, yet I don't think you were wrong to let her explore the library on her own. It was unfortunate that she found something so disturbing to read, but you aren't responsible for her choices."

"Thank you for understanding, Miriam. I wouldn't have encouraged her, as Susan and Helen have, to explore slavery and the treatment of Negroes, but I wasn't at fault to let her study on her own. I feel bad that Mildred's upset, but I shouldn't be blamed."

Within the hour, Susan arrived downstairs with reddened eyes. Deborah stood stiffly, expecting another verbal lashing. Instead, Susan apologized, "Deborah, I'm sorry I berated you. You were absolutely not responsible for monitoring what Mildred was reading. I shouldn't have turned my anger on you. Please accept my apologies."

"I really didn't do anything wrong. I just let her read, as you would have. It isn't my fault that she's taken on the plight of the Negro. I'm sorry she read something so despicable, yet I assume this will be just one of many upsetting articles she reads if she pursues this."

"You're right. I wish she was more interested in women's suffrage or something tamer, yet our girl wants to be a voice for the downtrodden Negroes in this country. I admire her perseverance, though I'm afraid there will be many tears and many angry moments as she learns more."

"What do you want me to do in the future?" Deborah asked, letting her shoulders fall from their defensive posture.

"I think it's great that she's accompanying you to the library. I'll talk with her about what she's learning and encourage her to discuss things with you when she's discovered something upsetting…if that's all right with you."

"She remained silent the whole way back today. Next time, I'll try to get her to reveal what's upset her."

"Parenting is not easy," Susan said.

They all nodded.

రా రా రా

The tension in the household eased, and everything went back to life as it had been since the epidemic and war had changed everyone's lives.

"Deborah, now that the war is over, I can concentrate on Hanukkah, which is just around the corner. I've been considering ways to make the holiday special this year," Miriam said softly as she ran her fingers across Deborah's face.

"And what might that be, sweetie?" Deborah said, kissing Miriam's fingers as they passed her lips.

"Maybe we could come up with something special for each evening of the holiday," Miriam said, shrugging and glancing sideways.

Deborah perked up. "Do you have something in mind that would be better than Hanukkah gelt?"

"We seem to make everything more important than intimacy these days," Miriam said softly.

"Oh my, are you suggesting that we share something intimate for eight days in a row?"

"Would that be too much?"

"We've not had that much closeness since we were first together." Deborah paused. "Remember what it was like when we first got to sleep together, when the Berkowitzes invited us to stay with them in Lenox during that first summer we were together?"

"That feels like a very long time ago. We couldn't get enough of each other then."

"That was a long time ago—seven years! Miriam, I like your idea. We had planned to be intimate each *Shabbos*, though that idea got lost soon after it started. Let's plan some special time together each evening after we put the girls to bed."

"I hope neither of them will be sick or have a bad dream and spoil our plans." Miriam sighed.

"It is not like you to be the one to worry. That is usually my role."

"Well, even if they wake up or interrupt us, there is nothing to say that we couldn't extend the eight days of Hanukkah a bit so we get our full eight days of pleasure."

"That sounds more like you!" Deborah said, grinning.

Thus began the plans for their intimate Hanukkah. They decided to split the holiday, each one planning something special for four nights. And even though the discussions made them more excited than usual, they agreed that they would have no intimacy until the holiday two weeks later. Even though they often went two weeks without intimately connecting, the air was charged between them as they plotted ways to pleasure one another.

అ అ అ

The first night of Hanukkah arrived. Deborah and Miriam closed the shop early, as they did on *Shabbos* each week. Sundown was early—4:15 p.m.—and they needed to be home to prepare the Sabbath candles and the Hanukkah menorah.

On the way home, Deborah said, "I can hardly wait until the girls go to bed tonight. I want to find out what you have planned for our first night of holiday pleasure."

"You'll enjoy it." Miriam smirked.

"I know I will. I'm ready!"

The first night of the holiday occurred on Friday this year, so there were extra rituals. A second menorah needed to be set up before *Shabbos* and readied for the next night when two candles would be lit immediately after sundown. On this, the first night, they quietly davened the *Minkah* prayers before lighting the Sabbath candles, then the Hanukkah menorah. After the first candle, the one on the far right, was lit, prayers were said for the first night.

Their housemates, Susan and Helen, joined them for this ritual even though they were not Jewish. After four years, with eight nights of Hanukkah each year, they had learned the holiday prayers well enough to add their lovely voices to the candle lighting. Sylvia, though five years old, had not mastered the tune or the words to the ritual chants, yet little Ida, at two years of age, was able to mumble the first few words of the prayers.

Together, they chanted, "*Baruch atah, Adonai Eloheinu, Melech haolam, asher kid'shanu b'mitzvotav, v'tsivanu l'hadlik ner shel Hanukkah.*"

Miriam interpreted for Susan and Helen, "Praised are you, Lord our God, Ruler of the universe, who made us holy through Your commandments and commanded us to kindle the Hanukkah lights." They then said the *shehecheyanu*, which literally means "that we are alive," the prayer said for the first occurrence of anything.

After candles were lit, Miriam placed the menorah high on the mantel, so their children's curiosity about the burning flames wouldn't cause a crisis. She hoped it was high enough that it would not be noticed by Jimmy, the mischievous cat that loved to explore anything new. Miriam brought out several small wooden dreidels for the children to spin. Neither child was old enough to play the dreidel game, though they enjoyed the spinning tops.

Helen and Susan then took over caring for the children, supervising dinner, and putting the little ones to bed while Deborah and Miriam headed to temple for *Shabbos* services.

Deborah and Miriam returned from shul to find the Hanukkah dinner awaiting them. Their cook, Mrs. Stern, had prepared their wonderful holiday meal, yet Susan announced, "We told Mrs. Stern to go home to have the holiday dinner with her own family. We'll serve dinner tonight."

"How sweet of you," said Miriam. "I'm sure she appreciated that opportunity."

"I love the Hanukkah meal," said Deborah, focused on the wonderful food on the table. "*Latkes* slathered with sour cream and applesauce could be my favorite food."

"You say that now," Miriam said with a smile, "yet as soon as they bring out the *ponchiki*,[38] you might change your tune."

"Nope. *Latkes* for me. Maybe *ponchiki* for you."

"Definitely!"

After dinner ended, Susan and Helen insisted they do the cleanup. Deborah and Miriam excused themselves. After all, they had their Hanukkah gifts to give one another…and it was the first of their eight nights of delight.

"I'm glad I'm in charge this first night," said Miriam with a twinkle in her eyes.

"And what have you planned, my sweet girl?"

"Tonight, I want us to remember the most exciting nights we've had in bed and to take turns telling the story of what happened on those wonderful evenings of pleasure."

Deborah smiled. "They might not all be evenings. One of my best memories was the afternoon we stole into the woods."

"Go ahead and tell me the story. But, first, I must tell you there is one rule for this first night. There is to be no touching of private areas, neither your own nor mine."

"Wait a minute. That isn't fair. I've been waiting for tonight for the past couple of weeks. I'm ready for some loving."

"Too bad!" said Miriam, grinning. "I'm in charge tonight, and those are part of my instructions."

"You're mean."

"No, not mean. I just want to draw out the excitement. Now, tell me the story as you remember it."

"You *are* mean." Deborah settled down on the bed and encouraged Miriam to lie down with her. "Can I touch you?"

---

[38] *Ponchiki*, traditionally Polish treats, are rich pastries filled with jelly or sweet custard. Immigrants brought them to the United States. For centuries, Jews in North Africa also served the doughnut-like confections. They are similar to *sufganiyot*, the Israeli jelly doughnuts that have been served on Hanukkah since the 1940s.

"Certainly, just not down there."

"Well, I remember we were still new. Every time I saw you, my body was ready. This one day, we went to the ice-cream shop to socialize with Ruth and her friends. I could hardly wait to be alone with you. I'd been obsessed with thoughts of you all day, and I was more than ready to touch you."

"Like right now?"

"Yes, though I don't want to imagine that. Shush. I suggested we go for a walk. All afternoon, I'd planned to take you into the woods near the ice-cream shop and kiss you."

"Is that all you planned to do?"

"No, I wanted to touch you all over. I imagined how I would begin by holding your hands and touching your face when we sat on a log. I would softly kiss you, because I remembered that you were still a little shy."

"And we were both still new, even at kissing," Miriam said. "I remember how surprised I was when I could feel wetness and excitement in my panties when I kissed you."

"Me also. Let's experiment. When I kiss you, can you feel the kiss down below?"

"Your kisses are so delicious," Miriam said, not giving away whether her body had responded as suggested.

The kisses went on for a few minutes, as their breathing became more rapid, and their hands began wandering over each other's bodies.

"Is it cheating to touch your breasts?" Deborah asked.

"No, it isn't cheating. Just below is off-limits," said Miriam.

Deborah pulled Miriam close and began caressing her nipples lightly with her fingertips, then with her tongue. Miriam's breathing became louder as she squirmed under Deborah's familiar touch. Deborah began to suck harder, while massaging Miriam's breasts. Miriam arched her back slightly, pushing her breasts closer to Deborah's mouth. Deborah began flicking her tongue over the hard nipples as she moved her hands lower. She massaged Miriam's belly through her nightwear, causing Miriam to squirm. She pulled at the nightdress, raising it so that she could reach underneath.

She continued to move lower, caressing Miriam's skin right above her triangle. Then she softly touched the hairs, causing Miriam to involuntarily gasp. She moved her fingers slowly to Miriam's inner legs, caressing lightly, careful not to caress the forbidden area. She sensed the wetness there. She listened to Miriam's breathing become ragged and noticed Miriam had repositioned herself, bringing the most sensitive area closer to her fingers. She followed the rules and continued to touch everywhere except the center of Miriam's excitement. She wondered if Miriam would be able to hold out. Miriam was definitely damp. Deborah could smell the excitement building. Still, she carefully avoided touching the center of Miriam's joy.

Careful not to move her fingers away from their constant pressure just a short distance from that sacred space, Deborah slowly moved her body into a position that would allow her to add her tongue to this game. At first, she licked Miriam's thighs as her fingers continued gliding near the swollen area. As she explored with her tongue, Miriam moved her body closer, trying to make contact. Deborah increased the pressure of her fingers, squeezing Miriam's flesh so she could feel the most sensitive place being massaged.

Miriam's hips moved rhythmically as Deborah caressed with her mouth everything near yet not on the tender place. She began to blow hot air over what she was not to touch and increased the pace of her fingers, massaging briskly, bringing Miriam closer and closer to the place of no return. She felt Miriam trying to move closer to create the touch that she so wanted. Deborah held back, withdrawing her tongue when Miriam pushed harder. Miriam was in a frenzy for contact. Miriam reached out to touch Deborah in her spot, but Deborah moved to just out of reach. They were both panting and squirming restlessly, chasing the release that was so very close.

Deborah backed off slightly and slowed the pace of her fingers without losing contact with Miriam's skin. Her tongue, licking the area nearby, was moist with Miriam's juices. Slowly, as if it were a mistake, Deborah's tongue made slight contact with the intended target. Miriam gasped loudly, clearly on the brink of exploding. Deborah continued touching close by as Miriam squirmed more, hoping to be stroked once again. After more torturous swipes near the target, Deborah again let her tongue make just the slightest contact. Miriam again moved closer.

On the third swipe, as Deborah's tongue just barely touched, Miriam pushed forward and yelled, "Please," as she forced her body against Deborah's mouth. Deborah obliged, flicking her tongue against the hard nub of skin, then grinding her mouth into Miriam. She sucked as Miriam arched her back and let out a loud noise as her body shook uncontrollably against Deborah's mouth. Deborah held on tight, pushing harder, sucking faster, as Miriam continued to writhe in pleasure. They stayed connected until Miriam's breathing finally slowed.

Deborah continued to lick as the stimulation drove Miriam to a second peak of excitement. With repeated gasps, finally Miriam calmed and lay perfectly still. Once she caught her breath, she whispered softly, "I guess we failed at our first night of pleasure."

"You call that a failure?" said Deborah, chuckling.

"No, not really. That was intense."

They both smiled as Miriam repositioned herself while announcing, "Your turn."

Deborah happily responded.

The next afternoon, following the appearance of three stars in the sky, Miriam lit the braided, multi-wick Havdalah candle, blessed a cup of wine, and handed the spice box around for each family member to sniff. Concluding the Sabbath, they blessed each other for a good week.

Deborah was pleased with the appearance of more latkes, this time accompanying roasted chicken. Deborah barely touched her chicken, instead choosing a second helping of latkes.

After dinner, while putting the girls to bed, Miriam kissed Deborah's ear and whispered a reminder of their second night of pleasure to come. As if she could forget!

Ida must have sensed their rushing the bedtime rituals, and in response, demanded an extra story. As Miriam read the book, Deborah touched Miriam's neck softly, letting a wandering finger caress the inner part of Miriam's ear. Deborah noted a few sighs inserted into the story as Miriam's concentration on the book wavered.

Finally, with both children asleep, they headed to their room. "And what do you have planned for tonight?" Miriam asked as soon as they were alone.

"Actually, I thought that I'd postpone my plans in favor of a repeat of last night. I couldn't imagine anything more sensational."

"You're cheating," said Miriam.

"No, I'm not. I just want my turn. Last night was luscious, yet although I got my share in the end, I want to be tempted, as you were."

"This is your night to plan, so you can copy me if you want."

"Wait a minute. If we repeat your plans, don't I get to choose tomorrow night?"

"So you want it all? I'll have to think about that," said Miriam.

"Let's have fun tonight, then see which of us has the better idea for tomorrow."

"Okay. Let's focus on tonight. Tell me what to do."

"First, you get to tell me one of your favorite memories. Let's hear..."

"At the top of my list was our first night in the turret at the Berkowitzes's new Berkshires home. I remember our excitement when we discovered there was just one large bed for the two of us."

"I remember you being upset with me," Deborah said.

"I forgot about that. I only remember our excitement when they left us alone for a short while before dinner. We took advantage of every moment, kissing and touching each other until we were in a frenzy. You could not get my clothes off quick enough. And when I touched you, I found you soaking wet, which was really thrilling."

"We were barely able to undress before we were fully engaged in loving each other's bodies. Matter of fact, I found that I still had a stocking on when we came up for air. That was exciting."

"And as soon as we were both satisfied, we started all over again," said Miriam with a smile.

"And then we heard footsteps—the four little girls rushing up the stairs to get us for dinner. I remember both of us pulling the sheets up over our naked bodies just in time for the children to come rushing into the room. I was really nervous they caught us."

"They thought we were just napping."

"I guess so, yet it really put a sudden end to our loving. It is funny that you remember this as such an exciting time, and I remember the worrisome parts."

"So I guess this has not put you in the right mood for tonight." Miriam frowned.

"Maybe we should start all over, and I should go back to my original plan, which was for us to say out loud exactly what we are feeling as we are being touched."

"I like that a lot. You start."

"You need to touch me, and I'll talk about how it makes me feel," Deborah said.

Miriam began with soft kisses, making certain to blow into Deborah's ear as she traced her way around Deborah's face.

"I love the sensation when you reach my ears. They're sensitive to your touch. You know exactly how to surprise me with a feeling that travels down my body. As you nibble on my ear, I feel my nipples harden."

Miriam continued, concentrating on Deborah's lips and neck.

"I love your kisses. They awaken everything, including a slight stirring between my legs. I can feel a throbbing just beginning." Deborah continued, "And your nuzzling my neck gets the same response. It sends shivers down to my breasts and then between my legs. I'm not yet wet, though I can feel sensations of pleasure. It is like a promise that soon you will reach my secret spot."

"Not too soon, my love. I want to wait until you are throbbing and wet."

"Then you should move to my breasts. You know how they respond to your touch."

Miriam did as asked yet touched lightly with just her fingertips. She kept her mouth focused on Deborah's neck, then lightly traced her way around her breasts. She circled them, then massaged the tender flesh, saving the nipples for special treatment. She felt Deborah arch a bit, offering her breasts. Miriam then massaged the orbs with her hands flat, squeezing tenderly yet insistently. Deborah was so lost to sensation that she forgot to describe what she felt.

As Miriam squeezed, she felt Deborah's nipples harden. Deborah remembered her role and said, "I love when you excite my breasts. You coax them into excitement. Please pinch my nipples a bit more, not hard, though with more pressure…there… Now they are fully aroused. My whole focus is on my nipples, and I'm beginning to ache down there for your touch."

"Not so fast, my dear," Miriam whispered hotly in her ear. "You must wait."

"I love it when you go slowly and make me wait until I'm desperate."

Miriam kissed lower, going from Deborah's neck to the place where her breasts began to swell. Again, Deborah arched, offering her deliciousness for Miriam's mouth. Miriam teased, at first circling the outsides of Deborah's breasts with her mouth, making Deborah wait for the pressure on her nipples.

"Please," Deborah begged, "suck on my nipples."

As Miriam lowered her lips to Deborah's right breast, she heard a moan of pleasure. She took the hardness into her mouth and sucked vigorously.

"The other one too" was all Deborah said.

Miriam pressed on the fleshy part of Deborah's breasts, massaging and bringing them closer together. She then flicked her tongue from breast to breast, making certain they both got their share of attention.

"Yes" was all that Deborah said before they became fully engaged in loving one another.

As they lay back on the bed, satisfied, Deborah whispered, "Happy Hanukkah."

∾ ∾ ∾

On the third night of Hanukkah, Sylvia had an earache and was very fussy. "You predicted that one of the children might get sick," said Deborah.

"And if you remember, we said that our gifts could go on past the eight days."

"Actually," Deborah said, "I wouldn't mind a night off. The past two nights have been delightful yet exhausting. If Sylvia feels better, I would love a calm night to recuperate and go to bed early."

"Oh my, have I worn you out, my love?"

"I'm not worn out, though a break might be nice," said Deborah. "Unless you're all worked up and want more tonight."

"Not really. I was teasing you. I would actually like tonight off also. I love the excitement we've brought to our intimacy. I'd love to continue. However, maybe not every night for eight nights in a row."

"What if," Deborah said, "we plan eight nights throughout the month for special play?"

"Or even through the winter. I'm in no rush to have this end. I'd like our special nights to go on for a long while. We've made everything else more important than intimacy. I really appreciate our return to a close connection."

"We could plan it for once a week. Maybe on *Shabbos*, since it is a mitzvah to have relations on the Sabbath."

Miriam remembered something. "We planned that before. We said we would have date nights on *Shabbos*."

"You're right. Let's try again."

"And I like that we take turns deciding how to make the evening exciting. Maybe by discussing these evenings ahead of time, it will keep us focused during the week about the excitement to come." Miriam smiled.

"What's it going to be?"

Just then, Sylvia began crying, and their attention turned to their daughter.

"I'll tell you later," Miriam teased.

Both of them went into Sylvia's room and took turns holding and rocking her until her earache subsided and she drifted off to sleep. As they returned to their bedroom, Deborah said, "I'm ready to hear about our next session."

"I bet you are. But maybe you should wait to find out what I have in store."

"Miriam, out with it."

"Don't get pushy. I'll tell you. I would like us to each pleasure ourselves in front of each other, as we did after our visit to the Palace Theater."

"I remember that. We went with Anna when she was in town. I learned about the laboratory in the same building, the one where Thomas Edison invented things."

"Deborah, let's not change the subject. I'm talking about ways to make our time in bed more exciting, and you're remembering Anna's vacation."

"You're right. I get easily distracted. Tell me more about your vision for our touching ourselves in front of each other."

"Now, you're catching on. But remember that this is not happening tonight. You get to ponder what it will be like and what fun we can have."

"I'm really glad we're finding ways to make our bedroom play more exciting."

❧ ❧ ❧

The week went by quickly, and Miriam made sporadic comments alluding to the experiences she was planning for Friday night. Deborah seemed a bit nervous, though she never considered turning down Miriam's proposals.

Friday evening was the last night of Hanukkah. They lit the menorah's eight candles with the *shammash,* and then they sang "*Ma'oz Tzur,*" the traditional Hanukkah song. After that, they watched as the candles slowly burned down then extinguished one by one. The children, pleased with their cache of Hanukkah gelt, built towers with the pennies. Neither had any concept of the worth of money, so to the girls, the coins were another shiny toy to stack.

As they were readying the children for bed, Miriam noted that Sylvia was rubbing her ear. She glanced at Deborah, who nodded. "I noticed her touching her ear during dinner. I hope her earache will not return tonight. Poor child."

After good-night wishes had been given to Susan and Helen, who never mentioned the new pattern of Deborah and Miriam heading to bed early on *Shabbos,* Deborah and Miriam went to their room and took off their dresses in great anticipation of what was to come. Suddenly, there was a scream from the children's room. They shook their heads, knowing their evening of excitement was about to be postponed.

"Happy Hanukkah," Deborah said in a low tone as they headed to the children's room to comfort Sylvia.

❧ ❧ ❧

Before the year ended, Miriam needed to have a difficult conversation with Marjorie. She decided to talk at the office since it was a work issue.

"Marjorie," Miriam said in an unfamiliar, serious tone, "we need to talk about baby Ezra."

"What's the problem? Is he making too much noise?"

"Actually, yes. He is a healthy, adorable three-month-old, which means that he is chattering quite a lot."

"I can try holding him more. He's quieter when I pick him up."

"No, I think it's time that he moves from the office. I've talked with Rachel, and he's welcome to spend his days with the other children at our house. She says she can handle watching another child."

Tears filled Marjorie's eyes. "I don't know how I can manage without him at my side all day."

"You'll be okay. It will be good for him to be around the other children. Rachel loves babies and is really excited about having Ezra join them."

"He's still drinking breast milk. How will we manage?"

"William can drive you home midday, so you can spend some time with him and feed him. Then, later in the afternoon, our new delivery boy will take you home for another feeding, and you can stay home the rest of the day."

"I just don't know if this will work."

"I know it will be a huge adjustment, so I'd like to suggest that we make the change gradually. In January, why don't we try this out for a couple days per week, and then increase the time as you're both ready."

"Thank you for letting me do this slowly. I can't imagine having him gone for so many hours of every day."

"I have an even better idea. Let's start with him being here in the mornings and with Rachel in the afternoons. Would that be better?"

"Yes, much better," said Marjorie with tears dripping down her face. "I'll make it work."

ॐ ॐ ॐ

Back at home that evening, Miriam said, "It was really hard to talk with Marjorie today about having Ezra at the office less."

"Were you worried she'd say no?" Deborah inquired.

"Not at all. And I certainly wasn't concerned that she'd be upset with me for asking. I know how attached she is to her baby and how hard it will be to leave him at home."

"Every mother needs to make the break from her baby if she has a job."

"I know that, but I think that's why so few women work. It can be wrenching to leave your child in someone else's care when they're so small."

"We leave our children with Rachel every day. Were you so torn up to leave Ida when she was a baby, Miriam?"

"Absolutely."

"You didn't talk about it. I knew you were sad, but I guess I didn't understand the depths of your emotions. Sometimes things like this just pass by me without notice. Were you upset with me for not being as devastated?"

"Not at all. I looked to you for help in coping with my feelings."

Deborah sighed. "I feel a bit embarrassed that I didn't have the same distress as you. Does that make me a less loving mother?"

"No," Miriam said, stroking Deborah's face, "I value you for your sensibility, especially when I'm so overly sensitive."

"Sometimes I think it terrible that I'm not as emotionally connected as you."

"I don't feel that way. You are my rock. I learn from you to take some of life's challenges in stride. I love you the way you are."

"I'm the luckiest woman in the world." Deborah kissed Miriam softly.

Menorah

Ponchick

Episode 25 ✢ *Great Molasses Flood*

January 1919

"Teddy Roosevelt died!" Deborah said as she opened the newspaper on January 6, surprised by the bold headline.

"The president of the United States? What happened?"

"Poor man had a history of many ailments, from serious asthma as a child to a throat condition that almost took his voice. According to this article, he was blind in one eye and deaf in one ear, and he recovered from a bullet to his chest from an assassination attempt in 1912. He was only sixty years old, so despite his medical history, it was a surprise to everyone that he died in his sleep."

"Why the focus on his health, rather than on his political accomplishments?" Miriam asked.

"Because you asked what happened to him."

"Tell me about his achievements quickly because I need to get ready for work," Miriam said.

Deborah responded, "I was most impressed by his establishing our national parks and forests."

"That's interesting, and you're very knowledgeable, yet I really need to finish getting dressed."

"You really have no interest in politics, do you?"

"Not really, however, I appreciate you keeping me up with important things going on in the world."

"I'll just tell you that he is considered one of the best presidents ever."

"Then I guess I should listen harder. Later, not now."

৯ ৯ ৯

"I smell something," said Deborah late in the afternoon, about a week after Roosevelt's death. Following a five-day cold front, with frigid weather no higher than in the teens, temperatures in the thirties were a welcome relief. "It smells like someone is making baked beans."

Micah sniffed the air in the office.

Deborah continued to wrinkle her nose as she walked from the publishing shop, through the door into the printing shop. Out loud, to no one in particular, she said, "Does anyone other than me smell something strange?"

"I do. It smells like cookies," said young Leah.

"Me too," said her companion Mildred.

Hannah, not wanting to take the word of the two young girls, decided to investigate on her own. She went to the front of the shop to scrutinize the situation. As soon as she opened the door, a distinct strong, sweet smell wafted in.

Everyone rose, as they heard a great commotion outside. People were gathering in the street, looking towards the waterfront about a half mile away, pointing, and lifting their noses toward the sky. Something was amiss. As they watched, the crowd increased, and speculation ranged from a fire at a bakery, to an explosion on a ship in the harbor. Some people talked of hearing a loud bang.

A young man ran into the street from the direction of the smell, climbed on a pile of boxes stacked on a street corner, and called for attention. He caught his breath as a hush fell over the crowd. "There's been a horrible accident at the waterfront. A huge tank of warm molasses broke, and a great flood of it killed many people. All strong men should head that way to help."

After a collective gasp, people ran in different directions, some towards the disaster to offer assistance and others towards their homes to ensure their loved ones were unharmed. Those at the publishing and printing shops stayed put and avoided getting caught up in the general panic. Miriam went back inside to tell Micah and Leah, the two unable to come out, what had happened. Deborah and Marjorie stayed outside for the latest updates.

One young boy seemed especially distraught. "It could have been me who was killed," said the boy of about ten. "I was on me way to the waterfront when this happened."

Marjorie asked him to tell her more.

"I go there to collect the molasses. Me mudder loves to bake with it, so she sends me to collect the smelly stuff. The tank was always leaking, so me and my friends always got a pail full. When it got on me hands, I had to lick it off. I hated the taste at first. Then I got sort of used to it. It was sweet. I really liked the cookies she made, and me favorite was the beans she made on Saturdays."

"I've made Boston baked beans with molasses," said Marjorie, trying to calm the boy down.

"Yeah, me mudder called it that too." Marjorie's attention seemed to relax the child, who said, "I'd better go home and tell me ma and da that I'm fine. I bet they have some worry on."

During the rest of the afternoon, there was lots of noise and activity downtown as people returned from the horrific scene with terrible tales to tell, including stories of several children being injured. They were graphic in their descriptions. They told of a huge wave of molasses that traveled through the neighborhood, covering everything. According to their reports, buildings collapsed, and even train trestles from the elevated railway were thrust to the ground.

There was lots of speculation about the cause, the number of people hurt, and which businesses were destroyed. People wondered how this mess could be cleaned up. The smell was intense, sometimes gagging people.[39]

The next day, Marjorie joined Deborah to see what had happened at the waterfront. On the way, Deborah mentioned the latest news reported in the morning newspaper. "Did you read that Prohibition passed?" she asked.

"No, I didn't see the paper this morning. Will we have trouble getting Manischewitz wine for *Shabbos*?"

"I don't know. Do you smell that odor?"

"Yes," Marjorie said.

By the time they walked the short distance to the shattered tank, they smelled more than the molasses. It was the smell of decay. They did not realize what the odor was, but the aroma was so strong that it turned them away.

---

[39] On January 15, 1919, a huge tank of molasses burst open on Commercial Street in Boston's North End. A wave of over 2,000,000 gallons of sticky, warm molasses flooded the streets, traveling up to 35 miles per hour and crushing buildings, people, and horses. The Great Molasses Flood killed 21 people and injured 150.

United States Industrial Alcohol, the company that built the tank, imported molasses from the Caribbean for the manufacture of munitions and the production of alcoholic beverages. They were charged with poor planning and lack of oversight that led to the tank's structural failure. The tank construction had been overseen by their bookkeeper, something that would never happen again because new laws were established to regulate the construction of the tanks.

Boston Harbor remained brown until the summer. The smell of molasses lingered for decades.

Once back at the office, Marjorie explained to those who gathered for an update, "It was awful. I heard that the huge wave of molasses was thirty feet tall and covered the whole neighborhood. Many people and animals were caught in it and drowned. The whole shipyard area was flooded."

"And I learned," said Deborah, "that the molasses was warm when it spilled from the tank. The very warm weather yesterday made it flow easily, yet the cooler weather today is making it harder to clean up. It's stuck to everything."

Marjorie arrived at work the following morning with more news. "A friend from my school, James, was hurt in the molasses flood. He was at the shipyard, delivering food to his dad who worked there, when the tank burst. His foot was injured badly, and he's in the hospital. Would you mind if I leave a little early to see him?"

"Not at all," said Miriam.

The news the following day, upon Marjorie's return, was grim. "His leg is horrible, and he is going to be in the hospital for a long time."

Over the next week, Marjorie went to visit James several times; she returned and talked about the pain her friend was in and the horrible stench from his infected leg. It did not surprise anyone at the shop when she announced that James had lost his leg.

"Maybe, when he gets better, he can talk with Micah, 'cause Micah has just one leg," said Leah.

Marjorie looked at Leah, uncertain how Micah would react to this request. "Let's see how James does. Maybe, once he's recovered, he can meet with Micah."

࿇ ࿇ ࿇

"What do you think about Leah's suggestion that the boy who lost his leg meet with Micah?" asked Miriam while she and Deborah were setting the table for dinner.

"I wouldn't bring it up," said Deborah as she placed the silverware around the table. "Marjorie heard Leah's suggestion. We should stay out of this and let her decide whether to approach her husband."

"I agree we shouldn't get involved. I just wondered how you felt about it," Miriam said.

"It might be good for him, as well as for the unfortunate boy. Micah has not talked about how his life has changed since losing his leg. No, actually, since he was first hurt. He talks about his pain, and he complains about how he can't do things he used to do. It's as if he wants to keep his disability a secret, though he obviously can't."

"I wonder how I'd be if I lost a leg," said Miriam, looking at the ceiling while deep in thought. "I wonder if I'd talk about it all the time or keep my feelings to myself, like Micah does."

"Does he discuss his feelings with Marjorie?"

"I know he doesn't. Marjorie tries to get him to talk, yet he resists. She's even asked him to discuss his loss with someone from the army, though he has no interest."

"I don't envy his life," Deborah said. "He's more independent since getting crutches. He isn't confined to that wheelchair all the time now, yet I wonder why he hasn't gotten a wooden leg. I would have."

"I would have too, though he's resisted every suggestion Marjorie's made. He seems stuck on being an invalid."

"I feel so bad for Marjorie. It's hard having a crippled husband." Miriam sighed.

࿔ ࿔ ࿔

Marjorie was thrilled when Micah agreed to visit James and several other boys badly hurt in the flood. They met at a house with a ramp to accommodate their wheelchairs; Micah was their special guest.

Marjorie secretly told Miriam of these meetings. "I'm really pleased these boys invited Micah to speak with them. I have no idea what they talk about; however, Micah seems different since that first meeting. He's gone a second time and plans to go again this week."

"Does he feel more accepted since being with others like himself?"

"From what he's told me, he feels like the expert. He likes that the others ask him questions and treat him like he knows everything. He hasn't felt like he has something to offer since his accident—well, except at the office. Everyone there always makes him feel like his contribution is valuable. Micah would never have attended the meetings had they invited him as just another participant. He was proud to share his success in being back to work."

"This sounds very good for Micah," Miriam said.

"There's more. They had a speaker last week, Philip Martino who founded United Limb and Brace, a local company specializing in artificial limbs. This man assured them he could fit every man with a prosthetic limb that would alter his life. One of the men at the meeting was a soldier who had been invited by a friend who was hurt in the molasses flood. He raved about how much more mobile he's been since being fitted with a wooden leg from the Artificial Limb Laboratory at Walter Reed Hospital. He told them that the army assured every amputee a modern limb."

Marjorie's face lit up. "Micah told me that every disabled soldier is eligible, though he's remained resistant up until now. He was quite impressed by Mr. Martino, and he's agreed to have an evaluation. I'm staying out of this since his new friends have agreed to take him, but I'm extremely hopeful."

"Oh, Marjorie! I'm so pleased. He'll be able to get around better. He always seems so awkward with his crutches."

"I'm really hopeful he takes action. And I'm very pleased he's begun to talk with the other boys about what it's like to be a cripple…and now with me too. It no longer feels like a secret or a subject we can't discuss. Truthfully, I think his new attitude is because of the baby. He wants to be more mobile so he can be a better dad."

"I'm as happy for you as I am for him." Miriam hugged her friend.

ॐ ॐ ॐ

One day, without any discussion, Micah walked into the office on his new wooden leg. Everyone made a huge fuss, congratulating Marjorie as well as Micah.[40]

ॐ ॐ ॐ

Although Marjorie was happy with her husband's new prosthetic, she was somber. Being away from Ezra for long periods was challenging. She wept when she dropped off the baby with Rachel and when she picked him up. He seemed perfectly happy.

Rachel's adjustment to the addition of Ezra in her care was also difficult. Caring for Sylvia, Ida, and Sarah had been manageable, but

---

[40] United Limb and Brace of Dorchester, Massachusetts, was a pioneer in the development of artificial limbs. Incorporated in 1972, and later renamed United Prosthetics, this company is committed to the betterment of the lives of disabled people. Following World War I, the United States government provided artificial legs, hands, arms, and feet to war veterans, helping them to return to the workforce and live productive lives.

a newborn made her days more complex. She wondered how mothers with large numbers of children managed. The most difficult part was entertaining all four children because their needs were so different from one another's. Sarah, at four, was quite independent and easily engaged in any project. Sylvia, now six, was more challenging, not because she was disagreeable—though she could be stubborn—but because she needed direct monitoring with any activity. For instance, if Rachel made a paste of flour and water, Rachel needed to watch both Sylvia and nineteen-month-old Ida carefully, or it would end up in a mouth rather than on the intended paper project. On the other hand, Rachel was thrilled to have a newborn to cuddle, though sometimes the other children got into mischief while she was changing his diapers.

Three half days were manageable, though Rachel worried how she'd manage when Ezra came to her more often. She feared the quality of her care would decrease proportionately to the number of children in her charge. She said nothing to the mothers, yet they were aware of her predicament when they came to take the children home.

They talked repeatedly with one another about possible solutions, though none was obvious. Deborah tried to be sensitive to the issue. Miriam was appreciative of Deborah's empathetic response when Deborah asked about how Rachel was doing.

≈ ≈ ≈

The end of the month brought a delightful surprise—Fanny came home. She was discharged from the navy just nine months after being sworn in. She returned to New York in a sour mood, devastated at having to leave Rina behind.

"I don't know what to do," Mrs. B. told Deborah in one of their regular calls. "Fanny is so upset that she's not even eating. She just sulks."

"I'm certain she'll adjust to being home. Just give her time."

"All she talks about is Rina. She's really taken with this young woman. I really hope I like her."

Deborah, not disclosing the incident when Rina had inappropriately kissed Fanny in the hotel lobby, hoped so too.

"She's asked that Rina move in with us when she returns, whenever that might be. Rina has her own family, so I don't understand why she would leave them to live in a strange city."

"New York just happens to be the most exciting city in the world. That's why she would want to live there. And Fanny's there. Also, it might be more likely she could find a job there."

"How will my other girls take to her? And what will Fanny and Rina do with themselves? Neither has anything to occupy her time."

"They'll have to entertain each other. That will be enough to start."

When Deborah got off the phone, she approached Miriam regarding plans for Fanny and Rina. "Remember when Fanny asked in a letter if she could move to Boston to work with us? I think that might be a good idea. Rina could come with her."

Miriam sat up straight. "Wait a minute. What are you suggesting? Are you thinking Rina could work for us like Fanny has? We haven't even met her, and we have no idea what her skills are. She might be more of a burden than a help at the shop."

"That isn't exactly what I was thinking." Deborah faced Miriam and looked her directly in her eyes. "Where we could really use help is with childcare. Now that Ezra has started coming here, Rachel looks overwhelmed."

"What makes you think that she'll be good with our children? Babysitting isn't a job you go to school to learn. Rachel is absolutely fabulous with the children, but there's no way to know how Rina would be."

"Slow down, Miriam. I know that. It's just a thought."

Miriam took in a big gulp of air and calmed herself. They sat in their wingback chairs and remained silent for a minute. Miriam broke the silence. "Where will they live? Even if we pay them, it will not be enough to get a nice place of their own. They'd end up in a place like Margaret and… What's her girlfriend's name? That couple we met at the first suffrage meeting we went to?"

"Abigail. And you're right. They'd end up barely managing a very basic flat. That's why I think they should move in here."

"What are you talking about? The room Fanny stays in is barely big enough for her."

"It would be enough for a young couple in love. Remember the turret room we stayed in at the Berkowitzes' Lenox home? There was hardly room enough for one, and we were fine."

"That was just for a summer. You're talking about them living here full time. And we haven't even met Rina. We'd have to like her a whole lot to have her move in and join our family."

"I hear what you're saying. It was just an idea. I didn't mean to ruffle you," Deborah said.

Several times, Miriam restated what a bad idea Deborah had.

∾ ∾ ∾

Rina was discharged two weeks after Fanny. After visiting with her own family for a week, she arrived at the Berkowitz home with enough luggage to appear she was moving in. Her things barely fit in Fanny's old room, which Ethel reluctantly released to the couple. Fanny and Rina were to occupy this room because it had two beds. Fanny's sisters never figured out that the second bed was never used.

The Berkowitz twins were delighted when Rina greeted each of them with buttery toffee, which she called butterscotch, ingratiated herself with them within minutes of her arrival. Ethel was harder to appease; she was ready to dislike this stranger who had ousted her from her bedroom. Yet when Rina pulled a Ouija board from her suitcase during her first evening there, Ethel was intrigued. Rina told them how this occult game was a means to communicate with the dead and predict the future. After dinner that evening, and every evening thereafter, they sat around the table, solving mysteries and predicting their lives for the next twenty years. When the two lovebirds asked to visit Boston, the Berkowitz girls were saddened that their new playmate would be gone for several days.

On the other end of the telephone line, Miriam bristled, assuming this visit had been staged by Deborah, yet she reluctantly agreed. As Miriam put sheets on Fanny's bed, she became determined to discourage Deborah's scheme.

From the moment Fanny and Rina arrived, however, Fanny's young girlfriend proved a delightful guest. She arrived with a ready smile, a warm manner, and treats to share. Rina focused her attention on Sylvia and Ida, engaging the youngsters in silly games before getting to know the others. Sylvia took to her immediately, not wanting to leave her side. Later that day, Rina pulled out her Ouija board, and quickly Mildred was enthralled, begging to stay awake past her bedtime to continue playing.

Rina encouraged everyone to share stories about their favorite people; she was using the game to gain insight into the people around her. During the week, she had private conversations with each person and asked questions about the people they'd mentioned while playing with the Ouija board. Her sweet yet assertive personality charmed everyone, including Miriam, who was pleased with this young woman. Additionally, Rina took responsibility around the house, cleaning up after dinner without being prompted. It was impossible for anyone to find fault with Fanny's girlfriend.

By the end of their stay, it was an easy decision. After consulting with Susan and Helen, Miriam and Deborah invited Fanny and Rina to move in and join the family on Homestead Street.

❧ ❧ ❧

All the Berkowitzes had been charmed by Rina, so they weren't anxious to have her leave. Fanny's sisters were reluctant to see her move. Even Ethel was sorry to have her depart.

Fanny and Rina moved into their new Boston home with more luggage than could possibly fit into their tiny room. Their first two days were spent sorting their clothing and storing them in a dresser they dragged up from the basement, three flights below, and placed in the tiny hall between their bedroom and Mildred's. The question of where to hang their dresses required ingenuity since their tiny closet could barely hold one woman's wardrobe. Rina set to work designing two racks, one to attach to the back of their bedroom door and the other to the front of the closet door. Fanny and Rina smiled as they hung their clothing, pleased to have figured out a solution.

Deborah and Miriam hoped the clothing covering the walls would help to soften the noises the two girls were likely to make. They were pleased Mildred was a sound sleeper, since it was likely Fanny's and Rina's passion would be audible.

❧ ❧ ❧

Having Fanny and Rina in the house added an unexpected thrill. Restraining their appetite for intimacy when around others, this new young couple usually kept their hands to themselves, yet their excitement was obvious. Sometimes, one squeezed the other's hand or slowly stroked her partner's arm. On other occasions, it was just a glance that gave away their excitement. Their desire was palpable.

They often retired to their room early, and occasionally their intimate sounds pierced the quiet and stimulated Deborah and Miriam.

One evening soon after Fanny and Rina moved in, Miriam pulled Deborah into a firm hug, followed by a deep kiss, after reaching their bedroom.

"Delicious," Deborah said, smiling.

"Hearing the sounds of the two young lovers upstairs has certainly charged our home," Miriam said with a grin.

"It certainly has. I think having them here will help us to fulfill our Hanukkah commitment to each other."

"I loved the feathers you introduced to our bed play last week. Did you have another idea? You seem ready."

"I am ready," Deborah said, blushing. "I've been thinking all day of how much enjoyment we both got from talking about what we were doing while we were doing it. That's my plan for tonight."

"I'll do my best with your idea, though you are several hours ahead of me in mentally planning our evening. I'm glad to participate, yet you may need to slowly entice me into this scheme of yours."

"I'll be glad to do that. The only rule for tonight is that we are both to talk about what we are experiencing." Deborah smiled.

"Right now, I'm just experiencing a little anxiety that I won't be ready fast enough."

"Silly you. We aren't in a rush. Now, you should take off your clothing and ready yourself for bed without putting on anything."

"But it's January, and it's cold!" Miriam said, shivering while thinking of standing at the sink with nothing on.

"I assume you'll arrive at the bed with your nipples taut and a desire for my arms around you."

"That's for sure."

Deborah climbed into bed first, smiling while watching Miriam in anticipation. As soon as Miriam climbed under the covers, Deborah checked that her nipples were as hard as expected. She covered Miriam's entire body with hers, bringing the heat back to Miriam's torso.

Deborah concentrated on Miriam's breasts, which were warming up, though still erect. "Tell me how this feels," Deborah coaxed, as she encircled each with her lips.

"It feels like my breasts are alive. The sensation is both in the nipples and in the throbbing between my legs. It is like they are attached to one another. The pleasure travels down my body and lands in my special place."

Deborah continued to suck Miriam's breasts for a few minutes, letting her enjoy the sensations. Then she replaced her lips with her hands, tweaking the nipples and massaging the flesh while traveling downwards with her mouth. As she reached Miriam's flat belly, she enjoyed making her whole body squirm. Again, Deborah took her time, slowly venturing south, never taking her hands off Miriam's breasts. As she reached the top of Miriam's pubic hairline, she stopped and trailed her hands down to join her mouth. Deborah's hands massaged at the very top of Miriam's legs, near her special spot, as she applied firm pressure to Miriam's inner thighs.

"What do you feel?" Deborah asked, reminding Miriam to put words to her pleasure.

"All my attention is on my sweet spot. I want you to massage it with your lips, though I love that you are taking your time getting there. I feel a pulsing, and it's getting very wet. I wonder when you'll finally get there. Part of me wants it right now, yet the other part of me wants you to take your time."

"I will most certainly take my time. You'll need to beg when you can't stand it anymore."

"I'm getting closer than you might guess," Miriam said between gasps.

"Not yet, sweetie."

Deborah massaged the area with her hands, never directly touching Miriam's most tender place. Instead, she moved the flesh so that Miriam felt her own body massaging and tempting the area.

When she removed her hands, Miriam said, "More."

Miriam's version of "more" was for Deborah to use her mouth. She blew on the area, adding warmth to an already-wet area. She pulled at Miriam's flesh rhythmically, careful to avoid the swollen nub that was the center of Miriam's pleasure. Then she parted Miriam's labia, pulling them apart, and exposed the wet area to the air. She looked down for a moment, watching the shiny, swollen clitoris glisten.

"Please," pleaded Miriam, getting close to frantic.

Deborah blew another gust of hot air over the inflamed skin where Miriam's parted legs met. Her mouth came close enough that Miriam could feel the warmth as she squirmed uncontrollably. "More. Touch me," she said.

"You want it bad?" Deborah teased.

"Yes. Now, please."

Deborah flicked her tongue quickly, making momentary contact with Miriam's tender spot. Miriam moaned loudly, "More."

Deborah repeated the flicking of her tongue, this time touching Miriam's body for a slightly longer time.

"More," Miriam begged again.

"Describe what you feel."

"I'm aching. The sensation when you make contact is intense. I want more."

Deborah slid her tongue along the length of Miriam's swollen area. She shivered involuntarily and raised her pelvis to meet Deborah's sweet mouth. Deborah finally gave in, lapping Miriam's sweet spot as Miriam began to pant. She was very close to exploding. Deborah placed her lips firmly on Miriam's pleasure spot and then rhythmically moved her tongue, darting in and out.

"Yes!" Miriam called out, out of control and moving her body in a frenzy as the area began to pulse rhythmically. Deborah held on, never wavering in her touch, moving her tongue faster and faster along the length of Miriam's excited flesh. As Miriam shouted, "Yes, yes," Deborah sucked in her sweetness. She carried Miriam through the peak of pleasure and never let go until Miriam collapsed on the bed.

Deborah moved up to kiss Miriam with her wet mouth. The lingering aromas and tastes pleased them both. They lay still for a short while, deeply appreciating the sensations as Miriam's breathing returned to normal. There was a smile on both their faces as Miriam took Deborah's fingers and gently kissed them. Deborah then moved Miriam's hand down to her own excitement. She was soaking wet and spasmed slightly at the first touch of her nakedness.

Miriam smiled as she lowered herself toward Deborah's sweet spot, which was ready and waiting. As her lips got closer, Miriam pulled Deborah closer so the next contact would be firm. Deborah could not wait; her joy exploded before Miriam barely had time to touch her. Deborah pulled Miriam's head firmly. She demanded pressure, and Miriam obliged by licking the area with a hard, insistent touch. Deborah immediately swelled. Miriam, as she knew Deborah would want, sucked vigorously, bringing Deborah to a prolonged peak of pleasure. Miriam continued lapping, and soon Deborah was frenzied again; she writhed with pleasure through another convulsion. Miriam continued, and again Deborah responded with waves of repeated delight. After the third time, Deborah pushed Miriam away from her sensitive pleasure spot, totally satisfied.

When they finally calmed, Deborah mentioned the sounds coming from the third floor. She speculated that Fanny and Rina had heard the sounds of their passion and had responded by creating their own. They listened silently to the music of love.

Teddy Roosevelt in MA

Episode 26 ✳ *Boston Suffrage*

February 1919

Noticing Mildred had arrived at the dinner table with a list, Helen asked, "What do you have to share with us, dear? Did you learn more about slavery?"

"No, I have other interests as well. I found out some things you probably don't know."

"Like what?"

"When I went to the library with Deborah, I found a magazine that had a really interesting list. I picked out the best things to tell you. These are the new inventions of last year, 1918."

"That sounds interesting," Miriam said, sitting next to Sylvia so she could monitor her eating.

Mildred unfolded her piece of paper, glad to have an audience. "There were a lot more things, but I didn't understand some of them, like the science stuff, and some were boring, like something called daylight time. I just picked out my favorite things to share."

"I'll be glad to hear what you found interesting," Susan said.

"The first thing on my list was something called wristwatches. These are like little clocks that people can wear on their arms."

"What's wrong with pocket watches?" Deborah asked.

"This is for girls too. Our pockets are too low and deep, so we can't reach into them easily. Wouldn't it be good to find out the time so easily? If I wanted to know if my homework reading time was done, I could just look down to find out."

"So if I wanted to know if it is time to check on the batch of cookies in the oven, I could just sneak a quick look at your wristwatch."

Sylvia perked up at hearing Miriam mention the word "cookies," and she looked around to see if there were some being served.

"Yes, I bet there would be lots of times it would be handy."

"What's next on your list, Mildred?" asked Miriam.

"Tea bags. These are little packets with tea measured out ahead of time. You just pop them into your cup."

"So we wouldn't make a pot of tea to share with everyone? Why would that be helpful?"

"What if we each wanted a different type of tea?" Helen said.

"Are there different kinds of tea? I thought we only had one choice, the tea from China," Miriam said.

"Maybe, with tea in bags, we'd get to learn about different teas. There are many kinds of tea. I once had tea made in India."

"Where's that?" Mildred asked. "Is it in China?"

"No," Helen explained, "it's near China, but it's a different county."

"I already like your list, Mildred. What's next?"

"Zips. It's a funny-looking way to pull clothing together or apart. I don't understand why anyone would want to use something they are calling a zipper."

"I'd love something for my dresses that wouldn't involve hooks and clasps."

"They call it the hookless fastener," Mildred said excitedly. "They used them for soldiers' boots and uniforms, and now they're suggesting they go on our clothing."

"What do they look like? I wouldn't want something ugly sticking out of my dress," Miriam said.

"I'll draw you a picture like the one in the magazine," Mildred said as she started sketching.

"I wouldn't want to be seen with that on my pretty dress," Miriam said, holding up Mildred's picture.

"Don't you want to be in fashion when everyone else is wearing them?" Deborah asked.

"No, thank you."

"The next one is about fashion too. It's not like fashion that you see, but what's underneath. It's called a brassiere."

"What's that?" Helen asked.

"Wait," said Deborah, "is this something that should be mentioned at the dinner table?"

"I think it's okay for me to talk about it because I don't have a bosom yet."

"Mildred, that's getting a little personal for our dinner conversation," Susan said.

"She asked."

"You're right. I guess you can go on."

"Some fancy lady in New York didn't want to wear a corset under her new dress. She made up this little strap to hold up her big bosom, so she didn't have to put on a whalebone corset."

"This is definitely not dinner talk, dear. On to the next thing on your list."

"This is the last thing. But I can't figure out why it's so special. It's called a pop-up toaster. Why would anyone want to spend extra money on a toaster that pops up? Isn't the toaster we have on the top of the stove good enough?"

Miriam answered, "Our toaster is old-fashioned. I was thinking we should get one of those new ones that you plug in, but now we could get the new pop-up kind."

"I still don't understand what's good about it."

"Think about how many times the toast is burned, and we have to throw it out," Deborah said. "If it pops up when it is done, it would never be burnt."

"Now I get it. Can we get one?"

"Maybe. Thank you for such an interesting list, Mildred," said Susan. "It's amazing to me how people come up with so many new inventions."

Just then, Jimmy the cat jumped onto Mildred's lap, knocking down the pencil she was holding. She could hear him purring as he jumped back off, pushing the pencil under the table. Mildred exclaimed, "Someone should invent a cat toy that would interest Jimmy more than my pencil. Maybe it could look like a little mouse and teach him that catching mice is his job."

Everyone smiled.

ȣ ȣ ȣ

One evening, Deborah entered the parlor after putting the girls to bed and found Susan and Helen deep in conversation about changes in the women's suffrage movement. Turning toward Deborah, Susan said, "President Wilson was not a supporter of women voting, but he's shifted his attitude."

"We think it had to do with the horrible treatment of women during the Night of Terror."

"You may think so, Helen, but I don't," Susan said sternly. "He changed his mind because he knew he wouldn't get reelected if he didn't."

"Whichever reason, on September 30, he announced to the Senate that they needed to endorse women and pass the Susan B. Anthony Amendment. The House passed it in January, yet it has not gotten through the Senate. We remain one vote short."

"I'm not certain I understand what this means," Miriam said.

Helen explained, "Congress needs a two-thirds majority vote to pass an amendment to the constitution, and they are shy just one vote."

"Now I understand."

෨ ෨ ෨

"I can't wait to tell you what we learned tonight at our women's suffrage meeting," Helen told Deborah and Miriam when she and Susan rushed into the parlor after their meeting.

"Good news, I hope," said Deborah.

"Brave news. Whether it's good or not will remain to be seen," Susan responded.

"Tell us."

Helen took a deep breath, stood upright, and began, "You know the Silent Sentinels, the group of suffragists who've been standing at the gates of the White House for the past two years?"

"Yes."

"Today, February 9, they took action. One of the women felt it important enough to spend the money to call a friend in our group to update her. She told our friend that while remaining quiet, they burned President Wilson in effigy."

"Did they get arrested?" Miriam asked.

"Surprisingly, they didn't. This was their latest effort to get attention about the constitutional amendment to allow women to vote. The next vote is tomorrow, and it's getting really close to passing this time," said Susan.

"Many other countries have passed women's suffrage this year. Germany, Poland, Austria, and the Ukraine have done so, as well as Russia," Helen added.

"And England and Ireland allow women over thirty to vote now."

"That's odd. I wonder why the age requirement," Deborah asked, but no one had an answer.

"I hope their actions tonight bring them positive attention, and that it passes tomorrow," said Miriam.

The next day, Deborah and Miriam waited for Susan and Helen to return from their second meeting in two days. They hoped to read success across their faces, yet the dim looks in their eyes told Deborah and Miriam all they needed to know.

"We're still behind by one vote," Susan announced. "The Senate passed the amendment, but not by the necessary two-thirds vote. The vote was fifty-five to twenty-nine, not enough to count."

"So close, but not quite enough," said Helen. "The fight goes on. Maybe next time."

෯ ෯ ෯

The month continued with focus on the passage of the Nineteenth Amendment. Boston suffragists met regularly at the National Women's Party headquarters at Number 9 Park Street. Susan and Helen attended many meetings as plans were made for President Wilson's impending visit to Boston.

President Wilson's ship was to anchor in Boston on his return from the Paris Peace Conference. A motorcade planned to take him down past South Station, down Summer Street, past Filene's Corner, down Park Street, to a special stand erected on Boston Common, where he was to give a speech.

The suffragists had ample opportunity to plan their moves. They created banners, including one which Susan worked on, stating, "Mr. President: You said to the United States Senate on September 30, 'We shall not only be distrusted but shall deserve to be distrusted if we do not enfranchise women.' You, alone, can remove this distrust NOW by securing the one vote needed to pass the women's suffrage amendment before March 4."

Prior to Wilson's arrival, twenty-two suffragettes were arrested near the Park Street headquarters. The arrest was for gathering longer than seven minutes, an odd city ordinance. As one woman was lifted into the police wagon, she waved to those at headquarters, causing quite a ruckus. This was the first arrest of suffragettes outside of Washington, DC.

෯ ෯ ෯

Back in their room, Miriam brought up the topic of the Paris Peace Conference. "I'm the least political of all of us. I've read some about the conference, but could you share a succinct version of what you know? It is confusing to me why this conference is happening after the war has ended, rather than before peace was declared."

Deborah took a deep breath. "I'll give you a very short version because it probably won't interest you a great deal. The Paris Peace Conference, held in the Palace of Versailles, began on January 19, was a meeting of the thirty-three countries that worked together to win the Great War. The intent of this meeting was to set the conditions of peace, which will be maintained by the five great powers—the United States, France, Britain, Italy, and Japan. The main result of the Paris Peace Conference was the signing of the Treaty of Versailles, which blames Germany and its allies for the war and sets a huge penalty Germany has to pay. Are you bored yet?"

"No, go on."

"The only other interesting piece of information is that I read President Wilson got sick during the conference and didn't participate much. He was not able to effectively advocate for the Fourteen Points, his strategy for achieving world peace."

"Thanks for your explanation," Miriam said. "Did they accept Wilson's proposal?"

"It is too early to tell, but I think the greatest point was his suggestion for a League of Nations, a way for everyone to work together to achieve peace."

"May it be so."[41]

---

[41] The Paris Peace Conference met for a full year. Both France and Great Britain were vehemently opposed to the huge reparations required from Germany, as laid out in the drafted treaty. Wilson wanted to spare Germany humiliation, so, instead, he focused on building the League of Nations, an international diplomatic group that was established at the conference as a direct result of Woodrow Wilson's Fourteen Points speech, his ideals for peace after the war. Wilson's Fourteen Points outlined ways for international conflicts to be resolved without warfare. Besides the League of Nations, Wilson's speech included proposals for open agreements, reductions in arms, freedom on the seas, free trade, and self-determination for oppressed minorities.

After the conference ended, President Wilson's personal physician reported that on April 3, the president suffered from a violent cough. His condition was bad enough that the doctor questioned whether Wilson had been poisoned. Later, it was determined

Reverend Brown and his family had become increasingly important to Mildred.

"I learned something fascinating," Reverend Brown said to Mildred during one of their get-togethers.

"Tell me," Mildred said. "You always teach me wonderful new things."

"This may be of great interest to your housemates, Deborah and Miriam, so I hope you'll share this with them."

"I wish you could come to the house to tell them yourself. I don't understand why this mourning period after Deborah's brother's death is so long." Mildred squirmed.

"It is not up to us to question religious traditions. Now, let me tell you about the wonderful family I met this week. They moved here from Cape Verde. Do you know where that is?"

"I've never even heard of it. Where is it?"

Reverend Brown settled into his chair. "Cape Verde is a set of islands off the coast of West Africa. Unfortunately, when people in different locations faced slavery similar to that in our country, many families fled their homelands because of the oppression they were experiencing. Spanish and Portuguese Jews emigrated to Cape Verde, hoping for religious freedom."

"Did they find it?"

"Yes. This small group of refugees were able to practice their Judaism and bury their dead in Jewish cemeteries. The family I met were of Jewish heritage, even though they are Negro, which is why I thought Deborah and Miriam would be interested in them."

"So how did this family get to the United States?" Mildred asked.

---

that Wilson's illness was due to the influenza of 1918. He was bedridden for much of the conference.

Wilson's change of tactics and attitude after contracting the disease was highly significant. As was true of others who had contracted the influenza, there seemed to be a great change in his affect. Some close to him noted neurological changes, which may account for his softening on the very points that had previously driven him. The flu had weakened both his body and his mind, and Wilson no longer stood his ground. Wilson became paranoid and was never the same after this illness. We will never know if it would have changed the course of history had President Woodrow Wilson not gotten the influenza and suffered such a significant shift in his attitude.

"Would you like to meet them and ask them all about their background?"

"Oh yes. Thank you."

Deborah and Miriam were fascinated to learn about this Jewish family of Negroes from Cape Verde. They told Marilyn and Julie, their Spanish friends who were Jewish, and they all wanted to meet with this family of Negro Jews to find out more.

Marilyn and Julie invited the group to their house for February 23, though there was a snowfall, so the gathering was postponed. It had been a mild winter, so a mere four inches of snow stopped everything.

When they were finally able to get together, the conversation was very animated, with everyone noting similarities in their family histories. The Cape Verdean family had emigrated from Morocco to Cape Verde, and later to Newport, Rhode Island. As Julie's family had also discovered, Newport was a welcoming community for Sephardic Jews.

On the way home, Deborah and Miriam discussed the interesting connections between Jews and Cape Verdeans.

"It seems we are everywhere," Miriam said enthusiastically.

"More places for us to be discriminated against," Deborah said, sighing.

"Deborah, you first see the negative side of each situation."

"And you, my dear, always look at the bright side. It's amazing that we get along so well. Or maybe we balance out one another. I keep us aware, and you keep us hopeful."

"We are good for each other."[42]

&ampampampampamp;amp; & &

As the day the President's ship was to anchor approached, the Boston suffragists plotted, knowing they only had eight days before the Senate was in recess. Susan and Helen discussed whether they wished to be among those who would be arrested in protest. They knew that if that happened, Mildred and those at the shop would be the ones who ended up paying the price, so they decided to do their best to resist arrest.

---

[42] In Boston, Cape Verdeans and Jews began celebrating a joint Passover Seder in 2003. The Cape Verde Jewish Heritage Project was established in 2015 to honor the contributions of Sephardic Jews and to restore Jewish cemeteries in Cape Verde, Portugal, Morocco, and Gibraltar.

Finally, at 10:00 a.m. on February 24, President Wilson's motorcade led the parade down the intended route; the crowds cheered loudly. The police were ready as the band of suffragettes proudly took their places on the bleachers. As expected, there were numerous arrests despite the quiet protest. The women proudly raised their banners as they were carted off to the Charles Street Jail and charged with loitering. Five-dollar fines were imposed on each woman, yet they refused to either pay or appeal the judgment. Four women were released after their fines were involuntarily paid—one by a brother and the others by an unknown gentleman who wished the ringleaders to be out of jail. The others were imprisoned for eight days.

During the next week, Susan and Helen spent part of each day with their comrades. Then they returned to the office with updated tales of those arrested.

"Guess what I heard?" Helen said as she burst into the shop. "One of the women in jail is our friend Katherine Morey. She lives in Brookline and is an officer of the Massachusetts branch of the National Woman's Party. She's famous because she was arrested in Washington, DC, with Lucy Burns; it was the first of the suffrage arrests."

"We've also met another of those arrested, Camilla Whitcomb from Worcester," Susan added. "Also arrested was Josephine Collins, who carried the sign 'Mr. President, how long must women wait for liberty?' She's unmarried and her tea shop is a gathering place for women without companions, so I wonder if she's like us."

Susan and Helen were proud to be part of this historic event, which they hoped would change the course of history for women.

President Wilson in Boston

Suffrage in Boston

Episode 27 ❧ *Music of the Great War*
March 1919

"Jazz," Deborah said, unaware she'd raised her voice.

"What are you talking about?" asked Miriam, wide-eyed and having just awakened.

"That's what I want to write a book about."

"Sounds interesting," Miriam responded, feigning interest.

"Well, not just about jazz, but about people's artistic undertakings following the war and flu epidemic. I've been awake for hours, jotting down ideas."

"Tell me more."

"You know I gave up my plans to write a book, *Unintended Victims of War*. Well, now that the war has ended and the whole country seems uplifted, I'm certain people won't want to read a book about the ravages of the Great War. What if I write a book about the positive effects of wartime?"

"What is positive about a war that killed so many people?" Miriam asked through a yawn.

"Lots of positive things have happened. There's wonderful new enthusiasm and patriotism, new music and dance, and women have become stronger and more independent. Also, I trust that we're getting closer to women's suffrage finally passing. I believe that women will vote in our next election. These are things to be celebrated. I could also include information about how women learned to farm as part of the Women's Land Army, how nurses were trained to meet the needs of wounded soldiers, and how women took over many tasks they'd never done before."

"Now I'm confused. Is this book to be about jazz or ways life has changed for women? I'm happy to help you with this book any way I can, but you don't need me yet. You need to sort out your topic first."

"I always need you. You are my strength, my conscience, and my advisor."

"I don't want to be your conscience, though I'm happy to assist you. Why don't you run the stories by me as you complete your first draft of each one?" Miriam said.

"Do I tell you often enough how much I appreciate you? You're always there for me, whatever my needs. And you've become an exceptional critic for my writing."

"That's quite a compliment from the young woman who complained I never critiqued her work and didn't help her to become a better writer."

"I was so wrong. I just needed to find a way to ask for what I want."

"And listen to me after I finally learned to offer suggestions," Miriam said with a gentle grin.

"I'm looking forward to showing you how appreciative I am," Deborah said, running her hands tenderly down Miriam's arm.

They agreed to continue this discussion after Deborah had a chance to jot down some of her ideas. Deborah's sensual touch had prompted other ideas.

Miriam lay back, opening her dressing gown to the waist, making it obvious that she wanted Deborah's attention turned towards her breasts. She assumed that Deborah's excitement about her new book would lead to enthusiasm in their bed.

Without hesitation, Deborah lowered her head to Miriam's nipples, lightly flicking her tongue to arouse them. Once they were hard, Deborah sucked vigorously as she moved her hands along Miriam's hips, a familiar introduction to more intimacy. Though Miriam often liked slow, seductive lovemaking, passion seemed to fit Deborah's elevated mood. Without waiting, she lowered her hand to Deborah's sweet spot and found it wet. Their hands massaged each other's scalps as their mouths met and they explored with their tongues. They wriggled with arousal. Quickly, they disrobed and clutched at each other's bodies in attempts to get closer.

Miriam moved one leg between Deborah's thighs, making certain that it rubbed Deborah's excitement. Her leg was wet as it stroked up and down, working Deborah into a frenzy. She reached one hand down, adding manual touch, immediately taking Deborah over the edge. Deborah's panting stopped abruptly as a huge spasm silenced her.

After a smile, without catching her breath, Deborah reached down to Miriam's tenderness, finding it equally awakened. She rubbed gently for just a moment, then began making circles with her fingers, which aroused Miriam until she too writhed into a convulsion. It had barely been fifteen minutes since Miriam awoke to Deborah's announcement about book ideas. They clung to each other's damp bodies, fully satisfied.

෴෴෴

Several days later, after spending many hours laboring at her desk, Deborah said, "I've drafted my first chapter. Are you ready to read it, Miriam?"

"Susan and Helen have the girls occupied, so I have a few minutes right now to hear what it's about. I'll be glad to read it once the girls are in bed."

"I've decided to focus on the arts and the creativity that was sparked during the war and the enforced quarantine due to the influenza. Musicians, writers, dancers, and actors used that time to reflect, and they came up with some of the most innovative art forms ever seen in one short period. I began by looking at the music of the war years and focusing on a totally new genre of music—jazz. Jazz is brilliant and may change the way folks write music in the future. It's captured my interest. I'll let you read what I wrote before I tell you more."

"I look forward to this. Even though it's a little early, I'll start the girls to bed as soon as Susan and Helen bring them upstairs."

"I'll work with Sylvia on her nighttime rituals while you read Ida her stories," Deborah said.

"Ida certainly loves her books. Even though she's not quite three, she's tremendously interested in everything we read to her. She's memorized many of her little stories and won't let me get away with skipping a line, or even a word. I think we should get her more books for her birthday."

"Good idea. And I'll go to the library soon and get some new reading material for her."

"You love any excuse to go to the Boston Public Library. I'm so glad it's easily accessible for you."

"It's my favorite place in the whole world, other than at home with you."

Just then, Susan came upstairs with a sleepy Ida in her arms.

"It looks like it'll be easy to get her to bed a little early. I doubt she'll make it through even one of her books tonight," Miriam said.

Helen arrived upstairs with Sylvia just a moment later. "Sylvia's worn me out. We played music and danced for what seemed like hours. I got tired, yet she didn't!"

"Come here, my sweet girl. You look very happy. Did you have a good time dancing with Helen?" asked Deborah.

"Dance," said Sylvia with a huge smile.

"And you're a very good dancer. Maybe you and I can dance tomorrow."

"Now!" Sylvia puffed out her cheeks and opened her eyes wide.

"We don't have any music upstairs, so I'll sing so you can show me your dance steps."

Helen joined in singing "Here We Go Round the Mulberry Bush." Sylvia pranced, and they smiled. Miriam poked her head out of the bedroom and put a finger to her lips. Ida was trying to sleep, so they shortened the dance party.

Once Sylvia was in her bed, sleepiness took over. After a couple of yawns, she put herself into her favorite sleep position and drifted off easily.

Once both girls were nestled in their beds, Miriam approached Deborah with an outstretched hand. "My reading, please."

Miriam sat on the wingback chair, and Deborah announced that she'd like to read the chapter out loud, rather than have Miriam read it herself. Later, Miriam could read it for punctuation and spelling corrections, though for now, it was the writing style and content Deborah wanted critiqued.

"I'd love to have you read to me. Sort of an adult story hour. I bet I'll enjoy it as much as the girls like their story time."

Deborah cleared her throat and began:

Music of the Great War

The Great War sparked both proven lyricists and fledgling musicians to write patriotic songs. The tunes were catchy and the words meaningful. American soldiers and their families at home delighted in ditties created to depict them as heroes. This music differed greatly from popular Victorian music-hall entertainment and had an infectious sound of its own.

The early war songs were focused on the recruitment of soldiers; then they shifted to stories of military life and dreams of returning home. "Over There," "Pack Up Your Troubles in Your Old Kit Bag," "Keep the Home Fires Burning," and dozens of other songs were written during the war. Patriotic songs served to raise the morale of soldiers and civilians alike. These hit songs talked of missing loved ones, the adventures of war, and details about military life. Humorous songs bolstered everyone's spirits.

Women gathered in groups around radios, riveted to the sounds they were hearing. The first regular broadcasts, which were immediately popular, began while the men were away. The songs portrayed soldiers as brave and noble, and described women as loyally waiting for their loved ones. The women learned the lyrics, ready to sing the tunes to their menfolk when they returned from battle.

"Do you mind if I interrupt?" Miriam asked.

"You already did, yet it's fine. I want to hear your comments. Is there something wrong?"

"Absolutely not. I love this piece. I just wanted to tell you how impressed I am with your writing. It's improved greatly. You painted a vivid picture of the women sitting around their radios. I worried this might be dry or dull, though it's not. You have made it personal, even though this isn't a novel."

"Thank you very much. Anything else?"

"No, but I think that was enough for tonight."

"I'm only halfway through. Are you bored already?"

"Not at all. But I'm tired, and I want to be fully awake to listen well."

Deborah agreed to stop for the night and continue the next evening.

∾ ∾ ∾

Fanny and Rina were glad to spend time with the children. Mildred often joined them, mostly to be with Rina, whom she viewed as a playmate. Rina had a lighthearted manner and was quick to respond to Mildred's enthusiasm. Rina was proving to be a tremendous solution to the childcare dilemma downstairs when Ezra joined the growing group of children in Rachel's care.

The small room where Miriam's Bubbie lived until she died a few years before was crowded with Rachel, Rina, and the children in their charge—Sylvia, Ida, Sarah, and Ezra. Rina, even on the coldest of days, took a couple of the children outside for adventures, valuing the opportunity to explore the city with them and easing the overcrowding. Their favorite place to visit was Boston's new Children's Museum located nearby in Jamaica Plain, right across from Jamaica Pond. The museum planned games and field trips for the children, and very soon the curator knew by name all the children of this extended family.

Some days, Rina took one or two of the children upstairs to the tiny bedroom she and Fanny shared, and they made up games they could play on the bed or on the small bit of floor space. Fanny learned to carefully watch her footing because small remnants of the day's play were often tripping hazards. Sylvia took a shine to Rina and often chose her companionship over that of Deborah or Miriam, easing a bit of the couple's burden.

Both Fanny and Rina were easy additions to the household, and they took over some of the daily household chores. They, too, were eagerly anticipating the day the women's suffrage bill finally passed the Senate, so they attended some enthusiastic suffrage meetings with Susan and Helen.

∾ ∾ ∾

Deborah and Miriam did not have to ask Susan and Helen to watch the children the next night because Fanny and Rina asked to play with Sylvia and Ida after dinner. Deborah was surprised when Miriam let them take over and didn't feel the need to monitor Fanny and Rina. Deborah was excited as they sat down to read, which Miriam hoped would again lead to intimacy.

Once upstairs, Deborah continued her first chapter from where she'd left off the previous night:

> Most soldiers would not hear these new tunes until they returned home. The men on the front lines would have loved the distraction of music, yet radio transmissions were unreliable, and there were long periods when silence was mandatory. Also, the weight of the equipment made it impossible to transport radios easily. The army developed a horse-pack set to be strapped on the side of a saddle; however, those radios were only used for important military communications.
>
> Troops on ships had more access to music. Thanks to spark-gap telegraphy developed in Massachusetts before the war, naval soldiers were able to hear the new war music. It became a way for people to share their messages with the world and to send words of encouragement to soldiers.
>
> The story of music was not all positive. Sadly, some composers died on the fields of battle, and many who survived were deeply affected by what they had seen or lost. Much music relayed the tragedy of war to those at home. Some melodies reflected the sounds of warfare, including the swishing of gas shells and spurts of sniper fire in the background.

Tastes changed, veering from the prewar fascination with ragtime. A new style of music emerged—jazz. Louis Armstrong, Duke Ellington, and the Original Dixieland Jazz Band tickled people's ears and caught their attention. As people heard this new sound, they were intrigued.

The first recordings of the new jazz music were released in New York in March 1917, the point at which jazz intersected with the war. It explored social tensions on the home front and the experiences of Americans at war. As this new musical form emerged, brass instruments took on leading roles.

"I see you making faces, Miriam. Is there something you want to say?"
"No. Sorry, I was just thinking about how we should listen to more jazz. Go on."

Also new was the explosion of nontraditional musicians. Women were introduced to the musical world in ways they'd never been before. With their men away, women broke into all-male orchestras for the first time. They played organs during silent films, including the war pictures and war-bond movies that filled cinemas. And some English women entertained the troops in performances organized by a British suffragette who believed in the therapeutic benefits of music.

As the fascination with jazz increased, so did the appearance of Negro soldiers. In 1918, the Fifteenth New York Regiment, an all-Black troop, landed in France to the accompaniment of a big regimental band. Led by James Reese Europe, the band played "*La Marseillaise*," the French national anthem, in its own distinctive style. It immediately became a hit abroad; everyone wanted to know how Mr. Europe produced those sounds from seemingly ordinary horns. The faster tempo, improvisation, and smooth sounds captured much attention. The world of music was set afire by the new music's inspiring sound.

Back home, Negro music didn't enter the mainstream. Most people did not consider jazz an artistic form of music. Jazz, still predominantly performed by Negroes, entranced some, but was viewed by others as disgraceful or sinful. Jazz was linked to dancing and drinking at Negro establishments that rarely welcomed White patrons. This exciting new art form still has many hurdles to cross before being fully accepted.

"Brava!" Miriam said, clapping her hands as she stood up. "You're off to a wonderful start. I love your description of how Americans could not help but be intrigued with jazz. And it was delightful that you paid homage to the Negro regiment that was partially responsible for jazz music's popularity. This book is going to sell well."

"Thank you for your praise. I'm waiting for your criticism."

"Sorry to disappoint you, but I've no critique. You've done a wonderful job of describing the current trends in music. I love the mention of 'smooth sounds' and the music being 'inspirational.' Your descriptive words bring it alive. Nice job."

"I'm glad you're pleased. I'll start on another chapter tomorrow."

"I look forward to hearing it…and maybe to some intimacy," Miriam said with a slight blush.

No additional words were uttered. The papers fell into a neat pile as Deborah and Miriam kissed deeply and were quickly caught up in passion.

In a surprisingly adventurous mood, Deborah came up with a seduction. "Let's pretend I'm a stranger, and you're trying to seduce me."

"How can I do that? I wouldn't ever be interested in a stranger."

Deborah huffed and sat back. "Then you decide something unique to excite us."

"Why does it have to be something different from the usual. I like it when we just lie down and get caught up in loving. Are you bored with the way things are with us in bed?"

"No, not at all. I love how we sense each other's desires. I just thought it would be fun to pretend something. What if you play the seductress? Ravish me as if it's the first time."

Miriam got a glint in her eye and started to take off her clothing.

Deborah stopped her. "Start with your clothes on. Make me want to undress you."

Miriam said, "I have a secret to tell you." She leaned in close and whispered in Deborah's ear as she nuzzled her. After blowing hotly into Deborah's ear, Miriam trailed kisses down her neck, moving as low as the restrictive clothing would allow. Taking charge, Miriam slowly undid the top buttons on Deborah's shirt so she could nip lower.

Deborah waited for Miriam to undress her, as she did expertly when directed to do so. Though Deborah couldn't help imagining the excitement of having her bodice ripped off, she treasured the slow seduction. Miriam bared Deborah's torso one shoulder at a time. She exposed the tender flesh, caressing and awakening each naked section. Sliding her fingers downward from the shoulder, Miriam slowly edged towards Deborah's nipples, never quite reaching them, but getting temptingly closer with each stroke. Miriam noticed them harden and become erect as she resisted caressing them roughly.

The flush rising on Deborah's neck urged Miriam to kiss even more softly, teasingly. Deborah strained upward, inviting Miriam's lips to her bodice. Finally, there was contact. The roughness of Miriam's tongue exaggerated the sensations on Deborah's flesh. Holding Deborah's wrists in a tight grasp, Miriam was intent on reaching Deborah's full bosom.

Deborah undulated uncontrollably. Miriam took further charge and initiated more teasing by stripping Deborah of the rest of her upper clothing. Still holding Deborah's wrists with one hand, she moved her other hand around the circumference of her ample chest. She squeezed and tantalized. Cupping Deborah's breasts, blowing hot air on her nipples, and barely hovering over her intended target, Miriam trailed soft kisses down Deborah's stomach and licked the tender skin. Writhing, Deborah tried to move closer for more intimate contact. A wave of ecstasy overtook her.

Suddenly, Miriam's mouth moved upward, and she took Deborah's nipples tightly in her lips, sucking hard. She let go of Deborah's wrists, and they went directly to Miriam's head, fingering her bun until Miriam's tresses fell to her shoulders. Miriam moved her head so her hair fell across Deborah's bosom, lightly stroking the already aroused nipples. Deborah wished these sensations could go on forever.

The adventure was a success. Miriam was pleased Deborah had been stimulated by her return to writing.

ॐ ॐ ॐ

Mildred's interest in Negro rights continued, and Susan and Helen proudly supported her. When Mildred selected the Jim Crow laws for a project at school, Deborah took her to the library to gather information. Deborah dried Mildred's tears when the children's librarian sneered at her, asking what she wanted with books about Negroes, claiming those stories weren't proper for a young lady. Mildred was outraged. The librarian wouldn't let Mildred have the books, so Deborah checked them out under her own name.

At dinner one night, Mildred asked about slavery in Massachusetts. Susan and Helen took turns describing the despicable practice of treating people as personal property and forcing them to work in subservient positions for their owners. They did not know a great deal about the treatment of local Colored people in the past, but assured her, incorrectly, that there were no indentured slaves currently in Massachusetts. Fanny and Rina just listened, getting used to Mildred's animated delivery.

"I know about slavery," Mildred announced, "and I know it happened here. But I want to know how it got stopped in Massachusetts."

No one had an answer, so Susan offered to go to the library with Mildred.

Upon returning, it was Mildred who explained to the others what they'd learned. "It was thanks to W.E.B. Du Bois's great-grandmother. He was a famous Negro, and he was one of the founders of the National Association for the Advancement of Colored People, that new group that helps Negroes get what they want."

"It isn't a new group," Susan corrected. "It started almost ten years ago."

Mildred made a face, not wanting to be challenged in her new role as lecturer. "All right, but he helped a lot of Negroes." Mildred pulled out her notes. "Mr. Du Bois grew up near Great Barrington, where Deborah's family lives in the summers. It was because of his great-grandmother, Elizabeth Freedman, that they made a law saying that Massachusetts couldn't have slaves no more."

"Anymore," Helen corrected.

They all applauded. Susan and Helen weren't the only ones proud of her. Deborah congratulated her on her research.

After this conversation, Mildred asked again about inviting the reverend and his wife to dinner, yet Deborah reminded her that there was still to be no company during this time of bereavement. Mildred was frustrated when Miriam reminded her that the mourning period would last a year, and she feared the reverend would feel slighted if he stopped being invited to their home. Helen had already explained this to the reverend and his wife. Surprisingly, Deborah conferred quietly with

Miriam, then announced that they would make an exception for the reverend and his wife because he was more like family than company.[43]

☙ ☙ ☙

Fanny and Rina had not made the reverend's acquaintance, so Susan and Helen informed them that he and his wife were Colored. Neither Fanny nor Rina had ever had much contact with Negroes. There had been none in their homes, other than occasional workers, and none in their military experience because Negroes were confined to their own regiments. Rina had no knowledge at all about racial tensions, so Mildred took it upon herself to educate their new family member.

The reverend's presence in their home was now comfortable. As everyone expected, Mildred was at the forefront of all conversations, both at the dinner table and as they sat in the parlor afterwards. She talked of her newest research, and Reverend Brown shared a personal story of slavery.

"My grandfather was enslaved," Reverend Brown explained.

"I didn't know that," Mildred interrupted.

"Yes, he was born in Alabama to a wonderful woman who was a housekeeper to a wealthy plantation owner. At age fifteen, she gave birth to him; he was fathered by a son of the owners."

"That's practically my age!" Mildred blurted out, not paying any heed to the comment about the illegitimacy of his grandfather or to the alleged rape by the plantation owner's son. "I wouldn't want a baby now. I'm too young."

"You are too young," said Helen, viewing the fourteen-year-old as still a child.

Reverend Brown went on to explain that his great-grandmother was freed from servitude, yet she continued to work for the plantation owners after her emancipation because she had nowhere else to go.

As the conversation continued, Mildred directed many of her comments to Rina, viewing her as a pupil. Rina participated fully in the discussion, pleasing Mildred, who hoped to encourage another voice for the oppressed Negro.

---

[43] W.E.B. Du Bois's great-grandmother, Elizabeth Freeman, was enslaved in Sheffield, Massachusetts, in the 1770s. After being burned when the mistress of the house hit her with a hot shovel, she fled the household. When her owner tried to reclaim his "property," she engaged a local lawyer who fought for her liberty, claiming the newly adopted Constitution of the United States disallowed slavery. This eventually led to the prohibition of slavery in Massachusetts.

Deborah tired of talking about slavery and began fidgeting. Then suddenly she made an announcement to the whole group, refocusing the conversation, "I've decided to buy us a Victrola."

"That's so exciting," Mildred called out, practically shouting, distracted easily from the intense topic of prejudice.

"And I intend to buy several jazz phonograph records," added Deborah.

"I can tell you about my favorites," Reverend Brown said, being pulled into this exciting new topic.

The rest of the evening was spent in a lively discussion of which records Deborah should purchase.

Original Dixieland Jazz Band

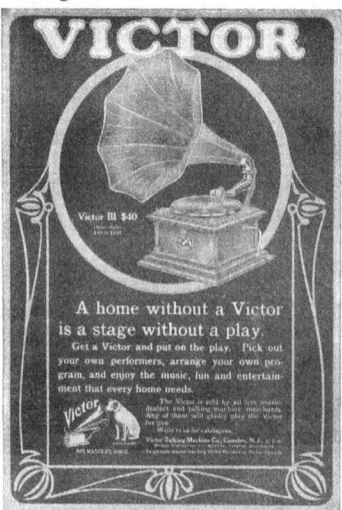

Victrola advertisement

Episode 28 ❦ *Prohibition*

April 1919

"What are we going to drink for *Shabbos* when our kosher wine runs out?" Deborah asked after Friday's dinner. "The law that just passed will restrict the sale of our *Shabbos* wine."

"I planned ahead," said Miriam. "This week, I bought three bottles and stored them in the basement. That should last us a long time."

"Prohibition may change our lives. I wonder whether the sale of liquor will ever be legal again."

"I doubt Prohibition will last longer than our supply lasts."

"Sometimes you surprise me. You're so naïve, Miriam."

"Don't call me that. And even though the law passed, it doesn't take place until the new year. We have plenty of time to create and stock a huge wine cellar if you're worried."

Deborah shook her head. "Actually, I heard the law allows for wine for religious purposes. Will we still be able to get wine at the kosher butcher? Or at the druggist? Will we have to prove we're Jews?"

"I've no idea. Maybe my idea of storing liquor in our basement is a good one."

"Will it put us at risk of robbery if someone sees you buying many bottles of wine?"

"Oh, Deborah! Do you really think there are potential robbers lurking around our house, ready to steal our sweet wine?"

"No, not now. Yet they may skulk around the stores that sell liquor as we get closer to the date for Prohibition."

"Let's not worry about that right now."

Just then, Susan and Helen came downstairs and joined them. "What are you two worried about?" Helen asked, having just heard the end of the conversation.

"We were just discussing the new Prohibition law," Deborah said.

"Everyone is blaming the suffrage movement for this law. I've been harassed on street corners when coming out of suffrage meetings," said Susan.

"People like to blame suffrage for everything," Helen said with an unbecoming snort. "Sorry." She put her hand over her mouth.

"I heard that the suffragists are pushing to ban alcohol," Miriam said.

"Everyone mixes it up. The temperance movement started many years ago and has nothing to do with suffrage," Helen said. "My mother belongs to the Woman's Christian Temperance Union, which supports suffrage, though she isn't a suffragette. And I've heard of Jewish groups opposed to liquor too."

"That's ridiculous. We drink wine every weekend. And there are several Jews from our temple whose families own liquor companies," Miriam said.

"I know," Deborah said. "It doesn't make sense, yet there are Jewish groups opposed to liquor that's not ceremonial. Those are mostly European immigrants who've seen in their home countries the harmful effects of the excessive drinking of liquor."

"What makes a wine kosher?" Susan asked.

Miriam sat up straight. "Importantly, it is made with kosher ingredients; the grapes are picked and crushed by only Sabbath-observant Jews. Also, kosher wine is *mevushal*, which means it is cooked. It is heated, so it can't be used as an offering by non-Jews for idol worship."

"Why would cooking it make a difference?" asked Helen.

"What my father told me," Miriam said, "is that cooking it for one minute removes some of the flavor, so non-Jews wouldn't find it acceptable to present to their idols. Also, Father and his friends would never allow a non-Jew to pour their wine."

"I never heard that," Deborah said, making a sour face.

"It was the practice of idol worshippers to pour some wine on the ground as an offering to their gods. *Mevushal* wine reduced their worry, although it was clear they didn't trust non-Jews."

"Is that why you pour our wine?" Susan asked.

Miriam blushed. "I guess it's just a habit. I trust you two."

"I certainly hope you do," Deborah said with a lilt.

Miriam turned to Deborah and asked, "Deborah, can you find out how we're going to prove we're Jews, so we can get our kosher wine?"

Deborah could not get that type of information from the library, so she suggested Miriam ask around at shul for the answer.

☙ ☙ ☙

When Deborah and Miriam were alone in their room upstairs, they discussed how Prohibition might affect Fanny and Rina.

"Although I've not seen either of them drunk, I wonder about their drinking habits. Remember that incident when they were in the service?" Miriam asked.

"Let's not hold that against them. Life was very different for them when they were in the military. They were newly in love and dealing with temptations they'd never encountered before. I've not seen anything worrisome since they've been here. I know they've only been here a couple months, but I assume we would have seen signs if drink was tempting them."

"I don't want to tattle on them, but several times I thought I smelled alcohol on their breath when they came home from a night out."

"So what? They're young, and they should be able to drink once in a while. You're sounding like an old lady."

"I guess I'm just not used to women drinking," Miriam said.

"And what about you getting quite tipsy on Purim?"

"We're supposed to overdrink on that holiday. The Talmud says that we are to drink to excess, to 'become fragrant.' In almost every chapter of the *Megillah*, someone is at a drinking party. Mordecai's instructions to the Jewish people are to celebrate these as days of drinking and rejoicing."

"And on Passover, everyone at the table gets a little silly after four glasses of wine, no matter how small their portions are."

Miriam shifted in her chair. "You've made your point. I'll not judge them unless there's a problem. Yet I'll keep my eyes and nose on them to make certain that drinking's not a regular practice."

"You are an old lady at twenty-six! I hate to see what you will be like when our girls are Fanny's and Rina's ages."

"I doubt Sylvia will ever be independent enough to have a drinking problem, and I hope to instill good values in Ida. I do wonder what will happen with Mildred, since she's already an independent thinker."

"Independence and overdrinking are hopefully not connected. I'll leave it to you to worry about her, and everyone else in our lives, because you are so good at it," Deborah said, smiling.

"Thanks for your confidence and giving me the role of enforcer."

"You're welcome."

❧ ❧ ❧

Over the next week, there were two pieces of news that shifted the focus from Prohibition. First was the story in the *Boston Globe* about the proceedings at the Paris Peace Conference, which was still going on.

"Have you read about the Racial Equality Proposal at the conference?" asked Helen over breakfast on April 12. Heads shook so Helen proceeded, "This proposal was to set standards on human rights, which certainly sounds like a wonderful idea. I don't understand why the Americans at the conference opposed it."

"Were we the only ones?" Susan asked.

"Japan suggested it, France and Italy supported it, and it was passed by a majority of the delegates. I'm unsure why Woodrow Wilson, the chairperson, overturned it."

"That makes no sense at all," Deborah said sternly. "Why would he do that?"

"The only comment in the paper is that he felt there was significant opposition, so he couldn't support it."

"I'm embarrassed that our president would do such a thing," Deborah announced, and everyone nodded in agreement.

The second piece of news just a few days later was something Mildred heard about and reported to the family. "There was another race riot. This one was in Georgia at a church. The riot followed a horrible event—two White officers were killed, and a Colored man was lynched. I hate to hear this is still going on."

Everyone concurred with Mildred. None of them knew that this incident was the first of many to happen over the next months, resulting in the summer of 1919 being labeled the Red Summer because of all the blood spilled.[44]

అ అ అ

---

[44] Racial violence escalated during the Great War, culminating in extensive riots during the summer of 1919, the Red Summer. Anti-Negro sentiments led to Colored people being blamed unjustly. Up to 120 deaths were attributed to the conflicts in over three dozen separate race riots, which began in Chicago and spread to New York and across the country. There were also over 100 lynchings during this period. Law enforcement officers did not quell White violence.

The conversation about liquor continued the next week with Deborah and Miriam seated in the parlor, Ida and Sylvia on their laps, and the cat cuddled close by.

"This weekend, I asked at temple," Miriam said, "about religious permission to buy liquor during Prohibition. I found that each Jewish person is allowed to buy up to ten gallons of kosher wine each year. I've now stored six bottles, which I think will last a very long time. We drink so little on Friday nights and never at other times, other than holidays."

"Your supply won't last us a whole year. We sometimes have guests for *Shabbos* dinner, and now there are six of us. And as we discussed the other day, our wine consumption increases during Passover and Purim."

"So how will we get more when that runs out?"

Susan said, "I heard that people who need liquor for medicinal purposes will need to get a prescription, just like they would get for medicine. It will probably be something like that for Jews."

"It will be another way for people to discriminate against us," Miriam said with a sigh. "Could we get arrested for drinking our wine on *Shabbos* if we don't have a prescription?"

"Miriam! Sometimes you sound so foolish. It is not illegal to drink liquor, just to buy it." Deborah threw up her hands in frustration.

"That's a stupid rule."

"Maybe. I didn't make it up, so don't blame me," Deborah said forcefully. The cat, bothered by her tone, scampered away.

"Let's not argue about this, Deborah. I wasn't finding fault with you."

"What are you two fighting about now?" asked Susan as she and Helen entered the room.

"We aren't really fighting," said Miriam. "Just disagreeing."

Deborah shook her head. "Miriam thinks we could get arrested for drinking wine on *Shabbos*. I told her that was foolish."

"I don't want to get in the middle of that conversation," Helen said under her breath.

Susan chimed in, "I saw a peddler selling liquor on the street near the office today. I was wondering what will happen to folks like him when Prohibition becomes law."

"He'll find something else to peddle, I'm certain," Deborah said.

"I suppose, but what will happen to the tavern owners? Those folks rely on the sale of drinks for their livelihood," said Helen.

Miriam became wide-eyed. "Or the men at temple who run liquor businesses? They're wealthy now, though their businesses will soon be illegal."

"And," said Susan, "We've not even discussed the men who frequent these places. I know some men who go to taverns every night."

"How do you know these men?" Helen asked.

"Just men from my hometown. Actually, my father stops at the bar every night on his way home from work."

"I didn't know that. Does he have a problem with drinking?" Helen asked.

"Not typically. Once in a while, he imbibes a little more than usual, and he can be quite loud and silly when he comes home. Mama frowns on this, though we kids always liked those evenings. He would sit around the table and sing with us. He was much more fun on the days he over-imbibed. Pa was harmless, and it didn't happen too often, or Mama would have put a stop to it. That's how I know that some men stop by the tavern regularly. He had a bunch of friends who were there every night."

"This is a world I know nothing about," said Miriam.

"My sweet innocent knows little about the world outside her neighborhood." Deborah smiled.

"Don't make fun of me, Deborah. I had a wonderful upbringing with little concern for the horrors the world harbors. I'd like to bring up our girls that way. Did you know about men who frequent liquor establishments?"

"I grew up in New York City, so certainly I knew about men who drank too much. They would line the streets in some sections. You could always tell who they were by their smell."

"Did they smell like liquor because they drank so much?"

"Yes, my love. And, unfortunately, they also smelled like urine, since they often…"

"No, I don't need to hear the details. My imagination is vivid enough. And now that you mentioned it, I smell a diaper needing a change."

❧ ❧ ❧

The next evening, the topic of Prohibition was still on everyone's minds as the four of them gathered in the parlor. Fanny and Rina had retired early to their room. Their plans were obvious because there was nothing in the room but a bed.

Miriam said, "I was thinking about your father, Susan. I can't imagine having a father who stopped after work, rather than coming directly home to be with the family. My father rushed home every evening to be with us. Dinner was always prepared, and the only waiting we did was to finish the Grace Before Meals before eating. Luckily that prayer is short, as opposed to the Grace After Meals, the *Birkat Hamazon*."

"That was certainly different than at my home," Susan said. "Pa never had dinner with us. As a matter of fact, Mama made certain all the children had eaten and our meals were cleared away before Pa got home. He would have been annoyed to wait for his dinner. My mother kept his warm, and he had his plate in front of him within five minutes of his walking in the door."

"Did all of you sit around the table with him?" Miriam asked.

"No. Once we were all fed, we were to entertain ourselves with quiet games in our rooms when we were little, or homework and reading when we were older. Pa would not have tolerated any noise while he ate, so we stayed out of hearing distance."

"What if you really needed something?"

"Pa would let out a *harrumph* when the little ones made a noise or needed help in the water closet. We learned to keep really quiet when playing together."

"Did you get to see your father before you went to bed?"

"Miriam, you're asking too many questions," Deborah said deliberately.

"It is fine to talk about this," Susan said with a dismissive pat on Deborah's hand. "Yes, as soon as Pa's dinner was cleared from the table, he'd call upstairs, and we'd gather around him. There was lots of excitement to finally tell him all the important things young children need to inform their parents about, like about the toad that jumped across the road or the boy who heaved during class. These events were important to us, and telling Pa all our stories was a treasured part of every day."

"It sounds lovely."

"It was. Somehow, telling Mama wasn't as exciting. And there was always competition to be the next one to tell Pa our stories."

Deborah refocused the conversation. "Helen, tell us some of your childhood memories regarding liquor."

"My mother would never tolerate drinking," Helen said. "As I mentioned, she belonged to the Woman's Christian Temperance Union, so she didn't believe in drinking liquor."

"Deborah's going to say I'm naïve, yet I never heard of that group. What do they do?" asked Miriam.

"It's the largest women's organization in the world, a social-reform group whose main purpose is to promote purity by abstinence from all intoxicating beverages. They see alcohol as the cause of most social problems. They also have a side group that helps men to avoid tobacco use, and they work on other social issues, such as prostitution and international peace."

"I like their values, though I wouldn't join a Christian group," said Miriam.

"You actually could join. It's not limited to just Christians, though there are few Jews."

"Interesting," said Deborah.

"I had a White Ribbon Recruit Ceremony when I was a baby. Someone from the group, which they call WCTU for short, tied a white ribbon to my wrist, and my mother and father promised they would raise me to be free of alcohol and other drugs."

"Have you been as pure as your parents hoped?" Miriam asked with a smirk.

"Miriam, that's none of your business," Deborah said.

"It is fine for her to ask. I've been fairly pure, which I guess, according to my mother, would mean I've been sinful. I've never been drunk, though I've had many glasses of wine, including on *Shabbos* with you. And I like it, which would be problematic for my parents."

"Good for you," Deborah said with a smile. "In my eyes, you don't have to be quite so extreme to be pure."

"I don't feel guilty because I doubt liquor would ever be a problem for me. Yet I certainly wouldn't tell my mother I'd imbibed."

They all chuckled, yet Helen told them more, which caused even more laughter. "This group can be a bit extreme. There were three years when they spearheaded a boycott of root beer because they considered that alcoholic."

"That's ridiculous," said Susan. "We've been drinking Tower Root Beer every time your friends Marilyn and Julie come over, and none of us has ever been drunk."

"I know," Helen said with a roll of her eyes. "I told you they can be extreme."

"We should toast each other with some root beer right now. To friendship!" suggested Deborah as she headed to the pantry to retrieve a couple of bottles.

❧ ❧ ❧

Friday night, after returning from shul, Miriam greeted Susan and Helen with news. "We learned something really interesting about kosher liquor tonight."

"While you were at temple?" asked Susan.

"Why, yes. It seems the rabbis are sometimes the ones to sell wine."

"The rabbis?" asked Helen with a look of astonishment.

"Yes, I learned that some of them import kosher wine from France and sell it to their congregants. It's a bit of an undercover business."

"They may benefit from Prohibition more than most if they can still sell their wine," Deborah said. "Would they sell it to others for a profit?"

"Deborah! You think the most awful things. Next, you'll be telling me Rabbi Feldman is making money off his whole congregation when he sells kosher wine for Passover."

"Be careful about spreading rumors," Deborah said with a snicker.[45]

❧ ❧ ❧

---

[45] Most Jews opposed Prohibition, believing it a Christian movement. The allotted ten gallons of wine per Jewish person per year may have accounted for a surge of people claiming the Jewish sacramental exemption. Jews accounted for a huge number of bootleggers during Prohibition.

The highest consumption of liquor in the United States occurred long before Prohibition. In 1800, each American drank an average of three times the amount consumed today. Prohibition came about in the United States at a time when the average per-person liquor consumption was approximately ten drinks per week. Heavy drinking is defined as the average consumption of more than seven drinks per week for women and twice that for men. After the end of Prohibition on December 5, 1933, the amount consumed gradually increased. The current per-person consumption of spirits is 9.5 drinks per week.

The next week was a huge week for the family due to the Jewish holidays, which overlapped with family celebrations. The Jewish calendar is based on the positions of the sun and moon, so it does not align exactly with the Gregorian calendar, which is commonly used throughout the world. The first night of Passover was on Monday, April 14, the second Seder on Tuesday, Sylvia's seventh birthday on Wednesday, and Ida's third birthday on Friday, which was also *Shabbos* and still Passover. Typically, they also gathered for the last two nights of Passover, which would be on Monday and Tuesday, but Miriam wondered how they would manage.

Their extended family came to the rescue. Even though the office would be closed during this time, it seemed impossible to plan so many events at once. Hannah was not much of a cook and wasn't really organized enough to manage the entire Passover meal, but she offered to do more than she typically did. Susan and Helen helped to clean the house, a major undertaking when having to rid the house of all *hametz*, nonkosher food, for Passover. They also helped Miriam change all the dishes, pots, kitchen towels, and other kitchen items to prepare for Passover.

Susan and Helen offered to make their own dinner for the two nights of Passover, though Mrs. Stern was pleased to provide food for them. Fanny and Rina went to Rina's family for the first night of the holiday and to the Berkowitz home for the second night; it was a relief for Deborah and Miriam to have two fewer at the table. Fanny and Rina promised to return in time for the birthday celebrations.

It was Marjorie's family who helped them most by inviting them all for Passover. It was a little scary to be gathering inside with so many people while the pandemic still loomed, but there was no alternative. And having two evenings with baby Ezra provided extra joy.

That left Deborah and Miriam with the two birthdays, *Shabbos* dinner, and the last two nights of Passover to plan. That felt reasonable. As usual, Mrs. Stern did much of the cooking, though Miriam participated. Miriam baked Passover sponge cakes for both girls' birthdays,

---

Overdrinking by Jews is discouraged, except on Purim, when they are commanded to drink until they cannot tell the difference between right and wrong, and during Passover, when each adult consumes four glasses of wine at each Seder.

adding strawberries to the top of Sylvia's cake and making a chocolate sponge cake for Ida's birthday. Ida would be disappointed not to have lots of gooey frosting, so Miriam drizzled a chocolate coating over the top, pleasing the little girl.

The custom for the seventh night was to stay awake all night, studying the Torah. Except for Mr. Cohen when he was alive, none of them had ever done that. The eighth night included the Yizkor memorial prayers, which felt especially important given that this was the first Passover since Deborah's brother's death. She knew her family would understand that she couldn't be with them, given that both her girls had birthdays. She shed many tears in the days surrounding this holiday, which had been Milton's favorite.

They made it through the week, exhausted but appreciative of their loving family of friends.

෨ ෨ ෨

Over dinner one evening after they'd all recovered from the Passover and birthday celebrations, Susan shared the letter she'd received from Grace Banker, their Barnard College friend who was still in the service after the end of the war.

> April 20, 1919
> Dear Susan and Helen;
> Though peace was declared on November 11 of last year, my girls and I have continued providing necessary communications as part of the US Army Signal Corps.[46] Now that the war has ended and my letters

---

[46] The Hello Girls, the group of military communications specialists lead by Grace Banker, were not initially given US Army discharge status, which meant they received none of the benefits accorded other military personnel. On November 23, 1977, sixty years after the first of the Hello Girls took the army oath, Congress retroactively acknowledged the military service of the women in the US Army Signal Corps. President Jimmy Carter signed the GI Improvement Act of 1977, approving veteran status and honorable discharges for the Hello Girls. When this occurred, only 33 of the girls were still alive to receive their official discharges. Grace Banker was not among them; she had died on December 17, 1960.

In January 2019, The Hello Girls Congressional Gold Medal Act of 2019 was submitted to Congress to honor the 223 girls who worked as telephone operators for the US Army Signal Corps. A detailed description of the work of these brave young women

are not censored, I can be more open about our experiences in France.

We frequently faced German bombings and difficult conditions, including extreme cold made worse by the lack of heat in our leaky barracks. One time, the barracks we'd recently vacated caught fire, and we were relieved to have escaped danger yet another time. Somehow none of my girls were injured, yet I still have nightmares and overreact to loud noises. So do many of the other girls, even though our lives are no longer at risk.

I think you'd also be interested to learn that since the end of the war, the Allied forces here in Koblenz have amassed a huge collection of German helmets and stored them in a warehouse near where we're staying. I heard they're to be sent to New York City to be put on display. It will be interesting to hear from you if they are of any interest to Americans.

Yours Truly,

Grace

"How frightening," Miriam said as she put down the letter. "If I'd known how bad their situation was, I would have been quite concerned about Grace."

"I'm glad you didn't know," Deborah said. "You are an expert worrier."

"Why would the army display German helmets?" Helen asked, changing the focus of their discussion.

---

acknowledged that they were among the last soldiers to return to the States. In 2021, a Congressional Gold Medal Act was introduced, and in March 2023, four senators introduced a bipartisan bill to award the women of the US Army Signal Corps with a Congressional Gold Medals for their service to the nation during World War I.

Carolyn Timbie, Grace Banker's granddaughter, said, "I am so proud of my grandmother, Grace Banker, and the women of the Signal Corps with whom she served in World War I. They fought for sixty years to get their recognition as veterans, and I only wish my grandmother had lived to see this day."

"I can only imagine that sending them to the United States was a way for war heroes to pridefully display this proof of their military success," Susan said.

"I find it disgusting that they would display the headgear of dead soldiers as an act of pride," said Miriam.

Deborah spoke up, "Helen, our soldiers want to honor their success in battle, and we should be proud of them."

Neither Susan nor Helen said anything further, worried Deborah was speaking with pride for her brother's courageous actions in time of war. Though he'd not fought, and his death was from the influenza rather than combat, they did not want to denigrate his military service.

The next day, after speaking with her father, Deborah had much news. "The helmets we talked of yesterday have been put on display right outside Grand Central Station. My father says they've collected eighty-five hundred German Army helmets! They've stacked twelve thousand of them in each of two pyramids in an area they're calling Victory Way, and selling them to proud New Yorkers for one thousand dollars each. Their sale is part of the Victory Loan program, an opportunity for citizens to reimburse the government for the extravagant costs of the Great War. My father read in the paper that there was a ceremony yesterday with speeches by many well-known personalities, including President Wilson's daughter. There was also a simulated battle reenactment, an air show, and an array of German war equipment on display. Patriotic spirit is running high after the war. Father read in the paper that more than $100,000,000 worth of victory bonds were sold in this city yesterday, the first day of the final war-loan campaign."

"That's impressive, but I would think that soldiers would rather forget the results of all that bloodshed, rather than making a display of the atrocities," Susan said.

Miriam said, "I don't understand men's behavior at all."

On April 29, Deborah tried calling her parents, but the telephone lines were down. She thought little of it until she had the same experience the next morning.

"There's something wrong with the telephone. I wonder what's going on."

Susan, who'd gotten to the newspaper first, explained, "There's a strike at New England Telephone and Telegraph. I'm certain that's why you can't get through."

"Why are they striking?" Helen asked.

"A Russian woman named Rose Finklestein, one of the strike leaders, is working with the Women's Trade Union League to argue for women's workers' rights."[47]

"A Jewish woman," Miriam piped up as she turned her attention back to feeding the children.

"Yes, but what does that have to do with it?" Deborah asked.

"It seems," Helen said, "that it does have something to do with it. Rose endured a lot of anti-Semitic attacks when her family moved from Russia to the predominantly Irish city of East Cambridge, and that experience made her into a fighter. Recently, she's been putting her efforts towards equal pay and better conditions for the women telephone workers."

Over the week, the telephone-operators' strike was a daily breakfast conversation. The papers explained that the women workers were highly regimented and closely monitored, though male workers were not. The strike was supported by eight thousand women and was extremely costly to the company. By the week's end, the strike was resolved by the women being given pay raises, schedule changes, and collective bargaining rights.

"This result is thanks to Rose and the other telephone operators who walked off their jobs to fight for better conditions for all the women workers," Susan said to a small round of applause as she read aloud from the paper. The children were confused yet joined in with the clapping.

---

[47] Rose Finkelstein Norman worked as a labor organizer for many decades, fighting for the rights of women to work once married and for women to serve on juries. She campaigned to unionize domestic workers, librarians at the Boston Public Library, and clerks at the downtown Jordan Marsh department store. In addition to her work with the telephone operators, she was proud to be president of the Boston Women's Trade Union League and an advocate for the elderly in her older years; she served on Boston Mayor Kevin White's Advisory Commission on Affairs to the Elderly in the 1970s.

At the end of the month, Miriam arrived home from a *Shabbos* walk with Marjorie and Ezra; she had news for Deborah. "Marjorie told me they are going to move into a little apartment on Cheney Street, just a few blocks from here. They are going to rent the first floor of a home belonging to Marjorie's aunt and uncle. Marjorie said her mother cried when they told her, not wanting the baby to leave their home. I'm pleased they'll have a place of their own, and they'll be so close to us."

"They've certainly come a long way from the horrible situation they were in after Micah's fall just over a year ago."

"That seems so long ago. They've suffered so much, so I'm really happy for them."

When Rachel's friend Roger heard of the intended relocation, he offered to help on the day of the move. He was working his way into everyone's good favor.

German Helmets in NYC

Rose Finkelstein Norwood

Episode 29 ❦ *Saturday Evening Girls*
May 1919

The focus on liquor was short-lived. The exemption of ten gallons per year for each Jew would provide them with more wine than was necessary for religious consumption, especially because the addition of Fanny and Rina had increased their household allotment by twenty gallons.

Deborah smiled every week when Miriam added another bottle or two of wine to the growing reserve in the back of the basement. Maybe Miriam was planning to supply the entire neighborhood…or the whole congregation.

❧ ❧ ❧

On the morning of May 7, when Rachel arrived to take care of the children, Miriam noticed Rachel's bloodshot eyes. "What's wrong?"

"You're going to think me silly to be so upset." With tears forming, Rachel said, "L. Frank Baum has died."

"Was he a friend?"

"Not really. He was the author who wrote *The Wizard of Oz* and all the other books in the series that Aaron and I read."

"Oh, sweetie, I understand. I remember those books are what brought the two of you together that first day you met."

"Aaron and I loved those books. It's ridiculous of me to be so upset about the author's death, but I've been crying since I read it in the paper this morning. It's reminded me of all the sweet times my husband and I discussed his wonderful works. But now that I have Roger in my life, I shouldn't be so sensitive."

"Not true at all. It's important to remember and value your marriage. Just because you have a new love doesn't mean that your time with Aaron wasn't significant."

"Aaron taught me so much. He was the first person to ever love me, other than my family, and I became much stronger when I was with him. I will always love him."

"And you should. It does not take away from your feelings for Roger to have loved before."

"Aaron made me a better person, and I'll always be grateful you introduced me to him."

"It was one of the finest things I did in my life. May his memory always be a blessing."

"Thanks for understanding. Now, I'd better go dry my tears so I don't upset the children."

"I'll say a little prayer for L. Frank Baum, in gratitude for bringing you and Aaron together and for the wonderful recollections his death brought."

"You mean so much to me, my sweet friend. You understand me. Now, on with my day."

꙲ ꙲ ꙲

Miriam was pleased that the threat of influenza had waned enough that she could return to her volunteer job at Denison House. Believing her life had special meaning when tutoring, she'd missed her weekly connection there over the last year. When she returned, she was greeted with great appreciation by the staff, the young girls she'd helped, and the other volunteers with whom she'd enjoyed a pleasant camaraderie.

When Miriam arrived home from her first day back at Denison House, she said, "I learned something fascinating today while volunteering." She looked around the parlor to see if Susan and Helen were listening. "One of the Denison House founders, Vida Scudder, has gotten involved with a special project. Have you ever heard of the Saturday Evening Girls?"

"Yes," said Helen, sipping tea. "A couple of my friends have been members for years."

"How come you never mentioned it before?" Miriam asked.

"I did," Helen said. "As a matter of fact, our friend invited us to a meeting once, and I mentioned it to you."

Deborah made a face. "I don't remember. Will one of you tell me what this is all about? Is it a private club?"

"Well, not exactly private," Helen said. "This is a group that has been meeting in Boston since the turn of the century. It began as a library club."

"Then you should know about it, Deborah, since you specialize in libraries," Miriam said with a grin.

"I'm still the only one who knows nothing about this silly library club. Well, go on then. Tell me."

"Fine." Helen began, "A librarian in the North End gathered a group of immigrant girls from the neighborhood every Saturday night to discuss literature. Mostly poor Jewish and Italian girls attended, valuing a chance to get out of their crowded tenements. They had no idea how important this small gathering would become to the world of art."

"Enough of the teasers. You still haven't told me anything. How does this group relate to the art world, and why are they still meeting almost twenty years later?" Deborah said with a huff.

"Patience, my dear," said Miriam, shaking her head at Deborah.

"Not my strongest quality."

"We all know that!"

"Please…" Deborah gestured towards Helen, encouraging her to continue.

"This program started in a small room at the North Bennet Street Industrial School, a branch of the Boston Public Library."

"I've heard good things of North Bennet Street," said Miriam.

Deborah slowly shook her head, reacting to the interruption of the story.

"The school was established to teach trades to young women, so they could get jobs. Soon, they had over one thousand students. They also provided other services. They named their weekly classes for the day on which they occurred—hence the Saturday Evening Girls."

After Miriam refilled their teacups, Helen went on, "A few years back, North Bennet Street hired a director for their ceramics program; that got the Saturday Evening Girls interested in pottery."

"Finally. Something concrete. So they make pottery?" Deborah asked.

"Yes, and they became very skilled at decorating it in their own distinctive Arts and Crafts style," Helen said. "The school attracted the attention of a wealthy woman, a Mrs. Storrow, who was so impressed that she bought a building to house the classes, and she began a camp for these disadvantaged girls."

"Where is this story going now?" Deborah huffed.

"Deborah! Calm down," Miriam insisted.

Deborah complied.

"Mrs. Storrow thought the girls could sell their wares to pay for their attendance at camp. She named the shop Paul Revere Pottery since the new building was near the Old North Church where Paul Revere began his famous ride to Concord at the start of the American Revolution."

"I thought the pottery was called Saturday Evening Girls Pottery," said Miriam.

"Yes, it was known by both names," Helen said.

"Finally!" Deborah shook her head. "This story is beginning to sound familiar. Didn't you bring home a small, broken piece of this pottery, Susan?"

"Yes, I did."

"I remember that little shard was quite beautiful and very distinct," Deborah said.

"It's artfully crafted. And I heard sweet stories of each girl having fresh flowers at her workstation and of the girls reading literature to one another, igniting their creativity," Miriam said.

"I'm sorry I was so impatient," said Deborah. "It really is a fascinating story, and now I understand why you wanted to tell me all the side stories—to have me understand the uniqueness of this pottery. I can't believe I didn't remember this. Next time, I'll try to be quiet and listen to the whole thing before interrupting."

"I'll remind you of this the next time you become impatient while listening to a story," Miriam said.

"Could I buy you a piece of this pottery to make up for my insensitive ways?"

"That would be lovely, though it's quite expensive."

"Then you'll just have to accept my apology."

࿆ ࿆ ࿆

A couple of weeks later, Susan came home from work excited, having just received a note from her friend Edith Guerrier,[48] who worked at the Paul Revere Pottery store in the North End. Edith invited the four of them for a tour the following Saturday.

"What will we do? It's *Shabbos*. We can't go on a Saturday," said Miriam.

"What if we go in the afternoon?" Deborah asked.

---

[48] Edith Guerrier, the founder of the library club that evolved into Saturday Night Girls pottery, was a pioneer in library science. Edith's role shifted from head of the nursery of the North Bennet Street Industrial School to the coordinator of a small branch of the Boston Public Library system. The school's initial intent was to train widows and wives of men during the Great War. Edith brought her artistic skills, her literary interests, and the principles of the settlement-house movement to enrich the curriculum. She founded the literary club, which prompted the pottery studio and eventually Paul Revere Pottery. While there, she met her lifetime partner, Edith Brown, who attended the Boston Museum School of Art, where Ralph Waldo Emerson's son of the same name taught art anatomy after retiring as a physician. He claimed that Edith Brown was the true artist.

"And miss our Havdalah service?"

"Miriam, God won't mind if we miss one week. This is a special opportunity."

"I concede. We've missed a few times. Do you remember when?"

"When my mother had a breakdown and once when Sylvia was sick. Thank you for being flexible," Deborah said.

On Saturday, Sylvia and Ida went to visit with their aunt and uncle, Hannah and William. Mildred was pleased to visit her friend Leah, down the street. That left the four young adult women free for their adventure.

Edith welcomed them into the large complex, informing them they were going to the studio where the ceramics were, rather than to the store. En route, she pointed out the various activities as they walked down the long corridors. Arriving at the ceramics studio, Edith opened the heavy door and let them in.

Attracting their attention first were walls of wooden shelves crammed with row upon row of assorted pottery pieces. Some appeared to be molded-clay shapes, others baked white vessels, and still others were covered with delicately sketched designs on bowls painted in hues of blue, green, and yellow. Workstations covered the floor of the large, high-ceilinged room. Each station had a flower vase, some with wilting flowers and others awaiting fresh posies on Monday morning. There were several girls in aprons at their stations, fitting in a little work time before their Saturday meeting.

"Welcome to our studio," Edith said softly as two girls took seats. "I'm glad to show you around. The walls of wooden shelves are crammed with pottery pieces in different phases of completion. We have room for about twenty girls. Please be silent if someone begins to read. It's still a practice of many of the girls to take turns reading prose and poetry to each other as inspiration for their creativity."

Miriam looked around, noticing the tools hanging next to each workstation and the pots drying on racks covering all the walls. The room smelled of fumes from burning clay, decaying flowers, and the sweat which clung to each apron. Somehow, the mingling of these acrid aromas was pleasant. Edith pointed to a huge oven in one corner, explaining the process of firing each piece in a special furnace called a kiln.

As several girls entered the studio and took with seats, a woman with gray hair falling into her face called the visitors over to her bench. She said, "I'm the other Edith. I began coming here as a young girl, seeking quiet. My crowded tenement gave me little opportunity for solace. That and a break from the oppressive heat of the summer were my initial motivations, yet what I found here was so much more. Most importantly, I gained the friendship of the other Saturday Evening Girls. I also developed a skill and later a job, which allowed me much freedom in my life. This is my work, my art, my family."

Miriam smiled and enthusiastically said, "Look at this extraordinary artistry. I love the designs, especially the plates with flowers. And the hue of the pieces is soft and soothing. I like how some of the girls have outlined their designs in black. It's really magnificent."

"It certainly is. Edith, how do you find so many talented girls?" Deborah asked.

"We have many creative women working for us; however, as you can imagine, not everyone has such fine skills. That's why some girls are assigned to mixing glazes, to working the kiln, or even to cleaning up. Only the finest artists create the pieces we sell in our shops."

Just then, one of the girls, ignoring the visitors, began to read from a small book she took out of her pocket. "Hope is the thing with feathers / That perches in the soul / And sings the tune—"

"I recognize that. It's an Emily Dickinson poem," Deborah said.

The girl stopped reading.

Miriam said, "Deborah, please be quiet."

Deborah stopped talking, and the girl resumed reading.

Then, turning to another girl, Deborah asked, "How do you concentrate on the pottery while someone is reading to you?"

Again, the reader stopped.

Embarrassed, Deborah pressed her lips together tightly.

The girl resumed reading, then took her seat when done.

Edith said, "I moved into a separate apartment with a friend I met here; we've lived together for the past fifteen years. We both work here full time, and we have a very rich life."

Deborah nudged Miriam as she listened to this story. Not noticing that another girl was reading, she quietly said to Miriam, "A Boston marriage? Could they be a couple like us?"

Though her voice was low, Deborah's mumbled words were a distraction to the new reader, who stopped.

Then Edith Guerrier walked up to Deborah and pointed to the door, escorting Deborah out of the room. After a few minutes, Edith returned without Deborah.

Miriam blushed. Hoping to distract the group from wondering about Deborah's absence, she asked, "How do you know which pieces are done by which girl?"

"Each artist signs her initials on the bottom."

Just then, Deborah quietly rejoined the group. No one acknowledged her.

"Why are many of the pieces on the workbenches wrapped up?" asked Helen, steering attention away from Deborah.

"To keep them moist until the potters have an opportunity to finish them."

"Here are some that are not wrapped," Miriam said.

Edith explained, "Those pieces have already been fired. They are probably sitting on the tables because the artist is planning to make another piece to match."

Miriam approached one bench that had a matched bowl, mug, and plate, each inscribed with the name "Moshe." "Look," she said, "these must be for a Jewish boy."

Edith read "Moshe" out loud in a manner that made it obvious to Miriam she was Jewish. Miriam smiled broadly as Edith explained that the set was called a milk-and-bread set and was quite popular in their shops. "It is an especially popular gift purchased by grandmothers."

"For a gift for a bris?" Miriam asked. By referring to the Jewish ceremony of circumcision, she wished to acknowledge that she, too, was Jewish.

Edith smiled and nodded.

Before they left, Miriam talked with Edith about making milk-and-bread sets with Sylvia's and Ida's names on them. She picked out a floral pattern in a soft-blue color and agreed to come back in a week to pick them up.

Susan and Helen talked with Edith about the possibility of Mildred joining a pottery class. They were all enthralled with this wonderful environment that encouraged young women to be their best.

Once outside, Deborah turned to her companions and apologized for embarrassing them. They brushed it off as unimportant, but Deborah was unusually quiet on their ride home and during dinner.

As soon as they were settled in their room, Deborah turned to Miriam to talk about what happened, but instead she burst into tears. She berated herself for not paying attention to others' needs, for being impulsive, for upsetting the potters, and for embarrassing them all.

Miriam held her until she calmed, then said, "I love you."

After another barrage of tears, Miriam said, "You are awfully hard on yourself. None of us would ever say such harsh things to you. You made a small mistake and learned a lesson, so it is time to move on. I trust you'll be more careful next time this type of situation occurs."

"I hope I can restrain myself."

The four housemates did not discuss their trip to visit the Saturday Evening Girls in front of Deborah, fearing that mention of it would upset her. Susan and Helen talked with Miriam privately, telling her more about their friend Edith. Along with her partner, the other Edith, she was the librarian who had begun the Saturday Evening Girls. The two women had lived together openly in a Boston marriage for many years.

In their room, Miriam said to Deborah, "I'm so grateful. I worried we'd never find anyone else like us, and now we are finding others everywhere."

When it was time to collect their pottery, Deborah resisted, yet Miriam persuaded her.

Deborah asked, "Should we drop hints to the potter about us being a couple too?"

"Yes, it's a wonderful feeling when we find like-minded women, so I'm hopeful she'll feel the same way."

By the time they left the pottery shop with their very special pottery for their girls, Deborah and Miriam had invited Edith to their house the following Sunday with her girlfriend. Their connections were expanding.

☙ ☙ ☙

The two Ediths arrived the next weekend with a special treat. Recent visitors to their studio had brought them a large box of chocolate cupcakes from the Taggart Baking Company of Indianapolis, Indiana,[49] which they wished to share.

Miriam looked at the cupcakes with substantial concern, assuming they were not kosher. Maybe they were made with lard, rendered pork fat. Even if beef fat had been used, they would not be kosher. Never before had nonkosher food entered their home, so Miriam was shaken.

---

[49] The small chocolate cakes from Taggart Baking Company were hugely popular in Indiana. In 1921, Taggart introduced a second popular product, which soon became the most popular bread in the United States—Wonder Bread. When the Continental Baking Company bought Taggart in 1925, they made the chocolate cupcakes a commercial success, eventually renaming them Hostess Cupcakes. Later, Continental produced another popular product, Twinkies. These products were made with beef fat and were not kosher.

Deborah noticed Miriam's pale complexion. When she disappeared into the kitchen, Deborah followed her. "What's wrong?"

"Those cakes are probably not kosher. I don't want to reject their kind offer, but I can't serve them. What should I do?"

"Everyone could hold them with a napkin, so they won't touch our plates."

"But I don't want the girls to have them."

When Deborah and Miriam did not return right away, Susan joined them in the kitchen to find out what the problem was. When Deborah explained the situation, Susan said she'd take care of everything.

Deborah and Miriam were awkward with their guests when they returned, yet the cakes were missing, and everyone seemed fine. After a lovely visit, Susan, Helen, and Mildred walked the visitors out the door. Deborah suspected they were all eating the cakes out on the porch, but said nothing to Miriam, who was too busy with the children to notice the group was gone for a while.

❧ ❧ ❧

Deborah missed seeing her New York family during the pandemic, fearing the train trip and increased exposure in the city would put her family at risk. Now that worries about catching the grippe were waning, she made plans to meet her family at Stonegate when they returned there next month. The shorter trip and a safer environment, given its rural setting, made this trip feel safer. Deborah knew they were suffering, as she was, over the loss of Milton, so it felt important they spend time together. To let Deborah have some private family time, Miriam decided to stay at home with the children.

During a phone call when planning the visit, Anna suggested she come to Boston prior to moving to their summer home. She stated her motive was to see the new Mary Pickford movie, *Daddy-Long-Legs*, which had opened to rave reviews on May 11. Anna said she wanted to see it at one of the magnificent Boston movie houses, yet Deborah knew that New York had equally extravagant venues.

Does Anna really want to spend time with her remaining sibling, or is she a little jealous that Fanny just moved in?

No matter what the reason, Deborah was pleased to have Anna visit. Accommodations would be more challenging now that Fanny and Rina occupied the upstairs bedroom across from Mildred, but Anna was willing to sleep in the extra bed in Sylvia's room.

They set a date for Anna to visit Boston in mid-June. They knew they would spend much of their time at home, given the needs of both children and Deborah's and Miriam's continued caution about being in public spaces. Deborah and Anna would then travel to Great Barrington together, meeting their parents there just after they arrived for the season.

North Bennet Street School

Edith Guerrier

Episode 30 ✳ *Third Wave*

June 1919

On June 4, the telephone rang. Rebecca answered the call from Mr. Levine, surprised because it was rare for him to call their workplace. She interrupted Deborah, who was deeply involved in a project at her desk.

Concerned, Deborah rushed to answer the call. While still holding the phone to her ear, Deborah yelled loudly, so the whole office could hear, "SUFFRAGE PASSED!"

The commotion that followed was memorable. Susan and Helen ran to each other and embraced with tears running down their cheeks. Never before had they shown affection publicly, but during this very special moment, all decorum was ignored.

Deborah repeated details from her father out loud, declaring that the Senate vote was fifty-six in favor to twenty-five opposed.

Susan told the group, "After forty-one years of debate, the Senate finally did the right thing."

Helen then explained that this was just the first step in the process, and there was still a great deal of work to be done because every state had to individually vote to ratify this amendment. Even with the Senate approval, it would not become law until thirty-six states passed it.

Deborah offered to give Susan and Helen the rest of the day off and to drive them to the homes of several of the other suffragettes on their committee to spread the word. It was a joyful afternoon.

The newspapers across the nation were surprisingly quiet about this historical event that mattered so much to American women. Susan found a photograph of Vice President Thomas Marshall, flanked by suffragettes, as he signed the Susan B. Anthony Amendment; she cut it out of the newspaper and tacked it on the wall of the office.

ॐ ॐ ॐ

Soon after the two Ediths' delightful visit, Mildred began attending pottery classes at North Bennet Street Industrial School. She wanted her friend Leah to join her, though they couldn't accommodate Leah's wheelchair. Mildred found a compatible group of girls in her class, causing Leah to be jealous. To pacify her, Mildred gave Leah several pieces of pottery she made. Miriam worried that Leah's disgruntled mood would affect the girls' devotion to one another. Yet there were bigger concerns about to affect them all.

❧ ❧ ❧

"I can hardly believe the virus has returned for a third time," said Miriam. "I thought it would be under control by now."

"I hoped it would be over. We all stayed home for so long and shuttered our business when the illness was spreading. Many businesses opened again, as ours did, as less people have been getting sick," Deborah said.

"I worried about all the celebrations after the war ended. People seemed to forget about the grippe as they celebrated peace."

"I know you were concerned, and it turns out you were right."

"It saddens me to be correct. After the war ended, the number of cases spiked, yet no one wanted to believe it had really come back," Miriam said. "As if it were over, the papers stopped tracking statistics on influenza casualties."

"The papers are reporting on illness and death again. I wonder if this influenza will ever be eradicated."

❧ ❧ ❧

"When will it finally be over? Illness and death have ravaged us for so long," Deborah said as they lay in bed a couple of days later.

"I heard today that one of Rabbi Feldman's cousins died of the influenza," Miriam said softly. "I also learned that one of my school chums died last week; she was pregnant. I read that pregnant woman have the highest death rate of anyone. There must be an end to this suffering."

"Even though we've reopened the shop, we must not lose our vigilance about staying well. Is it enough that we require face masks and that we use a barrage of questions to screen everyone who walks in our door? I still worry whether we're putting ourselves and our family at risk."

"I wish I knew. We're staying away from stores and from other people whenever possible. Other than those who work in the shop, we've hardly seen anyone." Miriam then said, "Should we ask Susan and Helen to restrict Mildred from going to her pottery class?"

"That would be awful for Mildred because she's really enjoying it. Yet if she stays away, it may calm her relationship with Leah."

"I noticed the two of them have been seeing each other less." Miriam described Leah's jealousy and her concerns for their friendship.

"Our visit from the two Ediths may be the last we see of guests in our home for a while," Deborah said with a sigh. "Even Marilyn and Julie have stayed away lately. I miss their friendship."

"So do I. And my return to Denison House was short-lived. I miss it once again." Miriam turned to Deborah with a blank stare. "I'm still afraid. As long as there are more cases, I'm fearful we're still at risk. We're doing the best we can, and, thus far, no one in our circle has become ill or died."

"Miriam, how can you say that? My brother died from the influenza...and Leah's baby brother died...and so many others we know."

"You're right. Maybe we should shut the shop again."

"Maybe."

"Deborah, how would you feel if I went to the pharmacy tomorrow? Sylvia's cold has been getting worse, and we've run out of the elixir we've been giving her."

"Is it helping enough to risk a trip inside a store?"

"It soothed her throat. And I worry that if she remains ill, she's more at risk of catching the dreaded flu. I'll make it a very quick trip."

"I'd be happy to go instead."

"No, I'll go. You go to the office, and William can stop by to pick me up on his way to work."

"No, I'll wait for you. We can both go in a little late. Just promise me you'll wear your mask and be quick."

"I promise."

ॐॐॐ

Early in the morning, Miriam headed to the pharmacy to be there as it opened. She forgot to take her mask, yet she was certain she'd be quick and safe. The pharmacist never took long to compound the elixir that soothed Sylvia's throat and calmed her cough.

Deborah dressed, fed the girls, and turned them over to Rachel. Susan and Helen, when hearing Deborah and Miriam would be going to work a bit late, decided to take the bus and train into the shop to get a head start on the day. Miriam said nothing about her fears for their safety on public transportation.

Deborah waited in the parlor for Miriam's return, leisurely reading the morning paper, an unusual treat. *What could be keeping Miriam? She never takes this long at the druggist.*

When the door opened, she looked up to see Miriam looking pale and frightened. "What's wrong? You look awful."

"Don't come near me. I just had an awful experience, and I'm afraid I've been exposed to the influenza."

"Where's your mask?"

"I forgot it."

"What happened?"

"I must go upstairs and hide in the bedroom before I tell you. I don't want to talk with you until I've isolated myself."

"You're scaring me, Miriam."

"I'm more frightened than I've ever been my life."

Deborah began to follow Miriam up the stairs; however, she was stopped by a loud, "No, you must not follow me. I need to take off my clothing and hang everything out the window. Then I'll bathe and clean my hair and every part of me that may have been exposed. I'll tell you when I'm ready for you to stand outside the bedroom."

"Miriam, I'm terrified."

"Please. Just stay away until I call for you."

It took a long time for Miriam to undress, bathe, and ready herself for isolation. Deborah paced, not knowing what else to do. She wanted to tell someone what was happening, yet if she were to call her parents or the shop, she'd just upset others. Fears swirled in her head.

Finally, Miriam called to her, "Come upstairs and bring a chair to sit outside our bedroom door so I can tell you what happened."

Deborah searched for a chair to carry up the stairs, settling on the one they kept in the kitchen, near the telephone. She took it upstairs and positioned it carefully next to the door. "I'm ready," she said with a heavy sigh.

Miriam was barely able to get out the story, but in words that would forever mark this as the most upsetting time of their lives, she finally said, "I can hardly believe I forgot my mask. How stupid of me. I should have come back for it when I realized. It was sitting right next to the door. I may have brought illness into our house, so I'll never forgive myself."

"I'll forgive you, Miriam. We've all forgotten our masks. Be kind to yourself."

"How could you ever forgive me?" She began to cry loudly.

"Calm yourself, my dear, and tell me what happened. Maybe it wasn't as bad as you think."

"Oh, it was very bad. As bad as it could be."

Deborah waited for Miriam's sobbing to slow as her own tears flowed, and her stomach clenched.

"It was senseless of me to go. We could have soothed Sylvia without the elixir. She could have managed. She would have gotten well, yet now I may have killed her by bringing home the disease."

"You did the loving thing any mother would do—search out something to benefit your ill child."

"Now I don't have the medicine, and we might all die."

"Let's not talk of death," said Deborah, her own fears mounting. Her voice shook as she tried to calm Miriam.

Miriam finally began the story. She was glad Deborah couldn't see her shaking with terror. She tried to keep her voice calm. "I went to the drugstore and told the pharmacist that we needed more of the syrup for Sylvia's cough. I was the only person in the store, so he set right to the task. After about three minutes, I heard a commotion at the door. It opened with a bang as a woman I've never seen before pushed it hard with her hip.

"'Please help!' she called loudly. Both the pharmacist and I looked toward the doorway. There she was, frantically trying to pull someone through the door with her. 'This is my daughter. Please help her.' Behind her, I saw a limp pile of clothes. 'My girl has the grippe. Please save her. She's all I have,' the woman screamed into the shop.

"I jerked my head toward the pharmacist, who was as frozen as I was. 'You must get her out,' he yelled. 'You cannot bring her in here.'

"She and the pile of clothing stayed still. I could not tell whether her child was dead or deathly ill. The mother refused to move from the doorway. I was petrified. There was no escaping. I was stuck in the store with no way out. The pharmacist had no answers."

Deborah breathed hard, hearing the fear and dreading the worst.

"We waited. The mother collapsed on her daughter—whether from illness or faint or fear, I didn't know. We were trapped."

"What did you do?"

"Nothing. I stood there as the pharmacist came near me. I didn't know if he wanted to support me or be supported. We stood there, fixed in our spots, just ten paces away, unable to move. I felt the air become heavy with illness. The disease headed towards us. I could feel it. It engulfed us as we stood there. The pile of lifeless bodies did not move. Maybe they were both dead. I just knew that they were blocking our escape. I was praying for release from this horror."

"How did you get out?" Deborah asked.

"We waited. We couldn't approach. We couldn't touch them. We were statues, unable to save ourselves. Finally, someone moved them. Suddenly, there was light in the doorway. An escape. I rushed towards it, finally free, running all the way home."

"Oh, my dear. How frightening it must have been. No wonder you're so filled with fear. You lived through a nightmare. I wish I could have been there to protect you."

"I couldn't think of anything other than escaping. Yet now, I may have brought the illness home to you. How could I do that?" Miriam cried loudly.

"You're where you belong. You're home with me."

"Illness and death were around me. I should have stayed away, rather than bring it to you."

"No, you did the right thing."

Although Deborah's words were soothing, Miriam did not calm.

Deborah repeated, "You'll be fine. We'll all be fine." The only truth Deborah could contemplate was what she said next—"I love you, and I'm glad you came home to me."

Miriam eventually stopping crying, and the silence frightened Deborah more than the tears. With tender words, she coaxed Miriam into bed, wishing she could be there, lying next to her and soothing her. She knew Miriam was right; she could have brought the grippe home, so it was unsafe to go inside the room. As painful as it was to sit outside the door, Deborah knew she must remain there.

Maybe Miriam fell asleep. Deborah did not. She sat in the chair, her thoughts and fears swirling. It seemed as if she sat there for hours. She vaguely heard the telephone ring, though she couldn't move from her position.

Rachel came up the stairs, having gotten a worried phone call from the shop. Where were Deborah and Miriam? Why had they not arrived at work? She approached Deborah, who was still sitting guard, protecting Miriam. Deborah's words were muffled, her explanation unclear. She made Rachel leave before she had a full story to tell. Rachel understood illness and fear, and that was enough.

Before long, there was a commotion downstairs as Susan and Helen entered the house. They gathered at the stairwell, trying to pull the story from Deborah. No one was able to get the whole tale, yet gradually they understood the gravity of the situation. They stayed downstairs, as Deborah insisted, while she sat vigil.

Eventually, Miriam woke. She was exhausted. Sleep had not lessened her fear.

Both Deborah and Miriam refused the tea, the food, and the kindness that was offered from those waiting downstairs. Deborah heard their hushed discussions and felt them as soft prayers.

After an hour, Miriam reported a dull headache and body aches. Over time, Miriam reported that her eyes were burning, and she was shivering from cold. Deborah offered repeatedly to come warm her, yet Miriam refused, knowing this was her illness to bear. She could not pass it on to those she loved.

After another fitful, short sleep, delirium set in. When she awoke, Miriam was making no sense and calling out to her mother and Bubbie. She spoke in Yiddish, screaming for Deborah to hold her.

Deborah knew the illness was flowing through Miriam's body. She peeked in the door as Miriam coughed and spit up small amounts of frothy, bloody secretions. She looked in horror as she noticed Miriam's face turning a ghastly shade of blue. Deborah knew, from tales of others, that she was already close to the end.

Deborah closed the door and defeatedly slumped against it. She moaned, "My Miriam."

As Deborah heard Miriam's gasping, she felt pulled into the room. A force was dragging her to the bed, begging her to embrace Miriam. She wanted to lay her body against Miriam's and feel the warmth bleed from her. Deborah wished the illness would be sucked into her also. She wished for the virus to invade her and pull her into those last moments with her sweet love. Together, they could pass through the eternal gates and float into death.

As these thoughts engulfed Deborah, she was brought back to the world by song as she willed herself to stay outside the door. The sound of lovely notes filled her head. *Is it the music of the angels calling to Miriam?* No, it was real music. Deborah realized it was the piano downstairs playing a soulful tune. *Is it lulling Miriam into the next world?*

Deborah realized she needed to raise her own voice to the sound of the Shema, the prayer that was to be the last words Miriam heard in this world, and the first words she would hear in the next. She opened her mouth, willing the words to come forth. At first, she could barely hear herself mutter, *"Sh'ma Yisroel, Adonai Eloheinu, Adoni Ehud."* She said the words in English, "Here, O Israel, the Lord is your God, the Lord is One." Then she repeated the Hebrew words louder, fuller, as if to sanctify the moment with this prayer. She repeated, *"Sh'ma Yisroel, Adonai Eloheinu, Adoni Ehud."* Softly, she continued the prayer as barely audible words left her mouth and traveled into Miriam's. Together they would chant this one last time. This was their last moment together.

Once the prayer was complete, Deborah sat still, knowing the end had come. She had heard the body needed to be removed from the house immediately to save the others. Suddenly, she was desperate. How could she rid the house of illness? Even though she wanted to linger, to hug, to kiss her sweet Miriam, she needed to save them all.

Deborah rushed from her spot outside the room, not knowing the tears streaming from her face were screaming the truth of her last moments with Miriam. She rushed down the stairs, past Helen at the piano, past the girls playing quietly nearby, and hurried into the street, searching for the cart that traveled through the neighborhood, assembling bodies of the dead. Surely it would be passing by right now. It would be waiting to escort Miriam to her resting place. No time for the psalms to be said to accompany her body until burial. No *Shemira*, as Bubbie had done for her husband, her son, and her daughter. No time to protect the soul. Deborah needed to protect her family. The illness must be scooped up and destroyed.

Deborah did not notice Susan follow her out of the house. As she ran down the street, Susan caught up with her. There was no time for words of sadness or love. Deborah searched for the wagon to take the sickness from their home. She glanced at Susan and just said, "The wagon. I must find the wagon."

Susan understood. She felt Deborah's desperation and understood Deborah was beyond mourning. Susan ran with Deborah, scouring the streets nearby, looking for the familiar sight, the cart of death that traveled throughout the day and night. When Susan spotted one of the health workers leaving another home that had been ravaged by illness, she pointed towards the nurse, luring Deborah in that direction. Susan approached, begging assistance, telling the woman that they needed the cart right away.

No other words were needed. The worker asked their address and told them to go home to wait. She would find the cart and bring it to their house.

Susan held Deborah's waist, guiding her toward their street. Their task was done. They walked the few blocks in silence.

Helen had instructed Rachel to take the children away, and she had summoned the neighbors to go to Hannah and tell her to come home. Susan and Helen talked quietly, wondering how to reach the rabbi. Prayers needed to be said even though none of the traditions could be followed. The body could not be washed. No shiva could be planned. These were desperate times.

In a daze, Deborah sat in the parlor. She did not want comfort. Then, suddenly, she got up and said that she needed to wash her body. Susan followed her upstairs and helped draw her a cleansing bath, understanding that Deborah needed to rid her body of potential disease.

While Deborah was bathing, the cart arrived outside. Susan quietly told Deborah, who did not move. She did not choose to be with the body being loaded into the wagon of death. Susan and Helen watched for her as the men, who were draped from head to toe in protective clothing, gently covered Miriam's body in a shroud and took her to their waiting cart. Susan and Helen were transfixed by every detail, bearing witness to these final moments and wanting to be Deborah's eyes should she ever ask what happened. They could tell her every detail and repeat the scene over and over until Deborah could save the memory as if she herself had watched it.

Susan and Helen then scrubbed the room, washing the bedclothes and every surface over and over. They washed as if their lives would be saved by every soapy bubble. They washed doorknobs and drawer handles just in case Miriam had touched any surfaces before heading to bed. They washed and cleaned until everything sparkled, leaving nothing but memories.

Susan then collected Deborah from the bath, where her body was shriveled from the long soak. She clothed Deborah in nightwear she was certain had not been near Miriam's sickened body, whispered to her of their cleaning frenzy, then placed her in their own bed in the room next to where Miriam had lain just a short while before. Susan and Helen then took turns watching over Deborah. There were no words, just love.

❧ ❧ ❧

The next few days passed quietly. No shiva, no mourners, no minyan to say prayers with the family. Hannah spent many hours at the house, saying little yet crying softly for the sister she'd loved so desperately. William stood by her side. Marjorie came by often, talking quietly with Hannah and William. Rachel watched the children. Mrs. Stern cooked their meals. Susan and Helen sat with Deborah, who mostly just stared straight ahead as tears dripped down her face. She muttered a little every now and then, but Deborah seemed to crave stillness.

The children added the only life to the house. Deborah forced herself out of her daze long enough to sit with them as they played. She could neither laugh at their antics, nor sing with them as Rachel led them in song. She left the words to Rachel when they asked for their mother. She did not know how she would ever explain where Miriam had gone or how she would manage being their only parent. She and the children were used to Miriam's kind guidance. The emptiness Miriam left behind filled the whole house.

When she headed to their bedroom each night, Deborah felt the enormity of her loss most keenly. Miriam was not there to sit across from her in the wingback chair, which still held her scent. Miriam was no longer waiting for Deborah's review of her day or the plans for her next projects. There was no one to dry her tears.

Deborah could not think clearly. She brushed the wetness from her cheeks, at times being keenly aware of each passing moment of loneliness, and at other times being lost in a haze of disbelief. *How will I live with a part of me missing? How can I make decisions without anyone to run my thoughts by? Who am I without Miriam?*

At times, between the tears, she thought of the empty world awaiting her. *Will I ever be whole again? Who am I without Miriam?*

☙ ☙ ☙

Deborah's Journal
June 28, 1919
I've been isolated, protected, and serene for the past few weeks. Following my sweetheart's unexpected death, I spent long days packing her things. At first, it seemed a chore, a necessity. I was anxious about the separation from everyone, wondering how I would tackle the long days of solitude. I feared being alone with my desperate feelings of loss and wondered if I would collapse into myself.

But soon after starting the overwhelming task of packing up her life, I discovered a calm. I was there with Miriam. I'd not yet lost her. She was all around me in every box, each drawer, every closet. She spoke to me through the letters she wrote to others and the words she wrote silently to herself. I entered her life through her diary, the details of the life I knew—and her secrets.

I put on her clothes as if to bathe myself in her smell. I slid into the fabric that she had recently touched, as if I was touching her. Her body held her dresses differently; they fell more softly on her hips. I felt we were together with inti-mate differences only she and I could know.

And now, as I scoured every item she ever collected, I brought them temporarily into my life. Each pen that she held and each book she read were parts of her. I felt connected. My heart raced at unexpected moments, and tears welled at odd times when some tiny piece of missing her came to the surface.

Vice President Marshall signing 19th Amendment

Epilogue

"Deborah, is it all right that I come by daily to spend time with you? I'm so lost without my sister," Hannah said, tears in her eyes.

"Certainly. I appreciate having you here. You and William are an important part of my life and my healing. I'd be lonely without you."

"I now understand the value of having a shiva. It felt empty without the gathering of loving people to support us in our loss. I need to be around you, who loved Miriam as I did, to share our grief. No one else feels the loss so acutely."

"I agree. Though Miriam touched many with her sweetness, you and I are alone in our desperation. She was the center of my world for nine years. She was my partner and the other mother to our children." Deborah burst into tears, which always sat just below the surface.

Hannah sighed and waited for Deborah to calm. "How are the children doing? They seem fine, but I know how devastated they must feel. How have you explained her death to them?"

"I've tried, but neither Sylvia nor Ida seems to understand. Every day, they ask for her, and I need to tell them all over that she isn't coming back. Every day, they see my tears yet don't understand. How many more days will it take for them to believe she's not returning? And how can I keep her alive in their hearts without breaking my own over and over?" Deborah closed her eyes, sighing deeply. She and Hannah held hands and wept quietly together.

Rachel arrived with the children, holding baby Ezra close to her breast. Ida, who'd recently turned three, asked for Miriam, though Sarah, a year older, seemed to understand something was amiss.

Sylvia could not grasp the permanence of Miriam's disappearance. Rachel was a wonderful support, helping to explain death and sadness to her charges. The adults agreed to avoid talk of illness, not wanting the children to fear even the common cold. They said the influenza took her away, a term none of the children could relate to anything else.

Susan and Helen took over some of the childcare after Rachel left each day and filled in with the household chores Miriam had previously done. Deborah seemed in a stupor, so they also assisted with some of her tasks. They wondered when it would be healthy for Deborah to return to her usual roles, and if she even noticed they were filling in. They did everything with love.

Marjorie stopped by frequently, seeming to need support as much as to offer it. Miriam was her oldest and very best friend, and she was unsure how to negotiate the world without Miriam's kindness and attention. No one knew her as well as Miriam, so the gap in Marjorie's life was huge.

Other than the appearance each day of Mrs. Stern, there was no one else coming by. The virus scared away all but those closest to Deborah and Miriam. Not that people expected the house to be filled with the grippe, but they all believed that staying apart from others and wearing masks were the best ways to avoid Miriam's fate.[50]

☙ ☙ ☙

Time moved slowly. Changes were barely perceptible until, one day, Rachel announced to Deborah that she was expecting. Although pleased for her and Roger, Deborah worried about how Mrs. Stern would take the news about her unmarried daughter. When she asked Rachel about whether she'd told her mother or anyone else, Rachel put out her left hand to display a small wedding ring.

"You got married?" wide-eyed Deborah asked.

"Yes. We are desperately in love, and as soon as we suspected there was a baby coming, we decided to marry. I'm sorry I didn't tell you, but I was worried about saying anything in case my mother heard. We told her of our marriage last night, and when she finds out about the baby, she'll be pleased that Roger did right by me."

"I'm so happy for you, Rachel," Deborah said, pained that she couldn't share the wonderful news with Miriam. She wasn't able to muster a smile.

---

[50] It is estimated that about one-third of the population of the world became infected by the influenza of 1918. At least 5,000,000 people perished, including over 675,000 in the United States. There were more casualties than in World War I, World War II, the Korean War, and the Vietnam War combined. It was especially harmful for children under five years of age and for the elderly, though many adults also died.

Death from this grippe was sometimes extremely fast, sometimes occurring within hours of infection. The infected person could develop a sudden high fever, a dry cough, sore throat, and fatigue. As the virus infected the person's lungs, they succumbed to respiratory failure. There was no cure.

Once alone, Deborah also worried about how Rachel's news would affect her own broken family. They relied on her consistency, especially now.

఼ ఼ ఼

Deborah was worried. "I suspect there have already been a few days when Rachel had to leave the children alone while she wretched," Deborah said to Hannah soon after Rachel's announcement. "Rina is wonderful, but not enough assistance. When Rachel's tending her own newborn, we'll be stuck. Having another child to care for may be more than she can handle when she's sleep deprived, as every new mother is."

They needed more help. Each day, Hannah and Deborah brought up names of young women they knew who had not been able to find meaningful work. None possessed Rachel's exceptional talents with children and her easy manner. Then, one day, it was Rachel who provided a potential answer.

"Would you mind if I invite my sister Rivkah to help with the children? You would not need to pay her. She has no work, and she'd be glad to assist me. She knows all the children well because she is their *Doda* Rivkah. She would love being an even bigger part of Ida's life, watching her little girl grow up."

Deborah and Hannah looked at each other and began nodding vigorously. Who would be a better caretaker than little Ida's own mother? And who would Rachel rather work with? They talked of how Rivkah had calmed and was no longer an unruly young girl. And they would definitely pay her, as they did Rina.

When the third wave of the horrible flu had taken the last of its victims, life settled into a new normal. Deborah found comfort in her daily routines, yet there was a huge hole in her chosen family.

There was minimal joy in any of their lives, until August 1920, when the world changed. The most important day in history for women occurred when Tennessee became the thirty-sixth state to approve the right for women to vote. Congress ratified the Nineteenth Amendment to the Constitution. "The right of citizens of the United States to vote shall not be denied or abridged by the United States or by any State on account of sex."

Deborah cried uncontrollably, missing Miriam almost more on this day than on any other single day since her death. She wished she could celebrate this momentous occasion with Miriam, to cry tears of happiness and imagine the world being a better place for women. But Deborah knew that life would never be whole again. She'd lost her true love, and they'd never again get to share joy.

Glossary

Yiddish

Shul　　Term used in daily conversation to denote a Jewish synagogue

Schvartze　　Derogatory term for Negroes

Tref　　Unclean or unfit food, according to Jewish law

"As di bubbe volt gehat beytsim volt zi gevain mayn zaidah."

Literal translation: If my grandmother had balls, she'd be my grandfather.

Meaning: Don't make predictions or plans based on assumptions.

Romance at Stonegate
(Deborah and Miriam's Boston Marriage Series)
ISBN Paperback: 978-1-63765-674-7

Deborah and Miriam, young Jewish girls vacationing in Massachusetts the summer of 1910, are immediately attracted to one another. As they explore their intense connection, they face challenges in their families, community, religion, and within themselves. These young women are products of turn-of-the-century values yet fall in love, a rarely accepted behavior in post-Victorian America. They explore ways to fit into a culture that is unforgiving of the choices they make, discovering what it means to be lesbian in a world which is not ready for them.

Struggles in a Boston Marriage
(Deborah and Miriam's Boston Marriage Series)
ISBN Paperback: 978-1-63765-675-4

True love knows no bounds . . .Deborah and Miriam are two young women whose love has survived the many obstacles life has thrown their way in their first years together. Now they find themselves in Boston, raising a young child whose been diagnosed as a Mongoloid Idiot, in an era where little was known about how to care for such a child at home. Deborah's thrilled that her writing is due to become published and she also pleased to be part of a growing and thriving business. Despite having found the woman of her dreams, she finds herself irritable and untrusting of Miriam's love.Miriam has given her heart and soul to Deborah and feels fulfilled now that she has a child and has meaningful volunteer work. She is proud of all their accomplishments at the printing and publishing shop and with her own ability to stand firm in her beliefs, even when Deborah challenges her. The world around them is changing. The Suffrage movement is trying to give women the freedom to vote and they feel guilty that they do not have enough time to continue their work for this cause. Also, people fear their country may go to war. During this time of uproar, Deborah and Miriam find their relationship becomes tested by an outsider. Will their love be strong enough to endure?

Chosen Family
(Deborah and Miriam's Boston Marriage Series)
ISBN Paperback: 978-1-63765-676-1

Chosen Family follows the maturing relationship of Deborah and Miriam, the lesbian couple who weathered rejection and isolation after falling in love in 1910. We watched them struggle as they learned to balance their relationship with each other and their families as they faced intense experiences of loss and jealousy.

They enter 1915, at ages 22 and 23, dealing with multiple challenges in their world. They create a family of choice by bringing those in their inner circle closer. As each person in their lives impacts Deborah and Miriam, they expand their ability to cope with and learn from new experiences, enriching them as individuals and as a couple.

Deborah's enthusiasm in this book centers around her developing skills as a businesswoman, a writer, a friend, and a lover. Her maturity is welcome, as she becomes more confident and less impulsive. Deborah learns balance and to express her desires clearly, with less demand. Will she be able to put aside her practical temperament to meet Miriam's desperate hopes?

Miriam's focus is on her family. Their chosen child Sylvia, her sister Hannah, and her best friend Marjorie are of upmost importance to her. Also paramount is her growing ability to express herself and stand firm for her needs, setting aside her natural compulsion to care for others. Her awareness of ways to live a life bigger than the protected one for which she was destined, brings her into conflict, an unfamiliar experience for this sweet young woman.

In this book, you will learn the importance of parenting for these two women, understanding their conflicted needs. You will watch their differing styles and desires, wondering whose demands will be respected and rise to the top. They face their demons separately yet come together when their equilibrium is challenged. Their relationship has stabilized, yet the demands on this young couple are enormous. You will root them on as they walk the unstable path towards adulthood.

Let's Connect

Get to know Ellen M. Levy

Email: ellenlevyauthor@gmail.com
Website: https://www.ellenlevy.net
Facebook: Ellen M Levy author
Instagram: Ellen M Levy author

www.ingramcontent.com/pod-product-compliance
Lightning Source LLC
Chambersburg PA
CBHW071156020726
47502CB00002B/430